Now, when I met Fiore, I thought myself a good man of arms. A
he disabused me of this, with many of the same lessons I'd had to learn
in pain with Jean le Maingre and du Guesclin and others, I learned
from him mostly by simple emulation. Fiore didn't teach in the way
a master-at-arms teaches. He simply stood in different ways – some
subtly different, like his version of the Woman's Guard, and some
startlingly different, like his low guard which he called 'The Boar's
Tusk'.

But it was in spear fighting that he departed most from the established manner. Yes? This interests you, messieur? I thought it might.
So I'll say this. Most men who fight with a spear fight with the long
spear; they vary in length, but in Italy we usually had them nine or
ten feet long. But long spears break easily, and have only a temporary
advantage over swordsmen.

Fiore preferred a shorter spear, just six or seven feet with a stout
shaft, octagonal in cross section. We talked about such weapons, but
it was not until we had a day in Milan that we were able to purchase
a pair, and then he was avid to fight with them.

By Christian Cameron

The Tyrant Series
Tyrant
Tyrant: Storm of Arrows
Tyrant: Funeral Games
Tyrant: King of the Bosporus
Tyrant: Destroyer of Cities
Tyrant: Force of Kings

The Killer of Men Series
Killer of Men
Marathon
Poseidon's Spear
The Great King
Salamis

The Chivalry Series
The Ill-Made Knight
The Long Sword

Other Novels
Washington and Caesar
Alexander: God of War

Ebook Exclusives
Tom Swan and the Head of St George Parts One–Six

Christian Cameron is a writer and military historian. He is a veteran of the United States Navy, where he served as both an aviator and an intelligence officer in the first Gulf War, Somalia, and elsewhere. He lives in Toronto with his wife and daughter. To find out more, visit www.hippeis.com

The Long Sword

CHRISTIAN CAMERON

An Orion paperback

First published in Great Britain in 2014
by Orion Books,
This paperback edition published in 2015
by Orion Books,
an imprint of The Orion Publishing Group Ltd,
Carmelite House, 50 Victoria Embankment,
London EC4Y 0DZ

An Hachette UK Company

1 3 5 7 9 10 8 6 4 2

A CIP catalogue record for this book
is available from the British Library.

ISBN 978-1-4091-3751-1

Typeset by Deltatype Ltd, Birkenhead, Merseyside

Printed in Great Britain by CPI Group (UK) Ltd,
Croydon, CR0 4YY

The Orion Publishing Group's policy is to use papers that
are natural, renewable and recyclable products and made
from wood grown in sustainable forests. The logging and
manufacturing processes are expected to conform to the
environmental regulations of the country of origin.

www.orionbooks.co.uk

For Guy Windsor, my first teacher in the chivalric martial arts, and Sean Hayes and Greg Mele, from whom I have learned so much and who have been unstinting in their provision of time and research; to Aurora Simmons and Christopher Duffy, who have suffered with all my mistakes, and to Michael Edgar, who set me on this road in 1980.

GLOSSARY

Arming sword – A single-handed sword, thirty inches or so long, with a simple cross guard and a heavy pommel, usually double edged and pointed.

Arming Coat – A doublet either stuffed, padded, or cut from multiple layers of linen or canvas to be worn under armour.

Alderman – One of the officers or magistrates of a town or *commune*.

Bailli – A French royal officer much like an English sheriff; or the commander of a '*langue*' in the Knights of Saint John.

Basilard – A dagger with a hilt like a capital I, with a broad cross both under and over the hand. Possibly the predecessor of the rondel dagger, it was a sort of symbol of chivalric status in the late fourteenth century. Some of them look so much like Etruscan weapons of the bronze and early iron age that I wonder about influences …

Bassinet – A form of helmet that evolved during the late middle ages, the bassinet was a helmet that came down to the nape of the neck everywhere but over the face, which was left unprotected. It was almost always worn with an *aventail* made of *maille* which fell from the helmet like a short cloak over the shoulders. By 1350, the bassinet had begun to develop a moveable visor, although it was some time before the technology was perfected and made able to lock.

Brigans – A period term for foot soldiers that has made it into our lexicon as a form of bandit – brigands.

Burgher – A member of the town council, or sometimes, just a prosperous townsman.

Commune – In the period, powerful towns and cities were called communes and had the power of a great feudal lord – over their own people, and over trade.

Coat-of-plates – In period, the plate armour breast and back plate were just beginning to appear on European battlefields by the time of Poitiers – mostly due to advances in metallurgy which allowed larger chunks of steel to be produced in furnaces. Because large pieces of steel were comparatively rare at the beginning of William Gold's career, most soldiers wore a coat of small plates – varying from a breastplate made of six or seven carefully formed plates, to a jacket made up of hundeds of very small plates riveted to a leather or linen canvas backing. The protection offered was superb, but the garment is heavy and the junctions of the plates were not resistant to a strong thrust, which had a major impact on the sword styles of the day.

Cote – In the novel, I use the period term *cote* to describe what might then have been called a gown – a man's over-garment worn atop shirt and doublet or pourpoint or jupon, sometimes furred, fitting tightly across the shoulders and then dropping away like a large bell. They could go all the way to the floor with buttons all the way, or only to the middle of the thigh. They were sometimes worn with fur, and were warm and practical.

Demesne – The central holdings of a lord – his actual lands, as opposed to lands to which he may have political rights but not taxation rights or where he does not control the peasantry.

Donjon – The word from which we get dungeon.

Doublet – A small garment worn over the shirt, very much like a modern vest, that held up the hose and sometimes to which armour was attached. Almost every man would have one. Name comes from the requirement of the Paris Tailor's guild that the doublet be made – at the very least – of a piece of linen doubled – thus, heavy enough to hold the grommets and thus to hold the strain of the laced-on hose.

Gauntlets – Covering for the hands was essential for combat. Men wore maille or scale gauntlets or even very heavy leather gloves, but by William Gold's time, the richest men wore articulated steel gauntlets with fingers.

Gown – An over garment worn in Northern Europe (at least) over the kirtle, it might have dagged or magnificently pointed sleeves and a very high collar and could be worn belted, or open to daringly reveal the kirtle, or simply, to be warm. Sometimes lined in fur, often made of wool.

Haubergeon – Derived from *hauberk*, the *haubergeon* is a small, comparatively light *maille* shirt. It does not go down past the thighs, nor does it usually have long sleeves, and may sometimes have had leather reinforcement at the hems.

Helm or haum – The great helm had become smaller and slimmer since the thirteenth century, but continued to be very popular, especially in Italy, where a full helm that covered the face and head was part of most harnesses until the armet took over in the early fifteenth century. Edward III and the Black Prince both seem to have worn helms. Late in the period, helms began to have moveable visors like *bassinets*.

Hobilar – A non-knightly man-at-arms in England.

Horses – Horses were a mainstay of medieval society, and they were expensive, even the worst of them. A good horse cost many days' wages for a poor man; a warhorse cost almost a year's income for a knight, and the loss of a warhorse was so serious that most mercenary companies specified in their contracts (or *condottas*) that the employer would replace the horse. A second level of horse was the lady's palfrey – often smaller and finer, but the medieval warhorse was *not* a giant farm horse, but a solid beast like a modern Hanoverian. Also, *ronceys* which are generally inferior smaller horses ridden by archers.

Hours – The medieval day was divided – at least in most parts of Europe – by the canonical periods observed in churches and religious houses. The day started with *Matins* very early, past *nonnes* in the middle of the day, and came around to *vespers* towards evening. This is a vast simplification, but I have tried to keep to the flavor of medieval time by avoiding minutes and seconds.

Jupon – A close fitting garment, in this period often laced, and sometimes used to support other garments. As far as I can tell, the term is almost interchangeable with doublet and with pourpoint. As fashion moved from loose garments based on simply cut squares and rectangles to the skin tight fitted clothes of the mid-to-late 14th century, it became necessary for men to lace their hose (stockings) to their upper garment – to hold them up! The simplest doublet (the term comes from the guild requirement that they be made of two thicknesses of linen or more, this 'doubled') was a skin-tight vest worn over a shirt, with lacing holes for 'points' that tied up the hose. The pourpoint (literally, For Points) started as the same garment. The pourpoint became quite elaborate, as you can see by looking at the original that belonged to Charles of Blois online. A jupon could also be worn as a padded garment to support armour (still with lacing holes, to which armour attach) or even over armour, as a tight fitting garment over the breastplate or coat of plates, sometimes bearing the owner's arms.

Kirtle – A women's equivalent of the doublet or pourpoint. In Italy, young women might wear one daringly as an outer garment. It is skin tight from neck to hips, and then falls into a skirt. Fancy ones were buttoned or laced from the navel. Moralists decried them.

Langue – One of the sub-organizations of the Order of the Knights of Saint John, commonly called the Hospitallers. The 'langues' did not always make sense, as they crossed the growing national bounds of Europe, so that, for example, Scots knights were in the English Langue, Catalans in the Spanish Langue. But it allowed men to eat and drink with others who spoke the same tongue, or nearer to it. To the best of my understanding, however, every man, however lowly, and every serving man and woman, had to know Latin, which seems to have been the order's lingua franca. That's more a guess than something I *know*.

Leman – A lover

Long Sword – One of the periods most important military innovations, a double-edged sword almost forty five inches long, with a sharp, armour-piercing point and a simple cross guard and heavy pommel. The cross guard and pommel could be swung like an axe, holding the blade – some men only sharpened the last foot or so for cutting. But the main use was the point of the weapon, which, with skill, could puncture maille or

even coats of plates.

Maille – I use the somewhat period term *maille* to avoid confusion. I mean what most people call chain mail or ring mail. The process was very labor intensive, as real mail has to have each ling either welded closed or riveted. A fully armoured man-at-arms would have a *haubergeon* and *aventail* of maille. Riveted maille was almost proof against the cutting power of most weapons – although concussive damage could still occur! And even the most strongly made maille is ineffective against powerful archery, spears, or well-thrust swords in period.

Malle – Easy to confuse with *maille*, malle is a word found in Chaucer and other sources for a leather bag worn across the back of a horse's saddle – possibly like a round-ended portmanteau, as we see these for hundreds of years in English art. Any person traveling be he or she pilgrim or soldier or monk, needed a way to carry clothing and other necessities. Like a piece of luggage, for horse travel.

Partisan – A spear or light glaive, for thrusting but with the ability to cut. My favorite, and Fiore's, was one with heavy side-lugs like spikes, called in Italian a *ghiavarina*. There's quite a pretty video on YouTube of me demonstrating this weapon …

Pater Noster – A set of beads, often

with a tassle at one end and a cross at the other – much like a modern rosary, but straight rather than in a circle.

Pauldron or Spaulder – Shoulder armour.

Prickers – Outriders and scouts.

Rondel Dagger – A dagger designed with flat round plates of iron or brass (rondels) as the guard and the pommel, so that, when used by a man wearing a gauntlet, the rondels close the space around the fingers and make the hand invulnerable. By the late 14th century, it was not just a murderous weapon for prying a knight out of plate armour, it was a status symbol – perhaps because it is such a very useless knife for anything like cutting string or eating ...

Sabatons – The 'steel shoes' worn by a man-at-arms in full harness, or full armour. They were articulated, something like a lobster tail, and allow a full range of foot movement. They are also very light, as no fighter would expect a heavy, aimed blow at his feet. They also helped a knight avoid foot injury in a close press of mounted melee – merely from other horses and other mounted men crushing against him.

Sele – Happiness or fortune. The sele of the day is the saint's blessing.

Shift – A woman's innermost layer, like a tight fitting linen shirt at least down to the knees, worn under the kirtle. Women had support garments like bras, as well.

Tow – The second stage of turning flax into linen, tow is a fiberous, dry mass that can be used in most of the ways we now use paper towels, rags – and toilet paper. Biodegradable, as well.

Yeoman – A prosperous countryman. Yeoman families had the wealth to make their sons knights or squires in some cases, but most yeoman's sons served as archers, and their prosperity and leisure time to practice gave rise to the dreaded English archery. Only a modestly well-to-do family could afford a six foot yew bow, forty or so cloth yard shafts with steel heads, as well as a haubergeon, a sword, and helmet and perhaps even a couple of horses all required for some military service.

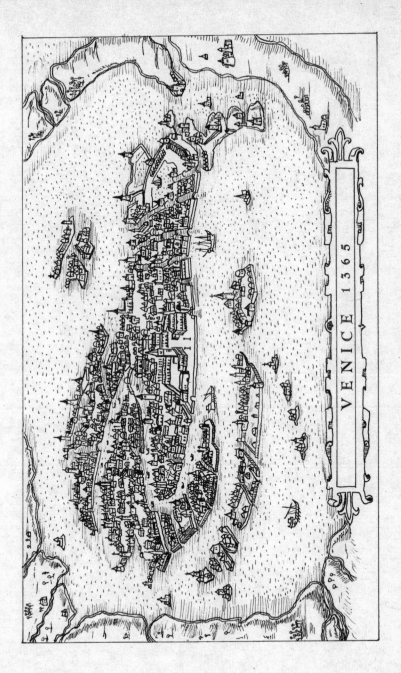

VENICE 1365

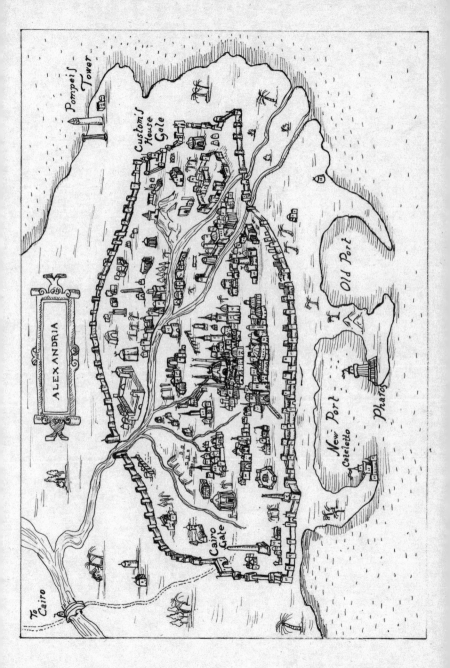

ALEXANDRIA

Pompei's Tower

Custom's House Gate

A noble

To Cairo

Cairo Gate

New Port · Coscietto

Old Port

Pharos

PROLOGUE

Calais, June, 1381

Evening was falling.

The air was soft enough for a man to stand outside clad only in his shirt, but winter's arm had been dreadful and long and the bite of a chill was close. Men took advantage of it to stand in the inn's yard and exchange blows with swords against bucklers, or to wrestle, or just to lift stones. When one of the inn's young women went to the well, every male head turned, but there was a discipline to their postures and their tongues that went with the matching jupons and the warlike equipment.

The inn-yard gate began to open, and the men in the yard stiffened at the sound of heavy hooves striking the cobbles.

An old archer put his flask of wine behind his leather bag on the ground and gave a sharp whistle. Most of the activity in the yard came to a stop, but two pages continued to wrestle, and a tall squire put his boot into a wrestler's hip.

'Sir William!' he hissed.

The gates came back against their wrought-iron hinges. The inn-keeper, a prosperous middle-aged man who could have passed for a gentle in any town in Europe, appeared in the yard, hat in hand. He bowed as Sir William Gold entered the yard, six feet and a little of scarlet wool and black, topped by hair that, though going grey, still maintained a sheen of copper. Behind him, his body squire, John de Blake, carried his sword and helmet.

The innkeeper took the knight's horse. 'Vespers any moment, Sir William,' he said. He nodded at the men in the yard.

'Thanks, Master Ricard,' Sir William said, and swung down from his horse. 'Do I smell apples?'

Master Ricard grinned. 'Apple *pies,* my lord. That have been making all the day. Last autumn had a fine crop.' In Calais – the jewel

I

in the English Crown of mainland possessions – Master Ricard's Flemish-English was the norm, not the broad Midlands accent that William Gold used.

'Well, it will have to wait until after Vespers,' Sir William said. He looked around the yard, eyes passing easily over two young pages, who stood bashfully rubbing their hips and glaring at each other. 'I'm sure you will all join me?'

A bell – from the church whose back wall overhung the inn yard – began to ring, carrying easily in the evening air.

'Was your meeting at the castle ... productive?' Master Ricard asked carefully.

'Hmm,' Sir William replied. He saw movement coming out of the inn's main door and he inclined his head. 'Master Chaucer.'

'Sir William,' the other man answered. He was thinner – almost lean – in the rich black of a prosperous merchant, but wearing a heavy-bladed basilard, the mark of a fighting man in most circles, and as he exchanged bows with the red-haired knight they might have been a mastiff and a greyhound.

Chaucer bowed, a tiny smile lingering around his lips, as if he found something funny but was too well bred to mention it. 'May I join you for church?'

'Please!' Sir William said. He took the other man's arm and they walked to the gate, the men-at-arms and archers in the yard falling in behind them in order of rank – military rank, and in some cases social rank. John de Blake was a fully armed squire, outranking the pages and counting as a man-at-arms; but his social origins outranked those of most of the other men in the company, and he fell in behind his master. And the company's master archer did not fall in at the head of the archers, but instead came last of all, using his will and his fists to move the slow and the unlucky past the long brick wall and into the nave of the church – the long, high nave.

The church, Notre Dame of Calais, started by Frenchmen and completed in a very English style, was big enough to silence even the most boisterous page. A trio of priests began to sing, supported by the chapter, who had seats. Everyone else stood – even famous English knights.

'You had trouble at the castle?' Chaucer asked.

Sir William was telling beads on his paternoster, his breathing deep and regular.

Chaucer looked away impatiently. He kept his head still and let his eyes wander – took in a pair of monks whispering where they thought they would not be heard; noticed a pretty nun smoothing her habit; eyed a pair of Sir William's pages the way a predator might watch prey: observing, cataloguing, listening.

The second psalm was taken up; the cantor's voice strong and powerful as a trumpet, and the chapter responded, and the congregation took up the *Agnus Dei*.

Chaucer sighed.

Sir William sang. In fact, he sang well, and his Latin was good. Chaucer smiled to himself.

Later, Sir William knelt, his arming sword's tip resting on the stone floor as lightly as the older knight's knees appeared to rest. Chaucer went to one of the mighty pillars that supported the nave and leaned against it to watch the nuns, who in turn watched the men-at-arms.

Sir William's lips moved slowly, and then his breathing deepened, and then he was a still as a statue, or a stone memorial to a dead knight.

Chaucer rolled his eyes and fidgeted. But his eye caught a pair of older nuns hissing at each other, and he shifted himself until he could catch their middle-aged invective, their careful avoidance of the appearance of anger, their false humility.

'You don't think very highly of your fellow man, do you, Master Chaucer?' Sir William asked.

Chaucer had to cover a start – the big red-haired knight moved very quietly. 'You pray for a very long time,' he said.

Sir William shrugged. 'I have much for which I should atone. A moment of prayer is a small sacrifice.'

'You had troubles at the castle,' Chaucer said.

Sir William's mouth made a curious gesture, as if it could not itself decide whether to frown or smile. 'Brian Stapleton is leaving to take up the captaincy of Guines.'

'That's Miles' brother? Surely you two are old friends and good companions?' Chaucer managed a genuine grin. 'You and Miles fought Saracens together.'

'He's being replaced by John Devereux. Something is afoot at home, and Sir Brian is unwilling to give me a passport.' Sir William shrugged again. 'I was summoned by the king. I am needed in Venice and my patience has limits.'

Chaucer nodded, and the two men walked past the nuns, who now kept their eyes down and their movements discreet. Outside, darkness was falling, the air was chill, and the smell of baked apples and sugar carried like the scent of love.

Sir William laughed. 'I'm imagining myself the centre of the world. Why are *you* still here?'

Chaucer grunted. 'The same. The French have not prepared me a pass, even though my business is to their good.'

'Peace?' Sir William asked.

'At least a longer truce. There are those at home who would push the young king to war – but the truth is, there's no money and no will to war in the commons.' Chaucer gazed into the darkness.

Ahead of them on the street, a woman was lighting the lamps on her house. She inclined her head as they passed, and Sir William bowed deeply to her and gave her the sele of the day, to which she responded by blowing him a kiss.

'You are the lovesomest man,' Chaucer said.

Sir William smiled. 'I do love women, it is true,' he said. He watched the goodwife as she stretched to light her last lamp.

'Adultery is a sin,' Chaucer said.

'This is very monk-like, coming from you,' Sir William shot back.

The two of them turned the corner of the church of Notre Dame and walked slowly toward the inn gate, visible at the end of the lane.

'If we're here another night, perhaps we can spin Monsieur Froissart more tales of our misspent youths,' Sir William said.

Chaucer laughed. 'I believe that the two of us are too far beyond Monsieur Froissart's views of the world.' He looked at Sir William in the torchlight. 'Do you remember him from Prince Lionel's wedding?'

Sir William nodded. 'No. But I was busy, then. Well, if he's determined to listen, we could do him some good. I could tell him of the Levant.'

'And the Italian Wedding,' Chaucer said. 'Sweet Christ, that was a horror.' He grinned mirthlessly. 'He was there, but he didn't see our side of it.'

'Not all a horror,' Sir William said. But when their eyes met, something passed – some shared thing.

'You tell tales for your living,' Sir William said. 'Why leave me to tell the story?'

Chaucer took his turn to shrug. 'I like to see what you do with it. You take all the blood and shit and make it into something. As if it mattered.'

Sir William paused, his hand on his paternoster. 'Of course it matters,' he said. Then he paused. 'It matters to the men who are in it. Even when the cause is worthless.'

Chaucer grimaced. 'You would say that.'

An hour later, and they were served a series of dishes – a meat dish with noodles, a game pie, a dish of greens. The inn's food was renowned wherever Englishmen gathered, but it was not all English food, and the greens showed the influence of the new French fashions: fresh food, in season, and especially vegetables.

Chaucer eyed his beet greens with a certain distaste. 'French clothes, French manners, and now French food,' he said. 'You'd think we'd *lost* the war.'

Messieur Froissart, on the other hand, inhaled his with every evidence of pleasure – or perhaps the hunger of a poorer man.

Sir William put a pat of butter on his and ate them quietly. 'In Italy,' he said.

Froissart quivered like a hound.

'My faith!' Sir William said, and laughed. 'I wasn't going to speak of fighting, messieur, but of food! In Italy, Sir John – Hawkwood, that is – has introduced an English dish, a true beefsteak, and it is all the rage, although they serve it with their own vegetables and salts. In truth, it seems to me that every country benefits in borrowing some food from their neighbours.'

Chaucer shrugged. 'Mayhap, William, but travel turns my ageing guts to water and I don't need a boil of green weeds to soften me.'

Froissart, endlessly fascinated by Sir William, ignored the English courier and leaned forward. 'And Saracen food? You are a famous crusader.'

Sir William looked up to meet the eye of Aemilie, the serving girl and the landlord's eldest. He smiled, and his eyebrows made a little motion; she returned the smile, and curtsied.

'My pater says to serve you this,' she said. 'And says to add that it was sent down from the castle for your enjoyment.'

Chaucer looked up. 'Come, that's handsome. Stapleton can't expect to keep you here forever, if he sends you a nice Burgundy.'

Sir William tasted the wine in the heavy silver cup set before him, and his eyebrows shot up. 'Bordeaux,' he said.

Aemilie poured for Chaucer and then for Froissart, and the three gentlemen drank.

'That's a fine vintage,' Chaucer said. 'But after all, you did save his brother's life.'

Again Froissart leaned forward in anticipation.

Sir William spiked the last bit of his meat pie on his pricker and ate it, drank some wine, raised an eyebrow at Chaucer. Chaucer shook his head. 'It's your tale,' he said. 'I was only there at the end.'

Aemilie was pausing in the doorway of the small dining room, waiting to hear whatever was said. Outside, Sir William could see his squire, John, and a number of other men. He swirled the wine in his cup.

'If I'm allowed a full ration of this apple pie,' he said, 'perhaps I'll tell a tale – but out under the rafters, where all can hear. Master Chaucer, do you play piquet?'

'Not with professional soldiers,' Chaucer said.

'Fie!' Sir William answered, and again they exchanged that look.

Froissart leaned past Chaucer. 'Tell us about your crusade,' he said.

Gold smiled his wolfish smile, and stroked his beard. 'Very well. But I hope you are no fan of Robert of Geneva.'

Chaucer narrowed his eyes.

So did Sir William.

VENICE

1364

In the spring of 1364, I had just been knighted on the battlefield by that two-faced bastard, the Imperial Knight Hans Baumgarten, for my feat of arms at the siege of Florence. Except, as you know if you've been listening, there was no siege and we never had a chance to take the city. Five thousand men against a city with a hundred thousand citizens?

And the aftermath of my great deed was bitter; most of the companions, the Englishmen and Germans who had formed the great company that had made war on Florence for Pisa, accepted bribes and changed sides. There were fewer and fewer of us with Hawkwood – even Baumgarten himself, one of the most famous soldiers of our day, took the gold and crossed the river to join the Florentines.

Sir John Hawkwood didn't change sides. Some say this is because of his honour. That's possible – he had a solid view of his own worth, and no mistake – but for my money, he stayed loyal to Pisa because they'd made him their Captain General and that meant promotion. He had never been the sole commander of an army before, and he knew that if he could stick it out and attract men, he'd make a name that would mean employment and real money, not the forty florins a month that most of the men-at-arms earned, if they didn't take a wound, lose their horses or pawn their armour or get the plague or fall prey to the hundreds of perils that beset soldiers.

At any rate, I stuck with Sir John. If you've been listening, you know he saved me once or twice, and despite being the devil incarnate in many ways, I liked him. And I still do. But by late May, we were down to two hundred lances or perhaps fewer. And that's when Fra Peter came into our camp – Fra Peter being a Knight of the Order of St John that most men call the Hospitallers. Fra Peter brought me orders from his superior, the Grand Master; from Father Pierre Thomas, who

7

had saved my soul, and from my lady, who I loved *par amours* – Emile d'Herblay. I won't tell you which of those three held the highest rank in my heart, but I will say that the three together pulled far more weight at the plough than Sir John. And since tonight's story will be about fighting the Saracens, let me begin where the story truly began; in Sir John's pavilion outside Pisa, in May of 1364.

Sir John seldom displayed any emotion at all, and if the loss of two-thirds of his lances troubled him, he never showed it. Neither did he drink, or wench. That is, he liked a maid as much as the next man, but he was unwilling to show weakness – any weakness. His clothes were always perfect, and his horse was always groomed, and he did not lie abed, nor did he let us spy a pretty thing between the blankets of his camp bed. If there was one such, I never saw her. Indeed, he kept much the same discipline of the brothers of the Order, with none of their piety or purpose.

His squire served me wine.

'How much have they offered you?' he asked.

I shook my head. 'It's Fra Peter,' I insisted. 'I'm off for Avignon.'

He fingered his beard. 'I can let you have a hundred florins if you stay.'

Now, this felt odd. First, I knew I was leaving with Fra Peter. If Emile was going on pilgrimage, I was going to be with her. And I had sworn to a living saint to go on crusade when my Order called me.

And a hundred florins was no longer so very much money. I had a surprising reserve of money in my purse, and a gentleman-squire to carry that money, and an account with the best Genoese bankers that could get me cash anywhere in the Christian world and pretty far among the *paynim*.

'I'm not going with Andy,' I said. 'I'm off to fight the Saracens.'

He held up an ewer of wine, voicelessly asking if I wanted more wine. I nodded.

'At least you have the honour to come and face me,' he said. 'But if you are riding with Walter Leslie, you might as well tell me.'

I knew of the Scottish knight, Sir Walter Leslie. I knew his two brothers, Kenneth and Norman, as well. We'd all served together in France. Sir Walter had the ear of the Scottish king, and the Pope, and he was across the river. That is, with the Florentines.

'I'm not going with Sir Walter,' I said.

'He says he's recruiting for the King of Cyprus,' Hawkwood said. He drank a little more. 'But right now, he's in the pay of Florence. Stealing my men. For the fucking Pope.' He looked at me. 'If you go with him, you are, in effect, leaving the service of the King of England for the King of France.'

I was used to this; Sir John had the habit of using patriotism against us. And I knew – none better, as Master Chaucer will allow – that Hawkwood was always the king's arm in Italy. 'I thought we were serving Pisa against Florence,' I said.

'Florence is aligned with the Pope, who is raising the French king's ransom,' Sir John said.

I smiled, then, because Fra Peter had passed me a titbit of news when he gave me Emile's letters, and I had assumed Sir John already knew it. But he didn't.

'King John of France is dead,' I said.

Hawkwood froze for a moment. And for the first time in the conversation, his eyes met mine. 'Says who?' he asked quietly.

'Fra Peter Mortimer,' I said.

Sir John pursed his lips, but he didn't protest. The Hospitallers had superb sources of information – they were the Pope's mailed fist, and their intelligencers, too.

'And you go to Avignon,' he said.

I nodded.

He took a deep breath. 'The Spaniard and the Friulian are donats, too. But I can't let you take my master archer and ten lances. Nor Courtney nor Grice nor de la Motte. I know they are your men, but by God, William Gold, if you take all your companions, I'll lose the rest by morning.'

'I'll come back!' I said.

He embraced me, one of perhaps three times he did so. 'Perhaps,' he said. 'If you don't – God be with you.'

John Hawkwood embraced me and invoked God. My eyes filled with tears, but I clasped his hand and left the tent.

Say what you like about John Hawkwood: he could have made my leaving him a test of loyalty and allegiance. But he didn't. Which is why, when the lines were drawn later, I went back to him.

*

Fra Peter agreed with Sir John. 'I'm not hiring your lances,' he said. 'You are volunteers for the Order, and you have to pay your own way. The Order will feed you and your horses; we'll find you lodging, but there is no wage.'

Crusading is a rich man's sport, and no mistake.

I sat down with Sam Bibbo and laid it out for him, and he laughed. 'You needn't make a fuss,' he said. 'I'm your man, but I wouldn't go to the Holy Land for all the fish in the sea. Italy is rich, the fighting is easy, and this is all I need.'

I had hoped that he'd insist. I relied very heavily on Sam Bibbo – he knew how to do everything, and when he didn't, I still felt better for his support while I made things up. But I understood.

Bibbo also embraced me. 'Bring me a piece of the true cross,' he said.

We were sitting at a camp table in a sumpter's tavern one of the wine shops that served the army. I shaved a splinter off the table and gave it to him, and he laughed and slapped my back.

'John Hughes won't want to go to the Holy Land,' he said. 'But he's had a message from home, and if you are headed north across the passes, he'll want to ride with you.'

I went and found John Hughes, a Lakelander from Cumbria or Westmoreland. I got to know that country later, as you'll hear, if this goes on long enough, but to me they were names, as alien as Thrace or Turkey, far off in the north of England. He was Milady's archer, and he was a damned good hand. He was also devoted to Janet – Milady – and seldom left her.

I won't prose on. He'd had word that his sister had died of plague and that he was needed at home, which was a village called Kentmere near Kendall where the green cloth comes from.

Milady Janet glared at me with her cat's eyes. 'If you leave, Hawkwood will treat me like a woman.'

I sighed. 'Janet, *ma vieux*, I have sworn.'

'Men and their oaths,' she said. She had her arming coat on, and her squire was trying arm harnesses on her. She was not the only armed woman among the English, but she was the only one who didn't make a secret of it. 'You leave, and John Hughes leaves. Mark my words, I'll end up married to some loutly lordling.' But she smiled, and she also embraced me.

That was odd, too, because Janet and I never touched. But there are few things less like lovemaking than rubbing steel breastplates together, and the moment passed. 'Andy Belmont—' I began.

'That cowardly shit,' she hissed. In fact, they had been lovers – at least, I *thought* they had been lovers. But now Andy had run off to fight for Florence.

She shook her head. 'At least you're taking Fiore,' she said. 'His love oppresses me.'

Indeed, I had to watch him kneel and swear his eternal devotion to her before we rode away.

There were too many goodbyes. This was, as I learned by leaving it, my home, and I was abandoning fame and fortune to return to lower rank with the Order. On the last night, we all shared wine, and John Courtney gave me letters from a lot of the Englishmen for Avignon, and Kenneth MacDonald, who now looked as Italian as the rest of us in fine hose and a silk jupon, gave me a packet of letters from all the Scots and Irish. Olivier de la Motte had letters for the Gascons and Normans. Avignon is a great clearing house for letters – priests come and go from there to every part of Europe, even Hyperborea.

At any rate, the next morning, with a hard head and an empty heart, I rode for Avignon. Listen, it is all very well to have a letter from your long-lost lady love, but it is damned hard to leave your friends.

We stopped on the old Roman road north of Sienna, well along toward Lombardy, for the evening, at a fine farm that has since been burned eight or ten times, I'll warrant. We sat at the farmer's table and ate his chickens and paid handsomely for the privilege.

After supper, Fra Peter prayed, and when we had joined him and said the office of compline, and when he'd looked at the two boys and the girl of the house and found nothing worse than some scrapes and some lice, then we sat under the grape arbour outside.

'You boys are too polite to ask me what's happening,' he said, leaning back against the stone wall of the house.

Fiore – that's Fiore dei Liberi, a tall, strong man of twenty with good manners and an ascetic manner and a tendency to forget anything that didn't involve fighting – Fiore raised both eyebrows. 'You did say there would be no crusade for five years,' he allowed. Fiore had the terrible habit of remembering everything you said; accurately. Unforgivable, in a friend.

Fra Peter laughed, though. 'Did any of you meet the King of Cyprus last autumn?' he asked.

We all shook out heads, and Fra Peter nodded. 'He came to the Pope and to King John of France too, and King Edward of England, looking for help against the Turks and the Mamluks of Egypt.' He took a sip of wine and smacked his lips. 'Italy, land of wine. At any rate, he's a good soldier and a fine man-at-arms, but the Pope thought him too young and of too little consequence to lead a crusade, so he chose King John of France.'

I snorted. So did John Hughes. Fra Peter was not much on social distinctions, and John was a senior archer.

Fra Peter raised an eyebrow at John and John shrugged innocently. 'Which he did so well, fighting us,' Hughes said in his Lakeland accent.

We all laughed. It was true. King John the Brave of France had lost to us, the English, every single time he'd faced us.

Fra Peter shrugged. 'The Holy Father has other concerns than ours, messires. At any rate, King John took the cross and then nothing happened. But now he has died. Father Pierre told me to gather my knights because the word in Avignon is that the Holy Father will re-declare the *Passagium Generale*. He has appointed Talleyrand as papal legate to lead the faithful, and he will offer the command to King Peter of Cyprus.'

Talleyrand, no friend of mine, was reputed to be the richest man in the world. And perhaps the most venal priest ever born.

Then he told us how he had spent the winter with Father Pierre, holding the city of Bologna to its allegiance for the Pope. In truth, I'd heard nothing of it, even though it had all happened two hundred leagues from me.

'You needed good men-at-arms,' I said.

'I fear the day that Father Pierre needs an escort,' Fra Peter said. 'He rides in among his enemies – at Bologna, he rode boldly in among men sent to take him, unarmed, holding aloft a cross. I thought we were dead or taken, but God supported his saint, and the mercenaries were moved to their knees.'

We murmured appreciatively. We all knew him: the force of his genuine conviction was like one of Fiore's smashing sword blows.

'And he made peace between the Pope and the Duke of Milan, where the King of France had failed. To some of us, it was a miracle come from God – one day, the Duke was threatening to hang us all, and the next day, he signed the peace. And the Pope held Bologna, despite all threats. Friends, I will not hide from you that the Pope had already sent letters to command a renewed campaign against Milan and a cancellation of the crusade.' He looked around at us. 'Even now, there is a powerful party at the papal court that attempts to cancel the crusade or to have it declared against Milan.'

Fiore recoiled. 'Infamous!' he said. 'A crusade against a Christian duke?'

Fra Peter nodded agreement. 'It would, to you and me, make a mockery of everything we hold dear about Christian knighthood and the crusade. But there are men in Avignon who hold the papal authority is the higher good – the true cause.'

Well, *we* were Pierre Thomas's men, and Fra Peter Mortimer's. We all shook our heads, or spat, or frowned. Even John Hughes. And he spoke for many men when he swore.

'By our Lady,' he said. 'The priests and the popes will be the ruin of the church. A crusade against Milan? It's like declaring a crusade against England.'

Fra Peter met Hughes's eye. 'It could come to that, if the papacy continues on this path.' He shrugged. 'Our Father Pierre has worked without pause for two years to make the *Passigium Generale* a reality. He made peace between the Pope and the Duke, and he's helped settle the Cretan Revolt. Now we're gathering knights and in two months, the army will meet us in Venice.' He looked from one to another. 'It's real, lads. We're off on crusade.'

Ah, Monsieur Froissart, since you treasure tales of deeds of arms, let me say that through that entire passage to Avignon, Messire dei Liberi and Juan Hernedez and I exchanged many blows, indeed, some evenings, if we had made enough miles, Fra Peter would join us. My new delight was fighting with the heavy spear, and Fiore loved it too, and where he might be blind to the glances of a pretty farm girl and deaf to the offers of a merchant looking for a guard, he was as avid for arms as a young priest in a university is for his theology. And he approached his study in much the same way, so that on that trip he began to sketch out a theory of – well, it is hard to describe. A theory of fighting, a theory of how to train.

13

North of the Alps, few men know of Master Fiore. But south of the Alps, we think him the best sword that ever was. And that summer, he was just coming into his own, growing in confidence in his own methods, and experimenting in how to teach them. He made us do the oddest things: we wrestled on horseback, of which you'll hear more, and we jousted, and we fenced with spear and sword and we wrestled and fought with sticks and fought with daggers.

One evening in Lombardy, with the mountains clear on the northern horizon, still snow-capped in late May, he and I were fencing with spears in harness in the yard of yet another farm. Let me add that my squire, Edward, was back with John Hawkwood, and that meant that all three of us were back to scrubbing our own harnesses – and Fra Peter's – like boys of fifteen. And that meant that getting thrown in the rain-soaked dung of an Italian farmyard was not just a petty humiliation – it represented the reality of an hour's work.

And in answer to your question, we fought with *sharp* spears. By our Saviour, gentles! We didn't carry blunts on campaign, and it is only by playing with sharp weapons that a man loses his fear of them.

Nor were we playing in visors. Truly, it is a miracle we made it to Avignon alive.

Now, when I met Fiore, I thought myself a good man of arms. After he disabused me of this, with many of the same lessons I'd had to learn in pain with Jean le Maingre and du Guesclin and others, I learned from him mostly by simple emulation. Fiore didn't teach in the way a master-at-arms teaches. He simply stood in different ways – some subtly different, like his version of the Woman's Guard, and some startlingly different, like his low guard which he called 'The Boar's Tusk'.

But it was in spear fighting that he departed most from the established manner. Yes? This interests you, messieur? I thought it might. So I'll say this. Most men who fight with a spear fight with the long spear; they vary in length, but in Italy we usually had them nine or ten feet long. But long spears break easily, and have only a temporary advantage over swordsmen.

Fiore preferred a shorter spear, just six or seven feet with a stout shaft, octagonal in cross section. We talked about such weapons, but it was not until we had a day in Milan that we were able to purchase a pair, and then he was avid to fight with them.

And he refused to fight as other men did – and still do. Most men, even trained men, face each other with their points crossed. On the battlefield, men will advance until the spears cross, and then fence with them as if they were long, stiff swords.

Fiore had different words for everything and he made us learn them. He called this tactic the 'Point in line'. He meant that it kept your point in line with the body and head of your opponent. It made sense to me, for this was the best defence against a spear, kept my weapon in the middle of the fight, and allowed me to push with my superior strength against the shaft of most of my adversaries.

Enough digression. That evening north of Milan, the light was fading, we were in harness, and there were six pretty farm girls pressed along the edge of the yard watching the knights duel with spears.

Fiore sprang into the yard and took up one of his fantastic positions – the boar's tusk, in fact – with the spear point low to the ground in front of him, right foot forward, spear on his left hip. I had mine up high across my body in two hands, right foot forward and spear point level with Fiore's unvisored face.

'Try to hit me,' he said. From another man, it would have been a taunt, but Fiore never taunted. He merely said what he thought.

I aimed my blow for the centre of his breastplate. Fiore was the fastest man I ever faced – thanks be to God for the mercy of never facing a man like him in mortal combat! – but not enough faster than me to have a decisive advantage.

I thrust.

He snapped his spearhead up from its low position, exactly like a Tuscan boar tossing its head to gore you. He slapped my spear out of line, and while I tried to recover, he stabbed me with the spearhead through the cheek.

I spat a tooth and sat down, blood pouring out of my mouth, and Fiore flung his spear down and started a steady stream of apologies.

I had been a single inch from death, and the shock of it was as bitter as the copper taste in my mouth. The cheek wound took a week to close and left me with this little twist on my mouth. And there are few things as hard to get off armour as blood! Sweet Jesu, it etches steel faster than acid! And of course, I sat in the wet dung.

On the other hand, Fiore was pitifully sorry to have hurt me, and yet from that moment he had his theory: the theory of the weapon 'off' line versus the weapon 'in' line, and the theory of the shorter versus the longer. I can say all this better in Italian. The phrase 'off line' sounds like something a scribe would say, but *fora di strada* conveys more. As if a common fight happens on a road, and you have had the courage to step off the road.

And, of course, there were the young women who had been watching. I have observed this many times: some girls relish the sight of blood, and some do not. Some desire the man who sheds the blood, and some seek to care for the one bleeding.

I compounded blood loss and trauma with fatigue by staying awake all night.

Fra Peter was not amused; not amused by my injury, and not amused by my lechery.

For three nights running, I was ordered to wash the dishes. And I was given several forms of penance, including standing with my sword by the pommel, held out at arm's length, while Juan prayed some rapid pater nosters and tried not to laugh at me.

The third day, my cut cheek hurt like an imp of Satan had it in fiery tongs, and my hips hurt, and my arms hurt, and I'd had enough of Fra Peter.

He came to see how I was doing. In fact, I could barely stand, and I was kneeling by the hot water in a tin basin, trying to wash his handsome Prague glass while keeping my hair out of the puss and blood coming out of my cheek.

'Let me see your cheek,' he said. He played with it, none too gently, and then smeared honey over the wound, which burned all over again.

'Fuck, that hurts,' I said, or something equally English.

He sighed.

That was enough to set me off.

'By Saint George!' I swore. 'I am a knight, not a squire! I don't polish armour and carry dishes! I fight! I do as I will!'

'Hush, you will split your cheek – ah, there, you've done it again.' He looked at me. 'Truly, William, perhaps it would be best if you went back to Sir John.'

'Sweet Christ, because I tupped a lass? I did her no harm, I assure you. Nor did I take her maidenhead.' I leered, as the young are wont to do when they know perfectly well that they are in the wrong.

'Really?' he asked. He sat back. 'And if she kindles, what kind of life will your red-haired bastard have, got on a serving wench in a barn? Is that the life you want to give to God?'

A thousand hot answers entered my head. 'She will not kindle,' I said. 'She knew her courses.'

'But you don't *care*, do you, Sir William?' he asked quietly, and his use of my title of knighthood hit me like a lance. 'I mean, whether she kindles or no is her loss, not yours.'

By God, I'd thought of those very words and almost said them to him.

'She should guard herself from lust, if she doesn't want to pay the consequence, eh, Sir Knight?' he said.

I was breathing as hard as a man in a fight.

'After all, knighthood does not lie in protecting the weak, does it?' he asked quietly. 'It lies in taking whatever you will. Does it not?'

He didn't threaten to send me back to Italy, where I would be rich, famous, and where pretty girls were available to me at any time. He didn't ask me to do any more peasant work; any more, that is, than we all did to get through the day.

In fact, he embraced me. 'It is hard,' he said. 'Please stay with us.'

I think I struggled against his embrace for a moment. Indeed, just then, I hated him more than the Bourc Camus. There is nothing worse than knowing that you have done wrong, and been seen to do it. Nothing.

Well, I still have the scar. Eh?

We were twenty days to Avignon, and mostly it was a wasted trip. But my cheek healed, to my relief and I saw my sin and my disfigurement together, and I swore a great oath to never fornicate again – an oath which I confess I've broken more than once or twice. When my cheek knitted we were high in the Savoyard passes, and I stopped at a roadside chapel and left a gold florin and a small silver cross.

We jousted. The weather was good, and I was a better lance than I had been, and Fiore was experimenting with lances and swords on horseback. He spent days trying to use his low guard with a lance against my lance, and I dropped him on one Savoyard field a dozen times before he snorted and agreed that his technique did not apply on horseback.

We arrived at Avignon and it, too, was like a home. The four of us had lived there almost a year, after all, and we got good rooms in the Hospital this time because most of the garrison had been dismissed. My room had a lovely glass window, a fine desk, a bed and a magnificent applewood and ivory crucifix of our lord in his passion that I admired so much that I took to using it as a focus for meditation. Fiore was excited by breathing that summer – breathing exercises, of course – and he taught us how to breathe in his own peculiar way as a sidelight to prayer, and the three of us practised it a great deal, because there was little else for us to do.

Father Pierre Thomas was there, too. He was in apartments at the palace, as if he was a great prelate, and indeed, I discovered that my spiritual father *was* now a powerful bishop with a magnificent amethyst on his thumb. When I met him, I kissed it, and he laughed.

'You know,' he said softly, 'I've lost it twice?'

'It is blessed by God!' I said.

He looked away. 'I could feed twenty poor women for a year on this ring,' he said. 'That is its value.' His eyes met mine.

I have heard of men with burning eyes – fanatics. Pierre Thomas was not one such. His eyes were brown and large and held nothing but love – all the time. But that summer he was deep in the matters of the Court of Avignon – the papal curia. The death of King John had thrown yet another blow at his crusade project, and again he had to repair the rent fabric of the church, cajole men to do their duties ... Indeed, it was at times difficult to watch. He was so absolutely humble that he would accept what we, his knights, saw as insults; would accept them with bent head and a smile.

At any rate, after my audience with him, he introduced me to his squire, Miles Stapleton. Miles was also a donat of the Order, younger than me, and far better born. And deeply pious, like Juan more than me. He was my size, with broad shoulders, blue eyes, and light-brown hair, another of Father Pierre's Englishmen, as they called us.

He had a smile as solid as his shoulders. 'Father Pierre has spoken of you,' he said, as if that was the highest praise a man could receive. Well, I suspect I shared that view, at least while I was in his presence.

Miles joined our little group – Fiore, Juan, and Miles and I. I was the worldly one, and a belted knight. Juan and Miles were better born, far richer, and far, far more religious. Fiore – well, he was what he was: tall, odd, and difficult to have around.

Unless you happened to be fighting.

We'd been a week or two in Avignon and nothing seemed to be happening. The rumour was that the crusade was cancelled because the King of France was dead. Peter of Cyprus – it was the summer of Peters, as far as I was concerned – was supposed to be in Avignon, but he'd stayed in Rheims to see the new king of France crowned and to persuade him to take the cross.

We were sitting in my favourite inn in Avignon, drinking wine.

'That coward won't take the cross. He'll make some excuse and send King Peter packing,' I said. Of course, at twenty-four, you know virtually everything there is to know.

'King Charles is a coward?' Juan was looking at a girl ... come to think of it, that girl looked familiar, and when she caught my eye, her face burst into a smile the way a sunflower faces the sun.

Truly, it is nice to be remembered. Her name was Anne, and she brought us wine, touched the back of my neck lightly with the back of her hand, and went off to avoid the attentions of other patrons.

Her touch caused me to lose the chain of my thoughts for a moment, and then I shrugged. I was watching Anne. 'I saw him run at Poitiers. In truth, if he had stood his ground, I think his father would have finished us.'

And I thought of the terrified man we'd seen at the Louvre in fifty-eight. Remember, Geoffrey?

Aye.

But the others wouldn't have it, that a king could be a coward.

We were having this conversation, and it led to another about Poitiers, and two young Scottish priests joined us. I remember all this because I wasn't too drunk, and since they were bound for Scotland, I thought of Kenneth's letters, and I rose, bowed, and ran to the Hospital.

And this whole incident only stays in my head because three men tried to rob me. I probably looked unarmed, and because I was running I looked like easy prey.

I had gone to the Hospital and bounded up the steps, barging into Fra Peter in his robes. He grinned.

'I've found some Scottish priests,' I said, as if that excused everything.

He went off to hear Mass, and I went to my little cell. I collected the letters and jogged out the gate, down the same alley ...

I saw the movement out of the corner of my right eye.

The smaller one had a heavy dagger in his right fist, point down, the way most men use a dagger, and he thrust at my head as he leaped. But he'd played this game before – he was a leering bastard with scars, and I saw all that by the flicker of the torches on the Hospital gate.

As I ducked and pivoted to face him, I raised my left hand to ward the blow, and he flowed around it, changing his blow to the other side, a backhand, descending blow at my right temple.

And four weeks practice on the road paid off in one heartbeat.

Unbidden, my right hand rose and covered his right wrist as my left hand passed close to my face, warding me from his point, and in fact he struck his point into the palm of my right hand because I was slow and it was dark, but I was already flowing on, ignoring the pain. My right hand gripped his, and my left rose, the point slipped out of my flesh, and I grabbed the blade and pushed at it, my fingers clumsy with blood and pain, but the grapple on his right wrist and the turning motion did its work and he let go the dagger as I spun him out and to my left, passing my left foot behind his, breaking his arm at the elbow and then throwing him to the ground, a foot on his arm, and his own dagger into his throat.

But there were three of them.

The other two had hung back, and I didn't go to the ground with the small man, but killed him with my back straight and my head up, so I saw the next pair come.

They had cudgels.

Cudgels are not to be spat on, friends. A stout oak branch can break a sword or turn a spear, and a strong man can break your arm right through your harness or break your head. Two big men with cudgels are long odds.

'He killed Jacques,' the nearest man said, as if I'd done him a favour.

The other man spat.

Both of them flipped their cudgels from hand to hand.

They didn't even ask me for money.

I settled my weight, and as the nearer of the two tossed his cudgel again, I struck.

He missed his grab at the cudgel, and he was stabbed. I used the blade in his body as a lever to move his weight into his friend's path – if such men have friends – and I left the dagger there and passed with my right foot, and the screaming man collapsed over his partner's blade in his chest, and the last of them cut at me and missed.

We were at an impasse.

He swung at me, half-hearted swipes from out of distance. And then he began backing away, and I followed him.

He was no fool. A soon as I followed him, he stepped in and swung.

I was ready and in time, and I stepped off line and avoided the blow, turning him.

He cut again, angry and afraid.

I moved with the blow, followed it, and caught his wrist; he pulled back sharply, and I rammed his elbow over his own head and threw him to the ground.

My own dagger, which I hadn't drawn, flowed into my hand.

I was standing on his wrist, as the Order taught, and as I had lowered my weight my knee may have already cracked a rib or two.

But I'd just had an interview with Father Pierre, I had other things on my mind, and I'd just killed two men.

I put my knife at his throat. 'Saint John commands you to change your life,' I said. I rose, sheathed my dagger while watching him, and walked away down the alley. The second man was already dead – my stab to the heart had indeed gone straight in.

I prayed.

I didn't see the third man get up. But I was aware, painfully aware, that I had killed two men. Letting the third live was a poor consolation to the other two. And yet ...

My hands shook.

My hands were still shaking when I reached the tavern. It is odd that always I react in fear after a fight is over. Sometimes, especially if there is a crowd, I'm terrified before a fight. Luckily, the fear never gets into my head *while* I'm fighting. But by the time I made it back to the table with the priests, I could barely walk, and my breathing was shallow.

I took a sip of wine and had to go outside and throw up my dinner. Glorious. All glorious. Isn't it?

I expected Juan or Fiore to come find me, crouched in abject misery by the stables, but it was Anne who came with a cup of soft cider and a hot, wet cloth.

'I'm sorry, my sweet,' I said.

She smiled. In fact, I think I scared her. 'What happened?'

'Men attacked me.' I drank the cider and it stayed down.

'Did they abuse you? Take your purse?' She put a hand to my head in the way of mothers the world over.

'No,' I said. 'I killed them.'

She didn't know what to say to that, so she said nothing, being wise. After a while, Juan leaned out the door of the inn and then came out and saw me, saw Anne, and bowed. 'Ah, Sir William, the priests must be abed, and crave your letters.'

When I passed him, he had the good grace to say 'Sorry, Brother!' Juan was never a prude about women. And he knew Anne from before.

But I bowed to Anne and mumbled something, used her cloth to wipe my face, and went inside, where I managed to say something civil to the two Scotsmen, one from Hexham, and one from the Western Isles, a place called Mull, which seemed such a commonplace name that it made me laugh. But, according to him, there's a great monastery there, and a nunnery, out on the very edge of the Great Western Ocean. Truly, God is great.

As it proved, they were passing so close to John Hughes' home that they engaged him as a guard and thus got him on their French passport, solving all of his travel problems. The Scots are far more popular in France than the English.

I hugged him. 'Go well,' I said, and I gave him twenty gold florins.

'Christ, I can buy a new farm for that,' he said. 'Milady gave me the same,' he admitted.

I shrugged. 'You've kept us both alive. I'll think of you, sitting by your fireside in whatever godforsaken hamlet in which you settle. Go be a farmer and forget your wicked ways.'

Hughes grinned then and we hugged, and hugged.

'To think I almost killed you in an inn yard,' he said.

'No, I almost killed you!' I answered, and we both laughed.

'Make me a promise?' he asked.

I nodded.

'If you see Richard Musard, kick him in the crotch for what he did to Milady, and then help him up. For me. I miss him.'

John Hughes shrugged as if he couldn't help himself. 'Good fortune out east, Sir Knight. Come to Kentmere and tell my children tales of the wars.'

'All right, John. I will,' I said. 'Go in God's grace and stay safe across France.'

I awoke the next morning and had no idea where I was, but my companion smelled like lavender and spices. I looked down at her when she rolled towards me, and she was Anne, and I was in her garret room in the inn, which meant her three friends were shivering out in the narrow hall or under the eaves.

She leaned over; we were on a pallet of linen filled with new straw, and it smelled healthy and wholesome, as Anne did. She drank water from a pitcher and gave it to me: it had mint leaves in it and I remember that trick still. Her breasts were heavy, white against her brown arms, and the mere sight of them aroused me, despite my painful awareness that I had just broken my oath. In fact, my cheek hurt.

I've known many a witty titbit exchanged between lovers at this point, the first sally of the morning so to speak; I've heard recriminations and I've heard love babble.

She lay back, unworried by her nudity. 'A girl does prefer a soldier to a priest,' she said. She rubbed a hand over the muscle in my belly. 'Do you know that Cardinal Talleyrand is dead?'

Cardinal Talleyrand had been appointed the Cardinal Legate of the crusade. He was leading it, and he was paying for a great deal of it. He intended to be Pope, after all.

Women are different from men in this way, I think. She was already flushed – I won't go into details – but she intended to start our day as we'd ended the last, and yet she could talk church politics with me.

I could see nothing but her lips, her nipples, the sharp line of her side where it met her hip.

At some point another girl pounded on the wooden partition. 'Stop your lechery and let us dress or we'll all be beaten!' she said.

Anne responded by pushing her hips up into mine and making a little emphatic noise.

'Marie had a customer, a papal courier,' she said. 'From the coronation at Rheims,' she went on, her voice raising a little, speaking in the rhythm of our lovemaking.

I'm sure we talked of other things. But I can't remember them.

See now, I've made Monsieur Froissart blush.

Almost the first person I met outside the inn while I was still tying my points of my hose to my doublet, was Father Pierre Thomas, with Miles Stapleton.

Miles waved. 'Did you spend the night in the inn?' he asked. Another boy might have said it with malice, but Miles was an innocent, and he looked at me without guile.

Father Pierre winced.

'I did,' I said simply, having learned a variety of lessons from my time at the Hospital. 'Father, do you know that Cardinal Talleyrand is dead?'

I hated Talleyrand – well, I disliked him, but he was in some ways the power behind Father Pierre. Pierre Thomas came from Talleyrand's home of Perigord, and had, it was said, been a peasant on his estates. And of course, he was the papal legate for the crusade. And the next Pope, or so we all guessed.

It was one of the few times I've ever seen the man hesitate. Then his face took on its habitual look, his eyes calmed, and he nodded. 'No,' he said. 'But this is not the place to speak of it. We were walking to the river, but now I think we will go to the Hospital.'

I had seldom seen Father Pierre agitated or walking more quickly than his determined, workman's stride. But now he did, and when he reached the Hospital, he sent for the Baillie, the local commander, Sir Juan di Heredia, and his own staff. Miles Stapleton was there, and so was Father's Pierre's Latin secretary, a nun called Marie. About whom you will hear more of later. But she was an exceptional woman – she would have to be, to be the Latin secretary to the best mind the Church had produced since Aquinas. Lord Grey was also there.

'Can the crusade survive this blow?' Father Pierre asked.

Di Heredia shrugged. 'And be stronger for it, truly. The King of France was always a broken reed, and Perigord (that's what they often called Talleyrand, after his title) would have used the crusade solely to further his own ambitions.' Now, di Heredia knew what he was about when he spoke of furthering personal ambitions – he was the most ambitious man I'd ever met, with a finger in every political pie. Related to half the crowned heads of Europe, he had been raised with the King of Aragon, and he intended to make himself Grand Master.

I see you both smile. Well, he *is* Grand Master, is he not? Forty years and more, the order was the servant of the Pope and the Doge of Genoa, eh? However much the truth hurts, let us face it. And the Catalans and the Aragonese had had enough.

But that's another story. Suffice it to say that I sat as a belted knight and a volunteer and watched di Heredia, who had once chased me out of Provence when he was the papal commander and I was a mere routier, a brigand. I might have hated him for that, or for his avarice and ambition, which contrasted so sharply with Father Pierre's saintliness. But di Heredia was a fine soldier, a good knight, and it was he who had made the decision to accept me into the Order. Knowing of my past.

Enough digression. Di Heredia twirled his moustache – he was very much the Spanish grandee – and smiled, leaning one elbow on a great table that clerks used to cast accounts.

'Now the legate will be *you*,' he said, smiling at Father Pierre.

Father Pierre made a face. 'I have no worldly interest,' he said. 'No one will make me the most powerful man on the Crusade, nor, I think, am I fit for the role. I would prefer to be the legate's chaplain, and try and keep him to humility and God's purpose. If a crusade is *ever* God's purpose.'

At this, Fra Peter and di Heredia both winced.

But di Heredia leaned forward, his dark eyes twinkling. 'I have the *interest*,' he said. 'My earthly king and your friend the Pope have the *interest*.' He sat back. 'Talleyrand was too powerful and too French. You are everyone's priest. Will you accept?'

Father Pierre leaned back and thrust out his jaw. 'With King John and Talleyrand both dead, surely the Pope will simply cancel the *Passagium Generale*. Or allow it to expire.'

Fra Peter glanced at me. 'Indeed, my lords. In England last year, the Prior there told me, quite frankly, that King Edward saw the entire crusade to be a false emprise. A mummer's play to hide the use of papal funds to pay the King of France's ransom.'

I remembered the trip to England – a very happy time for me, as I have said. Being young and full of myself, and my sister, I'd completely missed Fra Peter's deep disquiet. Indeed, one of the most difficult aspects of serving the Order was, and is, the divided loyalties. Fra Peter was a good Englishman. And to be told by his immediate superior, the Prior of England, that the King of England saw the crusade as a crass political manoeuvre to support the crown of France – by God, that must have hurt.

Father Pierre smiled, at me, of all people. 'I, too, have heard this. And perhaps it was true, although I assure you, my friends in Christ, that God moves men in mysterious ways, and that a *Passagium Generale* declared falsely to support the King of France might, in the end, serve God's will. Do you doubt it?'

Di Heredia nodded and twirled his moustaches again. 'That's what I hoped that you would say. I will suggest that the Pope appoint Peter of Cyprus to command the expedition, and you, my good and worthy priest, to be papal legate.'

Father Pierre's mild blue eyes met di Heredia's falcon's glance. 'As long as you and your king and the Pope understand that I have no higher interest than the will of Christ on earth, so be it,' he said. 'But I am not the man to listen to the Doge of Venice or the King of Aragon's interests.'

Di Heredia made a sound of annoyance and twirled his moustaches again.

Father Pierre looked around, for a moment more like an eagle than a dove. 'Why now, though? When to all, the crusade seems dead?' His eyes rested on Fra Peter's. 'Again?'

Di Heredia laughed. 'Sometimes, Excellence, you are the merest child to the politics of the rotten fruit that surrounds you. Listen. The crusade was only declared to collect the tithes to pay the King of France's ransom and to allow the Pope to recruit mercenaries for his war with the Duke of Milan. But now the Duke of Milan's daughter will be Queen of France, yes? Now the foolish but brave King John is dead no ransom is required. Talleyrand wanted the crusade as a tool of temporal power in Italy – now he is dead.'

'I know all of this,' Father Pierre said simply. 'I am a Christian, not a fool.'

'Then you should believe, as I do, that this is God's will!' di Heredia said. 'And that God can plot more thoroughly and more subtly than the Cardinal Talleyrand or the Pope of the King of France.'

Father Pierre wrinkled his nose in distaste at di Heredia's easy blasphemy.

Di Heredia snorted. 'King John is dead, and he has been replaced by *your* candidate, the King of Cyprus. Talleyrand is dead – who better to replace him than you? Now keep Genoa from going to war with Venice, and by Saint George and Saint Maurice, the crusade is a reality. And all the mercenaries that Talleyrand raised for war in Italy will be ours for the faith.' He smiled like the cunning fox he was: the Pope's version of John Hawkwood. 'We will have to restrain the French faction. They will lose much by Talleyrand's death.' He leaned forward. 'The aristocrats will not want you because you cannot be bought, and you are not one of them. There will be consequences.' He tapped his teeth. 'The Bishop of Cambrai has lost a great deal with Talleyrand's death.'

Fra Peter turned to look at his brother-knight. 'Tell us?'

'Robert, the Bishop of Cambrai, went straight to the Pope on word of the death of Talleyrand.' He made a face. 'I would wager a donkey against a warhorse he asked for command of the crusade, to take the soldiers for himself and his family.'

Well might you wince, monsieur. That was Avignon. That was our crusade.

No one even mentioned the Turks.

Juan was attacked. It began to seem as if we were being targeted.

Anne told me that the Bishop of Cambrai was intending to have a magnificent audience with the Pope. 'He thinks he will command the crusade,' she whispered to me.

'Who the hell is he?' I asked. I suspect I nuzzled her neck or tried to move on to other matters.

'The Count of Geneva's son, the Count of Savoy's nephew ...' She shrugged, which made her nipples move against my chest, and we moved on from church politics to other matters.

Another day of carrying messages for Father Pierre, and Anne told me we were to have an audience with the Pope. She laughed as she shrugged out of her shift. 'Do other girls talk about leaves and flowers and poetry?' she asked. 'I feel I have gone from being your light of love to your spy.'

Of course I assured her of my ardour.

She shrugged. 'You'll leave me soon enough,' she said. 'Your Father Pierre has an audience with the Pope. May I tell you something serious?

Your Father Pierre … people love him. But no one in Avignon can imagine how he has come to win the Pope's ear.' She leaned over me. 'Would you – could you – arrange for him to bless me?'

The path of love and lechery is never a straight one.

The next afternoon, I took a pair of scrolls to the Carmelite house, and another across the city to one of the Roman cardinals. I knew I was followed, and I was growing very careful. When I returned to the Hospital, I had time with Father Pierre. We prayed together, and he showed me a meditation that I still use with my beads, and then he asked me if I wished to confess.

I am a poor liar. It is one of my best virtues, I think. I confessed Anne, and begged him to shrive her.

He shrugged. 'I would bless her soul for her own sake, but for yours I will demand that you not sin with her again,' he said. He didn't smile, but there was a smile in his voice. 'The sins of the young,' he said softly.

On the eleventh of June, we were summoned to the papal palace for an audience with the Pope – Urban II, a French Benedictine whom I have mentioned before.

The last time I'd had an audience with the Pope, I'd stood in a dull brown cote and clean hose and had tried to listen to what my betters discussed while I looked at the wonders of the ceiling over my head and the rich frescoes on the walls.

Since then, I'd been to Italy and seen enough frescoes to dull the edge of my wonder. And men in their twenties are critical of everything; I was, by then, a hardened man of the world, and I looked at the frescoes with less awe and more judgement.

A pity. The awe was more worthy. I have the knowledge to judge a lance strike, a sword thrust, or the placement of a battery of gonnes, but I've never painted a stroke.

This time, I stood in the Pope's audience chamber in harness, with the red surcoat adorned with the white cross over my armour, and a small shield with my own coat-armour in the right quadrant: a knight-volunteer of the Order. I wore gold spurs and a gold belt of plaques and a sword. I'm quite sure that I looked very fine, perhaps finer than Fra Peter, whose scarlet surcoat had seen more wear and who eschewed the earthly vanity of a gold belt. I was not as splendid as Lord Grey, and Miles Stapleton rivalled me, but that only meant that our party looked martial and, at least in my memory, puissant. Sister Marie-Therese wore black, as did the two priests of Father Pierre's entourage, one Scottish Hospitaller priest, Father Hector, and one Italian, Father Maurice.

And then there was Fiore, in his plain harness and red coat. But we'd brushed him and mended him and I'd put him in my second-best doublet, and his golden hair made him look like a military saint.

Father Pierre, who was, of course, a bishop, nonetheless knelt and kissed the Pope's ring and there was a low murmur between them. Juan, my friend, the great Juan di Heredia's nephew, winked at me. He, too, was resplendent in gold and scarlet and harness, and as he was apparently the richest of the lot of us, he, too, glittered. In his case, he had a superb sword worth ten of mine, and a single ring with a ruby that was worth more than my warhorse and my harness.

Altogether, we made up Father Pierre's entourage. We were his household, and we'd been gathered for the crusade. Father Pierre was the least resplendent – despite being the Archbishop of distant Crete, he wore his Carmelite habit, and his plain dress was echoed by the Pope himself, who wore a magnificent chasuble over his plain Benedictine habit.

As Father Pierre kissed the Pope's ring, I saw that Fra di Heredia was also in harness, and that he held a magnificent white banner embroidered in gold. He was the Pope's standard bearer.

I think it was seeing the standard that made it all real. I had heard the talk. I'd been present for the negotiation. But Anne gave odds on the *Passagium Generale*, the crusade, being cancelled. Fra Peter was more cynical than I'd ever heard him, decrying the waste of time and money and manpower that had allowed the movement to be delayed and delayed.

But now, it was happening. One of the papal secretaries read out a scroll, and my Latin was good enough to make out that Father Pierre had just been promoted to be Patriarch of Constantinople.

A sigh went through the hall. It is an empty see, an appointment without a church, because, of course, the Emperor of Constantinople was a schismatic, a follower of the Greek heresy. But the appointment said *everything*. We were going on crusade to take Jerusalem, and I had heard rumours that we would go to Constantinople – or that the Emperor would join us. Why else appoint a Patriarch?

And then, in his slow, elegant French, the Pope appointed Father Pierre the papal legate. Legates were the commanders of the ancient legions of mighty Rome, and it was difficult to see the slight figure of my spiritual father, shoulders bent like a peasant's, as the military commander of the legions of Christ.

But Lord Grey was summoned and appointed the Gonfalonier – the standard bearer – of the legate. And Fra di Heredia placed the papal banner in his hands.

We bowed, and one by one we filed in front of the Pope, and he blessed us. When I bent to kiss the hem of his garment, he placed his crozier on my shoulder.

'I remember you,' the old man said.

I raised my head.

'Pierre, you seem to have a taste for Englishmen,' he said.

Father Pierre laughed. 'Perhaps they have a taste for me,' he said. 'But they are very brave.'

'You had the smell of a routier when last I saw you, young man,' the Pope said.

It is not easy to make a witty remark to the most powerful man in the world while you kneel at his feet in eighty pounds of armour. My memory is that I grunted.

'Well, well. Go with God, my son. I am pleased to see you are a knight, and still a volunteer. Will you go on this crusade?' Pope Urban II asked me.

'Holy Father, I will,' I managed.

He smiled. 'There,' he said to Father Pierre. 'One soul saved, if we lose the rest.' He put his whole hand on my head and blessed me.

I suppose we stood around for a long time, but I don't remember it. What I do remember is Fra Peter listening to a page, one of the Order's, I believe. I saw him stiffen, and I knew what that meant.

The Order has signals, hand signals, we use in the field. He made one to me, then.

The signal meant 'A l'arme!'

We were forced to stand on the steps of the palace by the arrival of prelate with an enormous retinue – a hundred men-at-arms and fifty religious – and I think that we were all relieved to be out of the palace. Father Pierre was silent, already, I think, planning his next step. Fra Peter was looking out over the plaza. I had loosened my sword in its sheath and checked my dagger.

Juan shook his head on the steps and hit me lightly with his beautiful gloves. 'I look like an angel come to earth, but the Pope talks to you!'

Juan thought his voice was low, but Father Pierre stopped and looked up. He was a small, slim man and his wool robes all almost buried him, but his smile pierced like a Turk's arrow. 'Juan, do you know the story of the prodigal son?' he asked.

Juan shifted. 'Excellency, I spoke only in jest.'

Father Pierre – really, the Patriarch and legate was far too powerful a man to be called 'Pater' – nodded. 'Listen, the Pope rejoices, as he should, in the redemption of a single sinner.'

Juan looked at me. 'Perhaps Fiore and I should commit more sins,' he said.

'Be ready,' Fra Peter hissed.

Fiore turned and loosened his sword. Juan looked at me.

Fra Peter was just raising a hand for silence when we saw the men-at-arms of the prelate's entourage approaching on the street before the palace, their flags a mixture of sable and argent on some men-at-arms and azure and argent on others, all riding behind a gonfalonier bearing a banner that bore the arms of the house of Savoy, a white cross of Saint Denis on red ground.

Is it happenstance that the great enemy of my youth bore the exact opposite of the arms of England and Saint George?

At any rate, they were on horseback, arrogant as Frenchmen, and refusing to give way to Father Pierre's smaller retinue.

My hand tightened on my sword hilt.

I had last seen that man lying in the mud, where Fra Peter had put him with a single blow while I sat with a halter around my neck waiting to die.

The Bourc Camus. He hadn't changed. That is, he was clean, neat, and his eyes passed over us with obvious contempt. 'Clear the steps, priest,' he ordered the papal legate. 'Your betters have need of them.'

The magnificent knight to his left on the caparisoned horse, in crisp dark blue embroidered with silver – that was the Count d'Herblay.

D'Herblay didn't see me at all. His eyes were on his kinsman (not that I knew that at the time), the Bishop of Geneva.

But the Bourc's eyes came back to me.

There is a great deal of worldly satisfaction in the shock of an enemy. He was dismayed and I rejoiced.

But I was no longer so very young, nor so afraid of all the world. Or perhaps I was simply inside the warm aura of my priest, and thus immune from the anger of Satan's messenger.

I smiled at him.

He was surrounded by his own men, and in the entourage of a prince of the church – if Robert of Geneva did not yet have the cardinal's hat, he would. Anne had told me that he was superbly rich in his own right, commanded all his family's connections, and was, in addition, one of the best minds the church had produced in twenty years.

The bishop was craning his head to see what had disturbed his arrival; he was in a chair, carried by eight liveried men. He was quite young, with a bulbous nose and no chin to speak of. His eyes were wide set, and seemed to question everything.

By my side, Fra Peter said 'Do *not* draw.'

I had already used my thumb to break the seal of sword to scabbard. I had slid the sword an inch free, ready to pull her free, all without any conscious thought. This, on the steps of the papal palace.

And yet I was not so far wrong.

The Bourc was still mounted. So was d'Herblay.

I could tell from the set of his mouth and the movement of his eyes that he recognised Father Pierre. And remembered him and his role. But more – his eyes kept going back to my priest, and I thought of di Heredia's warnings.

'Clear this hedge priest off the steps,' he shouted to his men-at-arms.

Then a great many things happened at once. All of us, even the nun, closed in around Father Pierre. We were his bodyguard and, even then, we had already begun to practice how we would defend him, if it came to fighting: on the crusade, of course. It had not occurred to any of us that we'd defend him from an animal like Camus on the steps of the papal palace, but we locked up around him in a few heartbeats.

Camus put spurs to his warhorse and aimed it at Father Pierre. He had a staff in his hands, the sort of baton that commanders carry, and he cut down at the nun who, by ill-chance, was in front of all of us.

She got an arm up, but he cut hard. I heard her arm break, but she didn't flinch, and her struggle cost him time. As her action bought us a few moments, I pushed past Father Pierre and caught Camus's blow on my crossed arms. My steel vambraces were easily proof against his oak baton, although I felt each blow. He threw three, very fast, and half a dozen of his other men-at-arms were charging us on the steps.

If this seems insane to you, remember who he was. And what he was. And what Robert of Geneva has become.

I had never faced a foe in full harness, but without a weapon or a helmet. A man can spend a great deal of effort protecting his own head; indeed, the piece of armour everyone gets first is a helmet. But by Camus' third blow, I had his tempo. My left hand trapped his descending right, just for a moment, and my fingers closed on the cuff of his gauntlet covering his wrist.

The oak staff carried on and smacked me in the nose, a light blow that nonetheless almost took me out of the fight, and my right hand closed on his baton and I almost screamed with pain. It was only a few days since I'd had a dagger blade in the palm – and despite all that I managed to get my left on to the flange of his right elbow cop. I pulled.

He came off his horse. The horse was trying to bite my face – a war-horse does that – but Father Hector put his crucifix into the horse's teeth with a two-handed blow that would have done honour to many a belted knight and the horse reared, finishing Camus's attempts to retain his seat, and they went down, the horse one way, and Camus at my feet.

To my left, Fiore had another man-at-arms flat on his front and was kneeling on the man's back, and Juan and Fra Peter had their arms up, covering Father Pierre. But more and more black and white men-at-arms were closing in, and it finally penetrated my head that this might be a real assassination attempt and not mere arrogant happenstance.

The blue and white men-at-arms took no part. They merely watched.

Miles Stapleton put a horseman down by throwing himself under the man's arm and lifting his foot. And Lord Grey opened the papal banner, so that every man in the Place de Palais could see the papal arms in glittering gold on white silk.

I had the Bourc at my feet. 'Call off your dogs,' I shouted, and rotated his arm a little farther in its socket. It was already dislocated.

He screamed. That scream got more attention than any call to arms – four paces away, a mounted soldier reared his horse and fell back. D'Herblay had his sword in his hand. He pointed it at me and shouted.

'Let him go,' Father Pierre said, gently. He put his naked hand on my armoured one, and lifted my thumb. My hand was locked in place on the Bourc's arm. I was rigid with anger, with shock – with not-really-suppressed violence.

'I'll kill you all,' Camus said. 'I'll kill you and then I'll flay your souls in hell.'

Father Pierre shook his head, his mild eyes unmoved. 'No, my son, you will not.'

'I am not your son!' roared Camus. Even then, his right shoulder dislocated, a swarm of men-at-arms around him, he went for his dagger.

I was too slow.

Fiore dei Liberi was not. He stripped the dagger from Camus's left hand as if he was taking a pie from a street seller. Fra Peter picked up the oak staff that Camus had dropped and held it high.

The Savoyard prelate was just watching. He wore his gown with long black gloves so that he appeared entirely black except his head, where his ferocious, inquisitive, bulging eyes and his narrow, chinless face made him look more like a cat than was quite right. If he cared at all that one of the captains of his escort was lying flat with his arms pinned and his own dagger at his throat, he betrayed nothing but an intense interest, as if we were a troupe of travelling players performing something vaguely obscene. Those eyes of his!

Fra Peter gave Father Pierre a gentle but very commanding shove away from the Bishop's men and towards the open steps to our left. 'Move, Excellency,' he said.

Now the blue and white men-at-arms were also moving, working their way to block the ends of the street. Robert of Geneva leaned down from his chair to speak to his cousin d'Herblay.

Father Pierre was not used to being called 'Excellency' and he didn't react at once.

'By Satan, I will find the peasants who are your father and mother and flay them alive,' the Bourc Camus spat at Father Pierre. This, let me say again, on the steps of the papal palace.

'You are like a child,' Father Pierre said. 'You seek to break things—'

'*Don't patronise me, you low-born hypocrite. You were born on the dung heap, and I will fling you back to it.*' Camus's voice had taken on an odd, sing-song chant and a sibilant hiss.

Father Hector had his crucifix in Camus's face, and Liberi had the man pinned, despite his demonic strength – demons, for all the aid of the netherworld, have a hard time with one shoulder dislocated and the other locked by an expert man-at-arms.

Fra Peter stopped talking, caught Father Pierre around the waist and carried him away.

I found that I was standing over the nun. Her face was white and her left arm was clearly broken, but she got to her feet without using either hand, rolling forward over her hips like a knight. She tucked the broken arm into the cord that bound her habit and met my eye. I moved my head, indicating that she should follow Father Pierre and then I looked past her at Liberi.

He had the tiniest smile on his face. With a look of pleasure on his narrow face, he rolled Camus off his hip and threw him down the steps and into his own men-at-arms.

Chaos ensued – shrieks, bellows of pain – and under their cover we slipped away to the left, moving fast. Juan was one step ahead of me. None of us had drawn our swords.

'At them!' shouted d'Herblay. But Fra Peter had chosen an alley, not the street itself. The sacrifice of our dignity gained us ten valuable steps on our enemies, and their horses only hampered them in the press.

At the base of the steps, I saw that Fra Peter was already running – in full armour, carrying a grown man – to the left into an alley, as I said, the Rue des Mons. The two priests followed, and then Juan and Fiore and the nun. I paused and looked back, ready to make a fight at the narrow mouth of the side street.

D'Herblay was coming.

I drew my sword. Father Pierre was no longer there to stop me.

The alley was so narrow that only one horseman could pass and that with his head brushing the overhanging houses. And d'Herblay's posture and his seat on the horse betrayed that he did not want to enter the alley first. He and another man jostled for position at the mouth of the alley, where the old palace gates had been forty years before.

I stood, my heart beating like a troubadour playing a fast dance. But I had my sword on my hip – Fiore's *dente di cinghiale.*

But d'Herblay reined in. He shouted something. I'm sure it was an insult, but I didn't care. He didn't dare face me.

There was no further pursuit – and the Savoyard bishop was still watching us.

As a group we were deeply shaken. Violence can impart a dangerous air of unreality to events, and the demonic – and I use that term deliberately, messires, for the nature of Camus's outbursts shook even the gentle Father Pierre.

Our Italian priest returned to the papal palace, escorted by Juan, to deliver a strongly worded protest that was written by Fra Peter. Father Pierre was already moving on to other things: to the revolt on Crete, which remained his see, and to his duties as papal legate. In an hour, he was a functioning prelate again.

I found it hard to breathe. The nun, Sister Marie, had her arm set in the hospital. I remember that part, because the Hospitaller cleared a ward for her, as if having a woman in the place might spread a contagion. But he also sent for sisters of his own order from their nearby house, and they came quickly, surrounding her with kindness.

I spent enough time with her to glean that she was not as shocked as one might expect from a Latin Secretary.

Fra Peter gathered us all in the chapel after vespers and we prayed together. The shock of the open violence so close to what we all thought of as 'home' didn't wear off immediately.

It was almost midnight before Fra di Heredia arrived from the palace. I was not included in whatever he discussed with Fra Peter.

But it didn't matter, because the crusade was a reality. We were going. And with the Bourc's threats ringing in our ears, it appeared we were leaving immediately.

I need to remind you that, whatever his reservations about the crusade, the Pope had sent men, trusted men, all over France and Italy, summoning the routiers and the men of the Free Companies to save their souls by going on crusade. It was said that the Archpriest Arnaud de Cervole, with whom I served before Brignais, was to gather the men who would serve, and lead them over the Alps to Venice. Sir Walter Leslie and his brother Norman, who were both famous knights and sometime mercenaries, were gathering men-at-arms in Italy. If the crusade was a charade, at the very least many powerful men hoped that the Holy Land would draw the Free Companies from France and Italy the way a leech draws poison from a wound.

The crusade was to depart from two ports, Genoa and Venice, both of which were being forced to cooperate each with the other. In fact, each of those cities hated the other far more than they hated the Turk; each city, in fact, sought only the best trade status with the very *paynim* we were going to fight. But let me add that of the two, Genoa was virtually allied with the Saracens of Egypt.

Hah! Messire Froissart, I know you have met Peter of Cyprus, and I know you wish for me to get to the meat of my tale: the fighting, the chivalry. But in truth, the tale is how anyone came to fight, and not the fight itself. Let me say this much without the spoiling of my story: I am not sure that the old French Pope ever intended the crusade to march, although I think Urban wanted it, and I'm damned sure that neither Genoa nor her arch-rival Venice intended a real blow to be struck. I'm reasonably sure that none of the routiers in France and Italy ever truly intended to save their souls and become crusaders, and I can attest to the desperate reality that not a single king of Christendom, save one, intended a blow to be struck, whatever they promised.

It was all lies and half-promises and empty titles and silk flags.

Listen, then. Sometimes, as Father Pierre used to say, Christ works in mysterious ways.

It is a flaw of the deeply self-interested men of the world that they assume that idealists are fools.

Father Pierre – I will keep calling him that, as he was always 'Pater' to us – moved like lightning when he moved. The Pope had appointed him to a dozen offices and given him various sources of income to enable him to gather the crusade. Whatever the Pope's real intentions, Father Pierre gathered his household and all the knights and volunteers of the Order who were in Avignon and led them to Italy. Less than two days passed after his appointment, and we were on the road with twenty men-at-arms and his whole household staff. To my shame, I barely had the courtesy to pay Anne a farewell visit.

Listen, it is not all war, the life of arms. Eh? I owed her better than a casual goodbye in an inn yard. As events proved, I'd have done better, far better, to have slunk away without a farewell, but I betook me to the inn and called her, and told her I was away on crusade.

She looked at me, yawning. And smiled her half-smile. '*Eh bien*,' she said. 'Some day you will come back here, too fine to speak to me.' She turned her head away.

Love ... love is a powerful force, but sometimes, plain liking is the easier emotion to distinguish.

'Don't be like that,' I said, somewhat pettishly. 'I'm a donat of the Order. I'll be back.'

She smiled a false smile. 'And your lady ... will she approve of me? Like your priest and your knight approve of me?'

I hadn't really thought of Emile in a month. The word 'lady' was like a blow. And of course, Anne was only guessing, with the unerring instinct of the young woman.

'I don't even know why you came to say goodbye, monsieur,' she said, casting her eyes down. 'I suspect I'm little more than a whore to you.' She looked at me with something of her usual twinkle. 'A badly paid whore, an unpaid spy. I have work to do.'

I hadn't even brought her a present. I walked quickly into the street of jewellers and bought her a good cross with an emerald, and the booksellers were only just opening their stalls. It was a lovely summer day in Avignon, and sin made me think of my sister, and I spent far too much money, almost all my available gold and silver, on a fine copy of *Cyurgia* by the Pope's doctor. The bookseller said it was new, the latest scholarship. He didn't have a plain copy, so I paid for a small illustrated one, with drawings in blue ink and scrollwork in the margins and some magnificent capitals.

Then I went back towards the inn. At some point, I began to wonder if I had been followed – I saw the same scraggly ginger beard for the third time since leaving Anne. I was cautious, and when I came to the fountain at the Place de Saints, I paused to drink water and wash my hands, and saw a boy that I had seen several times before.

I should not have gone back to the inn, but I misunderstood the threat. I found Anne washing tables.

'Anne,' I said.

'Go away! I'm working,' she said.

'I brought you a present,' I said.

She turned and her scorn was palpable. 'So that I can be a whore in truth, monsieur?'

She went back to washing the wooden table. The limp-haired innkeeper came down and leered at me, which did nothing to improve my mood.

I didn't like him listening from the common room, either.

'Run along on your crusade,' she said. 'You'll make me lose my place.'

'I *like* you!' I protested. 'Please, ask the innkeeper, and I will take you to Father Pierre.'

Her head turned. 'That's much better,' she admitted. 'I thought we liked each other. Remember the *auberge* at Chateauneuf? Last year?'

I smiled. 'With Juan?'

'One of my best days. Give me your present, monsieur.' She raised her head and put her hand to her back, and for a moment she was a much older woman. Remember that noble girls live longer, keep their looks longer, because they do not work from dawn to dark.

She went and whispered to the fat owner, and he shrugged. 'Don't come back too pious to help a customer,' he said, but he waved.

I paused and gave him a Florentine silver coin; it was bigger than most and unclipped. He took it with some respect.

I took her to the Hospital, where the gatekeeper looked at me as if I had grown an additional head. 'You cannot bring a slattern into the Hospital!' he said.

Chance had caused us to reverse positions, as men will when they argue, so that I was looking back down the street out the gate, and there was ginger beard.

Before I could cajole or intimidate the gatekeeper, Father Pierre appeared mounted on a mule, with Fra Peter Mortimer and Fra Juan di Heredia at his side. He didn't smile at me, but he smiled at Anne.

'Ah, Daughter,' he said, and he dismounted clumsily.

She burst into tears. I don't think she said a word.

He whispered to her, and she sank to her knees.

He made the sign of the cross on her and when he looked at me, his mouth twitched. His eyes cut me like knives.

I couldn't meet his eyes long, and I raised her and took her home.

In the doorway of the inn, she stopped and smiled at the ground. 'I really prefer not to think of you as a customer.' Then she lifted her eyes and they met mine. 'But really ...'

I put the cross around her neck. There was a pause, and I decided to kiss her neck.

She frowned, and then slipped away. 'Do you know that man?' she asked. She pointed out the door of inn.

Ginger beard saw her out-thrust arm – and bolted.

I shrugged. 'He followed me here.'

She sighed. 'Some footpad. Friend of the men you killed, perhaps?' She kissed me, but it was sisterly. 'I love your priest. He is everything people say he is. Go follow him. Be careful, *mon cher*. They mean him harm, the rich fucks, Geneva and his people.'

That's how I left her.

I left the medical book at the Hospital with instructions that it should go to my sister.

We climbed into the Alps, headed once more for Turin, and I had days to consider meeting Richard Musard, to fence with my comrades on the road, to joust, to share cups of wine – and to think of Emile.

I had, in addition to plain lechery, been repeatedly unfaithful to her; all very well when she was distant and thought dead, but a stain on my chivalry now that I knew her to be alive. I thought about her a great deal, because I knew it was possible that I would meet her at the Green Count's court. And because of Anne's barb. My 'lady'.

I had a number of reasons to be dissatisfied with myself. I pondered the twists and turns of the Bourc's attack on us, and the only conclusion I could draw is that, despite my best efforts, I had been afraid. And despite Fra Peter's exhortation, I was sure I should have killed him.

In fact, I thought a great deal about the two thieves I'd killed, desperate men. They had looked to me like brigands, and two of them at least had borne the stamp of men-at-arms by the way they moved, their strength.

I had been a brigand.

I hadn't dealt well with Anne, I had betrayed Emile, I had failed to kill the Bourc and I'd slaughtered a couple of down-on-their-luck routiers when I should have knocked them out or even handed them some silver.

I went to confession with Father Pierre again, in the same ruined chapel where we'd cooked dinner a year before. It is no pleasure to confess to a man who knows you, and whose good opinion you crave. Indeed, it is even less a pleasure to confess in the damp corner of a wet stone ruin with a flickering fire twenty feet away and a circle of professional ears cocked for your every failing.

That's just my fear speaking. God knows *I* never listen when some poor fellow is confessing, and I doubt they listened to me, but it made it all worse, and the rain fell on us. Father Pierre seemed immune; indeed, his patience was untouched by weather.

I confessed killing the two thieves and letting the third live. And I confessed my desire to kill the Bourc. And then I confessed to having lain with Anne, which he'd heard before – do priests tire of hearing men's sins? Does God tire? What can be duller than repeated sin, eh? And with the farm girl in Italy.

Emile I kept to myself.

Father Pierre heard me out, all my rambling, my disputations on my own sin; all the hollow arguments of the guilty.

He smiled in the flickering firelight. 'Killing thieves,' he said softly. 'Two thieves died by Jesus.'

I shrugged.

'Listen, William, what you'd like is for me to set you some strong penance, and then you'd push yourself to accomplish it, and be cleansed.' He shrugged and looked away.

'Yes!' I agreed.

'Let me ask *you* a thing,' he said, and his gentle eyes met mine. 'If you kill a Saracen on crusade, how is that different from killing a thief in the dark streets of Avignon?'

I rubbed water from my forehead. 'I don't know, Father,' I said. 'Since they are all unshriven, they go to Hell – is that what you mean?'

'No,' he said, and shook his head. He took a breath and then shook his head again. 'I don't know either, but as I am about to lead men to die and kill, I have prayed on this subject every night. And now you set me this.' He put his chin in his hand. 'Let me ask you another thing. The Bourc Camus. Do you think him to be … a servant of Satan?'

Just thinking of Camus made my breath catch a little. But I paused, and saw him in my mind's eye. 'No,' I said. 'No, I think he believes it himself. But if he were Satan's knight, surely he'd be ...' I found that I was grinning. 'Better? Or rather, worse? More ... *preux*? More dangerous?'

'He may yet serve the enemy in this world and the next,' Father Pierre agreed. 'But yes, he seems all too human to me. And yet ... he made me afraid. And for me to be afraid, I must, for a moment, have doubted God, because you know that a Christian who hopes for heaven has nothing to fear.'

'I have never met a mortal man who did not know fear,' I said.

'Perhaps battle teaches a wisdom and humility that the University of Paris lacks.' Father Pierre smiled. 'Perhaps fear and sin come from the same wellspring, then,' he said. 'At any rate, I can shrive you like any village priest. But you knights ... you kill. You strive hard to excel at it. You have fine words – beautiful, noble words like *preux* and courage to describe yourselves and your way.' He pursed his lips. 'Sometimes, I wonder if your way is not altogether wrong.' He raised a hand. 'Ah, your pardon, my son; tonight it is I who needs a confessor, not you. I do not like this mantle of authority thrust upon me. Listen, cut all the firewood from here until Turin, and while you cut dead wood, think of the living men you have killed, and say prayers for them.' He blessed me then. 'And stop your lechery. I am not amused by it – you are not a schoolboy. Wake up, or you will be awakened roughly.'

I went back to the fire, and he sat out in the wet.

The Green Count was not at Turin. He was at Geneva on business, but the word was that he was serious in his crusading vows, and intended to mount a campaign. Despite that, he was still very close to the Visconti of Milan, and the Pope was still on the other side of a deep political divide.

I tried to add it up in my head: Milan was the enemy of the Pope, and Savoy was related to Milan and an ally of the Pope, and Robert of Geneva, our erstwhile assailant, was part of the Savoyard clan, trying to take control of the crusade, and all the mercenaries that the Pope was enlisting ...

If the prelates thought that they could control the routiers this way, they needed to spend a winter with John Hawkwood. I had the notion that the Savoyards were plotting without understanding the consequences of their actions. As the great often do, the Savoyards had forgotten that lesser men might have better heads for plotting.

One of the ways that Italy had changed me was the way in which I saw the divides. Listen – when you are a London apprentice, the divides are simple enough: the Goldsmiths before all the other trades; Trades and Mysteries before the nobles; London before any other town; England and England's King above all other kings and countries. Simple.

As an Englishman, I had tended to see every conflict measured by the English side; so, for example, in the war between the Pope and Milan, the Pope represented the 'French' side and Milan the 'English' side, although as time went by it was clear to me that these simple views of Italian politics wouldn't stand up to scrutiny, and in the end, Milan married his daughter to the King of France. But Hawkwood assured us, his English soldiers, that when we fought for Pisa against Florence (an ally of the Pope) we were still fighting on the 'English' side. And that *mattered*.

It mattered, but a year in Italy had revealed a few things to me. One was that Milan was richer than all of England. I had yet to visit Venice or Genoa, but knew each city was richer than the whole of England including London and Florence was larger than Paris and hadn't endured ten years of near-constant starvation and war.

That meant that to see Italian conflicts through English eyes was like the plough dragging the ox. Edward III of England might plot all he wanted, but his schemes and those of Charles V of France were mere back alleys in the labyrinthine city of European diplomacy. I didn't come to this in one year, but I was beginning to suspect that there was more to Amadeus's quarrels with the Pope, or with Milan, than his relations with England and France.

So the divides were both true and false, and a mercenary, or a crusader, needed to be able to look at every plot from several angles. It was possible for a good man, a *true* man, to find himself on both sides of any question, because of divided loyalties or interest. As one example, Amadeus of Savoy, the Green Count, and his Savoyards hated the English and were at least in their hearts loyal to the French King, but the Green Count was a sovereign prince; he owed no fealty to anyone, king or Emperor, except for a few estates. He served the Pope, but he had designs of his own in Italy. He wanted a crusade – and he wanted to control it himself. He was not the sort of man who would abide another's commands. And his cousin Robert of Geneva, formerly Bishop of Cambrai, was a Savoyard first and foremost.

And my lady Emile was the wife of one of the Savoyard nobles.

At any rate, the Green Count was not at Turin, and neither was the Comte d'Herblay or his wife, nor Richard Musard. We stayed three days; Father Pierre had a long discussion on crusade funding with the Green Count's chamberlain, and we rode east and south, over the passes to Italy. There was still snow on the mountaintops, but the valleys were already in summer, with fields of flowers stretching away like the very embodiment of paradise.

And then we rode down out of the mountains into the plain of Lombardy, and I was back in Italy. By Saint Maurice, gentlemen, I hope I won't seem a worse Englishman to you if I say that I love Italy. It is warm and the wine is good.

We were bound for Bologna. To make the crusade possible, the Pope had curtailed his war with Milan, and his only concrete benefit from two solid years of war was that he had gained the city of Bologna. But let me put that in perspective. Bologna's taxes were roughly the same as those of the City of London. *Eh bien?*

Italy is rich.

Father Pierre had taken the city as papal legate while I'd been fighting for Pisa, and had proved himself both a fine governor and a Christian man in his dealings. Now he was going back to perform a good deed for the Bolognese, and to rally his own support for the crusade.

We were housed in the university. Bologna was not the most famous house of learning in Italy, but it had a mighty reputation for its doctors of medicine. The main palazzo was a magnificent building of brick and marble, and had frescoes better than anything in Avignon. I shared a room with Juan and with Fiore, and the three of us filled it to bursting with clothes and harness and horse tack.

The day we arrived, the three of us spent the entire afternoon going over all the tack – every mule saddle, every bridle. We were, in effect, the squires of the whole party.

In the evening, we laid out the knight's tack and several items that needed serious repairs, and Miles Stapleton came and joined us in the cloistered courtyard. Some of the men in gowns were scandalised, but most smiled to see us so industrious.

Half the bridles needed some repair, and Fra Peter's saddle was leaking stuffing and the tree was wearing through the leather so that it had to be troubling his mount. I went and fetched him, and he shook his head.

'I need a new saddle,' he confessed. 'I should have seen to this in Avignon. I hadn't expected to leave in such a hurry.'

I showed him the saddle for Sister Marie's mule, which was in worse shape than his. 'She must ride a great deal,' I said.

Fra Peter smiled. 'She does indeed. *Mon dieu* – that's bad. The tree is broken.'

Indeed, you could flex the saddle in your hands.

Fra Peter made a face. 'In Avignon, I could have us new saddles in a few hours.' He was frustrated, a face he never showed us.

'Can't we buy saddles?' I asked. 'It seems a mighty city!'

Indeed, Bologna was two-thirds the size of London and had shops and stalls and a great market and many leatherworkers.

Fra Peter smiled; not a bitter smile, but not a happy one, either. I noted that there was something of Anne's derision in Fra Peter's smile. 'I'm vowed to poverty, William,' he said. 'So is Sister Marie.'

Throughout the conversation, he was sitting comfortably on the stone between two columns of the cloister, while I continued to sew away at Father Hector's bridle.

'I'm not,' said a man from behind Fra Peter. 'Vowed to poverty. Ser Peter Mortimer, how fare you?'

The man addressing my knight was one of the handsomest men I ever saw, despite being more than half a century old, as I later discovered. He was also one of the most richly dressed men I'd ever seen, as out of place in the cloister of Bologna as a nun in a Cheapside chophouse. He wore a green silk pourpoint, stuffed and quilted, with a band of gold at each wrist and a collared shirt that emerged from the collar of his pourpoint like a white flower, a fashion I'd never seen before. He also wore a sword, which was unheard of in Bologna; a longsword, the kind that Fiore favoured, gilded steel on the cross guard and a jewel in the pommel, which was a wheel of gold. His hose were gold and green, and he wore a profusion of gold rings and a gold collar that matched the gold plaques on his belt.

He and Fra Peter embraced like old comrades. In fact, I discovered that this prince and Fra Peter *were* old comrades.

'Let me buy you some saddles,' he said. 'Peter, it is the least I can do.'

Fra Peter shook his head. 'Nicolas, I could not.'

'We accept!' I said, leaping to my feet. I had on my own plaque belt, the heavy belt that showed my status as a knight. Mine was silver with heavy gilding, and was worth roughly the price of my ransom: that's what we used to say they were for. I realised that I looked incongruous – knights don't sit about repairing horse tack and mule saddles.

But the prince took no heed. 'Here's a man of sense – your squire, I doubt not?'

Fra Peter raised an eyebrow. 'No one's squire, my lord. This is Sir William Gold—'

'Ha! The Cook!' cried the prince. 'But I know of you, of course! Knighted at Florence, attacking my home city! My bastard brother wrote and told me every cut, every blow. He said you were the best *caveliere* he had ever seen.'

Too much praise can be as confusing as an insult. 'My lord has the better of me,' I said, a little stiffly.

'Ah, my pardon!' he bowed.

Fra Peter laughed. 'William, this is the richest man in the world and one of the best knights I've ever met. Ser Niccolò Acciaioli, of Florence. And Naples. And the Morea?'

'I am no longer Baillie,' Acciaioli said. 'I remain Count of Melfi.' He raised his eyebrows. 'A fine accomplishment for a man who started as a baker's errand boy, eh?'

'I started a cook, my lord baron,' I said. Acciaioli seemed to boil with energy and good humour, and I had to like him. His neat pointed beard and perfectly groomed hair were the height of Italianate fashion. His eyes were large, and almost never serious.

'So this is true?' Acciaioli took my arm. 'I think we are both the better for humble origins. Eh? Do you love chivalry? My heart says you do.'

This man was an assault on the senses: rich, quick of wit, brilliant – and penetrating. 'Yes,' I said.

'He's not easy to share a campfire with, either,' Fra Peter said. 'Has Father Pierre brought you here?'

Ser Niccolò shrugged. 'I could make excuses, but yes. My Lady Queen has sent me with some letters of support, and I will arrange some funds.' He smiled at me. 'Do you like to spend money, Messire Le Coq?'

'At least as much as any banker I've ever met,' I said.

Ser Niccolò laughed. 'Well struck. Although let me tell you that in my family, they think my talent for spending gold a fault, not a virtue.'

Fra Peter interrupted him to introduce the other squires. He embraced Juan. 'I know your uncle,' he said. 'You must be close to your knighting?'

Juan blushed to the roots of his hair.

Ser Niccolò looked at Fra Peter.

Fra Peter shrugged. 'It hasn't been talked of, but he is ready.'

I felt like a fool – I had been knighted and I hadn't thought about Juan.

Miles Stapleton bowed to the Florentine. 'Messire is a famous knight,' he said. 'I have heard of your exploits in Greece from my father.'

Ser Niccolò made a face and grinned. 'It is good to be both handsome *and* rich *and* good at arms,' he said. He laughed. 'Come, *i miei amici*. Let us go to the streets of Bologna and see the papal legate's retinue better equipped.'

Fra Peter caught at his trailing sleeve. 'Niccolò!' he said in rapid Italian, 'You shame us! We can raise the funds for saddles.'

Niccolò put a hand to Fra Peter's cheek, an intensely familiar gesture, even from a Florentine. 'By God, if I buy you a saddle for every time you saved my worthless life, I would still be the richest man in Bologna when I was done, and you would be buried in Cordoba leather. Eh? So let us hear no more piss.' He looked at me. 'Tell me, English Knight. What are the seven virtues of Chivalry?'

I nodded. '*Preux!*' I said. 'Loyalty to my lord, Faith in Christ Jesus, Prowess on the field of battle, Love of a Lady, Courage to face the foe, Generosity to all, Mercy to my foes and to the weak.'

'Well said,' Ser Niccolò said. 'So when I practice generosity, is it enough if I give a few pennies to the poor? Listen, if a poor knight gives half his cloak to the poor, he gives more than I live when I buy you saddles.'

'You argue like a Dominican,' Fra Peter said.

Niccolò Acciaioli fluttered his eyelashes. 'But of course! I was to have been a Dominican!' He winked at me. 'Only the chastity was lacking.'

So the richest man in Italy took us out into a Bologna evening.

He was joined at the gates of the palace by a retinue of men-at-arms, a dozen, all well dressed. He had a squire dressed in his heraldic colours and his entire retinue wore his badge, so that they made a glittering parade.

Men and women cheered his name.

Shops opened that had closed. In the street of leather workers, all the saddlers knew we were coming before we walked to the corner, and every master was in the door of his shop, bowing to the great man.

Sister Marie received a fine mule saddle with silver buckles and a matching bag which buckled behind the back of the saddle, all in fine red Spanish leather and Fra Peter spent the better part of the hour before compline protesting various magnificent war saddles, each finer than the last, ivory plaques, gilding, heraldic decoration, matched reins and bridles and straps. In the end, though, while Fra Peter denied that he would ever use a brilliant saddle in Hospitaller scarlet, I nodded to my new friend, Ser Niccolò, and while Fra Peter protested, I was arranging to bring the knight's charger the next morning for a fitting, and promising to bring Sister Marie's mule as well.

It was great fun. Ser Niccolò's men-at-arms were as pleasant a set of men as the great man himself, and they were free with a jibe or a compliment. As they were all Florentines, I expected that they would hold some rancour for my attack on their city, but they seemed to have the opposite views, holding all their ire for Duke Rudolph, who they viewed as a poor soldier.

One young knight, Ser Nerio, had actually witnessed my feat of arms, and his flattery was effusive, and, to me, very sweet.

'Were you fighting, messire?' I asked.

He laughed. 'I was on the walls with the ladies,' he said. 'My harness was in Naples with my lord, and I was home for a wedding and a funeral.' He shrugged.

Another young knight, a blonde who had to be five years my younger, leaned over. 'Don't believe him! He's so rich he has ten armours, all different, spread across Italy like his women, and he was watching from the walls because he's a great coward.'

I thought there must be a fine pun on *amours* and *armours* but I couldn't get it right.

Ser Nerio didn't take offence. Rather, he laughed. 'I rode well that night and drank deep, Antonio. While you—'

Ser Antonio turned his blonde curls to me. 'I exchanged blows with two of your valiant gentleman, although I find now that one of them may indeed have been an Amazon.'

We all went to church together, laughing. I knew I was leaving Juan and Fiore and Miles to flounder, but I make friends easily, and I liked these men.

We heard compline sung in the Italian manner. Italian Latin is virtually incomprehensible to an Englishman and so I translated for Miles Stapleton, who gazed at the altar with pious devotion.

After church, we gathered around Father Pierre, and he and Ser Niccolò embraced. Then the Florentine lord departed, inviting all of us to dine at his house the next day.

I was up early the next morning. By then, I had discovered that Father Pierre was in Bologna to arrange grants and loans in aid of the Crusade and because he had a writ from the Pope to establish a chair of Theology at the university, which would, of course, greatly enhance the prestige of Bologna. But it meant that for the next three days he would be sitting with six other great prelates in examination of two candidates for the honour of a Doctorate in Theology.

The world is more complex than we often imagine. That the good men and women of Bologna were being pressed to provide funds for the crusade was true, but the Pope, and Father Pierre, who loved the Bolognese and had made many friends at the university, were providing value for money, a chair of theology would bring students from all over Italy and even all over Europe, and Father Pierre, himself one of the most famous theologians since Aquinas, would add enormous lustre to the founding.

At any rate, I had days to pass, and I had decided to apply myself to my new life. I curried Fra Peter's charger and emerged from the university's stable yard to find Sister Marie with her mule's reins in her fist.

She grinned at me. 'I'm told I have your intercession to thank for a new saddle,' she said. That was more words than I had heard from her altogether. She spoke in French, and her French had a very odd accent, which I couldn't place.

I bowed. On the road here I had decided that she was older than I had first thought, perhaps as old as forty. She had an upright carriage like a warrior and her eyes met mine with a frankness that was rare in women, even nuns. She never looked down. '*Ma soeur*, you owe your saddle only to the generosity of Ser Niccolò Acciaouli.'

She looked at me for perhaps twenty or thirty heartbeats. 'Are you bound there now?' she asked. 'To the saddlers?'

'Yes, *ma soeur*. I could take your mule.' I noted that she held her left shoulder stiffly and I guessed her arm still hurt.

She shook her head. 'I will be happy of your company,' she said, 'but I can manage my own animal. And have, the last thousand leagues.'

I nodded. 'Fra Peter said you had many miles in that saddle.' I wanted to convey that I respected her accomplishment. She lived in the world of men, which was no easy task. Janet had given me a taste of how hard that could be. 'Have you made many pilgrimages?' I asked, as that seemed the safest answer to why a woman would have travelled so far as to wear a mule saddle to the point of failure.

'I have made a few pilgrimages,' she said, and lead the way out of the yard.

I gathered I'd somehow mis-stepped. I elected to remain silent, but that only lasted through three crowded morning streets. A pair of carters abused her; she was a horse length ahead of me, and they yelled in their countryside dialect that she should stop fucking the Pope and move.

Just as I reached the offending peasant, she turned and smiled at him. 'The Peace of Christ to you,' she said.

The man fell back a step.

To me, she said, 'I fight my own fights, Englishman.'

We walked on. Eventually, because she didn't really know Bologna, I had to pass her. 'Don't I at least deserve the Peace of Christ?' I asked. 'The saddlers are this way.'

She narrowed her eyes. But she followed me.

At the saddlers, we had to wait while the apprentices tried the saddles on our mounts and then worked on the saddles, spreading the tree of my knight's and narrowing the tree on Sister Marie's. The shop had a wonderful smell of beautiful leather, wax, and oil and gilding and resin. The apprentices were well fed and cheerful, and I listened to the banter. My Italian was good by then, and I laughed when one young man let flow a stream of invective so pure and so malicious in response to a slip of his round knife that the swearing itself was an art.

I found Sister Marie looking at me.

I had no idea what I'd done to offend her, but as I felt guiltless, I answered her look with a smile. 'Sister?' I asked.

She frowned and looked away.

Her saddle was fitted first, and she took it and her animal and hurried away. I lingered, exchanged a few careful barbs with the witty apprentice, learned a little about leatherwork, and scrounged some leather thong and some scraps for future repairs. Leather work is a basic skill of arms, like wrestling. I imagine Geoffrey de Charny knew how to sew a good chain stitch, and I know for certain that Jehan le Maingre and John Chandos were both capable of touching up their own horse tack. A morning in a leather shop was not ill-spent. A few silver coins got me two new awls and a packet of steel needles better than any I'd ever used.

Back at the university, Fiore and Juan and Miles and I worked in the stable yard. Almost no one went there, and we had it to ourselves. Like every other part of the university, the stable yard was magnificent: bands of bricks and pale marble on two sides, with oak supports for the wooden roofing on the third and a great cobblestone yard comfortably padded in old dung. When we had all the horses seen to and all the new tack stored and all the repaired tack hung, Fiore grinned and produced a pair of blunted spears and a poleaxe.

We had been playing with spears all summer, but toward the end of our time in Avignon, Fiore purchased an English axe. The English have always been great ones for axes – the English Guard in Constantinople have carried them since King William's time, or so I've been told. But just about the time of Poitiers, many of our men-at-arms gave up the spear or the shortened lance for a long-handled axe, and many of them had a back spike and sometimes a spear point. Some men viewed the poleaxe as un-knightly, and others saw it as 'typically English'. In fact, one of the first men I knew to own one and wield it was Bertrand du Guesclin, and he was anything but 'typically English'. Hah! At any rate, Fiore had fallen in love with the thing.

So we took turns with it, and as we had no pell, we used one of the support pillars of the stables, an oak beam two handbreadths on a side. We left some fine marks in it, I promise you.

I showed Miles the basic postures of fighting with a spear. He was a careful, quiet young man. He listened. But he was not impressed.

When we had practiced various motions, most of which had to do with changing guards from right to left, which was one of Fiore's doctrines, we stripped to our shirts and hose and fought with sharp swords. I know that today men sometimes use blunts, but we were neither rich enough nor cowardly enough to fence with special swords. By then, I had ceased to be a contemptible opponent for Fiore, and we swaggered our longswords up and down the yard, stubbing our toes on cobbles, covering our hose in old dung, and enjoying ourselves hugely.

I had learned an enormous amount of postures and simple doctrines from Fiore. But he was still my master with the sword, and I remember that morning he finished me with a sharp tap to the side of my head that drew no blood.

At some point I realised that we had spectators. One of them was Sister Marie, and she beckoned to me.

'Do you know that the university has a law against public use of swords?' she asked softly.

The stable boys were on our side, so we organised them as a watch, and went back to our play after None. Fiore fenced with Juan, and pinked him through the doublet, which seemed funny enough at the time, although Sister Marie frowned.

Then Fiore turned to young Miles. Miles Stapleton was, if anything, worse than I had been when I arrived in Avignon, and Fiore took him on immediately, with his usual brusque impatience. Fiore had little understanding of other men and women, and he didn't see why young Miles couldn't *immediately* grasp the essentials of the postures he was shown.

I'd like to say that Juan and I leaped to help Miles, but what we really did was to spend an afternoon laughing our fool heads off as Fiore cracked a waster over the boy's head. Fra Peter joined us before vespers – he had attended father Pierre all day – and he laughed, too.

Fiore stepped back from poor Miles, who was a sweat-soaked bundle of nervous failure.

I had, despite my laughter, been watching carefully. I had seen that, despite our ridicule, Miles had learned steadily for over an hour. But as Fiore's criticism was relentless and accurate; eventually the younger squire could no longer concentrate on all the errors he was supposed to correct, and he began to fail. And as he failed, Fiore bore down, spitting out his criticisms fast and more insistently, because Fiore felt that somehow *he* was failing. Miles all but collapsed.

'And now you cannot even stop a simple cut to the head,' Fiore said, stepping back.

Young Master Stapleton didn't burst into tears. A lesser man might have.

I jumped up. 'Eh, Fiore, give the boy a rest and let's have another bout.'

Fra Peter gave me a slight nod, which was often his warmest sign of approbation.

Fiore was angry, feeling that he had failed, but he took three breaths – I told you, it was the summer of breathing – so he was outwardly calm, and we took our guards and engaged.

At the third or fourth pass, I got Fiore's sword in a bind at the crossing, but I was so surprised at my little triumph that I didn't move my hand correctly to place the blade on my cross guard, and got a nice cut across the back of my thumb even as I struck him lightly on the shoulder. Now, let me say, I had hit him before. He was not yet the master he is now, but it was a moment for personal rejoicing for me or Juan any time we landed a good blow.

He smiled and pointed his sword at my hand. 'Another pair of gloves ruined. You need to fix that.' He seemed to be ignoring that I had hit him. 'You rely on your iron gauntlets. In a street fight, you could lose your thumb.'

Well, of course he was correct, and I had just ruined another pair of three-florin chamois gloves.

I consoled myself that I had the thread and needles to fix them up, if the bloodstains weren't too bad. Gloves were expensive.

'Let me have some exercise, Sir William,' Fra Peter said. He nodded to me – we were all knightly courtesy when we had live swords in our hands, and I recommend such behaviour to any man-at-arms. Heightened awareness deserves heightened courtesy, eh?

Fra Peter began in a low guard, and Fiore began high. They met with a heavy crossing (I wouldn't have risked such a heavy strike) and Fiore leaped forward to strike with his pommel – and Fra Peter passed back and took Fiore's blade out of his hand as easily as a thief takes a purse on Cheapside.

Fiore grinned from ear to ear, while the rest of us clapped, and I discovered that I had Sister Marie behind me.

'Show me that again,' Fiore said.

Fra Peter grinned, suddenly one of us and very human indeed. 'No, I think I need to have something on you, since you have youth and speed!' But he relented, and began to demonstrate.

The laugh of it was that it was just like one of Fiore's dagger defences – in effect, the pommel strike turned the mighty longsword into a dagger. We all began to learn it.

I noted Sister Marie moving her hands through the disarm.

She caught me looking and turned away, a hot flush on her cheeks.

I went back to practising the turning of the pommel with Juan. Miles just shook his head.

Fra Peter put an arm around Miles. 'Just practice what you understand,' he said.

Miles looked at the ground a moment. 'I don't understand anything,' he said sullenly. I had never heard Miles be sullen. 'My father's master-at-arms says I am a very promising swordsman.'

Fiore looked at the younger man – they were, after all, only two years apart. 'I'm sure you are, to a provincial knight in rainy England.' He looked at us. 'You saw what Fra Peter has just done to me? Yes? And just like that, I am disarmed and dead. Yes?'

Miles shook his head. 'Yes.'

Fiore frowned. 'You know what the worst fault of most knights is? The one that kills them?'

I wanted to hear this. So, it appeared, did Fra Peter. He stopped wrestling with Juan.

Stapleton shrugged. 'They don't listen?' he said.

Fiore's frown turned to a small smile. 'That's not bad. But no. It is that they think they are much better than they really are, and they are not careful. You have only one skin, Messire Stapleton. If you are careful with your blade, you can win many fights against men who should have killed you. Did you see what Fra Peter did to me? Really did?'

'He turned your pommel strike,' Stapleton said.

'He used my arrogance against me,' Fiore said. He smiled. 'That's how to win any fight.'

Behind me, Sister Marie laughed. 'Women would rule the world,' she said.

That was the day that I discovered that mild Sister Marie, the Latinist, was an accomplished swordsman. She fenced with Fra Peter after he had us secure all the views into the stable yard. She was tall for a woman, but had nothing like the muscle or the height of a belted knight, and her weapon was an arming sword, the sort of weapon I'd grown to manhood using with a buckler. I'd seen her with her sword and her buckler while we were crossing the bandit-infested passes east of Turin, but what of it? Most women who travelled had weapons, unless they were so rich as to have men-at-arms or so poor as to have only a dagger or an eating knife. Many nuns carried staffs or even cudgels to discourage rape and thievery.

Sister Marie moved like a snake. I had never seen anyone move as she moved. She leaned well forward, so that whichever foot was moving, her weight was out in front of her, and her sword led everything. She passed forward and forward, changing from guard to guard, and it was all alien to me, but like a lethal dance.

Fiore's eyes shone. 'This is very interesting,' he said. 'She appears to strike from out of measure, yet it is all deception. She dances forward offering a *strada*, but it is all a lie. She has no line. She engages where she wishes.'

It was not so very different from the sword and buckler of my youth except that we tended to circle, refusing to take a guard until our opponent crossed some invisible distance. Sister Marie flowed from one guard to another, sword over her left shoulder, down by her left hip, up over her head to turn Fra Peter's cut, and then she was in at him, her little buckler over his sword arm. He wasn't having that, and he spun and kicked her and she leaped – and giggled. And cut backhanded at his arm. He covered with his pommel high and the sword falling over his hands, blade pointed at the ground to the right, and struck crisply with both hands and she covered with her sword and her buckler, a move I knew well. I suspected that if he'd cut with all his force, he'd have opened her head; even as it was, her buckler moved.

Each of them tried to bind, but her sword, while quicker, was lighter, and as the edges bit into each other, Fra Peter turned her blade down and touched her very carefully on her forward leg.

She leaped back and saluted him and bowed.

'Fra Peter, it is too seldom that I get to face a swordsman,' she said.

He grinned. 'And you a poor weak woman.' He shook his head. 'If I had to fight in a wool gown, I doubt I could do as well.'

She raised an eyebrow. 'If you plan to pity me, perhaps I should just shave you.' Her eyes glittered.

Fiore stepped forward. 'May I have the pleasure of a bout?' he asked.

She looked him up and down. 'I have to copy letters,' she said. 'You must promise to be careful.'

He frowned. 'Are you suggesting that I lack control?' he asked.

She shrugged. 'Messire, you have put a spear through Sir William's cheek, cut his thumb, pinked Messire Juan, and worn the poor English squire to a rage.'

Fiore looked hurt. But he bowed.

Fiore was so tentative that she mastered the first cross and touched him on his sword arm. And then she turned her sword in the same wind as she had lost to Fra Peter and although she didn't touch him, Fiore stepped back and bowed. 'You might have hit me,' he admitted.

'Yes,' she said, and stepped forward again, this time warding his guard with her buckler as she advanced.

Fiore lifted his weapon and struck her lightly on the side.

She stepped back and laughed. 'Usually, after I hit a man twice in two crossings, he folds,' she said.

Fiore frowned. 'Why?' he asked.

Fra Peter stepped between them. 'Juan is waving. Sister, put up your sword before the university provost arrests us all. Fiore, she played you. From the moment she accused you of having trouble controlling your blade, she was controlling your actions.'

Fiore wiped an arm across his face and frowned at me. 'It is like facing a rival fencing master,' he said.

As Sister Marie disappeared up the steps behind the stables, Fra Peter collected the swords. 'She *is* a rival fencing master, Messire dei Liberi. She teaches monks and nuns; indeed, she has a special licence from the Pope to do so anywhere she goes.'

I flushed. 'I see,' I said. 'I tried to protect her from some carters this morning.' I thought back over various other comments I'd made. 'She's old enough to be my mother,' I added. And then, 'If she has a licence, we were in no danger—'

Fra Peter stood up straight and put a hand to the small of his back. 'And I'm old enough to be your father. What difference does that make?' He nodded to me. 'Surely you have learned from your Janet that it is one thing to have official approval and another thing to be the woman in the armour? Eh?'

That afternoon, Fra Peter introduced Fra Ricardo Caracciolo, who had been the papal commander of the city and was now accompanying Father Pierre. He was a tall, grey-haired Italian, with heavy eyebrows and a lively laugh. We exchanged bows, and I liked him immediately.

'By the Blessed Saint John,' he said in accented English. 'It is good to see my Order can still bring the best young knights.'

Who doesn't like praise?

But his next words chilled me. 'My squire has just come from Milan,' he said. 'Do you know the Count d'Herblay?'

'Why?' I asked.

Fra Ricardo shrugged. 'My young Giovanni only mentioned it because we know you follow the good Fra Peter.' He shrugged. 'The man is looking for you. Or so my Giovanni says.'

That night, we dined with Ser Niccolò. He had a rented house – really, very like a palace. We did not eat peacock, nor was any of the food gilded. Instead, we ate a number of dishes I had eaten before, but served hot, and not on gold or silver, but on plain pottery dishes. The wine flowed freely, and was served in beautiful cups of brightly coloured glass, green and blue and yellow.

I can't remember everything we had, but I remember a fine dish with noodles and duck and truffles, and a game pie. And roast beef served the way the Italians serve it. Several times, Ser Niccolò would rise from his place at the head table and walk among us – there were forty men or more, and as many women, so that for me it seemed a feast in a royal court. He served wine to some, and brought a sauce to another, as if he were a page or squire.

I sat by Ser Nerio, and after the master had offered me wine – delicious red wine – I turned to Ser Nerio. 'His wife is very beautiful,' I said.

Ser Nerio laughed. 'That's not his wife,' he said. 'That's Donna Giuglia Friussi, his mistress and the mother of two of his children.'

Mistress or wife, she was the hostess of the evening, and she summoned minstrels, applauded a poet, and led the ladies in a fast-paced *estampida* that seemed more like a fight than a dance.

After a second dance, she came to our table and we all rose and she seated herself with two of her ladies. She was warm from dancing, and she had a scent I had never before experienced, something from the Levant. 'You are the famous Ser Guillaumo the Cook!' she said. 'Ah, every girl in Florence pines for you, messire. Do not, I pray you, break too many Florentine hearts.'

'Madonna,' I replied, 'I promise that, should I ever see a sign of a Florentine lady casting an amorous glance at me, I'd do whatever I could to make sure that her heart remained unbroken.'

She laughed, not a simper or a giggle. 'Your Italian is good, and so are your manners,' she said. 'I don't think you were ever really a cook.'

I liked this kind of game, always have. I sat back and played with my wine cup. 'Perhaps if we were to slip into the kitchen, I could prove myself,' I said.

The two ladies-in-waiting both giggled.

Donna Giulia leaned forward, and I could smell her scent again, more like musk than flowers, and yet at the very edge of perception. Her presence was ... palpable. I have known a few women like her, where up close, the impact of beauty and personality can rob you of breath. She put a warm hand on my arm. 'You play this game very well for an Englishman. What would you make me, in the kitchen?'

I sighed. Italian ladies can play this way for hours and mean nothing, or mean everything, where an English girl would be reduced to giggles – or a blow with her hand. I thought of Sister Marie, Donna Giuglia's direct opposite.

I leaned forward. 'I should make you ...' I said softly.

She smiled.

'... dessert,' I finished. 'Perhaps a nice apple tart.'

Now the whole table laughed; some at me, and some with me. Ser Nerio, beside me, gave me a look that told me I'd found the right path. We had skirted the marshy ground, for flirting with your host's mistress is a dangerous game at the best of times.

She threw back her head and laughed, not a ladylike simper, but almost a roar.

Ser Niccolò appeared at my shoulder. He poured his lady wine and she told him of the whole exchange, word for word.

He raised his eyebrows. 'But of course you must go make her an apple tart. I insist only that I have some too.' He grinned. 'Think of it as a feat of arms. Or a task of love.'

'He loves apples,' Donna Friussi said.

Juan glared at me, and Miles looked offended on my behalf, but given Ser Niccolò's origins, I didn't think he meant a slur. At any rate, I rose and took my beautiful glass of wine to the kitchen, following a page.

The cook was a big man with a pair of enormous knives in a case in his belt, and he frowned and then shrugged. 'Whatever my lord and lady require,' he said, 'it is my task to provide. You wish to make an apple tart? So be it.'

I found that the darker of Donna Giulia's ladies was at my shoulder. 'This may take an hour or two,' I said.

She shrugged and sipped her wine.

By the time I'd made my dough and was rolling it out, I had a little crowd. Ser Nerio was there, and Ser Niccolò, and Donna Giuglia. I had flour on my best doublet, and I was having a fine time. In fact, I was the centre of attention, and I like that well enough. And the cook had decided to humour me – better than that, he was actively supporting me, so that when I was at the point of forgetting salt in my crust, he slapped a salt horn on to the table beside my hand.

A pair of boys chopped apples for me. I discovered that the palazzo boasted a majolica jar of cinnamon, a fabulous spice from the east – you know it? Ah, everyone does, now. I ground it myself, and held my fingers out to the dark lady-in-waiting and she breathed in most fetchingly.

More and more of the guests found their way into the kitchens, and Ser Niccolò served a pitcher of wine to the cook's staff. He had rented the house, and none of the staff knew what to make of him: cook's apprentices do not usually mix with the guests. But Donna Giuglia brought musicians into the kitchen, and there was dancing, and a lady began to sing. And then, as I assembled my little pies, Donna Giulia took a tambour and raised it, and everyone fell silent, and she whispered to one of the lute players. Accompanied by only a single lute, she danced and sang to her own song.

She was magnificent. Let me add that she was so good that the fifty guests and twenty kitchen staff crammed into the corners of a great kitchen gave her both silence and room – and that she had an open strip of tiled floor no wider than a horse's stall and not much longer, and she held us all spellbound.

I finished my pies. I put Master Arnaud's mark on them – I don't know what imp moved me to do that. Perhaps just the memory of every other apple tart I'd ever made. The cook swept them away into the great oven by the fireplace, itself big enough to roast an ox.

Donna Giuglia finished, her honey-coloured hair swaying, and every man and woman whistled, shouted, clapped their hands or laughed aloud, and she stood and swayed a moment, eyes closed.

Ser Niccolò went and threw his arms around her and kissed her – a lover's kiss. I had seldom seen outside of army camps a woman kissed in such a way in public, but I gathered that there were few rules that applied to Ser Niccolò.

After the dance, it was difficult for any of us to reach the level that Donna Giuglia had set us, and we chatted. I began to tidy up the mess I'd made, and the cook and his apprentices began to look at me reproachfully, but in truth, it gave me something to do, and I didn't want to stand idle and silent among strangers.

Ser Niccolò came and put an arm around my shoulder. 'Now I believe that you were truly a cook,' he said.

'While I confess, my lord, that I have trouble believing that you were ever a stingy banker,' I said.

He laughed. 'Perhaps I became a knight because I was such a very *bad* banker.'

My little pies emerged from the oven, no thanks to me, and carefully watched, no doubt, by the professional. But they were golden brown, and the scent alone – I'd used more eastern spices in six small pies than one of Prince Edward's cooks would see in a month of Sundays – the scent alone suggested that the gates of heaven might be close.

I put one small pie on a wooden trencher and presented it on my knees to Donna Giuglia.

She laughed. 'I think I have been bested,' she said.

Ser Niccolò took a bite, and he looked at me over his pie with pure, unadulterated approval.

I cut the pies as small as I could, and almost everyone had a bite.

At the door, Ser Niccolò took my hand. 'I love a man who is not afraid,' he said.

I assumed he was serious, so I shook my head. 'My gracious lord, I'm afraid all the time.'

'You were not afraid to make the pies. In public.' He was serious.

'I was afraid that they might not come out. It has been a few years.' I smiled.

He didn't return the smile. 'But this is exactly what I meant. Wait, please. I want you to meet my son Nerio.'

I had seen Nerio all evening, and never known him to be the great man's son. But of course, when I saw them together, it was obvious. Nerio was my own age, as handsome as his father, and at this late stage he had another spectacularly beautiful woman at his elbow, this one thinner and more otherworldly than Donna Giuglia, but neither more nor less magnificent. I knelt to her and to him, and he pulled me sharply to my feet.

'By God, messire, you are a famous knight *and* a competent pastry cook, and I am neither!' He laughed. 'When there is steel singing in the air, I find a lady's lap and hide my head there like a unicorn.'

It has amused me all my life, the different ways men boast.

I had a fine night. After I saluted Nerio, I slipped around the palazzo and in by the tradesman's alley, and found the cook. 'Here's three florins to share,' I said. 'I know how much work you went to for me.'

He took the florins without hesitation and gave me a little bow. 'You were truly a cook?' he asked.

I looked past him at the circle of apprentices. 'Never,' I said. 'I was a cook's *boy*, and Master Arnaud would never have trusted me to cook a pie on my own.'

That made them all laugh, even the master. And as if he'd been drawn by the laughter, I saw Ser Niccolò appear on the servant's stairs.

'Sneaking into my house?' he asked.

'Offering my compliments, because these men made me look better than I am,' I said.

He nodded. 'If you always remember to thank the men that help you step up ...' He shrugged. 'Where do you bank, Ser William?'

'With the Bardi,' I admitted. My Genoese bankers.

He nodded and cocked his head to one side. 'They will fail – if not this year than the next. Your prince has served them but ill again and again.'

I was sitting on the same table where I'd prepared the pies. It seemed incongruous to me: Ser Niccolò was wearing the most magnificent *grande assiette* pourpoint I'd ever seen in crimson silk covered in gold embroidery, and he was leaning against the fireplace.

Well, I wasn't his squire, thanks be to God.

'Move your money to my family's bank,' Ser Niccolò said.

I grinned. 'My lord, I'd move only my debt. I'm owed some ransoms, but another knight collected …'

Ser Niccolò smiled and made a very Florentine gesture with his hands, a sort of denial of the very statement he was about to make. 'I know all this,' he admitted. He smiled at me. 'Give me your account, and I will find your money.'

I suppose I frowned. 'Why?' I asked.

Ser Niccolò tilted his head to one side like a very intelligent dog. 'You are a friend of Acuto Hawkwood. A good friend for me to have. A good knight. And you serve Father Pierre. Any one of these things might have made me notice you, but you now have all three things.' He leaned towards me. 'You can, I think, read and write.'

I shrugged. 'Yes. Latin or English.'

He nodded. 'Write me a letter giving me your account, and I will see to it you receive the money due you on your ransoms.' He slapped me on the shoulder. 'Really, I ask nothing more.'

As I walked through the dark streets with his linkboys lighting my way, I searched for the strings that would make this dangerous, but all I could see was that it would be a fine thing to be friends with the Florentine. He was the Queen of Naples's chancellor, a great knight, and a powerful lord.

And I had had a wonderful time.

If I've given another impression, I'm a poor storyteller. And back at the university, I had to tell all the tales of the evening to Fra Peter, who had stayed with Father Pierre. He laughed at my failure to recognise that Nerio was Ser Niccolò's son.

'By his wife, who stays in Florence,' he said.

Father Pierre came in behind us, carrying a pitcher of wine. He poured me wine with his own hands – he always did. He was the worst great church officer imaginable. He helped servants carry furniture and he liked to lay out his own vessels for serving Mass, even in Famagusta when he was with the king – but I get ahead of myself.

'Ser Niccolò wears his sins as well as he wears his jewels,' Father Pierre said. 'He would be more beautiful without them, but he never allows them to weigh on him.' He shrugged to me. 'I have known him ten years and more. The power he wields has corrupted him, but not so very much.'

'I liked his lady,' I confessed. 'His mistress.' I flushed.

Father Pierre laughed. 'Why should you not? God made her as much as he made you or me and she is a very good lady, despite her sins.' He shrugged. 'I am a bad priest. But as a celibate, what do I know of the world? Nothing. It is not for me to judge, but God.' He turned to Fra Peter. 'But Niccolò will accompany us to Venice, at least for a few days. I have word of King Peter. He left Rheims; not for Venice, as he promised, but for the court of the Holy Roman Emperor.'

Fra Peter went white.

Father Pierre sighed. 'I agree with your unspoken words. There are three thousand men-at-arms at Venice, and it is the most expensive city in the world. Every day he delays is a day he is not making war on the infidel. And those men will drift away to wars in Italy. Will they not, William?'

I blew air out of my lips. 'Unless Walter Leslie has a great many more ducats than he showed at Pisa, he can't keep them together for long.'

Fra Peter looked at the crucifix on the wall for a long time. 'What is King Peter thinking of?' he asked.

Pierre steepled his fingers in front of him. 'I am thinking that he was not informed that he was the commander of the crusade before he left Rheims.' He looked at me. 'But he is a strange man; a wonderful man, and a great knight. But very much a man.' Father Pierre looked over his hands at the table in front of him and finally shook his head. 'I don't think we can do anything. Any day, the Pope's appointment will reach him, and he will realise how essential is his presence. We must get to Venice now, and see to the men who are to be my flock.'

Fra Peter tapped a thumbnail on his lower teeth. 'You could send me to the king.'

They looked at each other for a bit. I drank my wine, which was delicious, and I poured more for my elders.

'What do you think of the wine, Ser William?' Father Pierre asked me.

'Delicious,' I admitted. 'As good as anything Ser Niccolò had to offer.'

Father Pierre's eyes crinkled with his smile. 'Denied all the other pleasures of the flesh, my brother priests and I can rarely resist a good wine,' he admitted. He looked back over his hands to Fra Peter. 'No, I need you at Venice. You and the other men of the Order are my ambassadors to the brigands and routiers who will be our phalanx of Angels.'

Sometimes, I suspected that the saintly Father Pierre had some cynicism lurking under the surface, but like some shy forest animal, whenever it peeked out with his rare half-smile, it was soon gone again.

I needed a new sword, and I spent some delightful hours prowling Bologna for the one I wanted, with Fiore and Juan and Miles, who had recovered from his sullenness to become one of us. But in three days, I knew every sword available for sale in the city, and none of them were quite what I desired.

I'm sure you will say that a sword is a sword, a tool for killing. This is true, and I can use any of them. But listen, gentles. There are many beautiful women in the world. Yes? Consider every charm, every allure. Consider the endless attractions: ankles, shoulders, the curve of a wrist, the top of a breast, the tilt of eyes, the corners of mouths. Consider also the subtlety that is the interplay – the conversation, the soul of a lady, so that some are dull and others sparkle like a fine jewel in any company.

So … every man has his taste, and perhaps every woman also. So many details that we cannot track them all or even remember what we like, and yet, at least with a sword, I have to no more than wrap my hand around a hilt and raise the blade from the floor and I *know*. Some blades demand to be swung up and over my head. Some hilts fit my hand as if they were some sort of inverse glove. And some do not. Perhaps they have warm conversations with other swordsmen, but not with me.

The perfect sword … it is a very intimate thing.

When I find one such, I think of it constantly. Listen, I remember once I saw a woman through the curtain of a shop; she was raising her dress over her head, trying something for a seamstress, perhaps, and all I saw was the line of her side, and that ell of her flesh stuck with me for two days, filled my waking thought, found its way into my head even while I prayed. And so it is with the right sword, so that the memory of the perfect weight across my palms will follow me out of a shop and into church.

Well, she was not to be had in Bologna.

But I did enjoy three days with Ser Niccolò and his knights, and I drank a great deal of wine with Nerio and was surprised to find how much he and Fiore disliked each other. I mislike it when my friends cannot make accord, and this was the most instant dislike between two friends I'd ever experienced. I suspect that Fiore resented Nerio's familiarity – and his riches. And Nerio was not used to being thought to lack anything, but Fiore found him wanting as a man-at-arms. I have no idea why. Nerio looked quite dangerous to my eye, and I'd killed a great many more men than my Friulian friend.

To complete the complexity of my existence, Fra Peter and Father Pierre had decided that they would arrange for Juan to be knighted in Venice. But as he was from a great Catalan family, this involved a good deal more preparation than a cook's boy from London got on a battlefield, and they wanted it kept secret, so I was handed a list of things to purchase and things to do and letters to write, all without letting Juan know. This, of course, had the unfortunate effect of letting Juan think I was ignoring him.

And finally, while I was writing letters, I mustered my courage and wrote to Emile. That is to say, I helped Sister Marie compose a circular letter from the legate to the bishops of the Duke of Burgundy about pilgrimage and crusade, and in it were dates for pilgrims who wanted to accompany the crusade to Jerusalem, assembly points at Venice and Genoa, and other points. When I copied the legate's letter out – to Sister Marie's surprise – I made sure that my name had been included among the list of routiers turned to soldiers of God, and she *had* included it.

It took me most of my last day in Bologna to copy that letter. Three hundred lines, and two small errors, and we covered them both. I had not entirely wasted my time with the monks in London, and no donat at Avignon escapes without some copy jobs, unless he is absolutely illiterate, which is increasingly frowned upon in the Order.

Sister Marie wore heavy Venetian spectacles to copy and they made her look like some avian monster, owl-eyed and beaked. But when she pulled them off she looked human, almost homey. 'Sir William, I would never have marked you down as a writing man. My thanks, I would not have finished in time without your clerking.'

'Sister Marie ...' I paused. My petty troubles with Fiore and Juan had suddenly made me more careful than was my wont with other men and friendship, but I am in general a blunt man, and I ploughed on, 'I would not have taken you for a sword hand, but as you are, can we not be friends?'

She met my eye – I've said it before, but she never flinched from eye-meeting like a normal woman. I suppose girls are trained to it and nuns, perhaps, are trained out of it. At any rate, she raised an eyebrow. 'I suppose we could be friends,' she admitted.

Well, she was not the warmest of women. But she wasn't my mother or my bed warmer; she was the legate's Latinist. And witting or not, she had been my ally in writing to Emile.

All told, I suppose we were a week in Bologna, although it seemed a year, and when we rode east for Venice, crowds cheered us in the streets. Leaving Bologna, we were a small army; two dozen knights and donats of the Order, brilliant in scarlet, Lord Grey at our head with the papal banner; Ser Niccolò and his score of men-at-arms as brilliant as angels from heaven; another dozen volunteers from Bologna with their harnesses and their warhorses and carts full of belongings they were taking east. And with another twenty priests and nuns and clerks, as well as squires and pages and servants we had at least three hundred horses in our cavalcade.

Fra Peter had command of the whole, and I found myself commanding the donats. The older Knights of the Order were quite content that I do so: they stayed close to Father Pierre. There were almost a hundred Knights of the Order heading for Venice that autumn, but only half a dozen chose to ride with the legate. Or perhaps that was Father Pierre's choice. A big column of knights ate up the countryside and devoured more bread and more grass.

I have not, up until now, described the intense faction that split Italy from the Italian point of view; I have to at least mention it to explain how I almost lost my life in the streets of Verona. The della Scalas were the lords there, and like every family of aristocrats in Italy, they belonged to one of the two competing factions – the Guelfs and the Ghibbelines. In brief, these two parties stand for allegiance to the Pope and allegiance to the Holy Roman Emperor. The quarrel is an old one and now has elements of the absurd, but the division remains lively.

Verona was a Ghibbeline city, and the della Scala, the local tyrants, were ancient supporters of the Pope. Since we served the Pope, you might have thought that we would make popular guests, but a rumour met us in Verona, to wit that the Emperor was coming to Italy with a large army to join the crusade. By some stretch of the popular imagination, that made us Guelfs – supporters of the Emperor. With papal banners at our head.

In truth, the London mob is every bit as fickle as the mob of Paris or Rome or Verona.

At any rate, we did not receive a hero's welcome to Verona, and while we rode in through the white Roman Gate and trotted by the marvels of the amphitheatre, and the magnificence of Saint Anastasia, we were watched by a sullen crowd. Father Pierre dismounted in the courtyard of the Carmelite convent, and the Knights of the Order closed around him, wary of the people. The nuns watched from the upper cloisters like curious birds.

Fra Peter watched the crowd for as long as it took the clock to strike three, and then handed me an ivory tube with many of our travel documents. He shrugged. 'This may be ugly. I need to be with the legate. Get to the castle and get our documents signed. Tell della Scala ...' He paused and looked at the ground. 'Never mind. But if you can find out what this is about, I'd like to know.'

Well, we had by then a dozen donats, all fully armed and armoured. I turned to Miles Stapleton.

'Will you play my squire?' I asked.

He nodded. 'Your servant, my lord,' he said.

Nerio Acciaioli caught my bridle. 'It could be murder out there,' he said, pointing to the gate.

It was my turn to shrug. 'I have orders,' I said. 'And Fra Peter is worried. He *never* worries.'

Ser Nerio let go my bridle and nodded. 'Do me the kindness of waiting on my father.'

I dismounted and bowed to Ser Niccolò, who listened while his son whispered in his ear.

'Do it,' he said. He smiled at me. 'You need a servant,' he said.

It seemed the oddest thing, at the time.

There were no women in the streets of Verona, that's the first thing I noted. The second was that there were a great many men of fighting age, all with swords. In Bologna, I hadn't seen a sword displayed in a week. University students who wanted to fight went outside the town.

We were watched in a heavy silence as we rode, and I suspect the sheer number and quality of the men-at-arms kept us safe – a dozen of the Order's men-at-arms and another dozen of the Accaioulos, with their green and gold banner and the Pope's, too.

The castle was the most modern, elegant, and imposing fortification I had ever seen. It is all red brick and white marble, with palatial facades and workaday walls; a magnificent design that is equally suited to holding the city against an invader or holding an escape route against a local insurrection. The della Scala were, after all, tyrants. Not really ill-natured tyrants, although there had been trouble.

We entered by the main gate and entered a courtyard, and my spine tingled: the walls around the courtyard were full of crossbowmen, and they were watching us, their bows spanned.

Fiore whistled softly.

Stapleton played his part perfectly, riding forward with my helmet and lance and calling for the captain of the fortress.

The man who emerged from the main tower was in full harness and had a poleaxe in his hand. I couldn't even hear him when he spoke, because his visor was down.

I didn't have a helmet on, and I was afraid. There were enough crossbows around us to kill us all in a matter of seconds, and I had led my friends into this. And I had led the life – I could tell how close to the edge all these men were.

I turned. 'Dismount!' I called. 'Everyone show your hands to be empty. Smile!'

Behind me, Nerio said, 'Smile?'

I looked at him and made myself smile. 'It's harder to kill a man in cold blood when he's smiling,' I said. I got an armoured leg over the cantle of my saddle and slid to the ground, then walked toward the armoured man with the poleaxe.

He backed away a step.

'Messire, I don't have a weapon in my hands, and I have no helmet on my head, and you have fifty crossbowman pointing at me this minute,' I said in passable Italian. 'I come in peace, with travel documents from the Pope, who is our spiritual father. I am sworn to the crusade, as is every man here, and if you harm us, you will be excommunicated. Please open your visor and let us talk like gentlemen.'

'Put your papers on the ground and back away,' he said.

'No,' I said. 'I represent the Cardinal Legate of the Pope.'

We stared at each other.

That is to say, I stared at his visor, and he stared at my naked face.

After some time had passed, I became angry. I took a step back, and turned slowly to face the walls. I held aloft my ivory tube and pointed at the papal banner. 'We are *servants* of the *Pope* and we are sworn to crusade.' I looked around. The impasse had lasted long enough that the crossbowmen – all mercenaries, and mostly Bretons – were tired of aiming their weapons.

'Shut up,' said the visored man.

'If you harm us, you will be excommunicated,' I said, and my voice rang off the stone. 'Whatever you have been told—'

'One more word and they shoot,' growled the Visor.

'Why?' I asked.

'Leave your papers and go,' he said.

'Why? This is an insult to the Pope.' I put my hands on my hips. I fetched a glance at Juan and he nodded. We weren't just young bucks with a message. We were soldiers of the papacy. I leaned toward the visor. 'And frankly, messire, you have done nothing to indicate that I should trust you with all of our travel documents. Which ...' I raised my voice, 'which are signed by the Pope, the King of France, the Emperor, and the council of Bologna.'

He stepped forward and placed the blade of his axe against my neck. 'You!' he began.

I grabbed the haft just below the head and pivoted on my back foot, gave the haft a sharp pull to throw him off balance and then slammed my unarmoured hand into the chainmail of his aventail at his neck, got my right leg behind his knee, and put him down with his own axe as the fulcrum. As fast as a crying woman draws a breath, I had his dagger under his aventail at his throat.

Everyone was very, very still.

'I can help you up, and we can start this again,' I said very softly. 'Or you can die. I may also die, but please understand that you will be ahead of me at the gates.'

His eyes were not daunted. 'You will *not* seize this castle while I'm its commander,' he said.

'I'm not here to seize your poxy castle!' I spat. 'I'm here to get the *papal legate's travel paper's signed.*'

All this while fifty Breton crossbowmen considered whether to kill me or not.

'Do you know that man over there?' I asked, pointing at Ser Nerio. 'He's an Accaioulo.'

'Heraldry can be faked,' he said. Then, 'Very well, let me up.'

The change was too sharp. 'Let you up? Why?' I asked.

He raised his head and opened his own visor. 'Stand down,' he shouted. 'Clearly been a misunderstanding. Stand down!'

The crossbowmen sighed all together, so that it sounded like a flock of birds landing on a pond, their wings all beating together. The knights in the courtyard watched the cup of death pass away from them, and they sighed too.

I probably sighed.

The man who opened his visor was Antoine della Scala. The lord of the city.

He poured wine with his own hand while a pair of boys in red and white livery disarmed him. 'The cardinal of Geneva sent word that you would attempt to seize the citadel and take the city for Milan,' he said. He passed this as if it was a pleasantry, a matter of little consequence.

I decided that he was quite mad. His eyes glittered, and his movements were curiously uncoordinated. He spilled a little wine almost every time he raised the cup to his lips and he had spittle at the corner of his mouth.

As I was now deep inside the castle, I was more scared than I had been in the courtyard. They had my sword and my dagger, and my armour was not going to keep me alive very long against a dozen trained adversaries. Men whose master was, as I say, a lunatic.

'The Bishop of Geneva?' I asked.

'The Green Count and Bishop Robert have always been a friends of this city,' della Scala said. 'He sent me a letter from Avignon ...'

I understood. Pardon, gentles. Now that it has all happened, it seems obvious – that Bishop Robert was our enemy. But at the time I scarcely knew him, and I had no notion that a bishop, a virtual prince of the church, would attempt to undermine a crusade.

'My lord, I can only promise you that if the weather is fair, we will quit your gates tomorrow on our way to Venice, the city of Saint Mark.'

The mad tyrant of Verona shrugged. 'I suppose,' he said. 'Cavalli, have all their papers prepared.' He turned to me. 'There, my English bravo. Is that enough for you?'

I bowed.

'And how exactly shall I punish you for the *lese majeste* of attacking my person?' he asked suddenly.

My hand went to the empty space over my hip where my arming sword should have been.

He shrugged again and turned away. 'We will see,' he said.

We made it back to the convent by riding quickly on the main streets with our helmets on and our visors closed. I dismounted in the yard, gave my horse to one of Nerio's pages, and ran, fully armed, for Father Pierre and Fra Peter. I found them at prayer.

I had never interrupted a priest at prayer but I cleared my throat a few times, and eventually Fra Peter and two of his knights turned to look at me, and he saw it in my posture and my face and came to the back of the chapel, scattering nuns and lay sisters as he came.

'I have the papers, but della Scala means us harm, I'd swear to it. He claims a bishop, Robert of Geneva ...' I paused.

Fra Peter let slip a nasty word.

Father Pierre's head came up.

Well, we're all merely mortals.

'If it were up to me, I'd take the legate and ride right now,' I said. 'Somehow the populace has been convinced that we are Guelfs and the guilds are arming under their banners.'

Ser Niccolò Accaioulo took a deep breath. 'Of course, we *are*

Guelfs. Famous ones, too.' He shrugged elaborately. 'Whether this is planned or happenstance, our presence is making it worse.'

I shook my head. 'Begging your pardon, messire, but Nerio's presence gave della Scala a little pause. It might have been what saved us. We rode into a trap.'

Father Pierre, clad only in his Carmelite robes, strode down the nave of the chapel to join us.

'You men of blood,' he said. He was angry. 'What have you done?'

I was more than a little crushed, I can tell you, to have my spiritual father assume I was to blame.

Fra Peter raised his hand. 'Your Excellency, this is apparently brought on by your brother in Christ, Robert of Geneva.'

The legate narrowed his eyes.

'They will use the Accaioulo as an excuse to attack us,' Fra Peter said.

'They would provoke war with the Pope, with Venice, and with Florence,' Ser Niccolò said. He pulled at his beard. 'Someone has told them otherwise, eh, messires?'

While we stood, the abbess and two senior nuns rose from their knees and went to the great oak doors of the chapel. There, a pair of novices whispered to them; the abbess looked stricken, and put a hand to the cross at her neck.

She approached the legate with her eyes cast down. 'Excellence, there is a rabble at the gates,' she said.

Fra Peter turned to me. 'You and your men are armed. You must hold them until the knights of the Order are ready ...'

Father Pierre looked at us – and smiled. 'No,' he said. 'I will not allow a single Veronese to be killed. Much less you gentlemen, who love me. God will protect me, messires.' He turned to me. 'Do not follow me, unless you are unarmed.'

Fra Peter gave me a look. It is surprising how much information a man or a woman can convey in a single flick of the eyes. I knelt before the legate, and he put a hand on my head and blessed me.

'Come!' he said. 'But leave your swords. Because I will neither live by one nor die by one.' He walked out of the chapel and I followed him into the yard. It was already dark, and we could hear the crowd at the convent gates.

'Mount,' I said. 'For the love of God, gentles, mount and draw your swords, but take no action unless the crowd strikes the legate.'

Nerio pressed his horse in beside mine. 'You know what you are doing?' he asked.

'Yes,' I lied.

Nerio saluted me with his sword.

Ahead of us, Fra Peter and Fra John of the Scottish priory – John Cameron, that was – opened the gates.

A cluster of nuns appeared around the legate with torches.

The legate wore neither cope nor chasuble, nor any garment of gold. But in the orange torchlight, he seemed to glow. The mob – the crowd, I should say, because they were citizens and craftsmen, not the poor – the crowd gave back a step.

'Brothers and sisters in Christ!' Father Pierre said. He said it gently, firmly, and his voice carried.

He took a small wooden cross from one of the sisters. They stood their ground with the resolution of English archers or Swiss spearmen – women can be stauncher than men. Behind them stood a dozen knights of the Order, all in their scarlet, but none armed beyond daggers.

'He's the Emperor's man!' shouted an educated voice safe in the heart of the crowd. A voice whose Italian was tinged with French.

'Brothers and sisters!' Father Pierre called again. 'Do you know that the Holy Father has preached a great crusade? Do you know that the princes of the West are even now gathering at Venice under the banner of the King of Cyprus to strike a great blow for Christ, and retake Jerusalem if it can be accomplished?' He smiled his gentle smile. 'I *would* serve the Emperor, if he would come to me and tell me that he would lead a thousand of his best knights to Jerusalem. In the eyes of Christ, there are no Guelfs and no Ghibbelines! There is only the flock of Christ – and the wolves that seek to divide us so that they can consume us. Brothers and sisters, shall we all pray for the state of Christendom?'

'He is a liar and a hypocrite!' the voice said, conversationally. 'The Pope will sell this city for gold – to barbarians!'

I knew that voice. I'd listened to it for too long – after Brignais.

It was d'Herblay. In Italy. Safe, deep in a crowd, and I was standing, head bowed, unarmed.

But Father Pierre ignored the voice as if it didn't exist. He knelt.

He was within a spear's length of a man with a heavy axe; there were armed apprentices even closer than that. The nuns drew back a little, so that all could see him. Then they knelt, ten women of faith.

The knights knelt. If you have never knelt in steel leg harnesses, let me tell you that it is God's own penance for the Orders of Chivalry.

After a pause of a breath most of the people in the crowd knelt, too, but my horse sensed my tension and began to fret, tossing his head and moving his back feet.

Father Pierre raised his hands and began the paternoster.

All the people in the street began to say it with him.

It isn't listed as one of his miracles. But I was there. He *glowed*. And not a man or woman died.

The crowd broke up quickly. I waited by the gate, eager to follow my quarry, but Father Pierre was on to me as soon as he rose to his feet and walked back in to the walls. He saw me and smiled.

'Your whole body speaks of violence,' he said. 'Jesus came to speak of peace. Walk inside.'

'But—' I began.

He didn't frown. He looked pained.

I took a deep breath, took my hand from my dagger hilt, and turned away from the gate.

In truth, had I killed d'Herblay in Verona that night, my Emile would have been a widow, and I might have been a much happier man. Yet, as Fra Peter said to me, the habit of obedience is essential to honour. Once you put your trust in a man, you must be prepared to obey. And perhaps, in my scarlet surcoat, I would merely have walked out into the streets and been killed.

We left Verona very early. I didn't sleep much, and neither did Fra Peter or Ser Niccolò, but in the end we had everyone saddled and ready in the courtyard as the darkness began its retreat from morning's light. We opened the gates on an empty street, and we rode into the next square, formed our column, and moved to the river as quickly as we could manage.

They were just opening the gates, a fine triple arch to the north. I presented our travel documents to the officer on the gate.

He flicked through them. And nodded.

The gates continued to open.

We passed through them, bags and baggage, in about the time it would take a man to say the Ave Maria. No one was disposed to linger. I saluted the gate officer, took our travel papers back, and rode through. When I emerged on the other side, I found I'd hunched my back against … well, boiling oil, which I feared all the way under the arch.

We passed Montorio, a Cavalli castle, a little outside of town, and one of the knights of that house rode up to us with his banner displayed. He knelt in the road and accepted the cross of a crusader, and we rode for Vicenza – and Venice.

Vicenza was beautiful, although not as beautiful as Verona. Padua was richer yet. The plains of northern Lombardy were, if anything, yet richer, and the hills were incredibly lush. Everything smelled wonderful – the hills smell of flowers and crushed grass even at the height of summer.

Fiore looked at the country north of Verona with a predatory eye. 'They say the cows give butter,' he said. 'That's how rich they are.'

Indeed, as we passed from town to town and city to city, I was struck nearly dumb by the riches. Every town had a cathedral and some had two. There were monasteries and castles on every hill; vineyards covered the hillsides, and there were almost as many olive trees as I had seen around Sienna and Pisa.

As far as I could tell, this country had never known war. And having just come from Avignon, the contrast with France couldn't have been greater – the difference between a beautiful house and a burned-out shell. The peasants wore good wool, and many had Egyptian cloth shirts; women wore fine gowns, often well fitting, and with enough buttons to pass as the gentry of England. They ate good bread and drank good wine and their sausages were among the best I've ever had.

And the closer we got to Venice, the denser the traffic on the roads. By the time we reached Padua, we were passing trains of merchant wagons and laden pack animals carrying cloth from the northern fairs, cloth that had come over the passes from Savoy and the Swiss cantons, from Germany and Flanders and England. And we passed a pair of wagons carrying Bohemian glass and armour, sword blades from Germany, and then load after load of grain from all the country about.

Fra Peter winked at me. 'Have you been to Venice?' he asked.

I shook my head. 'You know I have not,' I answered.

He laughed. 'You are full of surprises, William. But Venice is ... remarkable. And all of this is but a tithe of the products that flow through her port. Most of it comes by sea, or up the canals.'

Well, who has not heard of Venice?

We had planned to take a more northerly route from Padua and the legate had tasks in every city, but he received letters at Padua, one from the Pope urging him to haste, and letters from the bishops of England, Normandy and Burgundy.

That night in Padua, Sister Marie came to my room. She found me reworking the scabbard of my arming sword. It was a fine sword, and I prized it, but the leather was coming off the wood core of the scabbard where Juan had stepped on it. All the donats were gathered around my straw pallet, watching me, and Miles Stapleton had a stinking pot of fish-hide glue he'd got from the leatherworker across the convent yard.

'But the wood's broken!' Juan said in his Catalan French.

Sister Marie appeared at the door. I remember this as if it was yesterday. She wrinkled her nose at the smell and then pushed in with her intense curiosity about everything that characterised her.

I pulled a small, flat piece of bronze out of my shoulder scrip. It was a clipping off a larger piece, and I'd bought it for almost nothing the day before. I held it up so Juan could see it.

He grinned.

I used my eating knife, which was sharper than a razor, to shave the broken wood away. My eyes met Sister Marie's, and she smiled, so I went on.

I took the brush from the warm glue and spread the stinking stuff on the wood, and pushed the broken edges together. 'It looks repaired, like this,' I said. 'But it's like a man with a broken bone. If you don't splint it, it won't knit. So I take the metal plate ...'

Suiting action to word, I laid one small bronze strip on the back of the scabbard, and the second on the front, as if I was splinting a bone, indeed. Then I pulled the leather of the scabbard cover back into place. 'The leather makes a tight seal. You have to sew it up while the glue is still warm and wet.' I used a curved needle – a rare commodity, purchased back in Bologna for half a florin – and in twenty stitches, I had the whole scabbard fixed.

I used a little more glue on the mouth of the scabbard's chape, and slid it back on to the point of the scabbard; then I put two holding stitches through the leather. I turned the scabbard around. The plates showed a little under the thin-stretched red leather, but altogether, it was a decent job.

Sister Marie shook her head. 'The glue inside will dry and fill the scabbard,' she said.

I grinned; it's so nice to actually know something, when you are a young man. 'Miles?' I said, and Stapleton produced a second smelly tin, this one full of tallow. I took my arming sword and coated the blade a fingernail thick in tallow, and then slid it home.

'Good for the scabbard's wood; good for the sword. And now the glue has nothing to hold.' I smiled at Sister Marie, and she grinned.

'You are a useful young man,' she allowed. 'Can you fix a book cover?'

I shrugged. 'I imagine I can, *ma soeur*. I made all the fittings for a Bible once.'

'Hmmf,' she said, or something like it. 'Well, that was a good trick, that with the tallow. If I break my scabbard, I'll come and find you.' She turned to go, and paused. 'My old memory is playing me games,' she said. 'I came with a curious letter. Addressed to "Guillaume D'Or, Miles Dei".' Her eyes met mine.

I shrugged. And reached for it.

'The bishop of Nantes included it,' she went on, her eyes fixed on mine. She was withholding it.

I sighed. 'Truly, Sister, I have no idea.'

She placed it in my hand. 'The legate's couriers are not for your private letters,' she said. She raised one eyebrow, as if to suggest that she knew a thing or two, which I did not doubt for an instant.

She slipped out of the room.

Juan shook his head. 'She thinks all men are fools,' he said. 'She is too forward.'

Miles frowned. 'I like her,' he said.

I was starting to open the parchment, which was folded eight times and sealed with a heavy archbishop's seal in purple wax, when Ser Nerio pushed in the door.

'Christ, what are you doing? Roasting heretics?' Nerio wrinkled his nose and put a perfumed glove to his face.

'I suppose you would know the smell,' Fiore shot back.

Nerio ignored Fiore. 'What is this? Some foul English food?'

I raised my eyes, still struggling with the parchment. 'I fixed my scabbard,' I said.

Nerio laughed. He saw it leaning, point up, in the corner and went to pick it up.

'With stinking glue? Maria Star of Heaven, messire! Pay a leather-worker to fix your scabbards! I have to sleep here!' He waved his perfumed glove in front of his face.

I got the parchment open.

Juan said something about it being useful to know how to look after your own gear.

It was from Emile. Well, it seems obvious like this, but it wasn't obvious to me.

My heart paused – then it beat again, very fast.

Love and war – so different. But not, perhaps, so different.

Dear William,

My husband and I are determined to go on pilgrimage to Jerusalem. Our preparations are made, and he has taken every precaution, including the arranging of a special dispensation at Avignon. His intention is to join the crusade at Venice. My intention is to travel with my children. Please be kind enough to inform me when the legate thinks that the fleet might sail, so that I will not be late. I will come with my own household, and my own knights.

But be assured that I will come.

Emile d'Herblay

I looked up. Juan was glaring like a basilisk at Nerio. He turned and looked at me.

'He just said you were a peasant!' Juan said.

'No,' Nerio shook his head. 'I said he *worked* like a peasant.' The young Italian realised he'd gone too far.

I beamed my happiness at them all. 'Let's go out and have a cup of wine,' I said. 'On me.'

Under my happiness was the knowledge that she had also sent me a warning. But I'd already seen the man. I knew what I was up against. I thought of him as the man I'd bested at Brignais, the man who wouldn't face me in an alley in Avignon. He wasn't worth spit.

Or so I thought.

From Padua we turned back south, so that we had wasted two days travel.

Father Pierre merely shrugged and said it was God's will, and that he had reason to visit Chioggia. Now, today, every soldier in Europe knows of Chioggia, but then, it was merely a prosperous town, the southern land-link between the Serenissima and the mainland. The town was well walled, with a drawbridge and a long causeway road across a series of dykes all the way back to the mainland. It had a beautiful central tower of red brick and two fine churches, as well as a monastery on a nearby island and a forest of ships in her port. It was a fine place, with two central canals, and it gave me a taste of Venice without overawing me all at once.

We arrived late in the day, and Father Pierre went to the island monastery by boat with Fra Peter and Fra John and Sister Marie. The rest of us had to make shift. We stood on the central square – a square that would have graced London or York, let me add, with fifty palaces and great houses fronting on it. They formed an unbroken façade, and every house had a covered, arched portico on the ground floor, so that a man could walk all the way around the square and only be exposed to the elements at the places where the roads came between the houses. Most were three storeys tall, and fronted in stone. All had magnificent chimneys like Turk's heads atop poles, and in every case, curious to the English eye, the chimneys rose off the front of the house and came down almost to the front door. I later learned that this was a Greek style. The whole town smelled of fish.

I am prosing on. At any rate, there we stood in the main square, having just seen the legate into his boat at the piers, and Ser Niccolò grinned his evil grin at me. 'And where do you imagine you'll stay this night, Messire Englishman?' he asked.

'An inn?' I asked.

Ser Niccolò shook his head. 'There are two inns in Chioggia. They are fine establishments, but we will fill them both to overflowing.

Come, let me introduce you to my friends, the Corners of Chioggia.'

The Corners, a cadet branch of the mighty Venetian family, lived in mercantile splendour in a three-storey palazzo fronting on the square. It had room after room and the whole house seemed to me to be an endless profusion of blue and gold, bronze and aqua, over and over. The donna Signora wore jewels of lapis and aquamarine, and her husband was one of the richest men in the town. They were very deferential to Ser Niccolò and Ser Nerio, and I was delighted to be drawn in with them. I slept in a magnificent covered bed with Ser Nerio and Juan, and we drank Candian wine and played dice and went to Mass, which was said in a Latin so touched with the tongue of the Veneto that I understood little but the Kyrie.

Really, the only reason I remember Chioggia – except for what came later, of course – is that night, Madonna Corner was complaining to her husband that the house was overstaffed with male servants. This led to a long, rambling account of the process by which one man had been disciplined for some crime so arcane I couldn't get the gist, but was too old a family retainer to be dismissed. Again, they all spoke the Venetian dialect, *Veneziano*, of which I understood so little that I had to constantly ask my hosts to explain.

Ser Niccolò was his usual debonair self in green wool and gold silk and fur, and he was wearing tall boots – up to the top of his hose, in fact, which matched his clothes. I remember this, because when he rose he was oddly discordant with the blue and gold house.

He rose to his feet because the erring manservant had come in. The man was short and portly, but not fat; he had a cherubic face and a shock of bright red hair.

'Come,' Ser Niccolò said. 'William Gold, I have found you the perfect page.'

The man had the good grace to appear abashed.

'What's your name, sir?' I asked.

'Marc-Antonio,' he said softly. 'You are English?'

I nodded, a little surprised at his boldness. 'I am.'

He dropped his eyes, but he couldn't hide his smile.

'We cannot cast him out, as he is one of my husband's bastards,' the lady of the house said. She rolled her eyes. 'Judas Iscariot, I call him.'

Hah. When I was a boy, that's what they called *me*.

*

After evening prayer, I was throwing dice with Nerio and Fiore, who were still not friends. It was exhausting, keeping them from blows. But it passed the time.

'I had an eight, until you jarred the dice box,' Fiore stated.

'Why were you so clumsy as to strike me with it?' Accaioulo asked.

'Why were you so clumsy as to allow it to touch you?' Fiore asked.

Juan was lying on our bed, playing with the points of his doublet while I sewed a new metal aiguillette on one. 'Why don't you two get a private room?' Juan asked. 'Then you can have your lover's quarrels without troubling your elders.'

Believe me, his Catalan accent made him sound even more arrogant.

'I suppose you'd prefer if I was in the eaves with the servants,' Fiore asked, clearly stung. Fiore's relative poverty weighed on him far more than it need have, but he was very proud.

Juan swung his legs off the bed. 'I said nothing of the sort. William, you are a fine tailor, whatever I may think of you as a knight.'

Nerio was looking down his nose at Fiore, but he couldn't resist an opportunity. 'I hear he's a fine pastry cook, too,' he jibed. 'And he does leatherwork.'

The room was too small for so many young men. But rain was falling like the wrath of God on Noah, and we had nowhere to go.

Ser Niccolò knocked and was admitted, at which time everyone had to shift, we were packed that close. 'William, can you afford to keep a page?'

'Can he fight?' I asked. 'If so, yes.'

If I wondered why the richest man in Italy, the chancellor of the Kingdom of Naples, was working on finding me a servant, I didn't ask. I sensed that Accaioulo was a matchmaker at heart: it may have been the key to his success at negotiations.

Nerio smiled to himself and turned away.

Ser Niccolò nodded. 'I'm sure he can fight, or if not, you can teach him, or your Friulian can. But he needs to leave here. Madonna is a fine woman, but her natural inclination leads her to be ...' He paused, looking for a word that would not be indelicate or unchivalrous.

'To be petty?' I asked.

Ser Niccolò waved a hand in front of his face, the universal Northern Italian sign for a word or phrase that was too strong. The he frowned. 'Perhaps,' he admitted.

Well, I needed a servant.

Fiore glared at Nerio. 'Why is your father planting a spy on Sir William?' he asked.

Nerio stood up suddenly and put a hand on his dagger. 'Withdraw that!' he spat.

I stood up too. 'Gentlemen,' I said, 'I am going to meet this servant. Please try not to kill each other while I'm gone.' I looked back and forth. 'Really, friends, I am growing tired of separating you.'

Juan caught my eye and gave me the smallest head nod from the bed. I winked at him and walked out. Juan followed me into the passageway.

'Just let them fight,' he whispered. 'The longer you keep them from it ...' He shrugged.

He had some wisdom, did our Spaniard.

Marc-Antonio lived behind the ground floor loggia: that is to say, he lived in a room without heat, which stank of dead fish and canal water. He bowed when I entered.

'Christ on the cross,' I said without thinking.

Marc-Antonio made a face. 'I'm used to it, my lord. But I am sorry.'

I frowned. 'Do you *want* to be my servant?' I asked.

Marc-Antonio looked at the ground, and he flushed. 'No!' he spat. More softly, he said, 'But I'll take any road out of this fish-shit hole.'

'Boys used to call me Judas Iscariot,' I said.

'That's nice,' he muttered. Then he brightened. He was very young. 'You are truly English?'

I must have grinned, because he grinned back. 'As English as Kent and London can make,' I said.

He nodded. 'The astrologer – he was here a week ago! He told me an Englishman would make my fortune.'

Well, that was news. 'He may mean another Englishman,' I said. I was looking at the cuff of my jupon, which needed some work. 'Can you sew?' I asked.

'No, my lord,' he admitted. 'That's women's work,' he added with the reckless ignorance of the young.

'Do leatherwork?' I asked.

He all but spat. 'For tradesmen.'

'Can you cook?' I asked.

He frowned. 'No. I can toast bread on a fork. I can carve meat.'

'Start a fire?' I asked.

He sneered. 'Get a servant for that,' he said.

'Ride a horse?' I asked.

Marc-Antonio sighed. 'I would very much like to learn to ride,' he admitted. 'I was on a horse once.'

I paused. And watched him, from all the maturity of my twenty-four years.

'I can wrestle!' he said. 'And I can row a boat. I know it's not genteel, but I can row and cast a net.' He knew he was failing. 'Why do I have to know all those peasant things? Cooking? Sewing?'

I sighed. 'I'm a soldier,' I said. 'Those are the skills a soldier has. A page needs to know all of them, and in addition how to look after his own horse and his master's.' I thought, not for the first time nor the last, of Perkin, dead in a pointless skirmish. The best squire who ever lived.

'Know anything about armour?' I asked.

'It's metal,' Marc-Antonio said with affected disdain.

'Know how to use a sword?'

'Yes!' he said.

'Really? Ever had lessons?'

'No!' he said, louder. He was growing angry.

'Shoot a bow?'

'No! No, I don't know *anything* except how to read and write and count money, understand, my lord?' He stood and glared at me.

He was several stone overweight, and he didn't know how to ride.

I liked his defiance, but it seemed an odd virtue for a servant, much less for forming a squire.

'What do you want out of life?' I asked.

He glowered the way only a very young man can glower. 'I want to be a knight,' he said. He deflated.

I sat down on a bale of cloth. I didn't recognise it at the time, but it was illegal Sicilian cotton, smuggled from Genoa.

But that's another story. I looked at him carefully. 'Listen, Marc-Antonio,' I said. 'Will you obey me as if I was Christ come to earth?'

He looked at me with his head tilted to one side, as if I was a madman. 'Why?' he asked.

I took a deep breath. 'If you obey me, and serve me, I swear I'll do my best to form you as a knight,' I said. 'But it is a long road, and there's a great deal of work.'

Marc-Antonio nodded seriously. 'There's always a lot of work,' he agreed. It was the most likeable thing he'd said.

The next day, we caught a pair of small barques for Venice. Each had room for a dozen animals and twenty people, and the two small ships swore to return as many times as was required to get the whole party to Venice. Most of the party's horses made the short trip over to the Lidos, the barrier islands across the whole of the Venetian lagoon from Pellestrina to Lido itself, from which they would trans-ship for Venice. As it proved, we kept most of our horses on the grass and grain of Lido for months. But a few of us were ordered to keep our mounts to hand – I was, and so were Fiore and Juan and Stapleton. And Nerio.

From Chioggia to Venice is no great distance, and by midday, the dome of Saint Mark's was visible above the glassy surface of the lagoon as we rowed up along the Lido from the south, as people used to do in those days. As the city grew closer, my awe deepened. I had imagined that Venice would be like Chioggia writ large. Indeed, Fra Peter had been prosaic enough to say so, and the reality took my breath away. I had never seen so many stone houses all together in all my life.

If every noble palace and great stone house and church in London and York were placed side by each, and then we added all the best houses of Paris and Avignon, the resulting city would not be as magnificent as Venice. And a city with canals! No ditches, no stream of urine, no horse manure, no human excrement floating in muddy brown water. None of that. The sea washes Venice clean at high tide twice a day, and carries her effluvium out into the marshes that surround her.

Venice smells of nothing worse than the sea. She has a hundred stone churches and the greatest square in the world; the Doge's palace is one of the noblest structures in Italy, and the church of Saint Mark's is the rival of Hagia Sofia in Constantinople.

Hmm. Perhaps not. But I hadn't seen Hagia Sophia yet.

And let us not forget the forest of her ships. Every street is a wharf and all along the outer rim of the city, and indeed, up the Rialto and along the Grand Canal there were ships: round ships and great ships and galleys – more galleys than I'd ever seen. As our barge brought us to the steps by Saint Mark's and the Doge's palace, I counted sixty fighting galleys I'd seen.

Riches indeed. Spare me your counting houses and warehouses. Show me your galleys.

I admit I fell in love at once. And I have never fallen out of love, my friends. Venice has a hold on my heart the way London has, and England. My second country, though I did not yet know it. And truly, Venetians are more like Englishmen than any other people I have met. Perhaps it is the sea. Perhaps it's pig-headedness. Or a little liberty. But by God, the city of Saint Mark is a fine place.

We wasted no time: the barge took us to the Doge's steps, and we were welcomed into the palace.

I swear, the Doge winced when he saw Father Pierre. I knew from Fra Peter that there had been months of negotiations with the Doge and his council about the fleet that would carry the crusade to the Holy Land, and that, in the end, Father Pierre had had his way.

So now the Doge knelt and kissed the legate's ring, embraced him, and then frowned.

'Where's the King of Cyprus?' he asked without preamble. 'Your Dogs of War are emptying my kennels of food.'

With his arm around the legate's shoulders, the Doge escorted Father Pierre out of the loggia and up the great stairs. We were taken to a side chamber and entertained by a pair of lute players and a tenor who sang beautifully. It was in many ways the most elegant reception we'd had in Italy, and it was further reinforced with wine and cakes. Ser Nerio smiled over his glass – in Venice everything was glass.

'Welcome to the New Rome,' he said. 'They lie and they drive hard bargains, but they are far easier to deal with than Neapolitans or Genoese. Don't quote me.'

After an hour, a pair of Venetian knights came and courteously escorted us to our lodgings in the Count of Savoy's palace. I shared with the donats; eight of us in a single room, but the room was huge, on the *piano nobile* and elegant and full of light from windows of glass. We all had feather beds and trunks in which to stow our clothes, and we had another room in which to place our tack and our armour. The only difficulty was our horses; Venice has fewer than fifty open fields in the whole of the city, thanks to the population on the islands and the incredibly dense building. So our horses were, as I mentioned, to be kept on the Lido, and that meant that we had to rotate a watch to look after them. I found a pair of wax tablets and began on a watch bill, then carried my work to Fra Ricardo Caracciolo, who was sitting on his own feather bed, writing a letter while Sister Marie copied another.

I remember that I started to explain to Fra Ricardo , and he shrugged.

'Take yourself off the watch bill, Sir William,' he said. 'You are going to Prague.'

While we fought off assassinations and engaged in political discussions across Italy, the newly appointed commander of our crusade, the famous King of Cyprus, had not yet arrived in Venice, despite having set off from Rheims in France two full weeks ahead of the time we set out from Avignon. By the time we arrived in Venice, there were five thousand men waiting to go on crusade, eating Venetian food and drinking their precious fresh water, so that the Venetians moved many of them to the mainland at Mestre or above Treviso. They were nearly mutinous, being unemployed and unpaid. Unscrupulous or over-eager papal recruiters had promised them pay – money that the papacy didn't have, or at least had no intention of paying out. In the north, the 'army' of routiers that Arnaud de Cervole had raised for the crusade and led into the Swiss passes murdered peasants, ran riot and in the end, killed the archpriest himself. It's not my story, except to say that I have since come to believe that Arnaud de Cervole was intending to join us – and the Green Count and his minions stopped him. I mention this to say that we did not win every round, or even know what was happening out there in the lands north of the Alps.

All this news greeted us at Venice, and much more beside. If Father Pierre already knew of the state of near war that existed between the Genoese on one side and the King of Cyprus on the other, he knew more than his household, but we all learned more than we wanted in a few hours in Venice. Some Genoese sailors had been killed in a brawl, and Genoa was using the brawl as a pretext to demand that the Cypriotes cede new rights of justice and commerce to Genoa. And of course, Venice wanted no such thing.

A lesser man would have despaired. I *was* that lesser man, and I returned to the donats and did what I should not – I conveyed to them my sense of defeat. I cursed and complained and predicted the collapse of the crusade.

An excellent piece of leadership, let us agree. But it seemed that whatever Father Pierre did, the hand of man or fate was against him.

I was railing against the injustice of it when Juan's face changed and Liberi became very quiet. I turned, hand still raised to make another point, and there was Father Pierre.

He smiled, as he almost always did. 'My son,' he said.

I stood abashed.

'The crusade may or may not happen at the will of God, and not because we are so very mighty, nor so very clever.' His eyes had a glint of self-mockery. 'Despite which, we shall do all in our poor power to help the cause. Will you take my messages to the King of Cyprus, William?'

I remember how much I didn't want to go. Emile was coming, and I wanted to be with her – and with Father Pierre – although, like any young man, I didn't consider what it might be like to divide my time between the two of them. And I was aware that she had said that d'Herblay was coming.

But Father Pierre was more than just my commander. So I knelt and put my hands between his. 'Whenever you command,' I said.

His smile didn't waiver. 'That's my William,' he said to the room. 'I need you to leave now – today.'

Christ on the cross!

I suppose he'd been ready, because he'd made four of us bring our horses all the way to the city, when the guides had begged us to leave them. I had a hasty conference with Fra Peter about Juan's coming knighting, about the command of the donats, about my failings as a leader and, oh yes, the threat of our being intercepted.

'I have a fear heavy on me, William, that Bishop Robert and his faction will stop at nothing to end the crusade. Or rather, to subvert it to their own will.' He looked at me. 'Nothing.'

I nodded. Any faction that employed the Bourc Camus was blacker than pine pitch in my eyes, and I needed no warning, or so I thought.

In the end, I got Fiore and my new servant, Marc-Antonio, and Ser Nerio and his squire, Davide. I was handed a purse full of money and I got to repack the harness I'd just laboriously moved into a storeroom and placed on an armour rack, while I tried to teach Marc-Antonio the most basic elements of armour care.

An old man approached me as I handed my bags and leather trunk down into the boat that was to carry us to the mainland. He came down the water steps of the loggia and Fra Peter waved to tell me he was one of our own.

The old man bowed. 'Sir Knight,' he said, 'are you William Gold of England?'

Despite feeling especially surly – hard done by, unwashed and unshaved in the face of elegance and civilization – despite all that, I returned his bow and tried to comport myself as a gentleman of the order.

'I have that honour, my lord,' I said with a flourish.

'Ah, messire, I am no lord, but merely Francesco Petrarca,' he said with immense dignity.

Even I knew who Petrarch was: the greatest man of letters in Italy or the world, discoverer of Cicero's letters, poet, diplomat – hah, Master Chaucer, I see your surprise. By God, I know a few scribblers beside you! It is not all war and horses, messires!'

'A name that is a title in itself,' I answered.

The old man lit up like a church at Easter. None of us are immune to flattery, are we? And the older we are, the nicer it is when some young pup offers us some, eh? At any rate, the great man gave me a packet of letters to carry, for the Doge and on his own account. Those letters were bound to half the cities of Europe, but there was a packet for the Emperor and another packet for the King of Cyprus, and yet another for his chancellor, Philippe de Mézièrres, of whom more anon.

Darkness found me on the shore north of Mestre, with the magnificent city behind me. I'd been in Venice for almost six hours.

I hadn't even had time to look for a sword.

Fra Peter had laid out my route for me. I had every passport that a knight could need, and the first thing I did on reaching Padua – again – was to purchase three excellent horses. Then we rode the way Fra Peter had crossed France two years before: fast and light, with no baggage but our armour and weapons and a fat letter of credit. We climbed into the Swiss passes and blessed the weather, but at the top of the great pass, where a monastery's lights burn like the hope of heaven a thousand feet above the road, it was cold even at high summer.

We descended into the Grand Duchy of Burgundy, an amalgam of appanages and inherited towns owned by the King of France's brothers and uncles, a feudal empire that was partly French and partly Imperial and that shared territory and feudatories with Lorraine and with Savoy. But we continued north and east, following Fra Peter's instructions. We were careful, believe me. I used our Venetian passports and had reason to thank God for them. Papal passports had many foes.

It appeared that the King of Cyprus was his own man, and not the Pope's tool. And he had decided to enlist the Emperor in his scheme for a great crusade in the east. The Emperor and the Pope were not actually at war, but neither were they friends – the Emperor tended to side with the English, or anyone else who could weaken mighty France.

Fiore knew the roads of Germany, having spent time there learning from the German masters and having followed their tradition of fighting on errantry, travelling from town to town challenging strangers. Ser Nerio knew how to get good accommodations in any town, usually by showing a letter of credit and a Florentine ambassadorial letter. I truly think that we escaped harm because we had so many different letters of passage that no spy could pin down our 'side'. Nor were we much given to chatter.

In southern Germany, they took us for knights on errantry, and by God, gentles, we lived the part. We were challenged from time to time. Fiore was disposed to fight, but I had a mission and a fine sense of my own rank; well, arrogance is the specialty of the young, I think. I would flourish my various commissions and ride on.

But a day's ride east of Nuremberg, we passed through a small village and saw a party of knights whose colours we knew from the day before. They were obviously French; German heraldry is very different from French, and even the colours they use in a blazon are different.

I didn't know any of them, nor did I question how they'd got ahead of us on the road. But they barred the square, and tallest man – I called him the knight of the ship for the device on his shield – raised his arms and cried a challenge.

I sent him Marc-Antonio with my papal commission; I was chary of using it, but I did not intend to be delayed. I dismounted in the yard of the town's wine shop to have a bite with my bridle over my arm. Fra Peter had been correct – again. The Emperor had indeed moved his court east to Prague.

I was considering all this when the Ship Knight struck my squire to the ground with his spear.

I was not fully armed. In fact, I had on a habergeon and a good brigandine of many plates, my 'riding armour'. I had no leg harness and nothing on my arms, and wore only a light sword. Fiore was wearing even less – just a haubergeon. Germany is far too civilised a place to require a man to ride abroad in harness, and ours was packed in straw baskets on the panniers of our spare horses.

'Don't send me a peasant. Come and fight like a man,' Ship Knight shouted.

He meant business.

I drank off the wine in my cup – sheer bravado – and vaulted into my saddle. Fiore was two ells away, negotiating for a sausage, but he was alert and he knew we were attacked. With the ease of long practice, he reached on to the pack horse, extracted a spear, and threw it to me overhand.

The Ship Knight had his lance couched against me, set in his lance rest. He wore good armour on all his limbs and a heavy breastplate under a full helm. His heavy warhorse was half again the size of my riding horse.

Behind him, his friends lowered their visors.

Very chivalrous.

I rode at the Ship Knight, and as he put spurs to his horse, I shifted my weight as du Guesclin had taught me, and my horse sidestepped, the mounted equivalent of stepping *fora di strada* in a foot combat. His big horse leaped forward and I stood in my stirrups and threw my spear. It wasn't a full-length lance, but instead one of the six-foot spears we used to fight on foot, with a long, sharp head.

He could not ward his horse, and the spear went in by the horse's neck and the big horse stumbled and blew blood from its nostrils. I had my arming sword out; Ship Knight hadn't grasped what was happening and had no momentum, no forward speed, and my sword slipped unerringly along his lance shaft and flipped it aside. This, too, was the product of a spring of intense drill. Close in, my left hand closed on the haft of his lance, dragging it across his body and putting torque on his waist, and I dragged him from the saddle by his own lance. As his back struck the cobbled street, the lance finally came away from his lance rest and bounced once on the stones, and then I swung it by the haft, spun it in the air with a flourish – and turned my horse to face the other three.

Fiore trotted up by my side. 'Helmet?' he asked, and handed me my bassinet.

He covered me while I dropped it on my head.

'Caitiff! Coward! You killed his horse!' shouted another man, who I remember as the Knight of Coins.

Nerio reined in on my other side. 'I couldn't let Liberi have all the fun,' he said.

Liberi frowned. 'I don't need you to defeat these riff-raff,' he said.

'Could you two save the fight for the enemy?' I muttered.

We charged them.

I can seldom remember a fight that I enjoyed so much. We were better; simply, better men. Better trained. I think the best moment of the fight was that I hit my opponent squarely on his shield, having deceived his lance, and I rocked him flat across his crupper, so that his feet came up in his stirrups, and Liberi caught one going by and threw him to the street as if he'd planned this little manoeuvre all his life.

Truly, the only thing better than being a good knight is being one of a team of good knights. To have comrades …

Nerio, who was a fine jouster, put his man down, horse and all. Then his horse kicked the downed man. Their superior horses and armour were of no importance, and in seconds they were all lying in the dung-streaked stones of the square while Fiore collected their horses.

I rode straight to their squires and pages, who scattered. I shamelessly ripped through their pack horses, and I tipped a leather bag full of wallets into the muck, looking for letters, but I found nothing.

Nerio curled a lip in distaste. 'Is this your mercenary's chivalry?' he asked.

'I want to know if they are hired men,' I said. 'They are French knights and they attacked my squire. I suspect they are not what they appear.'

'Oho!' exclaimed Nerio, or words to that effect. 'This is more like Florence than I had expected.'

Then I checked on Marc-Antonio. He was deeply unconscious, and already had an egg on his head big enough for a duck. I got him over his horse, and Fiore had all the knight's destriers.

'Right of arms,' I called at the squires of my adversaries.

Nerio was for staying, perhaps to see if any of the downed knights was dead or needed a doctor.

'Let's move, before someone appears with a crossbow,' I said.

Two days later I wished that I'd ignored Nerio's aristocratic ways and scooped the purses out of the muck. Three destriers cost the earth and the moon to feed, and they were eating our travel money. However, they were beautiful horses, far better than those Fiore or I would usually have owned or ridden. We'd left our warhorses back in Venice – a perfectly sensible decision, given the cost of maintaining a warhorse on the road. Unless you have to fight, the warhorse is a useless mouth that consumes money.

We continued to speculate on who our late adversaries might have been, and then rode hard for Prague, crossing some of the most beautiful country I've ever seen – as rich as northern Italy. It was August, and the crops were coming; peasants stood in their fields, sickles in hand, to watch us pass their grain fields, which stretched away like a golden promise of heaven in the red light of the setting sun. Beautiful young women, the better for a sheen of sweat, wiped their faces and curtsied even as their fathers and mothers closed in on them protectively; indeed, some lay down and hid at the edge of the road so that we wouldn't see them, but we were old soldiers and we knew where to look.

What we couldn't fail to see was the lack of war. There were no burned towns and no crowds of starving beggars. Twice we passed roadside gibbets with men rotting in chains, but we never saw the tell-tales of regular banditry – sly informers, churned earth and heavy horse droppings on the roads like those left by a military column, columns of smoke on the horizon. Fire is the hoof print of brigandage.

Marc-Antonio took two days to recover, and then he was sick on horseback for two more and had real trouble speaking, so that I despaired of his wits. But by the sixth day from Nuremberg, he had again begun his litany of complaints in passable French, and devastating Italian. His riding improved drastically, and it appeared to us that the blow to his head had made him a better rider – a joke that didn't appeal to him for some reason.

At the very edge of Bohemia we were robbed in an inn, and all our purses taken. That was when Marc-Antonio's talents began to be seen; he had our travel purse under his pillow, and thanks to his preserving it, we weren't wrecked. Nerio was mortified to have no money of his own, and tried in every village to cash a bill on the family bank, but in Bohemia, at least in the forest, no one had ever heard of the Acciaioli and their bank, or indeed even of Florence.

But *par dieu*, my friends, the women of Bohemia are beautiful, tall and honey haired and deep-breasted. Nor are the men any the less handsome, and the knights we saw there were big men, skilled in arms.

We arrived in Prague in late afternoon, and as the next day was the Sabbath, we went to church in the magnificent cathedrals. We knew within an hour of entering the city that the Emperor was not there, and my heart sank within me. But our letters from Father Pierre and the Pope gained me admittance at the castle, and the chamberlain, as I think he was, told me that the Emperor and the King of Cyprus had gone east to visit the King of Poland and the King of Hungary and to hold a great tournament at Krakow, in Poland and we would find him there.

As we travelled east in Bohemia the weather grew cooler and the harvest was more advanced, but the women were not any the less beautiful and the grain was like a shower of gold on the land, the very manna God promised the Israelites. The land grew flatter and flatter until we were riding across the steppes that I had heard described by Fra Peter and by other knights who had fought against the Prussians: Jean de Grailly and the Lord of the Pyrenees, Gaston de Foix. It is one thing to hear traveller's tales, even from a courteous knight, of how flat the land of the east can be, but it is another thing to see it for yourself.

On the plains, there were no inns and few farms, and while we saw herds in the distance more than once, we were not accosted, but neither were we hosted and feasted, and we ran low on food and had to hunt antelope. Our spear throwing was up to the challenge, and I spent a happy afternoon teaching my squire to lay a snare and take a rabbit. And to cook it.

I cannot remember if I stopped to consider that I was riding across the world on a feckless errand to find the commander of a crusade that might never happen. Or why a commander would ride away from his crusade. I suspect I thought about it, but I was young enough to enjoy the adventure that was offered to me, and that day, that month, that summer, I was offered the steppes and the antelope, the golden wheat, and the matching hair of the lovely maidens of Poland and Bohemia.

We had been a month and more on the road when the spires of Krakow came into sight on the horizon, and such is the flatness of the ground that we had a full day's ride ahead of us yet, and we lay a night in the Monastery of Saint Nicolas, well out in the country. But the abbot put us immediately at our ease and told us that our quest was fulfilled, and that both the Emperor and the King of Cyprus were at Krakow, preparing a great tournament with all the best Knights of the Empire and Poland.

The abbot was a talkative man, with excellent Latin, our only common tongue, and he told us a great deal about what had transpired, and very little of it to the credit of the Emperor. If the abbot was to be believed, the Emperor had no interest whatsoever in a crusade, but was far too politic to say so, and was holding a tournament to allow King Peter to recruit knights – but Nerio, whose Latin was as much above mine as my swordsmanship was above Marc-Antonio's, came away with the impression that the Emperor's hospitality was wearing thin, and that the Cypriotes were expensive and perhaps troublesome guests for the people of Krakow. I remembered that Nan had told me when I was in London that the guilds had given a feast of four kings – the King of France, the King of England, the King of Cyprus and Jerusalem, and the King of Scotland – and how much it had cost the guilds and the alderman of the city.

When Nan told the story, I had been more interested in her, and her face, than in her tale. I had no idea, then, that I would meet Peter of Cyprus.

Any road, the last few leagues, I was as careful as I could be; I saw enemies behind every fence post and inn sign, and my hand was always on my sword and my purse, but looking back, I think we outrode our adversaries, if indeed Robert of Geneva *had* sent more than the one team of knights. So despite my caution, or perhaps because of it, eventually we reached the inn that bore the arms of the King of Cyprus, and several other blazons across the front.

We dismounted. It was evening, and the sun shining in long rays through the dust. In Krakow, and indeed all of Poland, the greater portion of the buildings are constructed of logs and wood, and the great inn was no different, although it smelled like any other inn from London's Southwark to Verona; that indefinable air of hospitality and good beer and flees.

We'd crossed half the world to get there, or so it seemed, and then we stood in the street while Marc-Antonio held our horses, straightening our clothes and sorting out all the packets of letters. The Emperor was in the castle and would have to wait for another day.

We paused to wipe off the dust. Nerio's squire, Alessandro, produced a brush and did his best. I was wearing a peasant's cote over my red surcoat, to protect it from the dust, and I stripped it off. Fiore emulated me, and Nerio looked meaningfully at our pack horse where we had good clothes. Italian clothes.

Marc-Antonio shrugged. 'It will take an hour!' he whined.

Whine or not, I knew he was right. 'Very well,' I said, or something equally masterful.

Brushed and combed and still smelling strongly of horse, we walked up the steps, past the porch that was packed with cut firewood, and entered through the great front doors that were pinned back, wide enough for a wagon and team to ride through. A door ward looked us over and made a face.

'What do you mean, sir?' I asked. He pointed mutely at my sword, and I unbuckled it off my heavy plaque belt. Fiore did the same, and then Nerio.

Nerio's sword was one of the finest riding swords I'd ever seen, all blue and gold with a heavy gold pommel that held a saint's relic, or so it was said. The door ward's eyes all but popped. He bowed to Nerio again, thus instantly reinforcing my desire to own the very best sword money could buy. Swords command many kinds of respect.

I tried to offer my papers, but the door ward merely bowed silently and indicated the inner door.

We went into the inn and found the King of Cyprus and all his court inside. There were twenty knights there, and as many noble squires, all dressed in the latest Italian modes, with tulip-throated pourpoints and collared shirts as if every one of them was Ser Nerio or Ser Niccolò.

Every head turned to look at us.

A handsome man in white and silver approached us from the right. 'By what right do you enter our lodging?' he asked.

I bowed and again offered my papers. 'My lord, I am a courier carrying letters for the King of Cyprus,' I said.

The man in white and silver frowned. 'You are not dressed for court,' he said.

By that time, my eyes had become accustomed to the light of the interior. The walls were whitewashed, the ceilings were high, even to the rafters, and two great fireplaces lit what, in England, would have been an old-fashioned great hall of logs rather than stone. The heads of deer and elk and bear studded the walls, with tapestries nearly black with age and a magnificent reliquary in silver and gold with jewels that had to have been the property of the king, because it was too rich for any tavern.

Between the fireplaces was a great chair with a beautiful fur of shining black sable hanging over it like a quilt, and sitting on the fur was a young man, not much older than me, in a cloth of gold jupon and hose of red with pearls in the shape of swans as embellishment. He was frowning, playing with a child's toy of a stick and a ball connected by a string.

He caught my eye. And rose with the sort of athletic fluidity that Fiore has, and Fra Peter. I strive for it: it is he mark of a great man-at-arms.

He moved like a greyhound, all long legs and stride. And he moved with purpose, crossing the great hall in ten paces, and his courtiers moved out of his way. He threw the ball-and-stick toy at one of them and the man caught it.

No one needed to tell me that this was Peter de Lusignan, King of Cyprus, King of Jerusalem. Men said he was the best lance in the West; the best knight in Christendom.

I went down on one knee.

Nerio and Liberi emulated me.

'De Tenoury, tell these three that I am prepared to imagine that they are here on important business,' the king said. 'But to enter my presence dressed as peasants is to dishonour their master, whomever he might be, and me as well.' He all but spat. 'I've had enough of being humiliated today.'

Silver and white leaned over me. 'You heard his Grace,' he said. 'Come back when you are properly dressed. Or come in by the servant's entrance.'

I was well trained – the order drills etiquette as well as all the other knightly skills. So I kept my head bowed, but I growled, 'I am a knight and a servant of the Order of St John and I am here with messages from the legate and the Pope.'

The king bit his lip and looked at an older man in blue and red standing near him. When I say older, this gentleman was perhaps forty, with grey in his blond hair and lines on his face. His blue eyes flashed over me.

'If your Grace wishes to order these men away, of course he may,' the man said.

'But, de Mézzieres? My faithful pilgrim? Always, your voice has that hint of censure. Please, share with us the nature of our failings.' The king's voice rose and fell a little more than was necessary.

De Mézzières bowed. 'Your Grace, it is not my place to put any censure on your royal head. Yet ...'

'Yet?' asked the king, and there was an obvious warning in his voice.

'Yet I will say that I would expect the King of Cyprus, the commander of the *Passagium Generale*, to fall on his knees and kiss any missive the Pope sends him,' said the older man, with his head high and his eyes boring holes in the king.

The king glared for a moment at the older Frenchman. I knew that the older man must be Philippe de Mézzières, the king's chancellor; I had letters for him and had heard him described. The king pursed his lips and stalked across the great hall, opened a door, and paused.

'It may be your fondest desire that I be shackled hand and foot to your damned crusade, Monsieur de Mézzières, but it was never mine.' He went through, and slammed the great oak door behind him.

The silence was like that of the pause between strokes of thunder.

'Let's go,' I said, very softly. My instinct was to obey the orders of the king, however childish, and not get caught up in some courtier's drama. I had been a squire for the Prince of Wales, and I knew something of princes. Quick to anger, and often deeply regretful later of letting the mask slip. But very conscious of the rules.

I was trained for this. I knew to bide my time, hide my emotions, and remain a knight. But I was angry.

I felt … humiliated. I had come a long way, and somehow had grown used to the armour of authority that was the habit of St John. Indeed, I felt that my *Order* had been humiliated. I was angry, and to my shame, I took it out on poor Marc-Antonio. Out on the street, he dared to ask what had happened.

'We were tossed on our ears,' I spat. 'Because our clothes are dusty and unsuitable.' My tone and my glare carried a clear message – he and his whining were at fault.

His face fell. In fact, it didn't just fall – it collapsed like an under-mined stone tower.

It's a small thing, for a man who has killed. You'd think I was hardened to it, but I had been with the Order for more than a year, and the collapse of his face, the twitch of his mouth – it was as if I'd kicked him.

I promise you, I didn't think of it at the time. I was so furious that I almost missed my mounting, and when I was up I found that I'd left my arming sword with the door ward. Fuming, I had to dismount and reclaim it.

He bowed. 'The king's had a hard day,' he said, in good French.

I considered a nasty reply, and thank God I bit my tongue and acted the part of a knight. I nodded, forced a smile, and bowed.

But between getting our own inn, finding our clothes and bribing a pair of maids to iron our things – we couldn't get back before darkness fell.

Nerio finally put a hand on my arm. 'Sir William,' he said carefully, 'I am going for a glass of wine and some beef. I recommend that you do the same.' He didn't wait for my expostulations, either, but took Fiore by the shoulder – took Fiore, for the love of the good Jesu; Fiore, who he affected to despise – and left our rooms and went to the head of the inn stairs without looking back at me. Fiore went with him willingly enough.

I suppose I had given them a difficult afternoon. In fact, I had behaved badly – disappointment and humiliation bring out the worst in most of us. I was left with Marc-Antonio. He kept his head down and kept laying out clothes and trying to boss the maids, who ignored him and went back and forth, heating their irons in a box by the fire. The box, of course, kept soot off the irons so that they were clean.

I still didn't apologise. I sat there, my black mood further darkened by the abandonment of my friends, until the maids lit tapers and I smelled the beautiful smell of resin in the torches. The smell woke me from my mood, and I went down and ate, but my companions were scarcely civil. Twice, Fiore looked at me in a way that suggested he was considering physical violence.

I went to bed early. As a consequence, I rose with the dawn. I dressed plainly and left a message that the others should not wait for me. My anger was gone, replaced, as it often is, with a sort of guilt complicated by fear – fear that I would be humiliated again and fear that I had behaved badly with my friends and it couldn't be fixed; a common fear for a young man, I think.

I had no experience of this particular world. I'd been a minor servant, and now, to all intents, I was a sort of ambassador. I didn't know the rules, but I knew damned well that if I went back as the Order's representative to King Peter, I would go alone, test the waters, and do my best to avoid public humiliation. And spare my friends. And, perhaps, apologise to them.

I was dirty, and I decided to wash. I managed to find a bathhouse. Like Bohemia and High Germany, the bathhouses of Poland are correctly notorious as dens of vice, staffed with scantily clad women whose single layer linen garments stick to their bodies in the steam in a most attractive manner.

Shall I go on? They really are splendid, and if priests don't want men to fornicate, why did God make women so beautiful? Eh? Answer me that. By Saint George, I was in a much better mood when I emerged, clean in body if slightly soiled in soul. The woman who washed me – I can still see her, because she smiled all the time and nothing so becomes a woman as a smile – she was a good leman, luscious and lovesome and very tall. And very apt for the game.

Hmm. I digress too much. I think perhaps old men think too much of the pleasures of the body, eh? But by Saint Maurice, sirs, I had my sport, and discovered that she spoke some little Latin, and we amused each other thoroughly, chanting prayers back and forth in the steam.

'You are a nun?' I asked her, and she laughed.

'Never in this life,' she said. 'And you are no priest.'

'I am a knight,' I said with all the pride of Lucifer. *Ego miles.*

She clapped her hands together. I suspect that it is a universal truth throughout the Christian world that women – working women

– prefer soldiers to priests. Mayhap not when the soldiers are burning your barn, but in a bath or a bedchamber –

'You are with the King of Jerusalem?' she asked. *Tu es cum rege Hierusalem.* Not the best Latin, perhaps. She was saying I *was* the king of Jerusalem – *su es* should have been *sis*. 'You will fight?'

I snorted water.

She said something in Polish, not to me but past me. Across the little linen screen that hid us from the other tubs, a girl's somewhat shrewish voice shouted back.

I must have looked my question. She swirled water and looked demure, a fetching trick for a girl wearing two yards of wet linen. She was in the tub with me by then. The better to wash me, of course.

The shrewish voice said something that caused my girl – Katerina, that was her name! – to look surprised. She shouted back, and a male voice shouted indignantly.

'King of Jerusalem's men fight last night,' she said. 'Drunk. Stupid.' She shrugged, indicating that this was the limit of her Latin and that any fool knew how stupid men were. 'drunk' and 'stupid' were conveyed with hand signs.

When I went to fetch my clothes, I found them neatly ironed. A closed-faced young woman, clearly not amused by the goings-on, was busy killing lice in a pair of hose with an iron so hot it made the wool sizzle and the insects pop. They were not, *par dieu*, my hose. But the service was good and I paid her. Who wants to put on dirty clothes on a clean body?

And at the desk, the table where money was taken, I counted over my silver cheerfully enough. The man at the desk was enormous – fat and tall. He smelled as if he had never used the services of his own establishment. Despite which, he had a smile almost as winning as Katerina's and I gave him a small tip as well.

'Speak French?' I asked.

'*Non volens,*' he said. *Not willingly.*

I laughed. The Poles are a nation of Latinists.

But I left with my mood changed, and sin made me humble. Aiming for the humility practiced by Father Pierre, I went back to our much plainer inn – although it still sported a dozen coats of arms, including, I say with pride, my own red and sable. I had Marc-Antonio dress me, ignored his sullen looks, took the packets of letters and went to the king's inn, which I entered through the kitchens. There, cutting capons and rabbits with heavy knives, were two enormous women at the main table, and at the next table, two equally fat women were putting eggs and bread in a basket with a tall pitcher of new milk and some cider. I couldn't understand a word they said – Polish is not in my list of languages – but they giggled a great deal and waggled a sausage at each other. I blew kisses at them and snagged a piece of bread and a cup of cider, and watched the great hall from the kitchen door while my eyes grew used to the gloom.

De Mézzières was there, and silver and white, now dressed in more practical clothes, and with his arm in a sling. With them were a dozen other men in arming clothes and younger men who looked to my practiced eye like squires. There was armour all over the floor and on benches long the far wall.

I could see that now I was the one who was overdressed, and my embroidered scarlet pourpoint, the very best of Bolognese fashion, was as out of place today as my dusty riding clothes and riding boots had been the night before. But it is far better to be overdressed than underdressed.

I could see the king, in his shirt, waiting while a pair of squires laced his arming coat. I caught de Mézzières' eye.

He nodded and came towards me. 'From where do you come, young man?' he asked. 'I must apologise for yesterday,' he said quietly. 'The king had had a very difficult day.'

'My lord, I am from the legate, Pierre Thomas, in Venice. I left Venice on the first of July.' I bowed.

De Mézzières looked at me and blinked like a man facing bright light. 'Legate? The Cardinal de Perigord is surely the legate,' he asked.

'My lord, the cardinal is dead, and the Pope has appointed Father Pierre as the Patriarch of Constantinople – and the legate of the crusade.'

French was the *lingua franca* of the Cypriote court. Every head turned.

I bowed again, keeping Father Pierre's humility before me. 'I have a packet of letters for you from Venice,' I said. I handed him a heavy set of envelopes. 'This one is from Messire Petrarca, as well.'

De Mézzières paused. He was about to speak, but the king waved at me.

'Ah! The courier of last night, now dressed in the latest Italian fashions to make us all feel dowdy.' But despite his words, the king smiled, and his smile was warm. 'Come here, sir, by me. And ten thousand apologies for my surliness of last evening.'

I bowed. 'It is nothing, your Grace. I have letters from the papal legate—'

'Who, it proves, is none other than our well-beloved friend and father in Christ, Pierre Thomas! I have ears, sir, and I can hear when you speak.' He held out a hand. 'We are impatient to read the words of our fathers, Holy and spiritual.'

I placed his letters directly in his hand.

'Were you charged with any particular message?' he asked carelessly.

I bowed my head. 'I was asked to tell you to come as quickly as you might, to Venice, where your army awaits.'

'Hmm,' he answered. 'Tell my legate that I will come when it suits me. Tush!' he said, grabbing my arm. 'Say nothing of the sort. That is only my surliness speaking. Are you by any chance a jouster?'

It was like talking to Ser Niccolò, except that if you were quick-witted you could follow the jumps Ser Niccolò made – his conversation was all connected, and often strung together with bits of scripture and quotes from the ancients. King Peter simply moved from one topic to the next without a shred of warning.

It was like fighting.

'Your Grace, I can run a course,' I said carefully.

'Do you have other men in your train?' he asked. 'That is, who can handle a lance and not make fools of themselves or me? Can drink a cup of wine and not cause an incident at a dinner?' His voice rose as he spoke, and silver and white – I assumed that he was the Sieur de Tenoury since I'd heard him so addressed – cringed.

'Your Grace—' de Mézzières said, and his tone urged caution.

'I will not be gainsaid in this, de Mézzières.' The king spoke with great vehemence. 'We are challenged and we will fight.'

No one in the hall was looking at me, or the king. All of them were attempting to slide under the oak floor. I had been a squire when the Prince of Wales was angry – I had even been the target. I knew exactly how they felt.

I was still kneeling in front of the king, and my eyes were cast down. 'Your Grace, I have two men by me who can run a course.'

'You have horses? Arms?' the king asked eagerly.

I wondered what I was getting Fiore and Nerio into. Perhaps I should have considered carefully, or been cautious. Or remembered the humiliations of the evening before.

Perhaps, but I am not made that way. 'Your Grace, we have horses and arms, and we are completely at your service.' Some devil made me raise my voice. 'The more so as you are the Pope's appointed commander, therefore I am your knight.'

Then the king turned the full sun of his smile on me. 'By Saint Maurice and the Holy Passion, monsieur, that was well said.' He nodded. 'I ask you, Sir Knight, to rally your friends and join us here; display your arms at my window, and serve with me this day.'

Yes, I fought in the Grand Tournament of Krakow.

Now, if you gentlemen have been listening carefully, you know that I had never actually participated in a tournament. I had certainly practised for them, and several times in my career I had the honour of fighting in deeds of arms, but I was – and am – a soldier, and tournaments are for the richest and most powerful lords.

I do not need to explain this to you, gentles – but Aemilie has never served in arms, have you, my sweet? So let me tell you how it is. To participate in a great tournament, you must first of all be invited. In the romances, of course, knights on errantry simply arrive at the tournament field, lance in hand, already armed – but that is pure fantasy. In this world, tournaments are very expensive affairs, with thousands of ducats spent on building the stands, on decorating an entire town, on the costumes of the knights, and on actors, *jongleurs*, bards, and food – and that's before a single course is run.

To participate, a man needs the bluest of blood and friends in the highest places and most tournaments are held by a team, who share the expense, usually led by a prince or a very great nobleman. To be invited to serve on the prince's team was a very, very great honour, and if you have been listening, you'll recall that I was going to fight on my own prince's team at Calais back in the year sixty, at the time of the great truce. But in the end, I was thrown off.

Tournaments are both socially and physically dangerous. Reputations are won and lost in a tourney. Chivalry is, indeed, tested. In fact, I think it is worth saying that, short of battle, the tournament, a great tournament, with kings and queens and great ladies watching, is the greatest test of a knight's virtues that there is. The whole *empris* is difficult, dangerous, expensive, and public. Bad conduct is instantly seen. Thousands of people, high born and low, are watching everything: the arming, the horses, the quality of harness, the techniques employed – everything.

The church has a very ambiguous view of the tournament, too. Most priests see the tournament as a sink of iniquity, where lechery, pride, and gluttony triumph and where the virtues of chivalry are seen to overwhelm the Christian pieties. Yet many churchmen come from noble families. And many churchmen see the tournament as a relatively harmless way to harness the men-at-arms without war. In some countries, men who fight in tournaments are considered to be outside the church for the duration of the deed and men who die in a tournament are considered unshriven. In some places, they cannot be buried in hallowed ground.

But, *ma petit*, there are jousts, and there are tourneys, and then there are deeds of arms, foot combats, *encommensailles* and *bohorts*. I could weary you with the language of arms, and truly, it differs from country to country. But in brief – a joust is two men with lances, tilting at one another. And in a greater deed of arms, the *encommensailles* may be jousts or even foot combats; they proceed the tourney, sometimes as many as three or four days of them.

But the tourney, the true tournament, is a different thing. It is a battle of equals, a team of horsemen on either side. I have been told that in King Arthur's time, men fought with lances in the tourney, but we are smaller, weaker men, and we fight with swords on horseback, and it is illegal to use the point. Indeed, in many tourneys the participants much use a special sword with a blunted point. In such a game, each team has a goal post – a heavy post, usually with a flag atop it. And the desire of every knight is to unhorse his opponent, take his horse, and lead it to the post. Once the horse is at the post, it is the property of the knight who took it.

You can make a fortune in minutes, taking warhorses from the great lords. And you can make a mortal enemy who will hate you all your life.

Well. I nearly burst with excitement, and I raced to our inn where I found Marc-Antonio eating in the kitchen.

'Where are they?' I demanded.

He took his time chewing.

I was fit to burst.

'Bathhouse,' he managed.

I ran in all my finery to the bathhouse.

The fat man laughed when I came in. 'Not got enough, eh?' he asked in his slow, accurate Latin.

'I need my two friends,' I said.

'Two?' he asked, and slapped his great thighs so that they wobbled like jellies. 'We're that busy this morning, my lord, I'm not sure I can spare you two.' He roared at his own wit.

I moved past him into the baths – you must see this, me, dripping self-importance, wearing a fortune in scarlet and black, pushing into the damp heat of a brothel-bathhouse.

'Fiore!' I called out. The bathhouse had twenty tubs and each was partitioned from the others by screens of birch bark or parchment.

Various Polish comments were shouted by male voices. Someone suggested how I might use my virility in a particularly offensive way – in French.

Fiore's voice carried perfectly. 'I am here, William,' he called.

'What are you doing?' I asked, unmindful of my friend's somewhat literal cast.

'I am in the very act of copulation,' he replied.

Only Fiore would *explain* that he was in the very act. I suppose I'm lucky he didn't elaborate on the mechanics of the thing. The sound of laughter and some very exact comments, more like coaching than anything else, favoured us from the other partitions.

'The King of Jerusalem has invited us to fight on his team. In the *tournament!*' I shouted.

A girl squawked, and cursed. I don't know what she said, but it wasn't nice.

'Oh, I beg your pardon,' Fiore said in Italian. I was at his screen, holding his towel.

'Where's Nerio?' I asked, while Fiore blushed and his girl cursed him. I had my purse on my belt – a nasty piece of poor leatherwork, my temporary replacement for the purse that had been lifted in Bohemia. I tossed her two silver pennies, and she was mollified.

'We are to serve?' Nerio asked, a trifle rhythmically. 'In the tournament? Against the Emperor?'

'Yes!' I said through his screen.

'Splendid,' Nerio said. 'I – shall – be – with – you – dir-ec-tly.'

I got the two of them back to the inn; collected our harness and our warhorses, our shields and our somewhat bedraggled papal banner, and transported them to the king's inn. By this time the morning was well advanced, and the king was none too pleased with us for the time we'd taken; he and eight of his knights were fully armed save only their helmets and gauntlets, and they were sitting on stools out in front of the inn, on the loggia.

But every squire present leaped to arm us. It was chaos for a few minutes, as the armour was laid out on the floor of the loggia and my harness and Fiore's were hopelessly intermixed. But Marc-Antonio had been paying attention as we travelled, and Nerio's squire Davide marshalled his master's harness, and then the steel fairly flew on to our bodies while the Sieur de Mézzières, resplendent in good Milanese and wearing a fine brigandine in dark blue leather, stood by us and explained.

'The king is an expert jouster, and he has borne away every prize these last four weeks – in Low Germany, in Prague, and now here. The Emperor has tired of seeing his best knights get tumbled, and has challenged the king to tourney – to a mêlée.'

And you don't like it, I thought. De Mézzières seemed cautious and old – but he was thorough, and he had a famous name as a crusader, having been knighted at the taking of Smyrna. He'd been a friend of de Charny and he'd held Caen against us in the year fifty-nine too. He was no parchment saint: he knew the business of war.

He looked at the three of us. At that moment, we had our leg harnesses on, and I was lacing up my mail haubergeon. Fiore was ahead of me, already getting an arm laced up.

'You are all knights?' he asked.

'I was dubbed on the battlefield,' I said.

De Mézzières paused. 'Ah,' he said. 'Sir, I mean no insult, but nothing – *nothing* – can be allowed to humiliate the king my master. Can this knighting be slighted or challenged?'

Well, that turncoat Baumgarten was good for something, after all.

'I was knighted at Florence in front of a thousand men-at-arms by the Count von Baumgarten – a knight of the Emperor, I believe.'

De Mézzières started. 'You are Sir William Gold?' he asked. 'I *thought* I knew the name.' He looked away and set his jaw.

I knew something was wrong. Battlefield knightings are for poor men and third sons and mercenaries.

'And the others?' he asked, his tone icy.

I tried to control my temper, because being on this tournament team was a gift from God. 'Ser Nerio is the son of Ser Niccolò Acciaioulo of Florence; also a Knight of the Holy Roman Empire,' I said.

De Mézzières nodded, but was not looking at me.

'Master Fiore is a donat of the Order of St John, a volunteer. His father is a knight of Cividale, but he has not yet been knighted.' I raised my voice. 'Have I offended, monsieur?'

De Mézzières took a deep breath.

But whatever he might have said, the king interrupted him. 'The thin lad's a squire? What is your name, sir?'

Fiore knelt, as the king was addressing him directly. 'Fiore Furlano de Cividale d'Austria,' he said.

The king exhaled. 'Only knights may play in this great game, Messire Fiore.' He looked at de Mézzières.

De Mézzières raised an eyebrow.

'I must have twelve, or forfeit,' the king said. 'And I will not forfeit, if I have to arm a serving maid!'

Fiore raised his hands together in a position of prayer – or homage. 'Try me, your Grace. I am a very good jouster.'

The king nodded. 'The *mêlée* is not a joust. It is a vicious game played on horseback.'

Fiore kept his head bowed. 'Your Grace, however it is played, I will be quite good at it.'

The king looked at me. He was smiling: an open smile, not a politic one, and his face seemed to glow like the sun. 'Well, Messire Fiore, seeing as you are so *very* sure of yourself ...'

Mézzières frowned. 'You are determined to do this,' he said.

The king nodded. 'Am I the king, de Mézzières?' he asked.

'Your Grace knows that he is indeed king.' De Mézzières still didn't look my way.

'Your sword, then.' The king took de Mézzières' sword – and knighted Fiore on the spot.

Lucky bastard.

By the time we reached the field that had been staked off for the tournament, there must have been ten thousand people in the crowd. The sun was high, and the king's squires were agitated because the judges had already cried for the *juges diseurs*, the judges, to come forward.

We were late. And the Emperor, according to Nerio, was *trying* to disqualify us.

The Empress sat on a great throne in the central stand, a tiered confection like a Venetian cake made of canvas and wood, more like a great galleys of war than a tent. She sat thirty feet above the crowd, with all her ladies about her like the lilies of the field, and there was many a pretty face there. Beside the Empress sat the King of Poland in robes of gold and ermine. He looked like a church icon come to life.

And seeing them made me realise that I had left Emile's favour back at our inn, folded in my clothes.

I was fully armed, and the judges were circulating among us, asking after men's lineage and the dates of their knighting. The crowd was cheering like the roars of a victorious army – the roll of the Emperor's team was being called, and one by one, the most famous Knights of the Empire were riding on to the field.

'Marc-Antonio!' I called.

He came with an ill grace. He had worked hard all morning and had scarce thanks, and if you don't think servants like thanks, perhaps you should spend more time serving, eh?

'Marc-Antonio, I have left something very important to me at our inn.' I leaned over, even as one of the judges approached.

'I'll get one of the foreign gents to loan it to you, whatever it is,' he said.

'I would take it as a courtesy if you would ride back to our inn, open my clothes press, and fetch me the small square of blue silk—'

'Now?' he asked and rolled his eyes.

I thought of a snappish reply but bit my lip. 'Marc-Antonio,' I said, 'I ask you to fetch me my lady's favour.'

He raised an eyebrow. 'The tatty blue thing?' he asked. Then he raised his hands in mock fear. 'And you want *me* to *help you*?' he asked with all the sarcasm of which a fifteen-year old Italian is capable.

The judge was watching me.

'Yes,' I said carefully. 'I humbly request it.'

'Hunh,' Marc-Antonio said.

But he turned his horse and began to push through the press – not, I'll note, with any particular vigour.

The judge spoke good French. 'You are one of the king's late additions?' he asked. His tone was offensive and his manner so superior that he should have been a doorman in Avignon – or a cardinal. 'Sir William Gold of England?'

I bowed. 'I am Sir William Gold,' I said.

'And who knighted you, Sir William?' he asked.

'Hannekin Baumgarten,' I said. 'A knight of your Emperor.'

That staggered him. But he was determined, and that gave his game away.

'Not my Emperor, sir, I serve the King of Poland. Can you prove this – this *field knighting*? Anyone might make such a claim.' He was being a prick, anyone could see it. If a king puts a man on his tournament team, no one questions his birth or his standing. Or so it is in England and France, but the Germans have a ceremony and a rule for everything.

'Sir, I am also a volunteer of the Order of St John, with my pass at my inn,' I said.

He shrugged. 'The Order of St John? Of no moment here.'

I struggled with anger; hot, sick anger that seemed to come out of my throat. He meant to offend. He meant to disqualify me.

He had two men-at-arms with him, and they looked sombre.

He meant to disqualify me.

That would be a whole pile of humiliations.

Very chivalrous.

But God delivered him into my hands as surely as he saved Daniel from the lions. Because at that moment, a bowshot away, the brass-lunged herald announced the next knight serving the Emperor, and it was none other than my recent enemy, Duke Rudolph von Hapsburg, last seen lying unconscious under one of his knights, a victim of my spear, about half a bowshot from the gates of Florence.

I pointed at the knight, who was in dazzling bronze-edged panoply with a scarlet surcoat that matched his beard and his caparison, wearing a link-belt of gold and looking the chivalric hero of every romance. 'Duke Rudolph was present when I was knighted,' I said. *Unconscious at the time, of course.*

The judge looked at me. He didn't collapse, or vanish in a puff of ill-smelling smoke, but my victory was total, and he could only cover it with a display of ill breeding. 'These battlefield knightings,' he said. 'Anyone can claim them.'

I bowed my head briefly. 'I'm sure it makes your work very difficult,' I said, emphasising work as if to imply that he was some sort of tradesman. I smiled at him. 'I'll try not to let it happen again.'

His eyes narrowed. 'You make light of serious matters, sir.'

I shrugged. 'Will you be fighting, sir?' I asked.

He shook his head. 'I am a judge.'

'Very convenient, I'm sure,' I drawled in my best Gascon French. 'But should monsieur at any time feel the urge to don his harness, I would be at monsieur's pleasure.'

Nerio, at my left side, choked on his laughter, and then threw back his head and brayed like an ass.

The judge turned a dark purple.

On my right, Fiore caught my reins. 'Ahem,' he said.

Fiore was not the best man at social complexities, but he was, in this case, right – I was not doing my duty by the Order in provoking some French functionary of the King of Poland. So I turned my head and managed to say nothing.

The Frenchman turned on Fiore. 'And you, monsieur? Were you also knighted on the battlefield? Perhaps by the Emperor himself?'

Fiore beamed with satisfaction. 'I was knighted this very morning, before all these worthy gentlemen, by the King of Jerusalem!' he said with such evident goodwill that it was hard for our Frenchman to be rude. But someone had set him his mission, and he was determined, like any petty court functionary.

'Knighted this morning?' he said, his voice rich with insinuation.

The King of Jerusalem and Cyprus, who, through all of this, had been moving among his team, discussing the contest, rode up behind the King of Poland's man so silently that we all missed him. He leaned over and tapped the Frenchman's back with his tournament sword. 'I knighted him this morning, yes. I'm sorry – is there a rule against it?'

The Frenchman sniffed – very like a princess of France I knew – a sniff of contempt. 'There is no *rule*, he said, implying the opposite.

'Excellent!' the king said. 'Then if you are done investigating our *noblesse*, perhaps you could let us have a chat, eh, monsieur?' The king's French was perfect – it was, after all, the native tongue of the nobility of Outremer.

The courtier bowed. He wasn't uncivil to the king, at least in form, but the tension was palpable.

The king backed his horse and waved the sword in his hand. 'Visors open. On me, *mes amis*. Come – press close!'

The judges were all conferring together, and the Emperor's team was forming for the contest. This was the first I had seen of the Emperor. He was in a fine armour, but not an ostentatious one – Rudolph von Hapsburg was much showier. The Emperor, Charles IV, was also King of Bohemia; a famous jouster and by all accounts an excellent king and lord. I couldn't see his face, but knew him to be quite old – almost forty or so.

Hah! Younger than I am now.

But our king leaned in. 'They want us to be afraid. The Emperor wants us to fail or withdraw or be disqualified.'

Mézzières looked pained.

The king gave a little shake of his head. 'Each time I win, it is that much harder for that cautious windbag to stop his knights from following me on crusade.'

Don't imagine I had anything to say. These were matters of high diplomacy, being acted out on a tournament field. Nerio and Fiore and I were the merest participants.

The king looked around. He glanced at the Emperor.

A judge raised his baton and shouted, 'The knights will now swear the oath!'

The king shook his head. 'Listen, the Emperor's men will form close about him – a wedge, I suspect. They will stay together like the expert fighters they are. I say we will fight them like Turks: we will divide at the first onset, scatter, and come at the ends of the Emperor's formation in threes. Do not abide! For their wedge will crush us if we allow it. Swing wide, stay off their front, and pick off the men on the ends. Remember, the only thing that counts is throwing a man to the ground, seizing his mount, and returning it to our pole. You may deliver as many blows to a man's head as you like – it is worthless.

A herald was riding in our direction.

Well, I had *seen* a dozen of these fights. I'd watched one in London with Nan, a thousand years ago, or so it seemed.

The king looked right at me. 'You three know each other – and we do not know you yet. Stay together. Don't get taken. I'll put enough Germans down to win the contest – don't you three lose it for me.'

His other knights nodded, as if this wasn't a piece of cocksure bravado, but a home truth. I glanced at de Mézzières. He looked away.

He did not like me.

Before the herald reached us, we trotted forward a few yards and formed a line. You can learn a great deal about a group of horsemen by how well they form and keep a line: by what horse frets, and what rider has to curb, or walk, or turn his horse. Right there, I saw that the Cypriotes were superb horsemen. And their horses were good.

Well, thanks to the Bishop of Geneva's best efforts, my horse was good, too. He was my favourite colour, a pale gold with darker gold mane and tail. He wasn't the largest horse I've ever had, but *par dieu* he was beautifully trained, and his best trick was that, at a weight change, he'd turn on his front legs, like my first great horse, Jack. He was also intelligent, for a horse.

Well, I called this one Jacques. He was like Jack, only French. Ha ha!

Fiore's horse was a rich black, the biggest of the three, an odd contrast to Fiore's shabby harness. Nerio's horse was a deep, dark bay with black mane and tail, which went perfectly with his family's green and gold arms. He had a caparison – God only knows why he brought it, but most of the Cypriote knights had them, too. His was an exercise in extravagance – a horse caparison embroidered in gold, with tiny gilt leaves attached everywhere. There was a motto running around the base, a line from Dante, I was told later. As it never stopped moving, I couldn't read it.

At any rate, he was without a doubt our side's most magnificent knight after the king, and the crowd – especially the Poles, who did not particularly love the Emperor – began to cheer him and the king.

The judges waved their batons, and we all raised our voices and swore the oath in unison, as if we were reciting prayers in church.

'Raise your right hand to the Saints!' intoned my French courtier.

'By my Faith! And on the promise of my body and my honour, I swear that I will strike none of this company in this tourney with the point of my sword, or below the belt or line of his fauld, nor will I attack by surprise, or an unarmed man! And if it should happen that a man's helmet comes off, I swear I shall not touch him. If I knowing do otherwise, I will be banished from the tourney, I will lose my horse and my arms, and I swear this on the faith and promise of my body, and on my honour!'

You see, I can recite that oath to you, seventeen years on. I've said it many times, now, but it's serious. And for me – for Fiore – the loss of our horse and arms would have been a catastrophe.

In truth, by the time I was done with the oath – my helmet off, my gauntlets still with Nerio's squire – I had had a good look around. There were ten thousand people, as quiet as a crowd that size can be. There were two queens, an Emperor, several kings, and a crowd of aristocrats and courtiers as big as the parade of the guilds in London.

If I hadn't had a horse between my knees, they'd have banged together like a tinker's pots. I stood to lose my horse and arms and professional reputation in front of a crowd of ten thousand commoners and another thousand of the most powerful people in Christendom. Any failure would be reported for the rest of my life.

Nerio leaned over. 'You look white, my friend, not Gold.'

I just shook my head. My breastplate was too tight and I couldn't breathe.

Nerio laughed. 'I'm used to this public performance,' he said. 'I forget that you are not. Listen; forget them. They aren't even here. It's just us.' He pointed at the Emperor's men, even then riding down the field to their flag on its pole – the great red lion of Charles IV. 'And them.'

I managed a deeper breath.

'Or you could just look at Fiore,' Nerio said with a wicked smile.

Fiore beamed at me. 'I'm a knight!' he said.

De Mézzières came by, arranging the team. Our trio went at the left of the line – the position of least trust and confidence.

To be fair, I'd have done the same.

I heard the king – our king – laugh and say to one of his knights, 'It's nothing, *mon ami*. We can take them, even nine against twelve.'

That stiffened my spine. The king thought we were worthless. No, to be fair, he thought we were a liability and he was planning around us. He'd made that clear when he told us to simply avoid capture.

I bit my lips and looked around again, still really searching the crowd for Marc-Antonio. I suspected that my lady, *par amour*, would forgive me some Polish girls if I wore her favour in front of the Emperor – but that really only shows how little I know about ladies.

Then I looked at Nerio.

Nerio was a popinjay, a dandy, a courtier. He wrote poetry and danced. I'd never really seen him in a fight, and yet he had my total confidence. That was based on small things – his demeanour when his purse was lifted, the way he rode, the way he handled his sword. Now, as the imperial squires handed us all the tournament swords – rounded points, light and flexible – he met my eye and winked.

'I'd like to take the Emperor,' he said. His eye twinkled.

On my other side, Fiore grinned. 'That's the most sensible thing you have ever said.'

I won't say my fear dropped away. That would be a lie. But Fiore's grin leaped to my face, and I laughed. 'You two are the best companions a man could wish,' I said, and I meant it. 'Let's take the Emperor!'

The judges came by, mounted now, and absolved us of our oaths. That actually mattered to Nerio. This meant that for the duration of the mêlée, Nerio did not have to feel any fealty to the Emperor. I had never seen this ceremony before – but I liked it, and I added it to the tournament at the Italian Wedding. Ah, we'll reach that in time, messieurs. If not tonight, than another night.

And then the judges called *Le Laisser*. My heart pounded again. I knew all these formalities from watching tournaments in Smithfield; from hearing about them in romances and from knights, all my life, but now I was the one donning my helmet, and lacing it up.

The world closed in to be the width of the slit in my visor and the height of the air holes from my brow to my jaw. I was already sweating, and my sweat ran down the back of my arming doublet inside my mail and my backplate – right to the base of my saddle. Cold as sin.

I swished my tournament sword through the air a few times. It was very light – but stiff enough, I thought. I looked around for Marc-Antonio—

And there he was, the blessed man. Even as I spotted his cherubic face, he passed under the ribbon that held back the crowd with more grace than you'd have expected from such a portly lad, and deftly evaded a halberdier's kick.

He ran at us.

Nerio's horse didn't shy. If you are a horseman, you know what I mean.

He ducked under Nerio's horse's head without getting bitten, and managed a bow to me. Really, he earned his right to be my squire and not some servant right there – it was a beautiful performance, and he had an audience. He handed me Emile's favour.

I had my helmet and gauntlets on, so I couldn't help, but he got it on my left shoulder, flashed a bow, and vanished back into the crowd before the three halberdiers could catch him.

The blank, cold stare of Nerio's sugarloaf helm turned to regard me. 'That was a pretty play,' he said in Italian. 'Now every woman in the crowd is watching you.'

And then there was nothing but the chief judge, and his white baton, held above his head.

All I could hear was my own hot breath inside my helmet. All I could see was the red lion on the Emperor's banner, and the solid wedge of horsemen in plate armour sitting in front of it. My hands were shaking.

The baton dropped.

Sometimes, when I tell my tales – bah! – perhaps I embroider. But this ... by the passion, friends, I remember that day in Poland as if it was happening today.

I just touched my spurs to Jacques, and he went forward. One of his many excellent qualities was his ability to accelerate, because he was trained to the joust, unlike almost every warhorse I'd ever had. So he went from the stand almost to the gallop in four or five paces, and that explosion off the line placed me a half-length in front of my companions.

I rode at a shallow angle to the left, where the crowd was. Fiore and Nerio followed me. We cantered, our horses throwing clods of earth – at least, I assume they did, because everyone else's did.

Off to my right, the king was the first off the line, and he angled sharply to the right, all but riding *away* from the oncoming metal wave of German knights. All the Cypriotes went with their king like a flock of starlings, leaving the three of us alone on the left.

The German wedge wheeled neatly – they were only moving at the trot – and the centre of the wedge point was about twenty yards in front of me.

They were coming for us. Excellent tactics. Break the weakest link in the chain. Start any fight with an easy win. Twelve to three; excellent odds. And in a mêlée, not the least unchivalrous.

Their wedge had some cracks in it. If they had practised together often enough, I imagine they could have ridden about, knee behind knee, for hours, without showing a fist of daylight between their horses, with their Emperor in front, and every man echeloning away, a single unstoppable wall of horseflesh and knighthood. That was the German tactic.

But in fact, they were a dozen great nobles, and there was a horse-wide gap between Johann von Hapsburg and his brother. I'll guess that Johann didn't see the wheel – the turning of the whole wedge – begin, and he was late to the turn, had too far to go to catch up …

I pointed my horse's head at the gap and put spurs to Jacques's sides.

He exploded forward.

He did everything. Because of his sure-footed turn and his magnificent burst to the gallop, I was on Johann von Hapsburg in less time than it's taken to say this.

I let him swing his sword at me. He hit me – *hard.* He put the whole weight of his strength and hips into that cut and he rocked me. The blow hit just on my left temple, and then my sword went past his head on the inside; I put my right knee into his knee – at the gallop – and my arm was around his neck and I ripped him from the saddle, just as Fiore taught. My beautiful horse threaded the gap and I let go of Johann before I shared his fate, and I was *through.*

Oh, but that's not the best of it.

Fiore was on my right, and he *collected the beast's reins.* Go ahead and practice that at a gallop in the tiltyard.

Nerio slammed his horse, chest to chest, into Rudolph von Habsburg as that knight turned to attack me or recover his brother's horse, and knocked them – horse and man – to the ground – and rode on.

The crowd *roared.*

Have you heard a crowd roar for you, messires? It is like strong wine and love and the touch of God all in one moment.

I turned Jacques to my right, and rode along the back of the German line, even as the wedge struggled to right itself and turn about. They had passed almost up to the crowd and missed their quarry.

I gave Jacques a strong left knee and made him sidestep – we were not moving fast yet – and slammed my sword into the Emperor's helmet as I went past him.

And so, of course, did Fiore.

And so did Nerio.

The crowd roared again. The first roar had, apparently, not been their best effort.

The three of us passed all the way across the German wedge, and cantered easily to our flagpole – the arms of the Kingdom of Jerusalem, gold on white. There were half a dozen unarmed squires there, and one of them grinned and grabbed Johann von Hapsburg's horse.

People cheered, and we were up, one to nothing.

We swung around the flagpole, saluted our squires – and the Cypriotes struck the far end of the German line. We were too far from them to take part, but it was sudden and stark. I had never fought the Turks, or I would have known.

The Cypriotes fought the Turks all the time. They came in at a dead gallop, caught the Germans halted, trying to rebuild their wedge, and they knocked the end two knights down, swept up their horses, evaded the German attempts to turn the raid into a general combat, and galloped away. They had two horses.

King Peter slapped his visor open a horse-length from me. 'Well fought!' he shouted. Then he pulled it down and turned his horse. He held his horse for the length of his speech, half reared, perfectly collected, his weight back – he looked like a centaur. He was, in that moment, the knight I wanted to be.

The Cypriotes fell in as if they were mercenaries coming for a pay call. They seemed to gallop their horses straight into the line and de Mézzières actually turned his horse on its hindquarters, with the beast's front feet off the ground.

We trotted into position – the last three, let me add.

The king was in the centre. We all looked at him, and he looked right, looked left.

He tossed his sword in the air – and *caught it.*

'*Pour lealte maintenir*,' he said. His knights cheered.

I had no way of knowing it was his motto, but I flourished my sword, and we started forward.

The Germans had pulled their wedge back together. The squires had helped the three downed knights off the field, and now their nine prepared to take on our twelve.

This time, the Cypriotes stayed together, and we had a more traditional clash. Guy le Baveux, one of King Peter's Cypriote lords, was slammed into the dust by the German wedge, and King Peter only avoided the same fate by charging his horse breast to breast with a Bohemian knight with a black lion on his golden coat. Both horses reared, the two knights swaggered swords, and I lost it all in the dust cloud.

We were almost off the end of the German line, and Fiore, on my right, swept in to make his capture. He met his opponent – Duke Rudolph, again – sword to sword. Rudolph cut hard enough to make sparks fly, and Fiore let him have the bind, leaned forward as his horse rose, and smashed his pommel into the count's visor, rocking the man's head back – but the sword continued its rotation, the pommel skidded across the visor and locked across the count's neck, and the relative motion of the two horses unseated him.

I reined in to pass behind Fiore and collected his new-won horse, but the next knight in the line, a big man on a big horse with barred black and yellow barding, grabbed at the same reins and leaned out to swing at Fiore over Von Hapsburg's now riderless horse.

Fiore took the blow on the back of his right shoulder and momentum carried him forward and I lost him in the dust. I changed leads over to the right and came up on what would have been Fiore's right side, and I could feel Nerio hard on my heels. Again the black and yellow knight reached across the empty saddle to cut, this time at me.

I covered, crossing my sword with his, hilt-to-hilt and close to my head. He was big and strong, and I let him press me, then I locked my free, steel-gauntleted hand on the flange of his outstretched steel elbow and used my spurs to tell Jacques to pivot on his front feet. I think I laughed aloud as I controlled his arm with my hand and my horse, dislocating his shoulder and throwing him forward over his saddle as I dropped him, dragging him *over* Rudolf's empty saddle as my horse backed. I swear to you that Jacques understood my intention all through, perhaps better than I.

I got my hand on to Duke Rudolf's bridle. Nerio was flank-to-flank with yet another German knight, but he had black and yellow's reins.

I had no opponent. I had a moment – there must have been a gust of wind – and I saw that the King of Cyprus was down.

Philippe de Mézzières was locked in a steel embrace with the Emperor, and three German knights were hammering away at him while a pair of the Cypriotes I didn't know tried to break into the circle around the king. The king's horse was – I assume – hit with a sword or a sabaton-clad foot, because he bolted instead of standing by his master. The king was on his feet, reaching for his horse, but the animal went past his reaching hands and ran for the crowd line.

Well, I had a great desire for fame and a captured horse in my left fist. I remember crossing the two horse lengths between us, and my only fear was that someone else would get to him first.

Philippe de Mézzières twisted, the Emperor rocked back, and de Mézzières' sword shot out and slammed into a German knight's head, rocking him back and opening a hole.

The king saw me and took two steps towards me. He was coming right at me, and he leaped – got his right foot into the stirrup and mounted without stopping the horse. Really, it was one of the most spectacular feats of horsemanship I'd seen, then.

Nothing beside what followed.

He swung himself like a door on the stirrup leather, mounting with the horse's stride, and then – as if he'd planned it every day of his life – he reached out his right hand and struck the Emperor in the helmet with his fist, pulled his arm back, reached under the Emperor's arm and pulled him back. De Mézzières let go his hold and got one of the Emperor's legs and lifted – and the mightiest monarch in Europe was down in the dust.

Nerio skimmed through the mêlée at a canter, plucked the reins out of the air, jerking the Emperor's horse's head savagely, provoking the great best to a lumbering gallop. The reins broke, and Nerio was left without his prize, but they were galloping along, side by side.

Headed for the Emperor's flag. By which I mean, the wrong way.

There were two Cypriotes down, by that time, and a third so badly injured – broken arm, dislocated shoulder – that he was staying at the edge of the fight, trying to avoid capture. But six of the Emperor's knights were out, and the other six were already breaking off, slamming their swords into the king's brother Hugh and riding clear of the dust.

Nerio was a patient hunter. He followed the Emperor's horse across the field, penned it into a corner of the crowd, and got its bridle.

I was riding flat out by then, because all six of the Imperial Knights had gone for Nerio. By my side were the King of Cyprus and his chancellor, and from the other edge of the field Fiore was galloping at the Germans and Swabians and Bohemians. The two Bohemian knights turned and faced us, and they were good. Better than me, I'm not ashamed to say. I locked one of them up, and he was dragging me from my saddle when the king passed his sword across the other man's neck and pulled him off me. The other Bohemian dropped de Mézzières, which was no mean feat of arms, I can tell you.

That left four Swabians on Nerio. But it was Nerio's moment – he cut and turned and cut, and he had his horse's back to the crowd, which limited the ability of the Swabians to get at him for a throw.

By that time I was riding for him again, although I wanted to throw up into my helmet and I'd lost my sword. The king was by me.

The second Bohemian – the one who had put de Mézzières down – was at our heels.

They were hammering Nerio as if they were armourers and he needed to be forged. Ever seen three master bladesmiths work a blade together? That's how they pounded him, and yet he was as light as air, dancing under them. He took blows, but he gave them, too.

I came up on a knight in red and blue, caught his sword hand from behind and beside him, and disarmed him as if he'd passed me the blade. I tried to throw it over his head, and he slammed his fist into my visor, and I bent back like a bow – he was a puissant man. I lost a moment, but in that time the king hit him, and I recovered my seat – Jacques had danced clear of the fight, may God care for that horse.

My nose was broken inside my helmet, and blood was flowing over the cloth of the padding of my aventail and down my breastplate and my coat armour. The pain was blinding. But I could see Nerio's green and gold, and I got my horse to do the work for me. I put spurs to Jacques – he didn't deserve that, but I was hurt and in a hurry, and Jacques exploded in outraged innocence, put his head down and crashed into one of the Swabians with a sound like an army of tinkers doing battle with an army of wooden spoons.

The Swabian reeled in his saddle, tried to regain his seat –

Fiore stripped him from the saddle as easily as a conjuror makes a scarf vanish. One moment there was a knight, and the next, there was not. Nerio still had the Emperor's horse. He was now free, and he turned and began to gallop for our flag, a bowshot away. There wasn't an imperial knight on the field to stop him that I could see.

Jacques followed Nerio's horse, bursting into a canter. I was recovering, but not as fast as I would have liked. Then something hit me like a butcher's knife hits a carcass – from behind.

I'd lost the Bohemian knight in the press, and he was the wrong man to lose track of. His first blow to my helmet stunned me. Then he hit me *three more times*. I couldn't get my sword up.

I fell. Suddenly, my knees could no longer keep the horse between them. I just couldn't continue. The fall seemed to take a long time.

I was only out for about as long as it took me to hit the ground but that was the last time I wore that helmet. Blows to the head are everyday business in war, or in the tournament, and you need to be able to take a great many of them. In a mêlée – whether of peace or war – men hit you; your guards are never perfect, and your opponents don't come one at a time. Many of my worst blows have come from behind or the side, and in a visor you cannot see those coming. I know men, good knights, who still prefer to fight in open-faced helms precisely because they fear the attacker they cannot see. My fancy bassinet with its long beak and light construction did not provide enough vision *or* enough protection.

But that was not my first thought as my eyes fluttered open.

I was lying on my back, and there was my lovely golden horse standing over me. He somewhat ruined the effect of his loyalty by voiding his bowels in the thoughtful way horses do, but he didn't do it on me – he was really a very intelligent animal, for a horse.

I raised my head, and a spike of pain appeared behind my left eye. I may not have *bounced* to my feet like a hero in a romance, but I got up fast, got a hand in Jacque's girth and let him pull me all the way up.

Once on my feet, I noticed that the king had his visor up and a pretty Polish maid was giving him water from a blackware jug. My Bohemian adversary was behind him, waiting patiently for the water – his visor was also up. Nerio was surrounded by people from the crowd.

The world swirled, my mouth filled with a salty taste, and then I was on the ground, throwing up inside my helmet. I don't recommend it, but I see glancing around that you've all shared this glorious experience of the life of arms, so I'll pass on.

Marc-Antonio appeared, sweating profusely, and got my helmet off me, then got a wet rag and began to wipe me down. The boy was going up and up in my estimation – apparently, he'd run along the crowd as we fought our way down the field, to be ready at hand.

Two young girls, one red and one blonde, appeared with a bucket of water. They were very young, and very determined to help, and dressed in their best clothes, covered in meticulous if not very well-rendered embroidery. But they wanted to help a knight, and I was chosen, vomit and all. And I admit they cleaned me up very nicely.

I drank a good deal of their water, and then managed to get back into my saddle. I did not vault, I promise you. There was a dent in my bassinet as deep as my thumb, and to the best of my ability to guess, my Bohemian adversary had struck the exact same place on my helmet three or four times.

I held it up to him and smiled.

He smiled back and rode over. 'I did my best,' he said in French, 'but it was too late. The judges called the contest.' He laughed. 'Because in a moment your Italian gentleman was going to take the Emperor's horse to the stake, and that would have been too humiliating!' He stripped the gauntlet off his right hand and extended it.

His goodwill was evident – he was as big as me, handsome as a God, and a year or two older. We shook hands, and people began to cheer.

He reached down and patted the redhead on the cheek. 'Oh, how I wish I had been on your team.' He smiled. 'Your king rides like a Turk or a Tartar. Or a Pole. The Emperor is too – cautious.' He shrugged. 'Or he assumed that he would be allowed to win.'

'Those were beautiful sword bows,' I said. 'You put me down – such a light sword!'

'My father says you can defeat any armour if you hit it repeatedly in the same place,' he said. 'Look, the judges are gathering us.' He gave me a lopsided grin. 'I wish I'd taken your horse. But I could not – your friends were on me as soon as I got you.' He nodded. 'We should fight again. I am Heřman z Hradce. In Latin, you might say Hermanni de Novadomo.'

I bowed, head throbbing. 'William Gold,' I said.

We rode to our respective teams – cheered, I'll add, by the crowd. I'll note here that I've seen this many times – the crowd *wants* to see men behave like knights, to exchange words after the blows, and behave with dignity and good cheer. Surliness is the very antithesis of chivalry.

There were five judges, and they sent us to our inns and pavilions. I managed to ride through the streets to the king's inn without tumbling off, and I waved and smiled as best I could, but my ears were ringing and I had a sharp pain in my head. By the time we dismounted, I had a lump in my scalp where the sword blows had dented my helmet that was soft and mushy and blood oozed from it each time I touched it, which was too often. And another on my forehead where I'd fallen face-first to the ground. I'll skip ahead in this catalogue of minor injuries and say that my neck was stiff for a week because apparently my bassinet's beak had dug into the soft earth when I fell and twisted my neck.

Ah, the glories of the tournament!

That night we entered the presence of the Emperor himself, who received each of us and gave us gifts. If he was bad-tempered from being unhorsed, I never saw a sign of it, and his behaviour was ... Imperial. He complimented Fiore, praising his skill, and he gave Nerio his hand. I received a warm smile and a beautiful golden cross, worked in enamel – this is it, here. I still wear it. I've pawned it a dozen times but always had it back, eh?

He said something very quietly to Nerio, who flushed and bowed and came back to us holding a beautiful gold and silver cup with a ruby in the base. Nerio whispered to Fiore and they laughed together.

'What's that?' I asked. I wasn't exactly stung – they were clearly the men of the hour – but suddenly they were whispering like old friends. I was used to arbitrating their quarrels, not to being left out of their confidences.

'We're both Knights of the Empire. Technically, we're his men. He said that it was a pleasure to see that the King's best knights were – ahem – his own.' Nerio glanced around.

Duke Rudolf was whispering in the Emperor's ear.

The Emperor – that's Charles IV, of recent and glorious memory

– was at the time about fifty years old, handsome, dark haired, and very strong. He was a cautious man, and he dressed elaborately and his court kept to complicated ceremonials, even at a tournament, so there was no easy approach to him, and as I have said, he was no proponent of crusade.

Rudolf bowed, the Emperor smiled, and Duke Rudolf swept down the room in his beautiful scarlet clothes. He paused near me and I bowed, knee to the floor.

'That's twice you've knocked me down, monsieur,' he said.

'Your Grace does me too much honour,' I said in my best Gascon-French.

He inclined his head. 'I've just done you a favour, I think,' he said. 'So that you will know I bear you no ill feeling. But listen, Sir Gold – take good care of your King of Jerusalem. There are those here who would do him harm.' He looked at a cluster of men I did not know, gentlemen all, in the older French style and long boots. They were the only men there in boots.

I guessed who they were. I guessed that they were a party of knights on errantry who'd lost their horses in a town square near Nuremberg.

Nerio was close enough to hear. I did the courteous thing and introduced him, at least in part to cover my confusion, and because the blows to my head had not made me wittier. I tugged his sleeve and gestured in the direction of the cluster of Frenchmen.

Duke Rudolf exchanged bows of near equality with Ser Nerio. 'Ah – Accaioulo the Younger? We were allies at Florence; how do you come to the company of this English Lancelot?'

Nerio smiled at me. 'I took a fancy to his red hair. In truth, Italy is better with Sir William in Poland.'

'Oh, my lords!' I protested, or something equally foolish. My head was not working well, and the room spun each time I drank wine, and I was thirsty.

King Peter came and we bowed again – knees to floor, hats off – and he paid us all sorts of compliments. I was still trying to work out who might do the King of Cyprus harm, or why, when the Emperor summoned the judges.

My enemy of the morning, for so I thought of him, opened a scroll and began to read, in courtly French, through a list of the achievements and encounters of the tournament and the jousts that had come before. I'll give the judges this much: they had sharp eyes for the encounters. The King of Cyprus was adjudged the best lance, and he went forward humbly to receive his prize, a hawk with gold jesses and bells. The hawk was magnificent – a true Icelandic peregrine. The victor in the foot encounters was none other than my Bohemian friend, who was showered with applause and kisses from a great many beautiful women, and who bore away his prize, an axe inlaid in gold with verses from Luke. There were prizes for archery, which I had not seen; for riding and for courteous behaviour and even a prize for the man who had been unhorsed the most times, given by the King of Poland to a German knight who bore the good-natured laughter with a sanguine air and seemed pleased to go away with a pretty gold-clasped purse and a velvet cushion which he flourished amidst laughter.

And then the Frenchman began on the events of the mêlée, naming the participants. The room fell silent. The Emperor was referred to as the 'Count of Luxembourg', which was, I gathered, part of an elaborate fiction by which a great lord might fight under a lesser title so as not to discomfit his opponents – a very courteous act.

I feel I have to mention, for Monsieur Froissart's delectation, that the King of Cyprus and the Count of Luxembourg bore the exact same arms – did you know that? What a herald's nightmare that must have been. But for the duration of our time in Krakow, the king displayed only his arms as King of Jerusalem – white and gold – and never the arms of the house of Lusignan.

I have strayed from my point like a courser leaving the lists. As my Frenchman described the mêlée, he and the other judges had it dead to rights, and in fact, my own description here owes a great deal to their observations. Heh, messieurs, you know that when the visors closes, you see little but the man in front of you! But they had seen it all, and every man received his due.

Even me.

I was surprised to hear the man I'd loathed in the morning mention my role, and my name kept coming up – Chevalier d'Or – and I began to grow uncomfortable as men around me looked at me. Well, I had been the first to put my sword on the Count of Luxembourg, and I had captured two horses, these things were true ...

And then they were cheering!

By God, messieurs, that was one of the proudest moments of my life. *I was chosen as the best man of the mêlée. Me!* I suppose I should have seen it coming, and Nerio and Fiore say they knew all evening, but in truth – in truth, I felt more than a pang of guilt, my friends. I think that either Nerio or Fiore was the better man – and certes, it was Fiore who taught me how to throw men to the ground from the saddle.

I blushed so hard that my skin felt as if it was on fire. Nerio told me later I was as red as an apple from head to toe when I went and knelt before the Emperor and the judges. Men cheered and applauded, and women curtsied and looked at me under their eyes.

The Emperor was seated on a throne of wood and ivory. While the cheering went on, he said, 'I understand that you were knighted by Hannekin Baumgarten?'

'At Florence,' I said, in something of a daze.

He touched my shoulder with a sword. 'Let no man ever doubt your knighting,' he said. His smile may have been a bit grim, but he was a good king, a good lord, and he played his role. He laid the sword he'd just used across my hands.

It was a miracle of red and gold that sword, and it had a belt and scabbard to match. It was a king's sword – I couldn't tear my eyes off it, and my right hand ached to grasp the hilt, but even a bumpkin like me knew that was lese majesty of the worst kind.

It was one of the finest swords I have ever owned. Eventually I'll tell you how I came to lose it, but for the moment, I can only assure you that I would show it to you gentleman if I still had it. A Tartar has it now, I'm fairly certain.

There is probably a sermon in what came next; there I was, with a magnificent new sword across my hands, burning to look at it, to draw it, to make it sing through the air; but, by the iron-clad laws of *courtoise*, I could do none of these things, but instead I stood patiently, accepting the plaudits of my peers, the good-natured insults of my friends, and the downcast eyes, lingering glances, and soft fingers of the maids of court, who gathered around me like moths to a summer candle.

Did I say *patiently*? I lie. I had Emile's favour pinned to my shoulder like a talisman, and I was acutely conscious that I had not spent the hour before the fight on my knees, or even considering God's existence. Instead, I had lain – well, swum – with a bathhouse girl.

Certes, messieurs, don't trouble yourselves on my account. It did not worry me unduly, except that I felt no urge to any of the fine ladies who surrounded me. And I was unprepared for the open friendliness of the knights. They praised me lavishly.

May I be frank? I was tempted to cry. It was so much the opposite of everything I had experienced with the Prince of Wales.

At some point, my Bohemian knight came and offered his hand and we embraced. He began a somewhat formulaic praise of my martial virtues, and my feelings must have shown on my face, because he smiled and paused.

'You dropped me like the butcher fells the ox,' I said. 'Why aren't you the best knight?'

He laughed. 'You and your friends won the game for your king, and no mistake. But no false pride. May I say a true thing? If you fight as long as I have fought, you will be the best man in a dozen tournaments, and then they'll never give you the prize. This one will have it because he is a king's son, and that one will have it because they don't like you, and a third will have it because the marshals didn't see the brilliant blow you threw.'

I laughed. I was new to the tournament, and I could already see the justice of his remarks.

'And then, when the judges see you as *better*, it is even harder to win. And men fight you differently; they do extravagant things to score on you, or they turn into hedgehogs and turtles to avoid taking blows, and they make it impossible for you to win. Yes?'

I nodded. Nerio nodded. Even Fiore nodded.

Sir Herman shrugged. 'So, today, at a great tourney, you took the prize. I, who am a great knight, say you deserve it, but I also say – take it! The next time you are the best, Lady Fortuna may not be so kind.'

I sat with him at dinner. His lady was a beauty – her name was Kunka, a Bohemian name, and she had long dark hair and great beauty of manners as well as of figure, making small motions with her hands as she talked, that looked like dance. Indeed, the Bohemians were some of the most elegant men and women I've ever seen, easily the rivals of the Italians or the French for courtly manners and sumptuous clothes, beautiful ladies and magnificent horses – and fighting. I would not like to face an army of Bohemians in the field.

His lady leaned over to me and ran her hand over Emile's somewhat frayed blue favour. 'This belongs to your lady?' she asked. She was the first woman to ask about it.

'Yes,' I said, or something equally short. I was not at my best; a pinnacle of knightly fame, and I was reduced to monosyllables. Especially in Latin.

She glowed with satisfaction. 'You love her?' she asked.

I grinned. 'Always,' I said.

'But she is not anyone here?' Kunka asked.

I shook my head. 'No. She is very far away. She is from Savoy.'

'Like those gentlemen who cannot take their eyes off you?' my Bohemian gentleman asked. 'They are all Savoyards. From Geneva.'

Well, I was dull-witted, but not so very dull-witted as that. 'Yes, she is from Savoy. But not, I think, with any of those gentlemen.'

Kunka put a warm hand on mine. 'And your lady ... will you be faithful to her tonight? With every girl at court ready to throw herself in your lap?'

I was looking for something courtly to say, but her eyes smouldered.

'Listen, Englishman. I am the very Queen of Love of this tourney, and I challenge you as you are a knight to remember your lady.' So the smoulder was not lust, but anger.

I bowed at the table. 'Lady, you are so wholly in the right that I can only swear on my honour to abide your challenge.'

She smiled, and her knight smiled.

Later in the evening, when my sword was still undrawn, and I was surrounded – indeed, I was cornered as thoroughly as a stag of fourteen tines is backed into a cliff by hounds and hunters; there I was, alone, with fifteen women about me. Their bodies were young and beautiful, their eyes open and shining. Their hair was uncovered, delicious to smell. Nerio had stood by my side all too briefly, engaged one fair maid in conversation and taken her hand, leading her away to discuss poetry, or so he claimed. Fiore was nowhere to be seen. My Savoyards were not even in the same hall, and I suspect I'd forgotten them.

Kunka appeared at my side, and all the ladies bowed – she was, after all, the Queen of Love for the tourney. Her husband unfolded a stool and she sat.

'Come, Sir William!' she said, and her smile was as wanton as any of the girls about me. 'Choose one of my handmaids to sit closest to you.'

I bowed. I was right willing to choose, and chose a young woman with jet-black hair and lips so red I wanted to see if they had paint on them. I didn't think they did. She blushed to her hair and into her gown, but she sat by me.

Kunka smiled. The wantonness was gone, replaced by a harder edge, and I thought that perhaps she was also a mother; she knew how to give orders as well as take them.

'Now, Sir William, welcome to the Court of Love.' Kunka laughed, and squeezed her husband's hand.

All the maids sighed. There were some poisonous looks for my raven-tressed choice. 'Before we dance, Sir William will amuse us by telling us of his Lady. He loves a lady *par amour*, and wears her favour on his shoulder.'

The maids looked abashed. I confess I was abashed myself, so soon had I forgotten her challenge and my promise.

I thought of Emile, and in truth – oh, this cuts me like a Turk's sword – I had trouble recalling her face. So many years. I could see her arrogant husband well enough in my mind's eye, but her face swam in a haze of associations.

But Kunka had every right to ask, as Queen of Love. And she was setting me a penance as well as recognising me as the knight who had won the prize, and I was being challenged. Chivalry is more than hitting men with a sword. Chivalry is there in every dealing with a woman, from the bath girl to the Queen of Love.

I thought of Father Pierre's strictures about the farm girl, and it made me blush, and the maids giggled.

'The lady I love must remain locked in my heart,' I said. 'But I will say that she is beautiful as – as ...' Once started, I could not be seen to stop, and yet no fresh image leaped to my head. A summer's day? A pox on that one. A flower? A rose?

I still had my longsword in both hands. I raised it so that it formed a cross. 'As beautiful as this sword – as beautiful to see, and yet as beautiful in her soul, strong as the steel and—'

'Your lady is as beautiful as a sword?' Kunka asked.

They were laughing at me.

I looked at the Bohemian knight, who shook his head and left me to my fate. 'Perhaps I must beg you to understand how beautiful I find this sword,' I said, hoping to win a smile, but the women all rolled their eyes and prodded one another with their elbows.

'Is she red and gold, this lady?' Kunka asked.

'No, blue and white like snow and the sky,' I answered, too quickly. Emile's arms were blue and white. I thought of her that way – I had been too open.

Kunka smiled, though. 'Now that was prettier, Sir Knight, and I think it possible that you are more than a boor. No more swords. Tell us what it is about her that won your heart, so that we poor women may strive to emulate that and rise in your opinion.'

'Courage,' I said.

'*Ma foi*,' Kunka said 'That is a fine thing for a knight to love in a lady. And far better than comparing her beauty to a sword. Let me tell you, monsieur, when you compare me to a sword, all I hear is that I am sharp and pointy.' She laughed, and all the maids laughed with her. 'But when you offer me *courage* as a woman's virtue, then I feel hope that a knight might see me as more than a leman and a mother. Can you tell us of her courage?'

I thought of her coming to my room in Normandy, during the siege, dealing with her husband ...

I thought hard, wanting to avoid revealing anything, and yet caught up in the game that was courtly love. And the girls were watching me differently, now, and in the distance, I heard the music begin.

'It is not that she fears nothing. It is that, when fearing, she acts despite her fears. Ask any man-at-arms where courage lies. It is not the fearless knight who wins our respect, but the one who, full of fear, carries on.' I shrugged, to end my little sermon.

Sir Herman gave me a small nod of appreciation.

Kunka put her hand on mine. 'As Queen of Love, I say to all that you are a true knight and worthy of your lady. Now I love her courage too.' She rose, and I kissed her hand, and she made a motion to the maids to attend her. 'It is my express command that none of you may dance with Sir William more than once. Or any other thing. Does anyone doubt my word?'

She swept away from me with a smile, having made sure that I would sleep alone.

But, like many of my other teachers, Fiore and Father Pierre and Sir Peter and Arnaud and more, she showed me something about myself.

Why is it that there is always so much to learn?

By our Lady! I danced three times, once with the Lady Kunka, and then, at last, I walked out under the stars, out the great gilded doors of the King of Poland's great hall, and into the cool of a Polish August night. I thought I was alone, but Fiore was at my shoulder.

He grinned like a boy. 'The sword?' he asked.

He was as eager as I.

We walked off into a garden, the two of us like secret lovers, and stumbled in the dark until we found what we sought: a little light from a lantern, probably left by real lovers earlier in the evening. And then I drew the sword from her red leather-and-wood scabbard, and her blade shimmered like Arabian silk in the candlelight.

She was broader than any blade I'd ever owned, as broad as a lady's wrist, and even broader. She had a different taper from most swords, and a flatter cross-section than the other longswords I'd owned, flatter and shorter. Had I seen her in a bladesmith's stall, I would not even have asked her down to put her hilt in my hand.

Listen: once I took a lady – we were both the worse for wine – who was, let us say, less than beautiful. Dumpy, short, a little overweight, I thought in my pride and lust. But when I undressed her, I found her body as beautiful as Venus herself. As that lady, so with the sword.

In my hand, she was quick and light and yet strong as a branch of oak.

Somewhat jealously, I handed her to Fiore. He brought her smartly to his shoulder and cut once. There was nothing showy or spectacular about his cut, but I felt like a man who has just watched his lady give a chaste kiss to a friend. Of course it is allowed, and yet … why is she smiling so much?

'Yes,' Fiore said. 'Yes!'

The next morning, my Frenchman's squire – the courtier, not the Savoyards – was at the door of our inn. Two hours later, I sat on Jacques with my helmet laced, and Lady Kunka was there, as were a dozen of the Empress's maids and ladies, and many of the Bohemian and Polish gentlemen, despite hard heads and the early hour. I had time to say my beads and to realise that if I had lain with one of the lilies of the court, I would be muzzy with lack of sleep and perhaps still little drunk. As it was, I was fresh.

The Frenchman said nothing to me, nor did his squire chat with Marc-Antonio. And Marc-Antonio was all but transformed by finding that I was the great man of the tourney, and I caught him, more than once, pointing me out and claiming me for his own.

You might think I anticipated a murder attempt or some such, but my Frenchman didn't seem the type, and none of the Savoyards were to be seen. Despite which, I checked every element of my harness and my tack for damage and interference.

We were riding along the barriers, which I had never done before. It keeps the horses straight, but requires some surprisingly false manoeuvres of the lance – common enough now, but new to me in the year sixty-five.

The first encounter was almost my undoing. My man could joust. His lance swooped like a stooping hawk, the point coming down from the heavens, and had his horse not faltered by a heartbeat in its course, his lance point would have taken me in the throat or left shoulder, but luck – Fortuna – was with me, and his point at my shoulder. I felt the impact on my shoulder, and I broke my lance on his shield.

He saluted me.

That changed the tenor of the contest. As we swapped ends, I returned the salute, galloped back to my place, and set myself. The salute meant, to me, that we were behaving like gentlemen.

The second course was accounted pretty by the crowd. My lance tore his left pauldron off his shoulder, and his – a beautiful strike, by God's grace – tore the visor off my bassinet. It did me no injury, but his point penetrated my visor almost a full inch. Yes, we were fighting *a l'outrance*, with weapons of war, unabated.

The heralds and marshals had to have a conference, as we had both scored.

Ser Nerio rather sportingly offered me his beautiful helm. I accepted gratefully; I didn't own a spare, and my bassinet had just met its end. Weakened by the Bohemian the day before, it now had two gaping holes where the visor pivots ought to have been.

Nerio grinned at me. 'That was a good course,' he said.

'Any advice?' I asked.

'Don't flinch. And don't miss. He's a better jouster than you, but not by much.' Nerio smiled wolfishly. 'If he kills you, I'll kill him.'

Fiore shook his head. 'No, he is very good, but you can take him.

Remember what we practiced at Avignon, the lance low?'

I looked back and forth. 'A parry with a lance? In a joust?' I asked.

Nerio raised an eyebrow. 'Too professional,' he said with a little of his old disdain for Fiore. But he softened it with a smile. 'For me, at any rate.'

Fiore shrugged. 'It is not against any rule.'

Nerio put a hand on Fiore's shoulder. 'My friend, there are rules that are not written down.'

Fiore frowned. 'If there is not a rule against it written down, it is not a rule,' he said.

I got the new helmet seated and the chinstrap buckled, and rode down the lists, still undecided.

Word of our tilt had spread, and other knights and squires were coming for their scheduled bouts. The 'great' men had had five days, and now the lesser knights, men like me and Fiore, were to be allowed three days of jousting and foot combat, and their own mêlée.

And all along one side of the list stood a troop of horsemen. I had never seen anything like them, and they were distracting me. They wore long coats, buttoned at the shoulder and edged in fur, even the least of them. Two of them carried hawks, and all had lances and bows.

I had never seen men with such deep lines on their faces. They looked like killers, every one of them.

I took deep breaths and took them out of my head, and then I set my thoughts on the lists and my opponent. He flicked his lance head at me. I returned the compliment, if indeed it was such.

When the marshal's white wand dropped, I put spurs to Jacques, and he blew forward with his usual explosive grace. Before his third stride, though, I had my lance in its rest – so different from my first years with the weapon – and I let the head fall low.

Lowering your lance head is bad practice. It is terrifying. A low blow, a blow to your opponent's horse, forfeits not just the run but your own horse and armour. It is considered cheating. With my lance across my body, under my right arm and couched against my lance rest on the right of my breast plate, but pointing to the left side of my horse's head and across the barrier, and now aimed down, almost at the ground, it looked as if I'd lost control of my lance. This happens sometimes in the joust.

My opponent still had his lance tip high in the air. He didn't couch until the last possible moment, just the way, let me add, that Boucicault used his lance.

We had heartbeats to impact.

His lance tip stooped towards my face and I did as Fiore had taught me and flipped my lance up, using my saddle bow as a fulcrum and my lance as a lever. It came up very fast, and our lances crossed, still in the air. But weight and the power of his lance on mine slapped them down again.

He missed his lance rest. With all the pressure my lance was putting on his lance, torqueing it, he'd have had to be Lancelot himself to maintain control.

My hit was unspectacular, just barely clipping his shield. But my lance-staff snapped cleanly with the impact, and he lost control of his lance three strides later and it fell to the earth.

The foreigners with the hawks were laughing and slapping their long whips against their thighs. One waved to me.

The judges all clustered at the centre of the lists.

Fiore slapped my back. 'That was nicely done,' he said, rare praise indeed. Then, 'We need to practice your seat and how it relates to your control of the lance, but otherwise – good.' He looked at Nerio. 'I wish some Frenchman would challenge *me*.'

'Find the man's wife and sleep with her!' Nerio said with a sneer.

'Why?' Fiore asked, genuinely puzzled.

Even Marc-Antonio laughed.

'They are calling for you,' Nerio said, and I rode down the lists to where my French adversary sat on his destrier. He had his helm off and looked as sweaty as I felt.

I had forgotten he *was* a judge. But he was smiling, not grinning, and his eyes met mine.

So, just by way of experiment, I returned his smile.

We were an arm's length apart.

'Is your honour served?' he asked me.

Well. That was the question, wasn't it?

I bowed, like one gentleman meeting another when mounted. 'Very well, monsieur. My honour is served very well.'

He urged his horse forward one single step. 'Sometimes, a gentleman is only doing what his liege bids him do. *Eh bien?*' He gave me a casual wave, and turned his horse, and rode away, neither angry nor afraid.

The judges held that I had been the victor, but on balance, I think he gave me the lesson.

Later that day, Fiore ran some courses, unhorsing men to the right and left until the judges forbade the use of his spear-crossing parry. Then he unhorsed more men.

He was spectacular to watch, and yet, at the same time, dull. He made one Polish knight very angry by unhorsing him on the first pass, and the man raged, claimed that Fiore had cheated, and looked like a fool.

Nerio, without my knowing, challenged one of the Savoyards to fight on horse and foot. I hate to think who was foolish enough to loan the Savoyard a horse. But Nerio took it.

The Savoyards had been loud in denouncing us to no avail, and after Nerio knocked their champion in the dirt on three straight passes and the man declined to fight on foot, no one would listen to them.

King Peter announced that we would leave for Venice after matins on the Friday, two days hence.

The two days passed in a haze of audiences, music, poetry, sweat and fighting. A few moments surface in memory. I remember giving Marc-Antonio my riding sword, and belting it on him, and Nerio and Fiore pounding him on the shoulders with their fists. Nerio bought him a pretty pair of iron spurs, and Fiore began to give him lessons. As of that moment, he was a squire. For a few days, he carried himself like a great lord and was very difficult, and then he had a fight – I never found out with whom. His mouth was cut, one of his eyes was black, and he became a much milder man.

I paid him his wages so that he could shop in the magnificent market, and he bought, of all things, a book. And a dagger. He was an odd boy, but he'd won my love in the matter of Emile's favour and a hundred other ways, and I was ready to tolerate him.

The other two encounters were just as pleasant. The first was meeting the Tartar lord who had laughed at me after the joust. He spoke no French and only a little Latin, but he had a Franciscan with him, booted and spurred, and the Franciscan translated.

The Tartar's name was Jean-Christ, or something like that. He was a commander of a thousand in the great army known to the Poles as the Golden ones or the Golden Horde. He had come as an ambassador to the court of the Emperor.

We were packing to leave: King Peter was travelling with only six knights, their squires, a dozen priests and servants, and my friends, and leaving the rest of his 'court' to follow after. At the time I didn't understand that the King of Cyprus was *not* the richest man in the world; that he did *not* desire to command the crusade as much as de Mézzières and the Pope wanted him to command it; that, indeed, the command was a massive imposition on the king. Nor did I understand that he travelled Europe with only a handful of his *own* knights; that most of his 'courtiers' were relations – French relations – of Cypriote lords, there only to make weight, so to speak. To give his entourage the appearance of riches.

I was an old hand at making war, but this was an entirely new game. The game of kings and princes and cardinals and popes.

At any rate, the Tartar duke rode up with a dozen of his soldiers and his Franciscan.

'My son, the Duke Jean-Christ wishes to address you,' the priest said. 'I am Father Simon, his confessor.'

I bowed, dismounted – after all, the foreigner was a Christian and a duke – and bowed. Father Simon blessed me.

'He asks, why do you dismount like a churl? And I tell him that you respect his rank.'

Father Simon spoke and the language was like the twittering of birds. Father Simon himself looked like a bird, a plain brown robin. He was as English as I am, and that made him easy to talk with. He had brown hair and deep creases in his face.

The duke threw back his head and laughed. He spoke straight at me, and his eyes twinkled like a jugglers.

'He says that if this is true, you are the first man north of the Volga to behave in such a way. But he says "be easy".' Father Simon smiled. 'For my part, I thank you. He is a great man, and has had but little respect here.'

I smiled at the foreign duke.

He spoke at length, and Father Simon followed as best he could. 'He says you are good at the lance. And this trick you do – pardon me, Sir Knight, but I really don't know quite what he's saying – this trick is not like any other Latin trick. But that all the People do it. By which he means his people, the Mongols and Tartars and the Kipchaks.' Father Simon shrugged ruefully. 'He said a great deal more than that, but I fear I don't understand the fighting words.'

'Fiore!' I called. Ser Fiore, as he now liked to be addressed, was packing his threadbare harness in wicker panniers for mules to carry. He came out into the yard, popped his eyes at the Tartar lord, and I repeated Father Simon's comments.

Before the next set of hours rang on all of Krakow's hundred bells, the two were riding up and down the street, demonstrating. Fiore picked twigs off the street with his lance point, and the Tartar Duke loosed his bow three times into a shield, striking with each arrow, and then flipping his lance off his back, striking a straw dummy with the point, rolling the thing over his head like a mountebank and placing it *under his left arm* and striking again against a target on the other side.

While he executed this deadly trick, Philippe de Mézzières appeared with two more mules and the king's compliments and two servants to help us pack. He watched the Tartar for a few breathes and then frowned.

'That is how the Mamluks fight,' he said.

'This man is a Christian and a lord,' I said with a polite bow. De Mézzières had fought at my side, but he'd been careful not to bespeak me. 'Yon Franciscan is his confessor and his chaplain.'

De Mézzières brightened. 'Come, that is glad news,' he said. 'Can you imagine the world we might make, if every man and woman might be brought to Jesus Christ?'

I had never given it much thought. I belonged to a crusading Order that was content to provide the protection of pilgrims to and from the Holy Places. I think that like practical warriors, the Knights of St John had surrendered any notion of the conquest of the Holy Land.

But I managed a smile.

De Mézzières met my eye. 'We must travel together,' he said suddenly. 'You have behaved well here, and to my liege lord, who holds you high.' His eyes bored into mine.

I think he rocked me back in the saddle as hard as my French opponent had done.

'I am at your lordship's service,' I said. 'On horse and foot.'

'I would like nothing better,' he said. 'But my lord has forbidden me to fight you. So I will withhold my hand.'

I'm an Englishman. Hating Frenchmen comes easily to me, but de Mézzières seemed both cautious and capable. And not a man I'd want as an enemy.

He clearly wanted a piece of me. I flushed, assuming he hated my low birth. As I remembered, his first dislike had arisen when I said I'd been knighted on the battlefield.

Of *course* it never occurred to me to just *ask* why he hated me.

At any rate, my usual reaction – anger – rose to choke me. 'I care nothing whether you withhold your hand or not,' I spat with all my usual restraint.

'That is the difference between us,' he said calmly, and rode away.

The other encounter was very different. I met the merchant who had brought the king's prize, the falcon. I was in the market shopping for something to send my sister, and perhaps something for Emile, since I might hope to see her soon. The king's new bird had stopped eating, and it was such a magnificent animal that we were all in a state trying to preserve it, and I said that as I was going to the great market, I would find the merchant and ask for his aid.

He was not a big man, but as broad as he was tall, formed as if from oak, fair-skinned and fair-headed and with one of the greatest beards it has ever been my pleasure to see. I could see, also, that he was a rich man, and a mariner. He wore clothes of blue and black, with furs even in a Polish August, and a magnificent hood, and carried an astrolabe around his neck. That's how they knew him throughout the fair: as Master Astrolabe. He was from the Kingdom of Denmark, which was as exotic in those days as saying the Kingdom of Heaven, and he had a scar across his face where it appeared that a finger's breadth of skin had been peeled away. I have seen some horrible things and I had a guess that he had been tortured. And lived. And for all that, his face was jolly, and his demeanour open and bluff.

I explained my troubles to one of his red-haired apprentices – we tend to hang together, we copper heads – and the apprentice led me to the great man. 'He's the only one who understands them,' the boy said.

Master Astrolabe, Carl Markmanson, as he was called by Danes, grinned and tried to break my hand. 'Ah, the English knight. Are the ladies through with you, zur? Have you fathered a hundred bastards yet?' He laughed.

I told him the king's problems, and he came immediately to the inn, and saw the bird, and fed it and talked to it. He spent a few minutes closeted with the king, and then I walked him back to the fair.

'Always best it is to council the great in private,' he said with his wide smile. 'Great men resent being taught, and yet no one needs teaching more, eh? Remember that when you are a great man, Englishman.'

I laughed.

But he fed me stew and wine by his wagons, and he and his journeymen told me about sailing to Iceland for birds. And how they had seen the Faroes, how they had come on Ireland from every direction under God's sun, and how they had seen great monsters and whales on the sea, and fought with Skraelings.

I may have looked doubtful. They told more tall tales in an hour than a roomful of Venetians in a day, and that's saying something.

But Master Carl put his finger to his forehead. 'I was taken,' he said. 'We had a fight on a beach, and my armour saved me, but the Skraelings took me.' He shrugged. 'They peeled an inch off my forehead, and a man in paint stood over me with a stone axe, and he raised it.'

I leaned forward. It was so real.

'And I was so afraid I began to sing. All I could think of was the Kyrie, you know?'

We all sang the Kyrie together.

'And the painted devil smiled. He smiled, and tossed the axe in the air.' Master Carl shrugged. 'So perhaps I was in the Kingdom of Prester John, and they were all Christian men. The next day they fed me and took me to another beach and left me.'

'Gospel truth,' said the tall journeyman. 'I plucked him off that beach in fear of my life and mortal soul, but we never saw a one of them again.' He looked shamefaced. 'We were off course – we thought we'd make a profit by taking a few as slaves.'

Master Carl shrugged. 'I'd wager they'd make terrible slaves,' he said.

I spoke more with them; they were all shipmen as well as traders, and they had adventures that would fill a good-sized book.

All I gathered from their stories was that the world was very broad indeed, and more full of adventure than a hundred tales of King Arthur.

We rode back west via Prague. Prague was, and probably still is, one of the most beautiful places in the west, with magnificent palaces and churches. Even the burghers' houses are as fine as those of Venice. But we stayed only one night, and then we were away west.

At Nuremberg, King Peter sent me to Avignon with his dispatches. I was loathe to leave him by then. Despite his mercurial moods, he was a natural leader and a fine lord, generous with praise and with money, even when he had very little himself.

I'll add that we cleared the road of bandits for the next several years, or so I've been told. King Peter would ask at every inn, and twice we left the road to hunt the robbers as if they were stags. One cold afternoon in the Tyrol, we caught a band that proved to be more like human scarecrows than like the demons of Satan we'd been led to expect. We surprised them, despite the late hour in the day, scattered them off their smoking fires and began to kill them.

There were only about a dozen of them. We were as many knights and then as many again —all the squires were mounted and armed by then. They had no chance, and a boy of perhaps twelve years old threw down his notched falchion and knelt at my feet.

I cut off his head.

I can still see it today. He was trying to surrender, and I had just fought another, older man, his father, perhaps. I saw his posture of surrender, but I didn't change my mind. My new sword severed his head as easily as a lady cuts pork at dinner with her eating knife.

He fell forward over his own lap. His head made an odd sound as it struck the sword he'd dropped. And it didn't roll anywhere.

I saw his eyes move.

I pray for his soul, even to this day. I had not *meant* to kill him. It was a wrong act, a murder, the sort of thing I used to do, when I was a routier.

When I was, in fact, like his father and his brothers. A brigand, if a better armed one. They didn't even try to rob us. They simply died.

I'm sorry if I cannot make a better story of that *empris*. It was, and is a lesson I have had to face many times. The line between knight and brigand is the width of the edge of the sword.

I left the king at Nuremberg. I took only Marc-Antonio, who was, after two months in the saddle, a decent blade and a good companion. He could cook a little, although I did most of it; he could make a camp and tend to horses; and if he tended to speak a little too loudly to his social superiors? Why, so did I. He couldn't sew to save his soul, and I did all the sharpening, but he was already a tolerable squire, and he was interested in learning more ... most of the time. But I noted that almost anything could distract him: a pretty face, an interesting song, a new poem, a handsome horse. I would ride along, piously enjoining him to something that seemed important to me that day – by our sweet Saviour, what a hypocrite I have been, and no doubt will be again – and I would look back and see on him that look that meant he was a thousand miles away. He was also a glutton. He ate constantly, and while I was following the Queen of Love's instructions and refraining from lechery, he made up for my chastity with a noisy relish that I came to resent. He was so soft-faced and angelic that girls trusted him – that's the only explanation I can offer.

We lay the night in Pont Saint Esprit, a day's ride from Avignon. The place reminded me of worse times, and it seemed odd to have the man at the gate salute me and bow to my surcoat. I dreamed badly: of the taking of the town and the rape of Janet. And the Bourc.

Dreams have purposes. Ah, Boethius – you have read him too, eh? That dream was a warning and, thanks be to God, I took it as one.

I entered Avignon as alertly as I had entered Krakow, and to better reason. Marc-Antonio watched my back, and I rode to the Hospital. The gate warden embraced me as if I was a prodigal son, and Fra Juan di Heredia embraced me and took all my messages. I had all King Peter's letters, as well as a dozen parchment scrolls from Polish and Imperial prelates, even one, the last added to my satchel, from the Archbishop of Nuremberg.

Fra Juan shocked me by opening and reading every letter.

He shrugged and raised his eyebrows. 'Welcome to the service of the Church of Christ,' he said. 'We have some mean bastards in my Father's house.'

I had never heard Fra Juan, or any other Hospitaller, refer to any churchman with anything but reverence. But the daggers were out in Avignon.

When he'd read through all the letters and scrolls and called in a pair of Hospitaller sisters who carefully – and expertly – repaired the seals he'd broken, he turned to me.

'Tell me of your trip,' he said. 'Tell me everything. Leave nothing out.'

Fra Peter had never cautioned me against Fra Juan in any way, and he was my superior. So I told him the whole story, as fully as I could: Bologna, Venice, Prague, Krakow and back, not leaving out a small encounter in a square east of Nuremberg.

He steepled his fingers like Father Pierre and nodded, but he didn't interrupt.

When I was done, he scratched his beard. 'Very complete. You won a tournament under the eyes of the Emperor? You know that our Order is expressly forbidden to fight in such affairs? Eh?'

I sat back, stricken. 'I—'

'Please don't tell me you didn't know. I believe I have taught you the Rule myself.' Fra Juan, for all his ambition and occasional venality, was a commanding figure.

I stuttered like a boy caught stealing.

He waved. 'A minor sin next to the fame you won us. I will get you a pardon and a light penance, I promise you, but as long as you are on duty and wear the Order's habit, it is forbidden. Yes?'

I swallowed.

'Sometimes, in this Order, we do things that are forbidden for the good of all. You know what the good Fra Peter says: it is possible that we will go to Hell? And that is a worthy thing for a knight to give his soul for others that they may see heaven. So much for the sin of pride. Are you strong, my son? In your faith? In your belief in God?' He frowned.

I sat very still.

He handed me a large square of parchment. It was stained brown. As I bent it, it cracked.

'This came wrapped around some meat,' Fra Juan said. His eyes met mine. 'It was addressed to you.'

I swallowed again. My mouth was full of salt.

'The letter is in Latin, and it was easier to read before the blood dried,' Fra Juan said. 'Did you know a young woman named Anne?'

In a moment, I couldn't hear him. Instead, I was seeing the

ginger-bearded man who had followed me and watched me with Anne.

I may be a damned fool when I have been hit in the head, but I'm accounted quick enough to do sums and audit the accounts of the Order, or to carry a message between cardinals. Or command armies.

'... dead,' Fra di Heredia said. 'I believe that this was to have held her heart.'

I was shaking.

Fra Juan leaned forward. He spoke very slowly, as if I was a child, and very quietly. 'These are bad men, even by my standards, Sir William. And very, very powerful men.' He put a hand on my shoulder. 'Their intention was to force you to meet with them. To turn you to their will.'

A small area of the parchment was legible, and in neat copyist's Latin it said, 'meet' and then 'To your advantage' and later 'unfortunate'.

'This wasn't the first letter,' I said heavily.

Fra Juan pursed his lips. 'No,' he said. 'There was a letter the same day you left. And when you did not attend their meeting, they meant to kill her.' He looked at me.

'You are killing *me*, my lord. Is she alive?' I asked.

'And very far away.' Heredia nodded. 'You owe me for this – understand?'

I fell to my knees, as the Order's spymaster no doubt intended. But I didn't care. I didn't care that he had two mistresses and more ambition than the entire college of cardinals.

'I took her from them. It is not important how.' He shrugged, and in his long, ascetic Spanish face I saw a man as dangerous as any I had known. He permitted himself a small smile of satisfaction, and then the smile was gone. His eyes were bland – and blank. 'I like you, Sir William. We have many things in common. You owe me one. That is all, except that the Bishop of Geneva means our legate harm, and this was but a small battle in that war.' The Spanish knight tapped his teeth with his thumb. 'Do not, I pray, offer this man or his minions any more hostages.' He leaned back. 'How is my ... nephew?' he asked.

At the time, I barely noticed his hesitation. 'An excellent man, my lord, and ready for knighthood.'

'Ah!' Fra Juan nodded. 'It is that time – indeed, the Crusade is a noble occasion. Thank you for the reminder.'

I went to my cell, lay full length on the cold floor, and prayed.

When I went down to eat with my brothers, I felt better, and that lasted for some hours, until I realised that Marc-Antonio was missing.

The Hospital was almost empty of knights and donats and even mercenary men-at-arms. They were all headed to Venice for the *Passagium Generale* and any knight worthy of his habit was with them except di Heredia, who was the Pope's commander in Avignon.

I went to him first, instead of running through the streets like a fool.

'I will send a message,' he said. He looked at me. 'Expect the worst.'

With the Bourc and d'Herblay, the worst was bad indeed. 'I will kill them,' I said. 'The Bourc Camus.' I paused. 'The Comte d'Herblay.'

Di Heredia shrugged. 'Just do not ask my permission,' he said. 'I command you not to leave the environs of the Hospital.'

While I fretted in my cell and tried to pray, I realised a number of things. I realised that Emile was a Savoyard, and that she lived somewhere in the debatable counties between Geneva and Burgundy. Her husband had served with the Savoyards at Brignais.

Her husband, who hated her, and knew the Bourc Camus.

Yet even in my panic, and as I began to understand the power of the coalition against Father Pierre and how I could be used against him, I was deep in panic. Still, I knew that Emile was a practical woman with a talent for controlling her husband. And that she would not have a will that would allow him a brass farthing if she were kidnapped and killed. I had to credit her with that much sense.

And further, it is difficult to protect a woman you have not seen in two years and more.

I prayed. It is one of the times that I'd say prayer helped me the most, in that with prayer came the clarity, sent, I think, by that fine soldier Saint Maurice: the clarity to see that my first duty lay to my squire.

And as I rose from my knees, a Turkish slave fetched me to attend Fra Juan.

'My friend Robert, Bishop of Geneva, has been polite enough to say that there has been some misunderstanding, that Marc-Antonio was rescued from some brigands and is safe, and will be returned to you unharmed. And all you have to do is go and fetch him.' Di Heredia tapped his teeth with his thumbnail. 'I am almost sure that they do not mean to kill you. But almost sure is separated from sure by the length of a dagger ... You know that expression?'

'I can handle myself,' I said, or something equally foolish and untrue.

He nodded. 'They can kill you. My question is: what can they offer you to turn you? Would you betray Father Pierre?'

'No!' I said, hotly.

'Good,' Fra Juan said. 'Try to remember that. If I don't see you in three hours, I'll pay them a visit.'

I rode to the bishop's palace and dismounted, leaving my riding horse with servants. The Bishop of Geneva had a palace as large as most of the cardinals, and larger than the Hospital. I wore the Emperor's sword – it was like a talisman, and it made me brave, but in truth, I was terrified. Battle is one thing. This was another.

The major-domo, a deacon, escorted me to the great hall. The bishop sat on a low throne, with men standing around him. The hall was hung in tapestries, magnificent weavings of war and the chase and scenes from the chansons. The blues were vibrant and alive, the reds stark. A hart bled out, and its blood pooled in scarlet silk almost to the floor.

I wore my surcoat of the Order, a little travel stained. It was, I thought, the best armour I had.

The bishop raised an arm from where he sat on a low dais. 'Sir William!' he called. His voice was a trifle high, but so is mine. His slightly protuberant eyes locked on mine. He smiled. 'Please grace us with your presence.'

The Bourc Camus was standing at his right side. D'Herblay was nowhere to be seen. Marc-Antonio was with them; he had a cut across his face and a black eye, but he was well dressed and he was smiling. I didn't know the other men.

I bowed, fully and respectfully. 'My lord, I came as soon as I received your message.' This was the tack that di Heredia and I had determined on. 'I am so relieved to see my squire in good spirits.'

The bishop smiled. It transformed his long, narrow face, pleasant enough to be considered handsome, to a devil's. If he had had fangs,

I couldn't have been more shocked. 'And for my part, Sir William, I am so glad you could come, as my last invitation ...' he glanced at Camus, 'went awry.'

Camus glared at me.

'I hope your shoulder is better,' I said sweetly. 'Fiore can be hasty.'

Camus's mouth worked. But no sound emerged.

'The Bourc has been forbidden to speak,' the bishop said. 'Because between his hatred and your adolescent posturing, I would be moved to haste. Please confine yourself to speaking to me.'

I bowed my head. 'My lord, that is too great a privilege. I will take my squire and go, leaving you with my thanks and saving you—'

'Shut up.' The bishop snapped his fingers at me. 'Do not speak until I ask you to.' He waved at the two men by him. 'Take the boy to the solar until we are done.'

I share with Marc-Antonio a certain willingness to spit at my superiors, but as they had him and I didn't, I thought I'd be meek. I bowed my head. My sword was already loose in my sheath and they hadn't taken it from me. Marc-Antonio threw me a glance as they escorted him down the hall and into a small room that opened off the great fireplace.

'The last time I summoned you, you chose not to come. This time you have come, and this is the wiser course. Agree?' His voice snapped like a silk flag in the wind.

'Yes, my lord,' I said.

'You suffer from weaknesses of the flesh. Many do. If I eradicate them, you will be a better man, will you not? Agree?'

'I agree that I suffer from weakness, my lord, I am a sinful—' I tried to sound contrite – and stupid.

'Save your false piety, Gold. You are a dog of a killer like the mongrel at my elbow. I know your kind. You have more loyalty than most, although I am not surprised that a man and not a woman brought you running. He's quite pretty and Camus wants him. Don't you?'

Camus spat something.

'You are forbidden to speak, monsieur,' the bishop said.

'I am not a sodomite!' Camus said.

The bishop laughed, and his ringed hand struck Camus – hard. The Bourc went a livid red-brown. Blood emerged from where the bishop's amethyst ring had cut him. 'Please do not speak,' the bishop said.

Camus mastered himself.

The bishop went on, 'I know your kind, as I was saying. I want you to understand that, and to understand that if you do what I tell you, you will be rich and well-contented, and if you do not, you will be dead and so will everyone you value. I am spending the time to speak to you in person because men like you and John Hawkwood are becoming very valuable. But not because you are valuable enough to me to make bargains. I give the commands, you obey. Clear?'

I met his eyes. Sadly, they were not mad. Not crazed. I had seen the poor creatures in London and Paris and Venice who are mad clear through, who believe they are Prester John. I saw one, caught in London, who had killed four women with a knife.

The Bishop of Geneva looked at me with the eyes of a banker, or a clever merchant. Or a bad priest. Or a great lord.

'No, my lord,' I said. 'I will not obey you.' I gathered courage and spoke. 'My spiritual lord is Father Pierre Thomas—'

'Spare me the recitation of your devotion to that penniless adventurer. He has no see and no hope of every commanding one. Patriarch of Constantinople – I wish he would go there and martyr himself with the schismatics!' His spit flecked me. Mention of Father Pierre made him angry.

'He is my lord,' I said.

The bishop smiled and squirmed in his throne, resettling himself. 'How much would it cost me to have you kill him?' he asked. 'Would a hundred ducats cover it?'

I made myself breathe. I was scared, but he had taken too long. My terror was past the point of incoherence. And I had my sword, given me by the Emperor. I stood. My knees hurt, and I had been kneeling in front of the bishop all through our interview. Camus stepped back – and drew.

I did not. Camus was too far from me to strike in one step. 'You have spent too much time with the carrion crow you employ,' I said. 'You imagine things that are untrue, my lord. I ignored your first summons, as you call it, because I was not here at all—'

'Please shut up,' the bishop said.

'I came this time to retrieve my squire, who I will now take, and if you, my lord, or the Bourc, your slave, crosses my path, I'll kill you right here.'

I'll give the bishop this much, he merely waved his hand at my threat, as if bored. 'Take your Ganymede and take the consequences,' he said. 'I enjoy punishing sinners. You will be fully punished, I think, for not knowing your place. You are a cook, not a knight. And God hates adultery, cook's boy.'

I still hadn't drawn, and I allowed my left hand to caress my hilt. 'The Emperor thought differently,' I said. I was ten steps from the Bourc, and my hand went to the door. 'Send for my horse, my lord,' I said.

He laughed. 'You are a bold rascal. You think you can just walk away?'

I looked about me carefully. 'If you had a dozen men with arbalests wound, I would see the odds as long.' I met his eyes. 'But even if you had them, I promise you that the first man to die would be you.'

'You wouldn't dare,' he said easily.

'Keep telling yourself that. *My lord.*' I pushed the solar door open. 'Come, Marc-Antonio,' I said, and turned and began to walk towards the bishop on his dais.

Camus, sword drawn, stepped between us.

Three steps from him, I flicked my eyes and saw Marc-Antonio emerge from the solar. I altered course, stepping to the right. Camus turned.

'Ah, Bourc. He has you leashed and muzzled, like the dog you are!' I said, and smiled. I licked my lips at him.

Marc-Antonio passed behind me, headed for the door of the great hall.

Camus's face worked and muscles bulged. I stepped backwards towards the door.

'You have no idea,' whispered the Bourc.

In a way, that was more frightening than any other part of the interview.

I backed out the door with my sword still in the scabbard. Because I knew that if I drew, I would kill, and I was old enough to know the consequences.

I heard the bishop laugh. 'Tell Madame d'Herblay to say her prayers,' he called. 'False as Jezebel, doomed to hell. Eternity in hell – for fucking a cook's boy!'

Camus slammed the oak door in my face.

My face went hot, but I got my girth done up.

'Guillaume!' di Heredia said, and he was coming around my horse.

'She's called Madame d'Herblay!' Marc-Antonio said. 'I'm sorry, Sir William!'

We three – four, with my horse – stood like a painting of saints for a long time. Di Heredia had his sword drawn.

That's how it was.

Finally, he sheathed it. 'I voted for you to enter the Order. I saved your little whore. If you betray Father Pierre and our Order, I will kill you if it's the last thing I do.'

This did not sound like an empty threat from the Spaniard.

I went down on one knee in the straw. 'I swear on the Emperor's sword and on the wounds of Christ that I will not betray Father Pierre. Or you.'

Fra Juan raised me and gave me a squeeze. 'Go with God, then. I will not ask who this Madame d'Herblay is. But I will ask you to carry the order's letters to the legate. And a letter of passage.'

When I looked sullen, he slapped my arm. 'You may do all the errantry you like, my young ingrate, but I suspect you'll find a letter of passage helpful.' He looked at me. 'You know the Count d'Herblay's wife?'

I was angry and afraid. My face was as red as my hair. 'I do,' I admitted.

'God save us all,' di Heredia said.

Marc-Antonio and I rode out through the most vicious of autumn weather, and if I say we were not faster than the wind, it is only because it blew as if all the devils in hell wished to slow us.

In truth, I didn't know where I was going. My love owned vast estates in Burgundy and I knew from making war there that Burgundy extended over half a continent. Further, I knew her husband had ridden in the van of the army of Savoy at Brignais, and Emile had described herself as a Savoyard.

The obvious place to start was Turin, and I went there. I knew the road, and I knew the inns.

The first night on the road, we were in the steep hills east of Avignon and we stopped in a tiny town, Saint-Marie d'en-Haut, or some such. Marc-Antonio was so scared he didn't even want to go to Mass, but the church supposedly had the relics of Mary Magdalene and we went to see them, armed as if for war, and we heard the sermon and took communion too, rare enough even then and probably the only reason I remember it,

After Mass I hired a linkboy on the church steps and we were still on the steps when I saw a man's head appear around the corner of the convent that fronted the tiny square. He put me on high alert: he was watching for someone, and I assumed it was me.

We made our way back through streets so narrow they were more like goat tracks, so sloped that you could lose a shoe going uphill and the streets were already dark. Twice at turnings, I glimpsed men moving parallel on other streets.

I tapped Marc-Antonio and gave him the Order's 'danger' sign.

He flushed and drew his dagger. The linkboy turned to see why we were stopped – and the sword bit deeply into his neck, and blood sprayed. He dropped his torch and screamed.

They were coming from both ends of the alley.

The closest man was one long pace behind me and coming fast. I raised my scabbarded sword, blocking the first downward blow of a club, and stabbed overhand, putting the gilded iron point of my beautiful red scabbard into the first man's face. In fact, I got his eye more by luck than skill, and killed him instantly. I pulled the scabbard off the sword with my left hand and threw it in the second man's face as he tripped over his dead comrade, turned on my hips without changing the placement of my feet, which can be chancy as hell in the dark, and thrust over Marc-Antonio's shoulder one-handed. I hit his adversary, pivoted back and ripped the sword out of my second kill and powered it forward in a strong overhand cut at the man who had tangled with my scabbard.

It's very, very hard to face a longsword in the dark. I had no compunction about killing these men – the odds were too long. They could only come at me from two directions, and I had the reach. And the training. I don't remember having a thought in my head, either: I killed, turned and killed, pivoted back and cut. My cut landed on a dagger and my blow blew through the man's guard and into his head.

It stuck. By a glint of light from a house's horn window, I saw that this victim was still alive with my sword two inches deep in his scalp even as I rotated my weight and kicked him off my sword so that a piece of his head came off his skull.

The other men to my front were now hanging back.

I could feel Marc-Antonio, still up and breathing, against my back. I flicked a glance back. He was holding his own.

Audacity is everything, in the dark. I abandoned Marc-Antonio and charged the men in the *traboule* – a tunnel through a house – behind me.

Two of them failed to turn and run, and they stayed there in their blood. The place stank like an abattoir, the copper smell of blood and the ordure smell of guts and I probably didn't even notice it until I had to go back to get Marc-Antonio and my precious scabbard.

He was shaking, I was not. I dragged him through the tunnel of dead men and we ran across the cobbles, lost in the streets of a very small town.

We went two streets over, or three – I was in a state of near-panic, which can happen to any man after a fight is over and Marc-Antonio was following me – and I ran full on into a man in mail.

'Where is he?' he asked in Gascon French.

I must have teetered stupidly, trying to work it out. Marc-Antonio got there first and put his dagger in the bastard. Then we huddled under the eaves of a low house and listened.

The town was full of men. There were shouts behind us.

In the dark, audacity is everything.

I got up on the roof of the house – it was not much higher than my head. From there, I saw the church spire and the tall, narrow roof of the auberge in which we were staying.

The alleys were very narrow, the roofs were low, and mostly finished in slate, with some thatch. Most houses had stone chimneys. 'Get up here,' I hissed at Marc-Antonio, and extended him a hand.

None too soon. A dozen brigands – or perhaps men-at-arms – came tearing down our alley. They turned at the base and ran off towards the church. We went over the roofs toward the inn.

I won't belabour it. I'm not good at being up high, and neither was Marc-Antonio, but we made it, roof to roof, stepping across the alleys and jumping the wider streets on to thatch. I suppose it was less harrowing than it feels now, but the streets were packed with mercenaries, and they were there to kill me. The roofs were safer, but they didn't feel that way.

We reached the roof across from the stable of the inn. There were no men at the inn yard, and I dropped into the street and caught Marc-Antonio down and we slipped into the stables and began saddling our animals.

'Baggage!' I hissed.

Leaving my armour behind would be tantamount to ruin. I left Marc-Antonio and crept out into the yard, moving from shadow to shadow. The auberge was really just a private house with a large kitchen and extra rooms, and I gained the kitchen unseen, slipped up the servant's stair to the main door, and threw the beam across. Then I went up the main steps to the top floor and pushed into the room in which we'd left our belongings.

God was truly with me, because the man my enemies had left to watch the room was asleep. I hesitated a moment, and then made his sleep last forever, and may God have mercy on him. I remember that he stank, and that I moved his head to keep his blood off my luggage.

I got my harness and our leather trunk, and ran down the steps just as there was a pounding at the door of the inn. In the street, a Gascon was shouting that the devil was loose.

I got our bags into the yard even as Marc-Antonio brought out our horses. I mounted my warhorse, and my fears were calmed. Mounted on Jacques, I was worth ten brigands. I got my bassinet and my gauntlets on as Marc-Antonio tied the baskets on our mule.

'All I want you to do is mind the mule,' I said.

Marc-Antonio nodded.

'You are doing very well,' I said, or some similar platitude, but really, he *was* doing well. His hands still functioned, he was alive, he'd put a man or two down, and we were on the last stretch of our escape.

'They're right outside the gate,' he whispered. His tone gave away his fear.

'Open it,' I said.

He slid back the bar on the stable gate, and there was a torch-lit crowd outside – at first glance, they appeared to be a hundred men.

One man said, 'Is that him?'

And then I was on them.

Jacques exploded into them and I might have killed them all, but one man knew how to fight a knight. Someone cut my girth and down I went.

That, my friends, ought to have been the end of this story. I fell heavily, and my helmet protected me from being knocked senseless, but I had no armour and I should have been meat.

Marc-Antonio and the mule had followed me out into the night and by luck and skill and the will of God, Marc-Antonio slammed his riding horse into the routier who'd put me down, staggering the man. I was already scrambling in the dark for my sword.

I was damned if I was going to lose the Emperor's sword.

I took a blow to the helmet that sharpened my perception of the threat. Jacques was still fighting – that's what a trained horse does. He bought me a moment and then another moment, and I still couldn't find my sword, and then I was fighting in the dark. My opponent had a dagger, and another man had a sword, and I had a helmet and gauntlets, which proved by far the best armament.

I found my sword with my booted foot, and cut myself badly. There's ancient satire there, something Petrarch might have appreciated. I thought it worth the blood to find the sword, and when Jacques rallied to my side I knelt and got a hand on the hilt.

I clutched it.

The night was full of shouts, and there were men running in all directions, and Marc-Antonio was shouting my name like a war cry. Jacques came up right beside me and I was up on his bare back in the time it takes to say 'pater noster' and we were away, our hooves echoing off the stone buildings.

For some reason I thought it was the Bourc Camus and his men, so I was shocked when I saw a man-at-arms by the gate in blue and white blazon. But he was badly mounted and his horse wouldn't face Jacques, and I put my pommel between his arms and broke his teeth. I had his sword arm by the left wrist, and I stripped his sword in the moment of shock, and I still had it in my left hand when we burst out on to the steep mountain road below the town. We rode hard for the time it takes to hear Mass, but if anyone pursued us, it was on foot, and not for very long. We could see every foot of road in the clear moonlight, and I changed to my riding horse after checking Jacques for wounds. The loss of my war saddle was a sore blow to my finances, but we'd escaped.

I handed the sword I'd taken to Marc-Antonio. He giggled nervously and pushed it through his belt.

And so we passed into the night.

We rode for three days without sleeping. We stank, and we didn't care. We stole a pair of riding horses from two monks in fur habits and riding boots, wandering mendicants who claimed a vow of poverty, and probably as much brigands as I can be myself. With spare horses, we could move all the time.

In the foothills of the Alps, Marc-Antonio reined in. 'Lord, I have to halt,' he said. 'I beg you.'

I shook my head. Fatigue and fear play strange tricks on a man, and the evils I had imagined and dismissed in Avignon now loomed as certainties in the light of day. I could no longer see Emile as a capable woman at no risk. I saw her now as the ultimate target of my enemies. D'Herblay was going to kill her – horribly. I could feel it, and dreaded that it had already happened.

'If you dismount, I'll leave you,' I snapped.

'Fuck you,' my erstwhile squire said, but it was more of a moan of protest than a curse. Marc-Antonio made me smile, and that's a good thing when you have fear all the way to the marrow of your bones.

'No one ever died of lack of sleep, lad,' I said. 'Change horses.'

Twenty leagues short of Turin, a day's ride past the abandoned chapel where I'd slept twice, there is a Benedictine house high in a mountain pass. We were allowed into the guest house after I showed my pass on the order and let in with a swirl of snow at the very close of day when there was only enough light in the sky for owls. We were wet through, so tired we must have seemed like drunkards, so cold that my hands and feet hurt like torture as they warmed.

Marc-Antonio was asleep as soon as he sat to take off my boots. I put a damp wool cloak over him and undressed and a monk brought me water.

I shocked the monk by stripping naked in front of him, and shocked him more by bathing with a sword by my hand. He brought me good wine, good bread, and a bowl of something with rabbit in it that was superb. Or perhaps hunger and fatigue rendered it superb. I ate that bowl and another and drank the wine and fell asleep in the bath, and the monk awoke me silently – he had some vow or other – and got me on to a pallet in a cell.

That's all I remember, except that I kept my sword by me.

Emile had a town house in Geneva. I learned as much from the monastery's abbot, and as soon as he said it, I realised that I was a fool, for I'd heard her speak of it as the place she spent the autumn and winter and lay in with her babies. More comfortable than her damp castles, she had said with her laugh that hid pain and pleasure equally. Few knights go to battle as well armoured as my Emile is in her laughter.

But the passes were closing with snow ...

I left Marc-Antonio with money and all my letters except those for local men, and I left my riding horse and took Jacques. I rode for Geneva.

I was three days too late.

That said, remember that it was Emile's courage – well, and her beautiful body – that first attracted me, and her good sense that held me. I was three day's too late to stop her abduction: luckily, she never needed me to save her.

I arrived at the door of her town house in as pretty a town as ever you need see, on the shores of the most beautiful lake in the world. The door had been hacked about.

The steward himself was in half-harness, and he only showed his face through a grill at first. I suppose that shaving might have helped me, but I looked like a routier after three days on the road, except for my scarlet surcoat. That got the gate open. Her steward still didn't like the look of me, and behind him in the entry way, I could see a brown blood-splash on the whitewashed stone.

'You say you are a knight of the order—' he said.

'Emile!' I roared. Or perhaps I squeaked it. I don't know. I got past the man in half-armour, roaring her name.

I might have expected that her husband was there or had let the attackers into the house.

I made it as far as the solar above the entryway, and I saw her.

She was wearing a breast and back, and had a sword in her hand. And the ice-cold feel of a sword pricked the back of my neck, too.

Some princesses rescue themselves.

It is very unsatisfying when two people in armour embrace. There is no warmth to it.

We managed.

I put my lips on hers and she turned her head away so that I kissed the nape of her neck clumsily. I stepped back.

'Emile!' I said. I'm still not sure what I felt: hope, fear, delight, despair? Why was she not kissing me? But she was alive.

'We were attacked,' she said, indicating the sword she'd dropped to embrace me. 'Oh, William. You came.'

'I'm late,' I admitted.

She shrugged. 'My esteemed husband gave himself away, and we were prepared. This is *my* house, the servants are *mine*.' She smiled gently over my shoulder. 'He's not an assassin, Amadeus. He is my loyal *servante*, Sir William Gold.'

I turned and saw the steward. He was as mad as an angry bull, and his sword was drawn. I had, of course, knocked him down. He was sputtering.

Well, there's comedy to be found in most situations, and I bowed to him and begged his forgiveness, which shocked him so much that he forgave me on the spot.

'*M'amoure*,' I said, 'you must leave. Now.'

'Do *not* call me that,' Emile said. Her smile said a great deal; injured and injuring too.

I took that wound like a blow. But I shook it off. 'Do you know the Bishop of Cambrai?' I asked. 'The Bishop, now, of Geneva?'

'The Lord of Geneva's younger brother? I should think so – I grew up with him,' she said. 'He pulled legs off flies,' she went on. 'Picked his nose and ate it.'

'He is my enemy and he means to harm you to force me to serve him,' I said.

She put a hand on my arm, and the gesture was warmer than her words had been. 'He may intend to harm me and then to harm you,' she said. 'But he won't care about the consequence. He is not the kind to make a deep and subtle plan. He's more the kind to wreak havoc and claim later it was part of a plan.' Her smile was the same difficult glimpse of the inner woman I'd seen when she told me of her husband. Not a smile so much as a defence. 'I grew up with this man, William. I know him.'

'Then he will not harm you – if you shared—' I imagine I stammered.

She sneered. 'Robert would sell his mother into slavery to advance his ends or satisfy his will.'

'Someone should put him down like a dog, then' I said.

She laughed, a true laugh, a hearty one. 'I promised myself I would harden my heart,' she muttered. 'But by God, William, it gladdens me to see you. Alive. A knight.' She shrugged. 'Even if you have forgotten me.'

I bowed. 'I wore your favour at the Emperor's tournament in Krakow!' I said. 'I have worn your favour in battle in France and Italy.'

'Did you wear it while you swived half the maidens of Europe?' she asked, and her eyes were blank, and I suspect I stepped back. I knew her well enough to know that she was angry.

Then she turned her head away. 'Pay me no heed, William.' She put on a false smile. 'We shall be friends and not talk of the past.'

Hot replies, defences and apologies bubbled to the top of my head, but I ignored them. By God, love can be like combat in this, that sometimes you must take a dangerous decision and live or die by the consequences.

'We must leave,' I said.

She looked at me.

'Emile, believe as you like. Three months ago, you were going on pilgrimage to Jerusalem with the *Passagium Generale*.'

She shrugged. 'A beautiful dream of another time.'

I shook my head vehemently. 'The *Passagium* is still active. My lord Pierre Thomas is the legate, and the King of Cyprus is to command us. I have only left him these two fortnights ago at Vienna. He will be in Venice by now.'

She looked at her steward.

He looked at me. 'I suppose it is possible that the bishop's brother is lying,' he said.

'We have virtually been under siege in this house for three weeks,' Emile admitted.

'Why would I lie?' I asked. 'There are four thousand men-at-arms in and around Venice. We will cut our way to Jerusalem or die trying.'

She smiled. 'You really have not changed, have you?'

'Come with me!' I said insistently.

She looked at me. 'I was attacked in my home,' she said carefully. 'If I leave, I will forfeit my right to bring my attackers to trial in the courts. This is my *home*. My people have owned a piece of this rock for six hundred years, William. I do not intend to leave that to Bishop Robert and his thugs.'

I had not considered that she was, in fact, of the *haute noblesse*. 'How could he imagine he could have you killed?' I wondered – that's how fickle the mind can be.

'He tried to have the bishop killed so that he could have the See of Geneva,' the steward said. 'That's how all this started. The old bishop was the count's enemy.' He turned to his mistress. 'I think you should go. If you trust this man, go.'

She blinked. 'Ah, Amadeus, I long for Jerusalem with all my soul, but I am a daughter of these mountains, and I will not be beaten.'

Amadeus shook his head. 'Take your children and go. If there are none of you left as potential hostages, we will be safe. I will get a notary, some fine plump black cock, to try your case.' He raised an eyebrow at me. 'Will your legate write us an indemnity?'

'Of course!' I said. It was against the law to seize or despoil a pilgrim or a crusader or their land or moveable property.

He looked down his long German nose at me. 'See to it that I receive a copy with a seal,' he said. 'Lady, take some men-at-arms and *go*.'

Emile looked at me a moment. 'Leave us,' she said. 'I thank you for your council, but I need a moment with Sir William.'

Amadeus withdrew.

When the door was closed, Emile looked at me under her lashes. 'With my children,' she said, 'I will have no scandal.'

I bowed and, I suspect, protested.

'Please give me my favour,' she said.

I was stricken. 'My love!'

She tapped her foot impatiently. 'You are a fool, William. Do you imagine that I, a countess, will ride to Venice in the company of a man who openly wears a favour I gave in my misspent youth? Do you *know* what a reputation as a wanton I had at Jean le Bel's court? I have two sons and a daughter to defend. I will not have them besmirched with foolishness.' She wore a look – a smile that included anger. 'You wore my favour at Krakow. People who know me were there.'

'Was it all foolishness?' I asked. 'I love you, Madame.' Then it struck me – what she had said. 'Oh, sweet Christ.'

'Were you thinking of me when you made love to your Italian girl? She figures prominently in tales of your amours,' she snapped. 'Pamfila di Frangioni?' She extended her hand. 'Nay, William, it will not wash. You are a fine knight and a bad lover, and I am no prize either. So help me get to Venice and we will be friends.'

Again, I might have complained, or set her down with a rebuke – surely she had slept with her husband often enough!

But age brings a little wisdom, and my battle sense was on me. I reached under my scarlet surcoat and unpinned the worn blue scrap and knelt. 'I am sorry I have been unworthy,' I said, and I meant it.

She took it and laughed. 'You really are too good to be true, William,' she said softly.

I was old enough not to berate her, but not old enough to do what I should have done.

She called for her servants to pack. I had a two hour nap, and when I woke and bathed, two of her men servants shaved me and dressed me in beautiful clean clothes and a pair of deerskin boots worth as much as a good riding horse.

I would like to tell you that the loss of Emile cut like a sword, but I was too tired and too sure that we were in immediate danger. And perhaps I was a cocksure young man who thought he could have his way with his woman in the end.

Bah. We're all fools with love, are we not?

The sun was high in the sky when six men-at-arms rode out of the alley behind her little palace – for her 'town house' had more rooms than half London. She wore her harness and we had no pack mule. We had a wet nurse with a baby boy, mounted on a donkey and wrapped in a dozen blankets, and two young children in the panniers of a second animal, a large Spanish mule with a nun mounted on it. She was the children's governess.

Her captain, Jean-François, told the gate we were bound with the children for the abbey on the heights above. It was a fair story, as we had no baggage and darkness was a mere four hours away.

The gate accepted the story at face value and we were away into the snow of late autumn in the Alps.

I longed for an ambush in which I could prove my love with my sword, but none eventuated. Men underestimate women constantly, and I'll guess now that Robert of Geneva never believed that a mere woman would take her babies and ride through the snow. I'm sure her husband didn't even see her as human. But she was. In truth, she would have been a great captain, had she been born a man. Did I not say that audacity is everything, in the dark? Hah! Audacity is everything all the time. And she had it.

We rode over the mountains and down the French side of the passes as far as Turin, and we were unmolested; indeed, we were virtually unnoticed. I had time to be jealous of my lady's attention to everyone but me and I had time to get to know her children. I was the odd man out: while I was forced to live with her men-at-arms, I was not one of them. They were professional, but not like my comrades in Italy nor yet like my comrades in the order. I suppose I was an arrogant prick, but they were scarcely friendly.

And not a single bandit showed his face.

An hour's ride north of Turin, I made my decision. I rode up to Emile in a shower of snow and bowed in the saddle. 'My lady countess,' I said.

She offered me a cold little smile. 'Monsieur?' she asked.

'I left my squire to recuperate in an abbey above the western gates of Turin,' I said. 'I should go and reclaim him.'

She nodded. 'Of course,' she said.

Well, *par dieu*, I could tell she was angry, but I was sufficiently a fool to not understand why.

'May I catch you south of Turin?' I asked.

She shrugged. 'I may stay in Turin some days,' she said. Her eyes met mine, and there was the rage again. 'But I imagine that you are none too anxious to meet Sir Richard Musard.'

That made no sense to me at all. 'I have no fear of Sir Richard,' I said.

'Really?' she asked. Her eyes touched mine again, and they were hot and full of the emotion she kept out of her voice. She had her youngest wrapped against her, and she looked down at her baby and smoothed his hair before pulling the wool wrappings carefully around the little head. 'My understanding is that he has sworn to kill you?'

I lowered my voice. 'Richard Musard was my best friend,' I said hotly. 'He betrayed me to the Bourc Camus and your husband, Madame. They sold me to the French authorities.'

'And when you escaped, you avenged yourself on him by taking his wife,' Emile said. 'Yes, I know it all full well.'

She rode on.

One by one, her men-at-arms passed me on the narrow trail. I thought of a dozen responses.

Par dieu, gentles, of *course* that's how Richard told the story. But I hadn't seen it coming and had no defence.

It took me a day of riding through the mountains to realise that when Emile reached Venice, I might be able to send for Milady. And then Emile might change her mind.

Because, in the meantime, I had hours to think about just what my love had heard of me. And even to consider those things I had actually done. I can remember riding, and wincing, physically, to think of the times I'd been unfaithful. Writhing in the saddle, cold and weary and *mortified*.

I have always been a fool for a fair lady, and no mistake.

Marc-Antonio was eager to go, having spent too much time on his knees and too much time eating gruel and, I gathered later, too much time defending his virtue from one of the more lecherous monks. Well, close a hundred men in a small box, and see what happens. But I had had time to think of many things, and I was profuse in my thanks to him for saving me in the village fight, and he was, perhaps unsurprisingly, delighted at my praise. When we camped, I made him go through the postures of defence, and we traded a few blows – gently, as our swords were sharp and he was inexperienced. But the sword I'd taken from the blue and white was a good one and all those days in the saddle were habituating my squire to life with and on horses.

At any rate, we made good time out the gate, and with the help of a pair of shepherds, we cut south and east, bypassing Turin on the plain below us and riding through an early snowfall. I was wary: we were no longer ahead of our foes, or so I reckoned. But we made the passes unharmed, and high in Saint Bernard we caught up with Emile and her party in a monastery. She was withdrawn, and in fact I saw her only at a distance. She was avoiding me, and that was yet another blow.

For the next four days, we travelled like two separate groups, the two of us, and the nine of them.

We were well over the pass, and on our descent, dismounted to lead our horses, when I fell. I was showing off every minute, I now confess, riding too hard, scouting too far, wearing all my harness all the time, trying to earn back her good opinion in the foolish ways boys woo girls. But high above the plains of Lombardy, I tried to ride over the narrow remnants of a bridge instead of crossing lower down at the temporary ford. I was driven by no nobler motive than that Jean-François, her captain, had ordered his men not to try the bridge as being too dangerous.

Three steps across and my riding horse paused, lost his footing on the icy logs, scrambled, and then we were in the rushing water. Autumn is not as bad as spring in the passes, but the water rises, and trickles of meltwater from summer can be swollen by rain to raging torrents.

I went all the way under, and my riding horse came down atop me driving my hips into the stone bed of the stream.

The shock of the cold stole my wits, and my full harness held me under for a long time, long enough that I might have screamed for breath; long enough to repent my sins, and wish that God had granted me time to commit more of them.

And then Raoul, my riding horse, shook himself and rose to his feet and his weight was gone, and the stream was narrow enough that I got my head above water by getting my elbows on a rock before the current swept me away. I went a horse-length downstream and was thrown on a sloping boulder. And there I might well have drowned except that Jean-François was there with a spear. He wrestled me from the grip of the icy stream. Water ran out of my harness, my helmet drained down my back, and my helmet liner was soaked through, all my arming clothes were inundated, and I was very cold.

Jean-François got me to the far bank, and Marc-Antonio had my horse. I was almost in another world: I had come so close to being dead, and I had the oddest view of the world.

Emile came up while I was mounting. 'We have to get him to a fire,' she said with her devastating practicality.

Perhaps I made some feeble protest. I felt terrible; terrible as a man who led men, and terrible in that the cold was like a vice on my feet, my head, my hands. Only the warmth of the horse between my legs steadied me, and when the wind blew I groaned.

'Thanks,' I managed to Jean-François.

He smiled, the first time I'd seen him smile. *'Bah! ce n'est pas rien, monsieur,'* he said. 'If you are not from these valleys, it is a simple mistake to make.'

An hour later I was all but inside the fireplace in a wealthy farmer's house at the top of the valley, and warmth began to make it into my hands and feet, but the cold had settled deeply and I was sick.

I do not remember much of that illness, except that I woke to find my head in Emile's lap. She looked into my eyes.

'You are a fool,' she said.

It was the nicest thing she'd said to me in two years.

Or perhaps I dreamed that.

When I returned to consciousness, it was to find that we were snow-bound. The snow lasted two more days, and we played cards and sang and I became friends with Jean-François and his men, close enough to exchange a few blows with them in the stable yard. They were very good for country trained men, and Jean-François had a cut to the hands with a feint that caught me again and again.

Thanks to Fiore, though, I had things to show them, as well.

And Marc-Antonio got better every day. He was still fleshy, but no longer plump by any means, and his angelic face now had a harder line to it. He'd been in the saddle for three months.

Where the Alps were in winter, Lombardy might almost have been in late summer. There was plague around Padua, or so we were told by frightened refugees, and I avoided Verona as if *it* had the plague. We had heard south of Turin that there were avalanches due to the sudden thaw, and I had a notion that if we were pursued, we had a respite. But I was cautious.

Despite my tomfoolery with the stream, by the time we left our snug farmhouse south of Turin, Jean-François and his silent companion Bernard were no longer sullen companions, and when I suggested a plan of march, they were perfectly willing to accede to my wishes, with due courtesy to their mistress. We made our way south of Verona, and it was almost painful to watch Emile bloom: sun, good food and wine and freedom conspired to make her almost luminous.

By Saint George, gentlemen. I loved her full well. And every moment brought me more to love. She was a mature woman now, grown strong, I think, in motherhood and ruling good estate. And yet sometimes she was still the young woman I had known in France – playful, determined, audacious.

And there was the matter of her children. She had three: a boy, Edouard, and two girls, one just a babe in arms, Isabelle, and one a little older, named Magdalene. At first, she was scrupulous about keeping them clear of me. Or rather, the nun seemed to have them whenever I approached the countess, and when she had care of her children, I was clearly not welcome. But then, one afternoon in the countryside south of Verona, I came upon her on the lawn behind an inn, sitting on the sheep-cropped grass in a kirtle like the embodiment of beauty. She had the older girl in her arms and the boy sat watching Bernard on the close-cropped turf and Bernard was whittling – he was a *preux cavalier*, but he was always making something – toys, dolls, wooden knights for the boy. I could already see the shape of the cavalier's great helm coming out of the billet of wood.

I could hear Sister Catherine calling her in her Savoyard French from a window of the inn. She shouted something about the child she had – Isabelle, as I remember – and something about blood. Emile leaped to her feet. Her eyes met mine – it's difficult to describe her look. Questioning? And yet – they held some promise ...

As if exasperated with herself, she put her babe into my arms, picked up the skirts of her kirtle and ran inside.

We arrived, a party of a dozen pilgrims, at Chioggia in late November. I showed my papal protection and my courier letter at the causeway and we were conducted like royalty along the edge of the lagoon into Venice's principle out-town.

I remember most the sound of the gulls, the piercing cry, so different from any other bird. And the good, wholesome smell of sea and foreshore and fish. I'm a Londoner, if not born then bred up, and Chioggia and Venice have a great deal of London in them. Of course, my Venetian friends would say that perhaps poor London has a little of Venice in her ...

Do you know Venice? Last year, during the great war – of which I'll speak in time, if we're stuck her long enough – I was in a position to view the Serenissima's accounts when she was at her lowest ebb, fighting Genoa to the death. *Par dieu*, messieurs, there is more gold in Venice than in all England. The merchants of the Rialto and the Lido have more commerce than all England and all France *together*. The customs intake at Chioggia, one small port, must rival Portsmouth. In England, most men have no idea just how rich Italy is.

At any rate, I rode along the causeway the allows Chioggia and the long, narrow islands of Pellestrina and Malamocco to be connected to the mainland – or almost connected – to the terra firma at Clogia Minore or Sottomarina, as some say. It would all be a major part of my life, one day. But for the first time in three weeks, Emile brought her horse alongside mine.

'You look happy,' she said.

I was, too. I had discovered that I didn't really need to sleep with Emile to enjoy her. That in fact, I loved her, and not that springtime, sap-rising thing that young people call love. I was also discovering the joy of riding, looking, smelling, tasting. It was a beautiful autumn, except for the poor people dying of the plague, God rest them.

'I love the gulls, Countess,' I said. 'They put me in mind of my home.'

She smiled and looked away. 'This town,' she asked. 'Is this such a place as I might buy a doll? My daughter has left hers over the mountains.'

I knew that. Every man in our party knew. The poor little sprite had wailed for fifteen days. She was not inconsolable; in fact, as long as she was happy, she didn't mention the missing doll, but the moment anything disturbed her, the doll became the focus of her outrage. She was two and a half and spoke well – eerily well, in fact.

I spread my hands. 'I will hope that we can stay with friends of my lord's, and of the Acciaioli who I am lucky to call friends.'

She made a face-raised eyebrow and the curl of her lip. 'The Acciaioli? Who do you call friend?'

'Lord Niccolò has long been a supporter of our legate and the order,' I said. 'Nerio rode to tourny with me in Krakow and even now—'

Emile laughed. I knew her well; it was the laugh that expressed more discomfort than joy. 'You know Nerio Acciaioli? The world is too small, indeed.' She frowned. 'I scarcely know him, only that my mother and his mother were great friends and had a – a falling out.'

This was the longest speech I'd heard from her in three weeks on the road. But we were almost to the gate. 'Countess, I will endeavour to find Mademoiselle Magdalene a doll.'

Emile favoured me with a smile, her real smile, the smile that struck me like a poleaxe to the head. 'I would be in your debt, if you would.'

Indeed, I felt a fool for not thinking to find the girl a doll on my own. Magdalene was a delightful child, as long as she got her way. Like most children, really. I was searching for a way to prove myself to my lady and here was one I'd overlooked. I was not good with children – but I was wise enough to see that I had better adapt to them.

In my own defence, I'll say that while there was some good wine and good cheer and staring at beautiful mountains on that trip, I'll also say that Bernard and Jean-François and I rode and scouted as if we were in hourly danger of our lives. I didn't know if d'Herblay was ahead of us or behind, or what other agents Robert of Geneva might have deployed against us.

Any road, on the causeway into Chioggia I felt we were safe. And I wanted to triumph with the doll.

I reined in and waved for Marc-Antonio, who was preening like a peacock. And why not? He was about to ride into his home town as the squire of a knight. Wearing a sword, even if it was in a plain brown scabbard. Bernard, Jean-François's silent friend, was not just a fine blade, he could work leather, and together the four of us had tinkered up a fair scabbard for my squire's longsword. He wore silver spurs and hip-high boots and he was long, lean, and a little dangerous looking – and he knew it. Women were already watching him with the appetite that belies many of the things men say about women.

At any rate, as he became more like a squire, so it was more of a pleasure to be served by him. He clattered up the causeway in a show of devotion and reined in by my side.

'Can you get us lodgings with the Corners?' I asked. 'Go and ask once we pass the gate.'

He bowed in the saddle. I was doing him a favour: now he could go to his home as my messenger, puffed in self-importance, his status on his hip.

The gate guards welcomed us like long-lost friends – an odd re-action, but due, I found, to the esteem in which Father Pierre was held in Venice, where they well-nigh worshipped him for his part in making peace between France and Milan and the Pope. At any rate, I covered my surprise. Gate guards can be officious, obsequious, venal or rude, but I've seldom known them to be friendly, and it put me on my guard. Marc-Antonio clattered away after exchanging a lewd jest with one of the guards, and we were in the wide streets and canals of Chioggia.

Emile rode with her head going back and forth.

'These houses are as elegant as those in Paris,' she said as we came to the grand central square. 'They must have a fine run of noblemen for such a small town.'

I nodded. 'Countess, these are all merchants. The town owns all the land; it is a commune. They rent the land on the condition that the merchants built rich houses.' I shrugged as if disclaiming my own knowledge. 'My squire is Chioggian, so I know a fair amount about the town.'

'By Saint Mary Magdalene, this town is a delight,' she said. We ambled along the main street with a canal on our left running on the far side of the church and the great town hall and the fine tower that could be seen all the way across the marshes. But we were on terra firma; the square was paved, and the houses around it *très riches*, with three-storey stone façades and arched entryways.

Marc-Antonio emerged from the Corner facade with the *padrone* at his back. Messire Corner bowed extravagantly on his own front loggia. 'The famous knight Sir Guillaume le Coq!' He grinned. 'Or perhaps you are too great to be a cook, eh?'

I shook my head. 'Master Corner, I am at your service. This is the Countess d'Herblay. This is her captain, Jean-François de Barre, and these gentlemen are all her men-at-arms.' I bowed from the saddle. 'May we impose for a night?'

'A night? You may come for Christmas if you want. My wife will be in heaven – a countess? I'll have to buy her new everything.' He smiled. 'Countess, I am entirely at your service, and my house is yours. What brings you to my humble town in the swamps?'

Emile dazzled him with her most gracious full-face smile; her eyes all but gave light, they sparkled so much. She spoke French – she had very little Italian, although like most Savoyards, she understood it well enough. 'My lord, I appreciate this welcome,' she said.

Jean-François and I translated together, and we both laughed.

'Tell your lady I'm no lord, but a free citizen of Venice,' Messire Corner said. 'But be gentle. Aristocrats are easy to insult. Eh? Come, there's food. I see you have taken good care of my scapegrace bastard. He looks like a man.'

'He is a man, messire. He has served me well, and I have made him a squire. Indeed, he served as a squire in front of the Emperor.' No harm in laying it on thick. This sort of thing can be a better reward than money. It *is* honour. Word fame is honour.

If Emile could be said to be luminous when she was happy, Marc-Antonio glowed.

The *padrone* glanced at his bastard son. He gave a long, steady nod. 'I am delighted, Ser Guillaume, and deeply in your debt. Will you keep him?'

'Indeed, I have undertaken to make him a knight, in time,' I said.

I was busy dismounting, handing Emile down – the first time I'd been allowed to do such a thing in the whole of our ride, and the touch of her hand caused me to miss the *padrone's* next words. But when I turned, he enfolded me in a velvet embrace. 'You are a true friend,' he said. He had tears in his eyes, and he led me by the hand into his house, shouting for his wife.

In England, a man, no matter how rich, does not brag to his wife of how well his bastard son by another woman has done. But Italy is different, I suppose, though no fool would call Italian women weak.

You might think that she would be angry, or spiteful – certainly she had no time for the boy when he was a servant. But now she sat Marc-Antonio at the family table and his sword was hung with pride by the chimney.

Emile favoured me with one of her smiles. *Par dieu*, it is good to play the great man sometimes, especially when you are young, and it is a pleasure to do a good thing, perhaps the greatest pleasure in the world for a Christian.

Emile went off with the lady of the house, whose French appeared equal to the occasion and who gave, as I can testify, every evidence of being delighted to host a countess – so much delight that I fear that every matron in Chioggia was treated to an evocation of Emile's gentility and demeanour for many weeks to follow. But perhaps I do the lady an injustice.

I remember that evening well. We ate a simple meal (so our hostess claimed) and I had octopus in a dark-brown sauce made with its own ink, which was delicious, and curiously like a succulent beefsteak. We had it with a heavy red wine, something local. Ah, messieurs, it is not all wading in blood, the life of arms, and we sat and listened to the Corner daughters play the lute and sing, and then we all sang some Italian songs. In those days, my Italian was far from courtly, and I did not know the fashionable songs, the ones Boccaccio and Dante made popular in the upper classes. But I knew several new songs by Machaut, in French. I sang 'Puis que la douce rousée' and Emile laughed so hard I thought she might injure herself.

'You are not the fair lady that Master Machaut expected,' she said when she recovered.

Of course, I'd only met Guillaume de Machaut through Emile, and she knew all his music. With only a little importuning from the company, Emile sang, and the elder of the Corner girls picked up her tune and even the words in one repetition – a quick ear and no mistake. They sang two rounds and a motet. Then I joined them for a third.

Alors, it was a fine evening. I was with Emile – how could it be anything else? And when the wine had gone round and the girls gone to their beds, the *padrone* rose and toasted me. 'You've made a fine young man of my wastrel son,' he said. 'My house is at your service. It is like a miracle from God.'

I shrugged; no man deals well with heartfelt praise. 'He was a fine young man to start,' I said.

Husband and wife glanced at each other and the wife's sister looked at Marc-Antonio and snorted.

But my squire rose and bowed. 'Thanks you, my lord, for your work. I am sensible of my debt,' he said, with more gentility than I had expected.

If I needed a reward for my labours – and I don't pretend I worked so very hard on Marc-Antonio – if I needed a reward, Emile's appraising look and smile were beyond price.

At any rate, a fine evening. And when the countess had retired, I took Corner aside in his hall and asked him if the shops of the town could produce a doll. In a story, he'd have produced one in the morning, but instead, he sent my squire out and he returned empty-handed and defeated.

Italians are the most hospitable men and women in the world – they will never allow you to buy wine, and Corner obviously felt that the failure to provide a doll was a slight on his good name. He offered to have the attic ransacked for one of his daughter's.

'They're all grown,' he said. 'All they think of now is shoes. And husbands.'

But somehow, in this *empris*, I suspected that little Magdalene needed a new doll.

That day, before we were ferried to the Lido, I sent a letter to Pisa, to John Hawkwood and Janet. And then we rode took the ferry to Pellestrina, and rode along the islands to Venice.

I think that, if the year of our Lord thirteen hundred and sixty-five deserves to be remembered, it is as the year in which nothing – nothing I imagined, anyway – ever seemed to occur as I had expected it.

I left Chioggia the happiest of men, and we rode the sandbanks and orchards of the outer islands like a company of pilgrims, telling stories and singing, and each time we dismounted for a cup of wine, I caught Emile around her waist, and her smile would take her like a flush of surprise. The gulls cried, the sardines were delicious, and I would have had that ride go on forever.

But all too soon we came to Venice. And in an hour, a boat ride, I lost Emile and her children and her men-at-arms to an island convent, where lodging had been prepared for them, and I was separated from her by a stretch of water that was as effective a barrier as the Alps. There was no goodbye, no touching farewell, no kiss. She was a great lady, and she and her party were greeted by officials of the Doge and I was treated ... well, as what I was, a gentleman-servant.

The Doge's secretary was kind enough to take me aside and tell me that the lapal legate wanted to see me as soon as I was at liberty. I sent Marc-Antonio to find us lodging with all our horses, and I walked across the square to the Doge's palace where the legate had been given space to work.

As homecomings go, it was quite good. Fra Peter embraced me in the guardroom, and there were Juan and Miles and a dozen other men

I knew, as well as most of the Knights of the Order that I had met and trained with at Avignon, here for the mounting of the *Passagium Generale*.

Fra Peter waited with what proved to be staggering patience while men embraced me, admired the Emperor's sword, or praised my fighting at Krakow or warned me of the dire penances that the order demanded for breaking the rule against private warfare. I might have been more terrified if these threats hadn't almost always been accompanied by a gruff laugh or a significant stare, and I had no idea I was in a hurry, but when I'd told my story three or four times, and I was just starting to describe the banquet to one of the Venetian captains, Fra Peter's iron-hard right arm locked on my left and I was frog-marched to the stairs. As soon as we were safe on the first landing, I handed over the leather bag of scrolls and letters from Avignon.

'Avignon!' Fra Peter bit his lip. 'We sent you to Vienna!'

I nodded. 'I went to Nuremberg, heard the king was in the east, and I chased him all the way to Krakow,' I said. 'He sent me back to Avignon with letters patent and missals for the Pope.'

Fra Peter's patience ran out. 'Where is he?' he demanded.

'The Pope? Still in Avignon – what in the name of all the saints?' I asked, as my misunderstanding had been genuine, and Fra Peter was breaking my arm.

'The king, you young fool. Where is the King of Jerusalem?' he demanded.

'On his way here,' I said, and shrugged. 'I left him at Nuremberg. I rode to Avignon. He should have been here three weeks ago.'

Fra Peter shook his head and put two fingers to the bridge of his nose. 'By Saint George and Saint Maurice and Holy Saint John, it has been a difficult two months. The soldiers—'

We both bowed to one of Father Pierre's Italian clerics, who returned my bow with a smile, and then I saw Sister Marie and she allowed herself a broad smile.

'Now that, my brother in Christ, is a sword,' she said. She grinned. 'When we have a moment, I'd like to fondle it.' She laughed and retired to her cubicle by the legate's office.

'It's very grand, after Avignon,' I said to Fra Peter. In Avignon, Father Pierre had owned a cell like any serving brother and in it he kept his books and his desk, his *prie-dieu* and his sleeping pallet. I have known eight or ten men in that cell, or in the hall outside, waiting to confess, or waiting with messages or looking to consult.

The Doge was considerably more helpful than the Pope. The legate had a suite of rooms, so that Sister Marie had a closet to herself, and a brazier to fight the freezing damp; Father Pierre himself had a room with beautifully stuccoed walls, a simple pattern in red and blue that pleased the eye and gladdened the heart like the cry of gulls. He was dressed in a plain brown robe, but he had a fur hood and a magnificent enamelled set of prayer beads on his belt. He still looked very plain amidst the magnificence of Venice, and I would say that it was not that he had made his clothing more sumptuous, as much as he had risen to the challenge of being a papal legate in Venice.

He rose and embraced me.

Then, after I had kissed his episcopal ring and knelt, he waved me to a chair. Italians have the best chairs. They have a dozen types, from thrones very like our own to my favourites, the folding chairs made of dozens of frame supports that fold into each other like two sets of human ribs interlocked and unfold into a chair. The Doge had provided the legate with a complete set of camp furniture for the crusade. He had set it up in his office and I confess that the Doge of Venice's camp furniture was better than anything I had seen in the palaces of Poland and Bohemia or England.

At any rate, I settled comfortably into my chair and told my story, leaving out nothing but venal sins.

Father Pierre motioned to Fra Peter to sit, and it was just the three of us, and Sister Marie, scribbling madly away. She wrote so fast that when she dipped her pen, she did so with her whole body, and her pen case, hung round her neck, would tap against the desk; our whole conversation was punctuated by that 'click' that came every seventy or eighty heartbeats.

When I spoke of leaving the king, Father Pierre winced and steepled his hands.

When I spoke of Bishop Robert, Father Pierre put his face in his hands for a moment and then exchanged a long look with Fra Peter.

Fra Peter was playing with his beard and staring out the elegant window at the lagoon.

'And this lady you escorted south – the Pope ordered this?' Father Pierre asked.

'No, my lord,' I said.

'Fra Juan di Heredia? He ordered you?' my legate asked. His eyes met mine.

Listen. Father Pierre was not of this world – he was then a living saint. But while he was above many worldly considerations, he was at the same time deeply knowledgeable of the world. Fiore liked to brag that in the whole of his youth he'd never got away with one trick on his mother – I suspect that Father Pierre would have made a frightening parent.

I knew that his look was neither angry nor amused. It was the look he kept for the condition of man. Which gave him pain.

'No, my lord,' I said. 'She is a friend. I had occasion to render her a service during the Jacquerie. And I had heard she intended to make the pilgrimage.'

'So you rode two days out of your way to greet her,' Father Pierre said.

Friends, I was a small boy with a nasty piece of work as an uncle – I can lie with the best of them. And as Emile and I had committed no sin – well, not outwardly – I had the feeling of somewhat hypocritical indignation that sinners get when accused of a sin they have not committed.

'Yes, my lord,' I said.

Our eyes locked.

He nodded thoughtfully. 'She is a very rich woman, and very powerful,' he said. 'And she brings six good knights.'

'Which is good, because we're bleeding men at arms like a beheaded traitor gushes blood,' Fra Peter put in.

Father Pierre winced again. 'My son—'

'If the King of Cyprus doesn't get here soon, we'll have no army, and it will all be for nothing,' Fra Peter said. I'd seldom seen him angry, but the last four months had aged him. And tired him.

'Surely the legate can hold the men at arms?' I asked carefully.

Father Pierre raised both eyebrows. 'I might,' he admitted. 'But our Holy Father the Pope has ordered me to suspend use of church revenues until the whereabouts of the king have been determined. So I have no money.'

No commander and no money. Most of the men gathered around Venice and living in peasant's houses, squalid, windswept camps and expensive lodgings were mercenaries. Men like me. Our purses are not bottomless and many had come to make a profit – well, to be fair, to make a profit *and* to save their souls.

'Tell him about the Genoese!' Fra Peter said.

Father Pierre smiled at me. 'I don't want to overburden his spirit,' he said.

Fra Peter laughed. 'I do. He runs about fighting in tournaments and winning beautiful swords and I get paperwork in Venice?' He glared at me, a mocking glare. 'Genoa has all but declared war on Cyprus.'

Since Genoa, Cyprus, Venice and Constantinople – the Eastern empire – were the supports of the crusade, war between Genoa and Cyprus would kill the *Passagium Generale* as thoroughly as a poleaxe blow to the head of an unarmoured man. 'Why? What for?' I could vaguely remember discussions about this – hadn't someone been killed on the docks in Cyprus?

Father Pierre looked away, almost as if he was disassociating himself from Fra Peter's answer.

'The charges against Cyprus are trumped-up forgeries. It is all tinsel and make-believe – but Genoa has a fleet in home waters for the crusade, and they are threatening to use it against Cyprus.' Fra Peter sat back, his nose showing white spots. He was angry.

I leaned forward. 'Are they in league with the *paynim*?' I asked.

Father Pierre laughed. 'In the name of the Father and the Son and the Holy Ghost also – Genoa trades with the Hagarenes. So does Venice, as the Doge never tires of telling me, even when I tell him of the traffic in Christian slaves, of the Greek boys and the Venetian gentlemen sold to the cruellest of masters ... My sons, Cyprus herself trades with the infidel.' He shook his head, not in sorrow but in rueful appreciation of the world. 'We are as God made us, and the world must be as it is,' he said. 'Sometimes I wonder if this is a false doctrine, but for the moment I am content with it. Venice, Genoa and Cyprus are all engaged in trade with the Saracens, despite which I am charged with this crusade and I will see it through. I need to travel to Genoa and force them to peace, but I cannot go until the king comes here, to reassure the soldiers.'

'The Lord works in mysterious ways,' Fra Peter said.

We all prayed together, and Fra Peter walked me out to the guard-room.

'Do we have beds?' I asked.

'I doubt that there's a bed in this city,' Fra Peter said.

Marc-Antonio found us both rooms in a decaying Byzantine structure near the new fish market. On the ground floor was a scriptorium where illuminated manuscripts were produced, and just walking through it was a dazzling experience for every sense with its gold leaf and size and resin and ink and lapis and turpentine and parchment. It was one of the smells of my youth: the monastery in London had a scriptorium, although neither this lavish nor this commercial, and I felt at home. The second storey rooms were in the hands of a prosperous grocer and his family: five daughters, a wife, and the wife's mother – a sort of commercial nunnery. They owned the building and the one next to it, where the grocery was on the ground floor.

Donna Bemba demanded *twenty* gold ducats for a month's rent, paid in advance. I'd like you to note that this represented about five years' wages for a peasant in England with his own farm; the cost of a *good* helmet made by a good armourer and half the cost of a decent warhorse over on the mainland. This, for two small rooms which were damp and whose windows sagged on their sashes.

'Just pay,' Marc-Antonio advised me. 'My father knows them a little. It is a fair price.'

'A fair price!' I all but shouted. I was down to the last of my money. Remember, I was not paid. The word 'donat' implies donation – a man donating his time and his body to the order. I had made a fortune in Lombardy and Tuscany, and now I was spending it on a failed crusade.

Had spent it. When I paid for the fodder for my horses and gave another month in advance and covered my debt to the tailor who had made up my clothes for the trip to Poland, my purse was empty.

Venice is a dreadful city in which to be poor. Food is expensive, trinkets are magnificent – and expensive – and everyone knows the value of everything to the last farthing. I needed a new helmet if I was to fight Saracens or really anyone except small children, and when I had a rower take me to the streets where the armourers plied their trade – that is, where both armourers and merchants dealing in Milanese or Pavian armour resided – I saw a dozen helmets I liked and two I adored, but the prices were now beyond me.

My favourite armourer was a Bohemian, a tall, handsome man with a fashionable forked beard who had earned his citizenship fighting for Venice in Dalmatia. I liked his work and I liked him, and we drank a cup of wine together while he tried to sell me a full harness in the new style, breast and back together, matching arms and legs. He had a helmet after which I lusted like a young man following a young woman, a *cervelliere*, or skull cap, in the new hard steel with a fine, light aventail lined in silk, and a separate helm, beautifully rounded and sloped so that it was all glancing surfaces, with a moveable visor. The best feature of the helm was that it slid on to the skull cap on little rails and locked into place.

My Bohemian, Jiri, nodded when I had it on. 'Not my work,' he admitted. 'But a good fit and it would keep anyone alive in a mêlée, eh?

He also had gauntlets that were lighter and stronger than anything I'd ever worn. Of course, they cost three months' rent on my third-storey hovel.

'Pawn the sword,' Marc-Antonio suggested.

I didn't.

I had been two days in Venice, and I had landed Juan to share my palace above the grocers, when Father Pierre sent me to Terra Firma to review the men-at-arms at Mestra and north around the lagoon. He sent Fra Peter north the same day despite the cold weather to see if the king was coming over the passes.

I visited Sir Walter Leslie and his brother, who were festering in Mestre and growing impatient. They had two thousand men, many of whom I knew, and I received a good deal of heckling while riding through the cold and muddy camp.

I have seen a troupe of prostitutes turn on one of their number who has married, screaming at her about the men she's had and the services she provided, as if these things should bar her from marriage. So too with some of my former comrades.

I noticed, though, that none of *my* lances was with Sir Walter. I saw this with mixed emotions; I would have liked to see friends, and have swords at my back that were closer than family. Yet, it meant they were still together and with Sir John, and I rather fancied that, too.

I visited the English and the Gascons, too, Among the Gascons I met was Florimont, Sire de Lesparre. He had served the King of

Cyprus before, but he'd also served the King of England. He had a famous name as a fighter, and an infamous one as a knight. I had been ordered to visit him in the legate's name and a squire pointed him out to me.

He was sitting under an awning in front of a great pavilion, playing chess with one of the King of Cyprus's nobles, when I rode up. I had a very small tail; just Marc-Antonio and Juan, both in the scarlet surcoats of the Order. Marc-Antonio was a penniless bastard and Juan was the scion of a brilliantly old and wealthy Catalan family, but luck, and some of my money, had given Marc-Antonio a fine horse and saddle and a good sword, and Juan had donated some 'old' clothes to the cause so that we did no shame to our order.

At any rate, Lesparre glanced up from his chess game and made a little moue with his mouth. 'By the Virgin's Holy cunt,' he swore. 'Some nuns have come to visit us.'

I have lived in military camps since I was fifteen and I had never heard a man refer in such a way to the Virgin, not even the Bourc. Juan's face flushed.

Marc-Antonio giggled.

Lesparre saw my stare. 'Eh, little nun? Does my bad language disturb you?' he roared. 'Perhaps you'd like to make me shut up?'

I slid from my saddle. When you most desire to make a good entrance, that is, of course, when your spurs get stuck in the mud under your heels. It never fails.

'Perhaps she has never worn spurs before, the pretty thing,' Lesparre said.

His companion laughed.

But I had spent years at this sort of thing and then been with the order for more. So when I'd sorted out my spurs, I said a little prayer to Saint George, put out my inner fire, and squelched my way to the awning and bowed.

'We are to be favoured with some—' Lesparre began.

I nodded and cut him off. 'If you want to fight, all you have to do is ask,' I said. It was, to be fair, Richard Musard's line – he'd trot it out when he was taxed for his colour. I always admired it.

Lesparre's mouth shut.

'In the meantime, the legate is solicitous for your comfort, and sends his greetings and blessing,' I went on. 'You are, I assume, Monsieur

Florimont de Lesparre?' I took a small twist of parchment with the legate's seal from my purse.

'Did you just challenge me?' he asked, and when he stood, he was a head taller than I.

'No, my lord,' I answered. 'I am forbidden to challenge while I wear this coat, but if you insist, I will be delighted to oblige you.'

He nodded. And as he drew, he stepped out into the drizzle from under the awning.

Marc-Antonio reached out my sword hilt – he was carrying my sword over the crook of his arm. I took it and drew, cut the air once, and rolled the sword over the back of my hand.

'You have beautiful eyes, sweet,' he said, and a dozen other fanfaronades to distract me.

When he struck, he meant business. He flicked his sword up from a low guard, back over his shoulder, and cut at my head.

Have I mentioned how much I hate facing big men? I'm as large as a man needs to be, *par dieu*! I caught his sword over my head on mine, near the hilts, and let it slide off like rain off a steep roof, but I felt his strength in my wrists.

I counter cut a *mezzano*, a middle cut, at his cheek, and he parried. He was fast, as fast as me, and strong like a wild animal, and he'd been well trained somewhere – he made his covers with the kind of precision that announces the trained man in or out of armour.

He tried to wind on my head cut, and after the rapid exchange we switched places and he flicked a tip cut at me to cover his retreat. I stopped his blade but failed to catch it with my left hand and got my fingers cut for my pains – not badly, but enough pain to distract me if I let it.

He raised his sword up over his head. It's German posture, although I've seen Englishmen do it, too. He strode forward, I stepped off his line, *fora di strada*, and I cut at his cut.

Our blades met with the oddest sound, and the resistance told me that I'd misjudged and his cut was a feint, the whole of his power slipping away from mine, and then I hit him. It's hard to describe, but my blade encountered some resistance but not enough, and my point slapped down on his right shoulder, cutting through his gambeson into his shoulder.

His blade had snapped. I'd never seen anything like it – it must have had a flaw near the hilt, because at our second crossing, with both of us powering our blades together, his had simply failed, and I was one push on my pommel from killing or maiming him. Even as it was, my point was two fingers deep in his shoulder.

He looked at his sword blade and said, 'Fuck me.'

I raised my sword and touched my knee to the ground in salute.

He was bleeding quite a bit by then, and a pair of squires sat him down. But he had no trouble meeting my eye. 'We must do that again, when this heals. A broken blade doesn't decide a fight.'

I shrugged. 'I remain at your service,' I said. 'Do you have any messages for the legate?'

Perhaps not my finest hour, but I felt I behaved with restraint.

I was only on the mainland a week, but I missed the arrival of the king and his magnificent entry. I might as well have been there, as Maestro Altichiero da Verona put me in the painting – it hangs in the Doge's Palace yet, I believe. But that's another story.

The King of Cyprus received an entire wing of the Doge's working palace. All of his nobles – those too poor to follow him around Europe, or too old or young to serve on his tournament team and embassy, now rallied to him from the towns around Venice and had their offices confirmed and set up for him a sort of government in exile to handle his business and the business of the *Passagium Generale* before we sailed. His appearance engendered respect; he looked rich, young, debonair and very competent. The Venetians liked him, and he loved Father Pierre, and suddenly, once again, the crusade seemed real.

I was delighted to have Nerio and Fiore back. With Miles Stapleton and Juan and our servants, we made a small company of ourselves. They all took sections of my little roost above the scriptorium, despite the fact that by then we knew that our grocers quarrelled every night, screaming like fishmongers about unpaid rents, bad debts, and infidelity. The process of reconciliation could also be loud, and the daughters were generally able to keep up with their parents, and the ringing battle cry of the youngest: 'I hate you! You want to ruin my life!' was so insistent and so frequent that we took to calling it along with her in our newly learned *Veneziano*, and on one famous occasion, when her mother called her a whore for wearing her hair down with a fillet to

Mass, Marc-Antonio roared it out before the maiden thought to say it herself. We all dissolved into laughter, even Miles Stapleton, who was the strictest stick to ever be thrust into mud.

It is odd how company can change a man. Among John Hawkwood's men, I was the mildest, the most chivalrous; the only man-at-arms in the company given to reading Aquinas or Malmonides or even Aristotle. But with Ser Nerio, Juan, Fiore, and Miles, I was the most adventurous, with the possible exception of Nerio, and the most raucous, and it made me see myself in a different way.

Venice is a city with a thousand adventures but a great deal of law. Perhaps too much law for my liking. Men are forbidden to bear arms in public, but there are a dozen exceptions to that law – the Arsenali, the guilds of ship's carpenters, shipwrights and caulkers in the arsenal where they build the great galleys for war, are allowed to wear swords, rather like London apprentices and for much the same reason; they are the militia. And the noblemen of the city are allowed to bear arms in public.

We, as members of the order, were perhaps not allowed to wear our swords. Or perhaps we were, but I did, and Ser Nerio, who had taken the donat's coat, did as well. Because we did, the rest did. Perhaps we swaggered a bit too much, but we were in a rich city, packed to the rafters with vicious cut-throats, seasoned by the shopkeepers, who instead of being soft-handed bourgeois, were in fact tough little bastards who cut an empire out of the guts of the Greeks and the Turks.

If it hadn't been for poverty, I'd have had the time of my life; well, poverty and the knowledge that Emile was a league away across the lagoon.

Like many good times, the scenes blur together, but I know that we were preparing for the Doge's Christmas court and the great masses at Saint Mark's. The city was covering many of the crusade's costs, invisible, inglorious costs, and in return they seemed to feel that the legate and his men, most especially the Order of St John, were at their personal service.

Beggars cannot be choosers, and the service was not so very onerous. We practiced for various processions in armour and I declined invitations from other knights because I couldn't return them, and ate what I could afford – fish.

Nerio took time to notice. I was too proud to ask him for money, although he seemed to have enough for us all. And I was busy planning Juan's knighting, which was to be included in the great Mass of the Eve of our Saviour's birth. I suppose that by that time I had heard, from Nerio, that Juan was actually Juan di Heredia's son, not his nephew, by one of the great ladies of Spain, to be forever unnamed. Once Nerio told me, it was so obvious as to need no hint – I can be a fool.

At any rate, it was in the days before the festival of Christmas. Every guild in Venice was working at full capacity to satisfy every customer and to prepare for their own roles in processions, passion plays, mimes and dances and feasts.

Venice was like an army on the eve of battle, except that everyone was happy.

I was searching the streets for an ecclesiastical vestment maker who would run up a new surcoat for Juan. Fra Peter and Father Pierre had left this to me, and I had been busy. My friend's knighting was ten days away, or that's how I remember it, perhaps less. Marc-Antonio was searching the tailors of the Judaica while I walked along the Rialto. Money was no longer an object, I was that desperate. I needed a tailor who would finish the garment by Christmas eve.

I had Nerio by me, and I was at a stand in a street so narrow that passers-by, apprentices and servants and great ladies in Byzantine turbans all had to press against the wall to avoid the four feet of steel that stuck out behind me like a scarlet tail. I'd just been laughed out of an establishment so squalid that I couldn't imagine how to proceed.

I was standing in front of a toy shop. Really, it was the shop of a fine leather worker, but his window displayed items he'd made that best showed off his skills, and one of them was a beautiful girl's doll wearing a fine gown of wool over a kirtle of real silk, some fancy eastern stuff with a pattern. The face of the doll was leather, and while not, strictly speaking, lifelike, it had a vivacity to it that most girl's dolls lack: the eyes seemed almost to cross, the lips to laugh. The body of the doll was cloth, and I shocked Nerio by striding into the shop, scabbarded sword bouncing off the lintel, and asking for the doll.

The master came out to wait on me, and he laughed to see my face when he told me the price. 'I thought you foreign nobles were all rich,' he said.

I shook my head.

Back on the street, Nerio raised an eyebrow. 'Well?' he asked.

'Too much,' I said. 'Too dear.'

Nerio walked several steps beside me. 'Give me your purse, brother,' he said.

'What?' I asked. 'I didn't come out with any money.'

He held out his hand and I unhooked my purse and handed it to him.

He used most of my worldly fortune to purchase a saffron-laced street pie with beef, and we walked along the Grand Canal. He was kind enough to give me a bite. Then he used the rest of my money to buy us a cup of wine from a very pretty girl whose wine was scarcely her only commodity. He let his fingers linger on hers when he passed her back the cup and she seemed to tolerate the familiarity with good humour.

He said something and she laughed and looked away, and Nerio came and grabbed my shoulder and we walked on.

He still had my purse, and as we crossed the narrow bridge over a side canal, he folded back the cover and emptied it into the canal – or rather, he up-ended it and nothing happened.

'Broke?' he asked. 'Destitute?' He tossed me the purse and went back to walking.

I shrugged.

'Why the doll?' he asked suddenly. 'Who is it for? You should have seen your face, my friend.'

'Why?' I asked.

'Bah! The disappointment of love.' He pointed at me. 'You have no money and you are in love. Every banker knows the symptoms!'

I don't know whether I glared or cringed or denied.

He walked off again, lengthening his stride as we crossed a tiny square with enough room for a man to walk fast. I followed him back to the leatherworker's shop. He walked in, exchanged a few sentences in rapid-fire *Veneziano*, and bought my doll for a third what I'd be told. He tossed it to me on the step. 'Don't play with it where the other mercenaries can see,' he said with a grin. 'You need money? Let me put some in your hands.'

Rich men borrow money. They are rich, so they get into debt. This is the rule of the street – no one loans money to the poor. And the poor know better than to borrow. I was used to pawning armour, pawning horses, but I was unwilling to pawn armour in Venice and besides, the army of the *Passagium Generale* had caused a glut of used armour in the shops. The value was practically nil.

My point is that I was, mostly, unwilling to borrow, even from Nerio and his father. He spent the rest of our walk trying to convince me that I was a good business risk. I took him to the armourer's quarter, and introduced him to my Bohemian.

He looked at the helmet and heard out the Bohemian's pitch on a full harness of new Milanese altered to fit, and Nerio shrugged. 'If you are going to keep me alive going to Jerusalem,' he said, 'come, what does this amount to, five hundred ducats?'

He wrote the Bohemian a note of hand.

I tried to thank him, and he declined. 'Listen, my friend, my father is the banker, not I. But I will not see a friend starve in Venice of all places. Here, he did it all for four hundred and seventy ducats. Take these thirty, and call it five hundred.'

I embraced him, and bought him wine. But I still hadn't found a tailor who would make a surcoat by Christmas eve.

I had, however, found an excuse to visit Emile.

'Where are you off to?' Nerio demanded.

'I have an errand,' I said.

'To the mother of a child who wants a doll?' Nerio asked. 'How very Italian of you, William. My mother used to tell me, when I was young and amorous, only lie with matrons and never virgins, and no damage is done. Eh?'

I suppose I flushed. I'm a redhead with a vicious temper and my face often gives me the lie.

'Well, be back by tonight,' he said. 'Remember Juan!'

Which made me feel a guilty fool, a bad friend. We had all decided to throw Juan a little feast before he was knighted – Nerio thought it would be amusing to make the Spanish boy drunk.

'I'll be back,' I insisted. In fact, I was too fond of Juan to want to make him drunk and foolish.

In the end, I had to ask Sister Marie for help. It was she who provided me with the visiting hours of the *convento*, although she did so with a wry look that told me that I'd intrigued her a little too much. Or that she saw right through me.

It cost me six solidi I could ill-afford to get a gondola to the island, but my gondolier was young, tough, talented, had a fine singing voice and new many of the newest songs. I gave him wine from my canteen and we had a fine trip out from Saint Mark's.

Landing at the convent's brick pier gave me pause. But Jean-François rescued me from a sense of sacrilege by greeting me like a long-lost brother. Escorted by a silent sister, we walked past the great convent church to the two dormitories as I regaled Jean-François and Bernard with my doings.

I invited them to join me – and my brothers – for a dinner.

'We're all of us ready to die from boredom,' Jean-François allowed. 'I went to Mass three times yesterday.' He rolled his eyes, and our escort glared at the brick walkway.

Bernard smiled his soft smile. 'What brings you, messire?' he asked.

I produced the doll, and both men clapped their hands. '*Par dieu!*' Jean-François said. 'Perhaps we'll have some quiet out of miss yet! Where'd you find such a treasure?'

I was part way through my story and had got to the tale of the search for Juan's surcoat as we reached the dormitory receiving room. I must explain: this was a convent for well-bred Venetian girls, and most of the sisters were from the best families of the lagoon. No one was sworn to silence, and some novitiates wore fashionable clothes and had servants. Each dormitory had a fine parlour with good oak panels and paintings or frescoes as fine as the piano nobile in a Venetian palazzo for receiving brothers and fathers – and lovers.

Our escort blushed and didn't look at me, but she bobbed her head for my attention. 'Perhaps my lord has been led here,' she said. 'My sisters and I make ecclesiastic vestments. Indeed, we have just made a chasuble for the new Bishop of Aquila, even though he is no friend of ours.'

I unlaced my own and the nun sat down and turned it over. She wrinkled her nose, but smiled, and I imagined her as someone's sister.

'You wish a line of gold edging the cross, perhaps?' she asked.

'It is for his formal knighting,' I said.

Emile came in through a barred door. I felt her enter the room, turned, and bowed.

'So,' she said. With the smile for which I would die.

She was happy I had come. What more did I need to know?

'Are you the same size?' my nun asked. 'Oh, my lady countess, I did not mean to intrude.'

I grinned – Emile was so prettily confused. 'Countess, this pearl among Christ's brides thinks that she and her sisters might solve my pressing duty to have a surcoat made for my friend's knighting.' Emboldened, I said, 'It is on Christmas Eve, at Saint Mark's. You should attend!'

Emile laughed. 'Indeed, my people would accept an invitation from Satan to get off this island, although we have been treated with every courtesy.'

I produced the doll. She *pounced*.

'You didn't forget!'

I confessed. 'I did forget, madonna. My lord sent me on a mission, and it is only this morning that I found this. But I came as soon as I could.'

She wasn't listening. She swept out, and there were peals of laughter, giggles, a shriek!

And then nothing for so long that I feared that I had lost her again. I filled the time explaining to the sister that yes, I was very much of a size with Juan.

She went out and came back with an older woman.

'For the Order of St John?' she asked. Her voice was flat, and a little shrill.

'Yes, my lady,' I said in my best Italian.

She unbent a little. 'This is an impossible task, but all my little reprobates love a knight. Very well. Thirty ducats in a single donation on completion, and ten for me to dispense as I see fit.'

A month's rent. But I had no choice; it was cheaper than some of the tailors.

'We'll have to keep this,' the older lady said, holding up my surcoat. She sniffed. 'Perhaps we'll return it clean.'

Emile came back with Magdalene at her apron strings, clutching the doll. The little girl wouldn't meet my eyes and kept turning away, but she managed to mumble her thanks for 'Lady Guinevere' very prettily. I bowed my very best bow to a lady.

Then I made bold enough to meet her mother's eye. 'May I expect you on Christmas Eve, Countess?' I asked.

She half-smiled. 'Perhaps,' she said. She looked at me with a little of her old self. 'We are so *very* busy.'

Strong in the knowledge that I had saved Juan's knighting, I helped my gondolier to pull over the choppy water of the lagoon. There was rain, a cold rain, with a little sleep mixed in.

I came back to my cramped rooms by the fish market to find Juan on the wooden steps with a young Moslem girl in a red shawl – a slave-prostitute of the kind favoured by the gangs that ran the water-front brothels and wine-houses for foreign sailors. Behind them on the steps was Marc Antonio, wearing a heavy cloak.

He read my expression and bridled. 'I'm a grown man and can sin as I like,' he said. His voice was thick with angry wine.

'Where did you get her?' I asked.

He wouldn't meet my eye. 'I ...'

Marc-Antonio's eyes gave him away.

I turned on him. 'You? You went and bought—'

Juan shoved the girl down the steps and put a hand on his sword. 'I will take no moralising from you, Sir William. You have a doxy in every town.'

'You've paid her?' I asked, raising an eyebrow.

Juan's cheeks flushed. 'Of course I've paid!'

I turned to the girl. 'Run along, now,' I said, and she bolted.

'You fucking hypocrite,' Juan said. He said more, in Spanish, about my affair with a notorious married woman.

Nerio, called forth from his den – he paid the most, and in return he'd arranged for our room to be divided by panels so that he could have his own snug chamber – stood in his shirt and hose on the landing. 'Can you children be a little less noisy?' he asked. 'Juan, come back to your party!'

'I was *taking my ease* with my friend—' Juan said.

'He arranged to have my squire buy him a strumpet on the docks,' I said. 'Juan ...' I thought of a thousand things to say: about the life of a Moslem slave in Venice, about women, about prostitutes.

Nerio laughed. 'For a fornicating adventurer, William has a fine sense of moral outrage.' He raised an elegant eyebrow at me. Juan brightened, and Nerio turned on him, 'But gentlemen – at least, gentlemen in Italy – do not hand over coin for access to a whore. At least, not in such a way as their friends can mock them for it.'

Juan, caught between us on the steps – it was almost like one of Dante's poems – looked up and down, and his rage returned. 'You have some bitch in your room this minute!' he spat at Nerio. His use of language, the way he spoke – he was very drunk. I'd never seen the younger Spaniard as a man dedicated to any of his appetites and I'm not sure I'd ever heard him use foul language. He lived like a monk and his piety was proverbial, even if he was less a priest in armour than Miles.

'How long have you all been drinking?' I asked.

'You thought we'd wait for you?' Juan snapped. 'I assumed you'd be stuffing your baggage all night.' He looked back at Nerio. 'You are all the same!' he shouted. 'Liars and hypocrites!'

Nerio laughed. 'But mine is not paid, and comes there of her own free will, my dear *caballero*, and if you call her further names, I will be forced to—'

Fiore appeared behind Nerio and said something which included the words 'not helping'.

Nerio winced and withdrew, and Fiore came down the stairs. 'Come,' he said. 'Let's take Juan out for a walk.' He looked at me. 'Can't you tell something is wrong?'

This from a man who thought that swordplay was a form of human communication.

We walked most of the way around Venice that night, and discovered nothing except that Juan was very unhappy, and in some ways very naive.

'You all have your loves,' he said. 'I have nothing. And no one.'

He had been quite smitten with a girl in the company the year before, but the plague had taken her. I didn't think of Juan as inexperienced; he had been a year or more with the companies, and two years with the order. But before that, he'd been raised mostly by religion, and as we slopped our way from bridge to bridge in the icy rain and fog of a Venetian winter night, I heard a great deal about growing to manhood in a Spanish monastery.

Ascetic monks, fanatical monks, and sexually predatory monks in equal doses; an automatic hatred of all things Moslem, and a healthy dose of pride and the fear of his true parentage, his bastardy – itself a sin.

I had known him eighteen months, and I truly had no idea. Until that night, he had always seemed young, courteous, a fine blade and a virtuous man. But the thin ice of virtue sat atop a steaming pile of dung: mistreatment, abuse, and two busy, arrogant parents pursuing worldly careers – a knight of the order and an abbess, neither interested in acknowledging a child.

Fiore proved himself as a friend that night, not that he needed to prove himself to me. But he listened, and in the end it was our ability to listen rather than speak that measured our friendship and worked what healing there was. Juan vomited his childhood like a man spewing bad wine, and we listened.

"I'm not fit to be a knight,' he said in the grim first light of day. A tailless cat rubbed against our boots, sensing a trio of soft touches who might provide food.

Aha I thought. At last we are to the essential wound. 'Don't be a fool,' I said. He was sobering up. 'No one is *worthy* of knighthood. Think of all the bad men who are priests.'

Juan looked at Fiore.

Fiore looked at me.

'None of us is Galahad,' I said, all too conscious that I had just returned from a day spent with Emile.

'I am afraid, all the time!' Juan said.

'So am I,' I said.

Fiore looked at me across the back of Juan's head and raised his eyebrows. Well, I suspect that Fiore was so very much himself that he was *not* afraid most of the time.

We walked Juan around and fed him a little more wine, and by the time the cocks were crowing on the islands, we undressed him and put him in bed.

Nerio had one of the grocer's daughters in his room, I discovered, and she emerged, shy but triumphant, to display her cooking skills.

Triumphant, and certain her mother would never catch her.

Nerio grinned with masculine accomplishment. Anna was, in fact, very pretty, with a round face and dark curls that were, I think, genuine and not the product of fiddling with an iron, and they had certainly survived a night's athletic entertainment with Nerio.

She began to heat milk for us to break our fasts, and Nerio and Fiore sat with Miles at the table. Miles looked distant, as if he was pretending not to be there at all. Fiore was untroubled. He was repairing a shirt.

Nerio had eyes only for the shape of his conquest, and she was shapely, and delighted enough, or simply appalled enough, at her new role to carry off the part: she was naked under a single shift, and most of her was on display.

'You made him drunk,' I said, with a nod to the cot where Juan tossed and snored.

'We promised him a festivity,' Nerio said. 'We are soldiers, not monks.'

I looked at Miles. 'Well?' I asked.

His eyes were large. 'I – that is – my lord—'

Nerio laughed. 'You are all such children!' he said. 'Life is for living. *Carpe diem.* If the next lance stroke goes through my visor, I want to have sported every maiden in Venice – in Italy! What use is chastity to a corpse?' He looked at me. 'Eh? William?'

'When he confesses all this to Father Pierre,' I said. It was a weak thing to say, I admit.

Nerio shook his head. 'A fine man, but you fear him too much. Let him live a life of chastity if he will.' He smiled at me.

'*Par dieu*, brothers!' I said. 'In a few weeks, we'll be going on crusade! To Jerusalem!'

Nerio licked his lips. 'I'm quite sure there will be women there, as well,' he said.

Later that day, or perhaps the next, but still with a disturbed and unclean spirit, I went to the Doge's palace to meet with Fra Peter. I feared the summons was about Juan, but I was mostly incorrect.

'Father Pierre is going to Genoa,' he announced.

'In the winter?' I asked, and probably blasphemed.

'Now that the King of Cyprus is here – and he's been asking for you, William – Father Pierre feels free to try to move Venice on the matter of war with Cyprus. I must be here, to help the king with the men-at-arms – those who are left.' He shook his head. 'Do you have a few thousand ducats lying about that you could loan me, William? If I could make even the smallest of payments to our "crusaders", I could hold this army together. We don't have the great nobles that we expected. Indeed, the Green Count has obviously decided to spurn us and go his own way: he's raising his vassals, but not for us.' He gave me a withering look. 'All we get is his useless cousin, the Count of Turenne.' He looked at me – a look I knew meant trouble. 'And we hear we are to be graced with the Count d'Herblay.'

I thought of them – both from Geneva, both cousins of Robert the Bishop. I hadn't considered that such obvious enemies would be travelling with us – fighting beside us. I entertained Fra Peter for a quarter of an hour with my thoughts on the alignment of that bishop and the party in the church that had been Talleyrand's. I thought of having d'Herblay with us and something in me just ... broke.

Fra Peter tugged his beard, sent for wine, and heard me out.

'This is all your own?' he asked. I suppose my tirade was emotional.

It is a great pleasure to be flattered by your mentor, and his response was flattering. He was taking me seriously.

I shook my head. 'A great deal of it is from Fra Juan di Heredia.'

Fra Peter's face altered. His pleasure in my explanation evaporated, and he frowned. 'Yes,' he said. 'You like him?'

I shrugged. 'Yes, my lord, I do like him, although he is a difficult man. He helped me in a – a personal matter. And he is absolutely loyal to Father Pierre.'

I heard his sandals before I saw him, and suddenly Father Pierre was there, gliding into another of the beautiful camp chairs. 'But William, I need no man's loyalty. I am not a secular lord. I do not request or require your commitment or Fra di Heredia's to anyone but the Saviour and the Church. The rest is mere vanity.'

I understood what he said, and yet, in a way that is difficult to explain, I thought it was likely that Fra Peter and Father Pierre, two of the men I loved and trusted most in the world, were fools, and Fra Juan, who I suspected was as venal and ambitious as the Bishop of Geneva, was a man like me: a man who could accomplish a goal. For good or ill.

Father Pierre was still talking, explaining to Fra Peter that the Venetians would not rent a single ship, by last year's terms or any others, to the King of Cyprus while Genoa threatened war.

Fra Peter stretched his booted feet towards the fire and leaned back. 'William has just favoured me with an explanation of events which would stretch to fit the Genoese business.'

For the second time in an hour, I found myself explaining Robert of Geneva's role in Avignon, and his family stake in the bishopric of Geneva and the papacy and the crusade.

'Genoa is a pawn of France,' Fra Peter said.

'France *and* Egypt,' Father Pierre said. He looked at me, and his eyes told me that he had read my thought, and that his love of man included an understanding of how much the animal man could be. 'Imagine: a hundred years ago, Saint Louis led a crusade to Cairo, but now the King of France conspires with the Sultan in Cairo to stop a crusade.'

I looked at my feet and ran my fingers though my hair. 'Does the King of France even know what's afoot?' I asked.

Fra Peter looked at me, then the fire. 'Probably not; it is enough for him to get a Frenchman as the next Pope. He won't trouble himself about the ways and means.'

'Fra di Heredia said you might be the next Pope,' I said. I knew it was bold.

Father Pierre's wide eyes met mine. 'If they make me Pope, I will fling the moneylenders from the temple,' he said. 'I will burn their fingers on their own ingots of gold.' He smiled.

Fra Peter laughed. 'I pray I may live to see the moment you receive Saint Peter's crown,' he said. 'I for one would like to see what you will make of Mother Church.'

Father Pierre raised an eyebrow. 'Enough. I will go to Genoa.'

Fra Peter nodded to me. 'After complete impasse, and some very underhanded dealing, suddenly Genoa invites Father Pierre to address her great council and make a case for peace.'

I suppose we should have seen the connection, but we did not.

Nor were we fools. Fra Peter ordered me to take a few volunteers. We thought we would be gone just three weeks, back in time for Juan's knighting. King Peter intended to keep Christmas court in Venice; there was to be a tournament and a foot combat in the square of Saint Mark's. We had three weeks to get the legate over the rain-swept roads of northern Italy, to an inimical city, to make a treaty.

A week passed, and we still hadn't left. These things happen; the legate was held up every day by the press of business, and now that we had the king in person, it was increasingly likely that there would, indeed, be a crusade.

There were further letters from Avignon. The letters told the legate that the Pope was still interested in the expedition, but they told me that the passes above Turin had opened again, however briefly, and that Robert of Geneva's agents would be abroad.

I attended King Peter. The Venetians had moved him from the Doge's palace and now housed him magnificently in a private one, and he kept court. Many of his men who hadn't had the coin to travel Europe had come this far, and now he was surrounded by a phalanx of noble Franco-Cypriotes. Jehan de Morphou led them – he was the best dressed and the most arrogant. The admiral, Jean de Monstry, had been on the king's team at the tournament of Krakow, and I knew him a little, and of course there was Phillipe de Mézzières. But none of them were overtly rude; Monsieur de Mézzières was distant but courteous enough, although I didn't much like the way he watched me, and Morphou was full of praise for my exploits with the king at Krakow – praise that I found as insubstantial as a pimp's promises of a wedding.

However, I invited all of them to Juan's knighting. I was determined to pack his ceremony with good knights.

It was also while visiting the king's court that I first met Nicolas Sabraham. He was older than I, grey-bearded and as plainly dressed as a monk, but he wore a heavy sword and spurs. I was briefly introduced by a French knight, Brémond de la Voulte, who was serving King Peter as a volunteer with ten men-at-arms. Brémond and I had crossed lances on several occasions, or at least, we'd been within yards of each other in fights in France, especially Brignais, and we probably bored a number of Cypriote knights to tears with our reminiscence, but we were instant comrades, and swore to each other to go to Jerusalem come what may. He knew Sabraham, who often served with the order. I had never met him. Sire Brémond walked off and left us in order to flash his Poitevan smile at a Venetian lady, and left me with Sabraham.

'You're English,' he said.

His English was as good as mine, and pure Northerner, like John Hughes.

I suppose that I grinned. 'I would never have taken you for a Londoner, sir,' I allowed. He was dark-skinned and dark-haired under his grey.

'Nor should you,' he said. 'My family is from the north.' He smiled and tugged at his beard. 'Or do you mean I'm dark? It serves me in good stead here.' He shrugged. 'Men say our forefathers were Jews in York.'

He said it with such simplicity – listen, I have not, myself, ever held with those who attaint the whole of the race of Jews with the death of Christ. Father Pierre said once in a sermon that we should never mind the Jews, that we kill Christ ourselves, every time we sin against another man, and I take that as a gospel. But Sabraham's easy admission marked a kind of courage – or indifference – and yet instantly educated me about the man: he was surrounded by a circle of emptiness. A few men, like Sire Brémond, were not afraid of whatever taint might stick to such a man, but most of the Cypriotes left him a wide berth.

It was their loss. He was a witty man when he spoke, yet careful and dignified. In ten minutes, I had learned that he had read the Koran in Arabic and the Bible in Hebrew and Greek, that he had travelled all over the Holy Land, and that he knew Juan di Heredia.

I invited him to Juan the younger's knighting, and he smiled. 'Are you sure?' he asked, eyebrows pausing as if to check my intentions independently from his eyes.

I wanted to tell him that I had no truck with the Jew-haters, but that might offend him doubly – perhaps from a convert family he was, himself, one of them? Men are hard creatures to know.

About the same time, we were joined by two schismatic converts who served as knights with Father Pierre. They'd been on a mission for him to Constantinople, and they returned with Imperial bulls written in gold on purple parchment. Father Pierre had spent a great deal of time out in the East while we were fighting the French, and he knew the Emperor, John V, and many members of his court, and he had converted two of the Emperor's noblemen – Syr Giannis Lascarus Calopherus and Syr Giorgos Angelus of the Imperial family. They were darker than Sabraham, as dark as Moors, with curling black beards and dark brows, but they were good men-at-arms. I had never really met any of the Greek Stradiotes, although there were already a few serving with the Hungarians and Venetians in the wars. These two were the first Catholic Greeks I met, and they spoke as many languages as Sabraham. And of course, the three of them knew each other – Venice is full of Greeks, and they attend the same churches and drink wine in the same houses and probably use the same brothels; and Sabraham was more readily accepted by the Greeks than by the Cypriotes.

At any rate, we played dice with them and they taught us card games and we all practiced at arms together. The Greeks were a revelation, even to Fiore; they, too, had a martial tradition, and as Venice was afire for anything even obliquely Classical, and as Greeks claim a classical ancestry to anything they do, Fiore was at first amazed, and later at least interested, by their exercises, which they claimed to come from Galen, and their swordsmanship, which they claimed came from Roman manuals.

In private, Fiore practised some of their exercises and mocked others. 'The Romans never had the longsword,' he said. 'It is an invention of this age. Yet they both wear them, and their teacher was a High German, or I'm a Moslem.'

Whatever their martial antecedents, they were good swordsmen, and they were amazing horse-archers, as we had cause to

display they put on for the men-at-arms at Mestre. Fra Peter and the legate and the king all wanted the mercenaries and volunteers to see what the Turks and Saracens could do, and he used our Byzantine gentlemen to act as Turks. Later, when I saw real Turks, I realised that they were pretty good imitations, although Giorgos never rode as well as Giannis, much less as well as a Turk bred to it from birth. But I digress.

Twice I had notes from Emile. Jean-François and Bernard joined us, and we had a feast in an inn, with a dozen Knights of the Order and another dozen volunteers, with Sabraham and the two Greeks and Sire Brémond. We drank and told lies and promised each other we'd kill all the Saracens on the face of the earth, which made Sabraham wince.

'Why so solemn, Sir Nicolas?' I asked. 'We all go to fight the *paynim* together.'

I think he shrugged. I was more than a little drunk and he was not. 'They are all as God made them,' he said.

The only thing worth noting about that evening, beside the quality of the wine, was that we all agreed to share the cost of renting a small warehouse with a dry sand floor, well along the Rialto, for the balance of the winter, so that Fiore could exercise us. We had twenty knights and almost as many squires. I mention this because I'm quite sure it was the foundation of his fame as a teacher. We subscribed to pay for the warehouse and wood for wasters and a few ducats for Fiore's time.

And at dinner, Giannis leaned past Juan and informed me that he was taking letters for Avignon, and did I have any messages?

I took the time to write the situation as carefully as I knew it, and send it to Fra Juan di Heredia. I had imagined that he would come to Venice for his 'nephew's' knighting, but I reckoned without the man. He didn't come.

Sometimes it is hard to like the men you value most. His own son? I mentioned the coming knighting twice, and no doubt made a hash of it.

Father Pierre informed me that we would not leave for Genoa until after Epiphany, and I laid down my last borrowed ducats for clothes for Juan's knighting, and borrowed more from Nerio. It was almost evil, the extent to which he enjoyed giving us money. I hated to be owned, but I was poor, and there is no level of self-denial in Venice that can keep a man-at-arms fed and housed. When I look back at that happy time, surrounded by my friends, living comfortably, and seeing or hearing often enough of my love, I am pained to know that in that moment, unaware of what was ahead, I was afire to leave Venice just to save a little gold, and horribly lusty, eager to end my self-enforced chastity. Every girl and every woman looked appealing to me, and Nerio's infatuation with our grocer's eldest daughter and her wantonness – I know no other way to describe her eager acceptance of the role of mistress – was sapping my resolution to be faithful to Emile.

Yet even while I watched Anna and Nerio bill and coo, I knew that there must be a thunderclap waiting in the wings. It is one thing to buy a Moorish girl on the docks, and another thing to deflower a merchant's daughter of marriageable age. Or rather, it may be the same thing in the eyes of Father Pierre, or God, but in the eyes of the world ...

I sent two notes to Emile and one to the sisters of the convent, and worries about the state of Juan's soul and my own were replaced, as young men do such things, by the constant worry that Juan's surcoat would not be done for his knighting. But the day before Christmas Eve, I received a note from Emile promising her attendance and delivery of the surcoat, and the next day I met her at Saint Mark's in time to take silk-wrapped package from Jean-François and another from Bernard. The first proved to hold Juan's surcoat, resplendent in new red silk, with a perfectly white cross-edged in magnificent gold thread. I ran almost all the way back to our rooms in my arming clothes, untied laces flapping like the gills on a fish.

The second package held my own surcoat, or rather, all that was left of my original surcoat. I assume they kept the lining, which had been used as a pattern. My new surcoat lacked the gold thread along the cross that distinguished Juan's, but that was replaced with a tracery of embroidery – red on the scarlet and cream on the white, some verses of the New Testament in gold, and a magnificent embroidered rendering of my arms on my left breast, just as Juan's had his on his left breast.

It was magnificent. But I didn't have time to stare, and I shrugged it on over my harness and Marc-Antonio laced the sides, but from the quality of his swearing I knew that he was impressed. I sent mine down to the grocer's to be pressed, and one of the daughters returned, breathless and delighted to have played her part.

On Christmas Eve, we all attended Mass, and Juan stood his vigil all night. We had all stood with him – Miles, Nerio, Fiore and I; as well as Sir Norman Lindsey, Jean-François, Bernard, Ser Brémond and Fra Peter and a dozen other Knights of the Order, too, so that we ushered in the dawn of our Saviour's birth by making him knight. The King of Cyprus gave him the accolade and Fra Peter struck him the blow, and I buckled on his spurs. And then we all squired him, lacing the new surcoat tight, and it fitted him over his new breast-and-back like an outer silken skin, and he stood in the light of a hundred candles and glowed.

But of course, between the vigil and the services and the Mass, I had missed Emile, who was gone back to her island.

Ser Juan di Majorca, as we now called him, glowed all the way through the Christmas festivities. The guilds of Venice feted us, we fought for the pleasure of the ladies and the crowd, and we drank wine for free in every tavern in the city, although it made Fra Peter and the knights of the order frown. I saw Emile three times in a week.

To say she seemed distracted would not fully do justice to her state. The third time I met her was at the Cypriote court, and when I had bowed deeply to her, she glanced around and drew me aside, making my breath stop in my chest as she seized my hand.

'I hear you are to leave this beautiful city for its rival, Genoa,' she said. Her attempt at dissimulation couldn't hide the darting of her eyes.

'Yes, countess,' I agreed. 'I regret it, but I have never had a chance to address you.' Even as I spoke, I felt as clumsy as a young knight. I wanted to tell her what I thought of her deliberate avoidance of me, of her indifference. To remind her of what she wrote in her letter, when I had been with Hawkwood. To thank her, because, having puzzled out the verses on my surcoat – gothic script can be nigh on impossible for a layman to read – I knew whose hand had embroidered them.

Her slight frown blew all that away like the rigging is stripped from a mast in a gale in the channel. 'I do not know how best to state my … reservations,' she said carefully. 'But I do not think it is merest happenstance that while I wait here for a ship to the Holy Land, my husband has gone with a French embassy to Genoa, or so I am told.' She paused. 'And my chamberlain believes he is coming here.'

She would offer no more, but I treasured the warmth of her hand and the slight pressure of her fingers. We were drinking in each other's eyes when the King of Cyprus cleared his throat. 'Madame la comtesse,' he said with an elegant bow, 'as you are the fairest flower to adorn my court this season, perhaps you would come and teach us the latest songs? I gather that Maître de Machaut claims your acquaintance?'

She looked up under her lashes and flashed her most engaging smile, and something in my heart froze.

But I was to go to Genoa.

Even as the worm of jealousy, the black serpent, began to gnaw at me, still I treasured the information she offered, as well. I passed it to Fra Peter and he made a face.

'See to it you protect the legate,' he said. 'Who is this Emile d'Herblay to you? I seem to remember the name.' He looked up from a list of warhorses and feeding costs. 'I hear her name linked with the king's.'

'I took her husband at Brignais,' I said. They say that no man can hide three things – love, sorrow, and sudden increase in fortune – but I'll add a fourth: no man can hide jealousy.

Fra Peter's eyes cut into mine. I knew he was not buying my evasion, that he had read me. He spat as if he'd tasted bile. 'Listen to me, lad. You be cautious with our legate's good name, here and in Genoa. The Venetians are all smiles, but they'd like to cancel the *Passagium* as much as the Genoese would. *Do you understand?*'

Again, I had a sort of false outraged innocence. 'I have done nothing of which I need to feel ashamed,' I said.

Fra Peter raised an eyebrow. And waved me away in dismissal.

We were both wearing our splendid surcoats, as was Fiore, now a knight of the empire, and Nerio, when we escorted the legate. As donats of knightly status, we had scarlet coats, our own arms emblazoned in the upper canton, otherwise marked by white crosses. We wore gold belts and gold spurs, and we looked superb! Red is the most martial colour.

We took boats to Mestre and then rode across the Venetian plain to Padua, where we were well enough received, although there was still plague in spots, poor souls. From Padua we rode to Vicenza, and from Vicenza to Verona and thence via Brescia to Milan.

I was very conscious of our danger and of our dignity. The legate cared little for outward show, which was very holy of him, to be sure, but his very lack of show made him a target where he needn't have been one. In some ways, the outward display of the richest churchmen was a protection from thieves and brigands. It could awe the populace in a town, too.

Our legate in his brown Carmelite robe was far from an awesome figure. Further, other churchmen resented him. He had almost absolute powers in Italy; in any town in which he stopped, he had the power to take money from crusading funds, even to dictate the manner of collection of those funds. He could use revenues brought in by pilgrimage and donation – in cathedrals, for example. These were, in fact, funds that were intended for the crusades, going back two hundred years, but the bishops of these places looked on those revenues as their own money, and their resentment was dangerous.

I think that perhaps they would have found Father Pierre easier to deal with had he been one of them, had he travelled with pomp, and a hundred men-at-arms. Instead, he wore an old brown cloak over his robes and had an escort of ten. In Brescia, we had an incident that was only averted by Nerio's connections. In Milan, we owed our protection to Nicolas Sabraham, who appeared at dinner in the Episcopal residence and ordered me to change our lodgings, which I did, despite the cursing of all of our pages and squires. We carried every trunk halfway across the city, and moved the animals.

Sabraham was not mistaken. That night there was an attack on our former beds. A dozen men, masked and hooded and carrying crossbows, killed two Episcopal men-at-arms and stormed our rooms – and found them empty.

That was my introduction to Milan. We hadn't been invited to the palace, yet. If Vicenza and Verona had tyrants, the Visconti of Milan were the greatest tyrants of all. We'd made war on Bernabo Visconti just two years before, and we were aware – at least, Sabraham and I were aware – that he was allied to the King of France, he was the most powerful man in northern Italy, and he was the inveterate foe of the Pope.

I see you smile; yes, because there were not just two sides in Italy, or anywhere else. The Pope was the ally of the King of France, and so were the Visconti. But the Visconti and the Pope were enemies, and this fracture went deep – the Green Count of Savoy was friend to both the Pope and the Visconti – and the King of France. A remarkable balancing act. States like Florence tried to balance the Pope and the Visconti and cared nothing for the King of France.

Our legate had an audience with the tyrant at the palace. I went with him, and stood at his shoulder while Bernabo, Lord of Milan, openly fondled a magnificent courtesan and promised thirty knights for the crusade. He meant to insult Father Pierre, but failed. On the way out of the palace, one of the more sinister buildings I've ever known, and perhaps I'll describe it more fully in due time, the legate smiled his rare impish smile at me.

'I am not here as a man, but as the legate of crusade,' he said with a twinkle in his eye. 'Thirty knights? I may be sorry for his sin, but I needn't bridle at it.'

Milan was full of men-at-arms, almost an armed camp, and I suspected, as did Sabraham, that our attackers had been Bernabo's men. I wondered if he would send us the very men he'd asked to assassinate the legate, but Sabraham laughed.

'You don't understand Italy as well as you think, my young apprentice,' he said.

I rather liked that he called me his apprentice. 'Why?' I asked.

Sabraham laughed his thin-lipped, grim laugh. 'It would humiliate the Visconti if the legate had been killed in Milan, in the centre of Visconti power.' He looked at me and winked. 'Visconti has just discovered that his arrangements are penetrated and one of his men has sold himself to France. He's in a rage – against the French.'

I watched the houses like a hawk – and then it hit me. 'You!'

Sabraham smiled. 'Never,' he said.

I didn't breathe until we were in the countryside, riding west.

Sabraham joined us with a pair of soldiers and it is difficult to describe them. They were not, strictly speaking, archers, although in England I think they might have been. They were both very professional, their kit clean and neat and well-cared for, weapons well-oiled. They rode good horses and had no badges. We called them George and Maurice. They accepted these names with a good nature.

I had been around. I was getting an idea what Sabraham did, and I was delighted to have him with us. At an inn west of Milan, with half my friends on watch and all the precautions I could manage, I told Sabraham of my fears – Robert of Geneva, the Bourc, d'Herblay, the papacy, and the legate.

He nodded and agreed. Finally he rubbed his beard. 'You have done well to puzzle this for yourself,' he said – warm praise from a master. But his next words chilled me.

'The legate shouldn't be here,' he said. 'The Bishop of Geneva means him humiliated or dead.' He gave me a rueful smile. 'The safest place for him is on crusade.'

'Does the legate know what you did?' I asked, looking around. 'In Milan?'

Sabraham frowned. 'I have no idea what you are talking about,' he said. 'And neither does the legate.'

The next morning, over watered wine and stale bread, I put some of this to the legate, who smiled his saintly smile.

'You are going to tell me that God will provide,' I said.

Father Pierre nodded.

My faith, much abused, sinned against, and manipulated, was as strong as it had ever been. Despite which, I suspected that God's will would function best – as it did on crusade – if we were worthy, took precautions, and avoided ambush.

Two days west of Milan, I sat in a chilly arbour – no grapes left – and read an old itinerary that the inn kept, a list of destinations and distances. I called Sabraham who had already scouted the road with his two professionals. I wasn't sure which of us was in command: he was without a doubt the more experienced, but I was a knight. He was retiring, almost mild. He never stayed to drink wine in the evenings, and he was all but invisible in a group.

I showed him the itinerary. 'What if we approached Genoa from the south?' I asked. 'Two days extra travel ...'

Sabraham nodded, really pleased. 'This is well considered. What a valuable little book.'

Sister Marie overheard us. She nodded to Sabraham and stood with a false demure hesitation. 'I could copy it,' she said, riffling the scroll. 'Two hours.'

The little scroll covered Northern Italy as far south as Florence. It looked to me like a mighty resource, and Sabraham agreed. Sister Marie sat and copied. To speed us on the road, Sabraham and I both joined her, and before we were done, Ser Nerio sat down and stained his hands with ink. We paid the innkeeper to make that copy and I have it yet. Listen, knowing the fastest way from one place to another is all very well, but for a soldier – or a spy – it is useful to know all the other ways, too. And whenever I learn one, I add it to the scroll.

Thanks to that little book, we went south, skirted the marches of Florentine territory, and arrived on the coast. The road wasn't bad and the people were delighted; they had pilgrims in summer, but winter was a hard time. Twice we heard of brigands, but they were elsewhere or thought better of an armed party.

At the southern extent of the Ligurian coast, we caught a small trading ship, a Pisan, and he dropped us on a wharf in Genoa, unannounced and safe.

Genoa is a very different city from Venice. Perhaps the principle difference is in the people. In Venice, the small trades share the prosperity of the city. Our grocers were prosperous people; the guildsmen were rich, by English standards, and not just the Masters; the men who owned ropewalks were rich, and so were the men who owned boatyards.

In Genoa, only the rich are rich. A handful of men own everything, just thirty or forty families. The caste of workers derives no benefit whatsoever from the riches of Genoa's overseas empire. Let me give you the simplest example. On a Venetian merchant ship, all sailors, even the oarsmen, are allowed a space to ship their own cargoes, even if that space is only a single small chest as long as your arm and as wide as the span of a man's hand. But fill that chest with spice at Alexandria, the richest city in the world, and sail it home to Venice or to England or Flanders, and an oarsman might make ten years wages in an afternoon.

Genoese oarsmen are not allowed anything. Their masters feel that to allow them to trade might cost the owners some profit. The guilds derive little profit from the sea trade, because their wages and their products have set values: values set by the men who rule the city. They call themselves a republic, but they have fewer men involved in government than the Savoyards, who call themselves a feudal state.

I think my dislike – nay, hatred – of Genoa began on the docks. *Par dieu*, docks are heartless places. The same vices rule every set in the world, from Southwark in London to the stews in Constantinople: prostitution of girls and boys too young to even know what their trade is about, drunkenness and dangerous drugs that rob a man of his senses, and thieves to take the rest; sheer greed, so that workers are underpaid and merchants are fat. Lust, gluttony, greed, pride –dock-yards are, in most cities, nastier places than battlefields, and that's saying something.

Venice's docks had Moslem slaves and tired stevedores. But the stevedores were mostly citizens and the slaves – well, they ate.

The Genoese docks were peopled by men and women at the end of despair. It was the middle of winter, and there were beggars in women's cast-off shifts and no shoes, backs hunched to carry bundles of rags. They looked as bad as the poorest French peasants, or refugees from the height of our war in France, when our armies burned a hundred hamlets a day and drove the villeins to the fields and forests.

Father Pierre stopped on the quay, in a cold wind and light rain that cut through my harness and my arming clothes and froze the marrow in my bones. He began by blessing the poor, and to my great shame, I shifted from one foot to another, worried about my warhorse and wishing he would move on, my eyes scanning the crowd.

I needn't have feared the poor and the desperate. They were not my foes or his.

The Pisan captain got our horses unloaded with professional competence, and I paid him with the legate's money, having almost none of my own. He spat. Pisans hate Genoa, for good reason, and we had been lucky with him. 'I may have to jump in the ocean to get clean,' he said, when my Jacques was out of the cradle of the winch. 'You would do well not to linger here.'

Indeed, as soon as he had our florins in his purse and a small cargo of hides he picked up on the foreshore, he was away, his sons poling his small ship off the quay. I'd only known him two days, and I felt as you do when you have a sortie outside the walls in a siege and you see them lock the gate behind you.

Father Pierre was saying Mass for the beggars on the docks.

I gathered my knights and ordered them out into the crowd. In full harness, with a longsword, every knight was worth any ten attackers. Marc-Antonio and Nerio's squire Davide held the horses. Sabraham nodded to me and vanished with his two henchmen, and I was, if anything, more comfortable for knowing that I didn't know where he was.

The legate's religious retinue helped him with Mass. They were steady, reliable men. Father Antonio was another Carmelite from Naples; Father Hector was an Scottish Isleman, and there were nigh on a dozen others, mostly servants, all of whom had religious offices as deacons and sextons and the like. Sister Marie had by that time acquired an assistant secretary, a young Frenchman from the University of Paris named Adhemar. He never spoke; his eyes were always downcast, and I scarcely noticed him, but he was clearly well born and he wrote beautifully.

At any rate, we got through Mass. I dare say it was beautiful, to the clerics, but to me it was a nightmare, as I was all too aware by then that the legate's life was threatened, and there he was surrounded by riff-raff. Truly, I tried to see them as men and women. I have heard the sermons, that there is Christ in every man – but I looked into the open sores, the missing teeth, the black rot, and the hard, closed faces, the malignant cunning that comes of a life lived at the edge of death, the false humility of the professional beggar and I *knew* Christ was there, because Father Pierre had told me many times. But I *saw* a thousand criminals, any one of who could be bought for a copper, close enough to put a dagger in my lord.

No one did, however.

We did create a bread riot. The podestà turned out his army of thugs and drove the poor back under the piers and into the chicken coops and barns and sewers where they lived. I met him in person; I had mounted my friends and our squires and we made a living wall of armour and horseflesh that covered the legate and his people as they served Mass to the last stragglers of the poor.

'Who the devil are you?' he swore.

I pointed to the man in a brown habit, apparently impervious to the vicious wind. 'This is the papal legate for the Crusade. He has come to negotiate with your lords.'

The podestà's horse was nervous. It was the smell of blood that was worrying the animal: the podestà's men-at-arms had killed a dozen of the beggars. Just behind the podestà, a small woman was pounded to the ground by a man in armour with a steel mace, the sort I grew accustomed to seeing in the hands of Turks, later.

She was fifty, or even older, with no teeth and wisps of white hair and he caved in her skull with a whoop.

'This thing is fucking perfect!' he shouted, and tossed his bloody mace in the air.

Some of the other men-at-arms had the good grace to look away.

Some laughed.

At my back, Marc-Antonio had the legate mounted.

'I'd thank you for an escort through the streets,' I said to the podestà. In powerful Italian cities, the officer who commands the garrison is usually a foreigner. That way, he can't get mixed up in the endless internal quarrels of house against house that divide the Italians as much as money unites them. Looking at this man's hat, his gleaming harness and his sword, I guessed he was Milanese.

He frowned. 'Papal legate? Never heard of him, but if he makes another riot ...'

One of Sabraham's men appeared by my left boot, on foot. He tugged at my stirrup to get my attention. When I looked at him, he gave me the Order's sign for a direction and I nodded.

'Your men cannot be armed in the city,' the podestà said.

I bowed. I made no answer, but hoped that my bow would cover the exigencies of the situation.

Even as I spoke to the podestà, two more beggars tried to run to safety behind us, risking our warhorse's legs to get away from the podestà's men. Both were men – one a leper, with no lips and no nose, and the other a poor deformed mite, a very small man or even a boy with something awry with his face.

The leper got away – no one likes to catch a leper – but the mite was trapped by the man with the bloody mace. He caught the little man in the corner where two warehouses came together in a jumble of garbage and old roofing, and he grinned.

'Watch this, messieurs!' he shouted with glee, and the mace rose—

Fiore stripped it out of his hand. His horse pranced out of our line, he flowed through the other mounted man and dumped him in the gutter and backed his horse to our line before the podestà's men, still milling about like a stag hunt at the kill, could react.

The podestà's face grew red-purple. He pointed at Fiore. 'Arrest that—'

I put a hand on his reins. 'It is bad manners to attack people during Mass, my lord. You have just attacked these poor people while the Patriarch of Constantinople, the Ambassador of the King of Jerusalem, was saying *Mass*.' While in my head I applauded Fiore's action, I would have traded the life of a beggar for a little peace.

The podestà opened his mouth. Some men despise anything that brooks their authority and this was one such. He didn't hate me as a Milanese or as the podestà – he just hated me for not cringing.

'We are knight-volunteers of the Order of St John, if you are too *fucking* ignorant of the habit of the Order to know.' I'd had it with trying to be polite. 'Unless you want to see your whole city under interdict, kindly clear the way.'

The podestà glared at me, but short of ordering his men to attack mine, there wasn't much he could do.

The man-at-arms in the mud got to his feet cursing. He stomped to his horse and called to Fiore, 'I'll know you again, fuckhead!'

Nerio laughed. 'And we will know you by the smell.' His contempt was beautiful. It hurt the podestà's thugs more than our blows might have.

And I was sure that we could take them. Just at that moment, I would cheerfully have made the streets of Genoa run with their blood.

Sometimes I think I am the wrong man to command an escort for a living saint.

On the other hand, we got to our inn alive.

I had nothing to do with the negotiations, which is probably for the best. I had developed an instant contempt for Genoa and I've never changed my mind.

Everywhere in Genoa, there are slaves. In Venice there are a few, mostly Moslems. In Genoa, there are thousands. They displace the working poor – anyone of any power has slaves, not servants. Men have slave mistresses and when the slave woman bears children to the master, they are also slaves. Our innkeeper told his wife that every time he fucked their servants, he was making them money.

Need I go on? Slavery rotted their families, undermined their morals, and made them petty tyrants. To say nothing of the sins it engendered in the slaves themselves. I have seen slavery in many places – God knows that Moslems themselves will enslave anything that moves – but a Christian slave in Egypt has every possibility of freeing himself by work and is protected by laws even as a slave.

Bah! I've been told that it is worse elsewhere, and that my hatred of the Genoese is as foolish as any other hate. Perhaps. But I hate them the way most Englishmen hate the French – they are a nation of slavers and tyrants, with the morals of merchants and the courage of assassins. False, treacherous, cunning without wisdom, vulgar in display, ignorant, utterly without honour!

You can see why it was best I had nothing to do with negotiations.

The legate met with their senators for eight days. During those eight days, we guarded our inn and fought the podestà's men.

They never stopped coming at us. Their honour, or whatever honour they felt they had after careers attacking the weak, had been threatened, and every man-at-arms on the city payroll made it his business to gather near our inn and make comments. By the fifth day we were threatened with outright attack.

The innkeeper wept and wrung his hands and said they'd burn the inn. I distrusted him utterly, and while I was off escorting Father

Pierre, Sabraham knocked him on the head and locked him in the basement.

After that, we were under siege. The difficult part was getting the legate through the streets to the palace each day. Sabraham and his men scouted routes every night, after dark, and I began to go out with the man; he clearly knew things I didn't, and I was eager to learn.

I learned a great deal about roofs, and how to climb them; about ambush sites in a city, and about stealth.

And about ruthlessness.

I think it was the fifth night; we were prowling near the market, looking for a safer route to get the legate to the northern part of the city. I climbed across a board that had been left over an alley by one of Sabraham's men, got my feet under me – heights are not my best thing – to find one of Sabraham's soldiers, Maurice, cutting a man's throat. The man died hard – terrified, pissing himself, with a look of horrified unbelief on his face.

'Thief?' I asked.

Sabraham spread his hands. The motion said more clearly than words that Sabraham didn't care a damn who the man was. 'We cannot be observed,' he said.

Later, as we went up the corbels of a church with a rope, Sabraham said 'One of the podestà's men.'

On the sixth day, we got the legate through the streets by misdirection, using Sister Marie's apprentice as our bait. The French monk was hit with a rock and brought back unconscious. I'd been with him, as part of the misdirection, and my beautiful surcoat was smeared in excrement.

By mid-afternoon, they were all around our inn, and threatening to burn it. The arsonists were the podestà's men, of course – responsible for keeping order.

We were all in full harness. Juan was with the legate, as was his new squire, a Catalan boy of good family, who had relatives in Athens. Nerio had found him for Juan, but that's another story.

Sabraham was out with his killers, and I had Nerio and Fiore and Marc-Antonio and Alessandro and a dozen unarmed clerics to protect.

We'd shuttered the windows. The yard was defensible, but we needed a garrison twice the numbers we had.

'What can we do?' Marc-Antonio asked. He was in his breast and back, formerly my armour, now his. He'd lost so much weight that he could fit my old harness. I was in my new stuff.

Nerio was, for once, at a loss and we could hear them clamouring outside.

'They burn the inn, and then what?' Fiore said.

'Then there's no one to defend the legate. They *invite* him to stay at the palace. He sickens and dies.' I shrugged. That was Sabraham's scenario.

Nerio's eyes met mine.

'Anyone you can buy?' I asked.

He smiled. 'I wish. This is Genoa. They hate Florence.'

'And they hate the Church,' I added. 'At least, the Guelfs do, and they seem to be in power right now.'

A window broke.

I had a moment of clarity. I asked myself how John Hawkwood would deal with the situation, and the whole thing revealed itself to me. It unrolled like a carpet.

It may have been the first pickaxe of the first pioneer undermining my devotion to the order, but at the time—

'I have it. Are you with me, gentlemen? It won't be nice.' I looked around. 'It is a routier's solution.'

Fiore grinned.

Ser Nerio laughed aloud. 'Good,' he said. 'I've about had it with doing the right thing.'

I went out the main gate of the inn with one of the matron's caps tied to a roasting spit. Fiore was at my shoulder, looking humble, and Sister Marie followed us, demure and harmless.

We were mocked, and yet, in the process of telling us that we were sons of whores and mere children and various forms of sexual deviants, our tormentors emerged from their cover. I knew the man across the street immediately, and so did Fiore – the whoreson Fiore had dropped in the muck.

I leaned out. 'Send someone to talk!' I roared.

Whoreson laughed. 'Come out and surrender.'

I shook my head. 'I have priests and nuns here. Tell us what you want.'

Whoreson swaggered towards me, master of the situation, and

slapped his gauntleted hand against his cuisse. 'What I want is that catamite right there!' He stepped to the right to get a better view of Fiore, ignoring Sister Marie.

She tripped him, Fiore slammed a fist into his head, and we had him. But I wanted more, and I took a long stride into the confused rabble, kicked a man in the knee, got a hand under his aventail and dragged him back.

Fiore put Whoreson on the ground with a knife-tip at his temple.

Now the little square in front of the inn gate was as silent as a tomb. I pushed my prisoner through the gate and Nerio slammed him into the gatepost and then dropped him.

'Go away,' I shouted. 'Or come at us, and see what happens.'

Naturally, I said nothing of all this to Father Pierre, but there was no hiding the two men bound to chairs in the common room.

He raised an eyebrow. 'Let them go. I have what I came for. I would like to leave as soon as possible.'

I pushed them out the gate with good humour. They had heard nothing of our planning, and we were free to go. Sabraham and I had made a plan – not an elaborate plan, but one that would have appealed to every routier I knew – in the kitchen.

Back with the legate, I said, 'No dinner at the guildhall? No solemn Mass to mark the occasion?'

Father Pierre looked away. He was shattered; I could see his eyes full of tears. I had missed the signs, and I was frightened. You have to understand, he was a pillar, a tower. I don't think I had ever seen him so used up, and so unhappy.

'I have paid a high price for the crusade,' he said. 'These men …' His eyes met mine. He was struggling against saying what he felt. Father Pierre's lapses of hot-blooded humanity were both a relief to us – and a terror. But he knelt down on the inn floor and prayed for guidance, and then he rose. 'Let us leave this place,' he said.

I found Nicolas Sabraham looking at me from the kitchen door.

We smiled at each other.

Our smug self-assurance lasted as long as it took to draw a breath, and then we heard the unmistakable sound of breaking glass.

Marc-Antonio ran for the stairs, but he was too late.

The innkeeper had escaped.

I was the third man into his room, and I instantly realised two things – that his room was over the kitchen, and that someone had unlocked his shutter. There was no other way he could have got out the window.

He'd jumped on to the stable roof and then was gone.

'I think he knows what we plan,' I said to Sabraham.

He frowned. 'If we're quick—'

'True as the cross,' I said.

It took long minutes to get the horses saddled. Sabraham and his men went out the back of the tavern. We'd lost our hostages and our plan was betrayed – someone had let the innkeeper go. Who?

Before the legate's horse was out in the yard, I could see men in harness moving in the alleys.

But I had two cards to play, as well. No, to be fair, Sabraham had the cards.

In Genoa, every free man has a crossbow. It is their favourite weapon; silent, mechanical, good at sea or on land. Every free man from Monaco to Liguria has one, and my greatest fear was a storm of bolts. It was evening in winter, already full dark. That had to cut the odds a little.

And the podestà's men were overawed. They gave us space, and they were not well-organised. I'm going to guess that their Milanese master didn't trust his lieutenants, so, as he could not appear himself, they were rudderless.

The quarter hour struck in the neighbourhood church. We had ten mules with all the legate's goods, mostly desks and a portable altar and other necessaries.

We kept the gate closed.

Father Pierre looked at me. His face was pale and he was deeply unhappy.

'I must ask you what you have been driven to do,' he said.

As if in answer, the first part of Sabraham's plan came to fruition. Down on the docks, a warehouse burst into flame.

Bah. Arson has an ugly name, but war without fire is like sausage without mustard, eh?

The same free citizens who own all the crossbows are the same men who fight the fires – and own the cloth. They left us, if they'd ever been watching us, and ran to fight the fire on their waterfront.

We opened the gate to the inn and started through the streets.

The podestà's men didn't fight the fires. They were still out there, and the innkeeper had spoiled our surprise for them. We'd planned to start a nice little riot between the local Guelfs and Ghibbelines, but the podestà got there first, or so a panting Sabraham reported to me as we cut north.

It was Verona all over again, except that I had my doubts that we'd be allowed out the gate.

Two streets north of the cathedral, we had our first fight. A mounted fight in the dark is no joy at all – the noise of the steel-shod hooves on the cobbles is so loud that you cannot hear commands, or screams, and the sparks from the horseshoes and the swords give the whole thing a hellish feeling. We were hampered by a long tale of mules and non-combatants. Our opponents were not hampered by the least notion of honour, as they demonstrated by killing Father Hector at the first encounter – a priest, and he unarmed.

The second attack occurred a few streets from the northern gate. Of course, by then, my legate and most of his people were gone. Fiore took them to the left suddenly, so that the legate would not know that we'd divided our efforts in the darkness. I was willing to lose a few priests and deacons, to be sure.

I had a few second's warning as my opponent's horse caught a lantern's light and I felt the vibration as he charged.

I killed his horse.

It's not done in polite circles, and I'm sure it is the last thing the bastard expected from a knight of the order, but I was down to the training that lets a man survive the hell of France. I put the Emperor's sword through the horse's head and down he went. The rider behind him tangled with the first man's dying mount, and I was backing. I gave them a moment, and then I attacked. I think I killed them both – I certainly left some marks. This in an alley so narrow I couldn't turn Jacques. But a good horse is the best weapon; I backed all the way to the mouth of the alley even as crossbow bolts began to rattle against the stone walls.

The whole time I had been fighting, Ser Nerio had taken the rest of our feint, our pretend convoy, north to the wall. I saw motion in the right direction – my visor was down, and when your visor is down at night, you almost might as well close your eyes.

But I'd bought time.

I had bought time, but when I turned Jacques, I'd lost my bearings. One scout, even with someone as professional as Sabraham, is not enough to ensure real knowledge. I got the visor open – my new helmet had a wonderful visor.

Nothing. Except that my foes in the alley were coming, and a crossbow bolt – thanks to God, some of its force spent against the alley wall – slammed into my shoulder and ripped the pauldron away.

There were armoured men on horse coming from behind me.

Time to go I said to myself. I picked a direction and put Jacques at it.

It must have been the wrong direction. Or rather, not the direction that Nerio and Marc-Antonio and the Italian Carmelite had taken, but I was too desperate to care over much. I rode as fast as the alleys and streets would allow. Once I burst through a crowd of footmen – for all I know they were innocents just out of vespers, but I was through them and into the mouth of another street.

It was only when I emerged into the central square that I realised where I was, and how desperate my cause had become. I was almost a mile from our gate and I had a good idea what capture would mean.

A dozen of the podestà's men-at-arms burst from another street, fifty paces away. They weren't chasing me, unless they could see in the dark like cats.

Off to my left, by the cathedral, I heard a war cry.

The podestà's men reined in.

I had no idea what was going on, but I sat on my horse, letting poor Jacques draw a breath while I did the same. Under my very eyes, two groups of footmen rushed each other with clubs and swords. In less time than it takes to tell it, a man was down, another lost his hand, and the first group broke and ran for the cathedral, hotly pursued.

I had my bearings. I turned my horse, picked the archway that looked right in the shadows, and trotted poor Jacques up a narrow street that turned twice before running almost straight uphill. We went up and up, the houses growing narrower and more crowded, and twice I had a glimpse of the gate towers in the moonlight. I stopped in front of a fountain – really, no more than a spring in the naked rock – and let Jacques drink, but not for long. I couldn't let him get a cramp in the middle of this.

I heard shouts, muffled by my helmet liner. I backed Jacques. It may sound foolish, but you can hide a warhorse and a knight around a corner, at least in the dark. Two men fled past me, on horseback. They could have been the Pope and Father Pierre for all I saw of them, and then they were gone, their hoof beats ringing like the sound of hammers on anvils.

I went the other way, up the hill and around one last corner–

There was an open square in front of the gate, no wider than a bowling green. Men were fighting.

None of them were mine.

Far below me in the dockyards was a red glow where the fire still burned.

It illuminated Genoa with the sort of flickering red that monks and nuns put into manuscript pictures of Hell, and made the armour of the men fighting in the little square seem as if made of liquid metal.

I consoled myself that in the dark they were all Genoese, and put Jacques at the gate. It was open – I could see the lower tips of the portcullis drawn up above us. Jacque's hooves slammed into soft flesh and hard armour and we were through the square and out the gate, and I was uninjured.

I sat in the darkness and breathed, and so did Jacques.

I must have lost an hour on my party, but it was obvious they'd made it out the gate. There were a dozen little signs – the most obvious was a pack donkey I found half a league on in the moonlight, strayed from the convoy and placidly standing in the shadow under a palm tree that grew in a village square.

But riding into the mountains above Genoa in the darkness proved to be as daunting as carving my way out of the town. I was lost twice, and the donkey, which I was leading, was no help, braying in the darkness like a trumpet and standing stubbornly against a wall and refusing to budge.

In the end, I found myself back in the same town square where I'd found the donkey – showing I have no more sense than an ass – and I dismounted to give Jacques a rest. I got some water from the town's spring, hung my helmet from my saddle bow, and sat down.

I awakened to find myself looking at a sword held at my eyes. Beyond the sword's point was the Count d'Herblay.

*

I'll pass over the beating. They took my armour and the Emperor's sword and Jacques. They stripped me naked, and then they beat me.

Let's just say that I had several humiliating hours.

On the other hand, d'Herblay wasn't the Bourc. He ordered me beaten and went elsewhere. The men who beat me never really worked themselves up and, thanks be to the good God, they were hard men, but not evil. None of them particularly enjoyed the work.

They were thorough enough, though. I had broken ribs, broken fingers, and a broken nose quickly enough.

Eh bien. I won't mention it again.

By mid-afternoon, the pain had become a sort of constant haze; time had lost its meaning.

At some point, d'Herblay came back out of wherever he was. They brought him a seat – my eyes were swollen almost shut.

'Christ, you are ugly. If only Emile could see you now,' he said. He laughed, nervously.

In fact, he wasn't really tough enough to destroy me, even to accept the consequence of his own orders. He fidgeted.

And talked.

'Really much more satisfying,' he began, smiling, 'catching you, instead of that pestilential priest. I'm not even sure these brigands I've hired would kill a priest.' He nodded. 'Tell me, where is my wife?'

I'd lost an eye tooth – this one – and I'd bitten my tongue because, despite my youth, I'm not as good at being beaten as I ought to have been. And my lips were so swollen I couldn't speak well.

I didn't even try to say anything, and to be fair, I suspect I just lay huddled, whimpering.

'I gather that she is now spreading her favours around the court of King Peter. Perhaps she's warming the king's bed.' He shrugged. 'I suppose there's some consolation in knowing that one's wife is not just unfaithful, but a whore. I suppose she suffers from some sickness.' He leaned over me. 'I married her for her lands. I knew she was soiled goods, so I suppose I got what I deserved.' He shrugged. 'How'd your people slip past my ambush, Gold?'

I suspect I whimpered. Let's just take it as read throughout this reminiscence, eh?

'As I say, perhaps for the best. But some people want your legate dead.' He leaned over. 'I really only want you dead, Gold. Although it brings me a certain joy to see you like this.' His riding whip flashed. He struck my head, and I covered up, and his next blow went between my legs.

His heart wasn't in it. He could have exploded my testicles. He could have torn the nose from my face with his whip. He didn't.

This is the part that I remember. He didn't laugh, or groan. He sighed. As if bored, or from simple revulsion.

I'd like to say I spat in his face.

I did not.

He spoke. I couldn't see, but I could hear.

'Just take him somewhere and cut his throat. Kill the horse and bury all his kit.' I could hear him shift his weight.

I hated that they would kill Jacques.

'Don't be a fool – any of you. The sword looks good, but every knight in Italy will know whose it is, the same with the horse and any part of the harness. Off a cliff is best.' I heard him walk away, and then I heard him mount his horse. And I heard every hoof beat as the horse walked right over me.

'Goodbye, Cook. I find that I get very little in the way of pleasure from this, but I expect the knowledge that you are dead will cheer me up immensely.' He cleared his throat. 'By now, your legate will be as dead as you will shortly be. I'll go and join my wife. Goodbye. Send my regards to hell.'

To hell.

I was unshriven.

I had most certainly sinned.

The brigands – let's be fair, they were men just like me – tied my hands and feet to a spear and strung me, naked, between two horses. It was cold, although that was so little a part of my troubles that I don't think I noticed until the swaying had stopped. My parts felt as if they had exploded and I couldn't breathe.

Gradually, though, I grew cold.

Who knew that getting beaten keeps you warm?

A freezing rain began to fall and I wondered if a peasant would rescue me – some brave, resourceful lad who hoped to be a knight.

They carried me to the edge of a precipice. Far below, I could see Genoa sparkle beyond a rain shower. It was a long way down.

The men who had beaten me had no contrition in them. No one offered me water, even with vinegar in it; no one eased the ties on my hands.

They dumped me in the road.

And then one said 'I'll take the horse.'

I cannot remember when hope began. But after they bickered about the horse, and the barrack-room lawyer – there's always one – argued that keeping the horse would see them all hanged, the first voice roared out, 'Shut the fuck up!' and they all fell silent.

The man must have been bigger. He had a little authority, not much, but enough. 'Listen,' he said. 'Listen and keep your fucking gobs shut. This piece of shit is someone famous. I'm taking this horse, which is worth more than all the rest of you combined, and I'm walking away. I don't want to fucking lay eyes on you leprous lads ever again, understand me?'

'We'll all be caught!' Barrack-room lawyer piped up.

'No, we won't. That's a tale for children. It's fucking Italy; we can do whatever we want. I found this horse grazing by the roadside. Eh?' I heard a rustle, and then the sound of Jacques' heavy hooves.

'Then I'm keeping the Goddamned sword,' said the barrack-room lawyer. 'Mister high and mighty can give himself the shits for all I care.'

'Why do you get it, then?' said another voice, a Gascon. When there's trouble, there's always a Gascon.

'Perhaps because I have it in my hand, fuckwit?' said the barrack-room lawyer.

Something wet hit the road.

Men laughed.

Barrack-room lawyers are seldom popular. I didn't need my swollen-shut eyes to see what had happened.

'I'll just take this,' said the Gascon. 'I can get a good price for it in Lombardy, or Aquila.' He had an odd laugh, like a dog's bark, and his Gascon-French was strangely accented. Catalan, I might have thought, if I'd had a thought in my head.

That started it, as the removal of Jacques had not. They tore into my kit – my rosary, my surcoat, and my harness.

In a way, it was like death. Everything that made me a knight was taken: my golden plaque belt, my beautiful spurs. It took the routiers only as long as it takes a hungry horse to eat everything in a nosebag, and they'd stripped my pile. One old man only got my arming clothes.

The Gascon's *servant* got Charny's dagger.

And then it was all gone, and men were riding off into the gathering darkness like stray cats taking scraps of food.

There were dead men on the road, too. Three of them.

And one hard bastard kneeling at my side with a dagger. 'Who'd have thought you'd outlive Sweet Willy? Eh, laddie?'

He spoke English.

'I'm English,' I said. I suspect it sounded like 'Mmm gagliff.'

I felt his dagger touch my throat. 'George and England!' I assayed. Which may have been a mumbled 'org n' gagle'.

So he cut my throat, and I died.

And blessed Saint George came in all his glory and raised me to heaven.

Bless you, friends, it was not quite like that.

In fact, he knelt for a long time. Long enough for my hope to ebb and flow a dozen times. I mumbled things, and he listened or didn't. I couldn't see.

'Somewhere, you must be worth a *fuck* of a lot of money,' he said quietly.

I nodded.

'In your place, I'd say the same,' he agreed. 'Still, that was a nice harness. And a horse to match.'

He slung me over his horse. Thanks be to God, I passed out.

Greed. There is something wonderful in God's will, that I was saved by the greed of a dozen hard men. Mind you, in their place, I suspect I'd have done the same.

I never learned my captor's name. And I never got to thank him, because three days later, he sprouted a crossbow bolt in the chest and fell off his horse, stone dead, without another word. I saw that, but then there passed a period of waiting, and then something spooked the rouncey over which I was thrown, and I was gone again.

When I came too, the man leaning over me was Sabraham.

Nerio Acciaioli got the legate back to Venice. He had the money and the authority, and he gave orders and was obeyed. He ran south, almost to Florence, and hired fifty English men-at-arms from the break-up of the White Company – Sir John had been badly defeated in the south. But the Englishmen got the legate home to Venice alive. Juan rode with him so that one of them was awake at all times.

Fiore and Sabraham doubled back to find me. I can't bless them enough. I had missed the road – in fact, as best any of us can make it, I left Genoa by the wrong gate, and my finding the pack animal was a miracle of bad navigation. But the road I chose was the one that the innkeeper had thought we meant. Later I learned why. I'd ruin the story by telling you now.

Sabraham and his henchmen killed my captors, of whom there were two. I never saw the other, but that doesn't mean anything. My left eye has never been quite right since then but my right recovered well enough. I'm told it gives me a good stare, eh?

Sabraham splinted my broken bones. He was ruthless – I've said that before – but he had the sense and the guts to re-break my arm and set it straight, otherwise I'd still have a ruined left arm. Christ, it makes me shake to think of it.

They wrapped my hands. Most of my fingers were broken and so swollen they were like puffballs, those giant mushrooms. They got a tinsmith to make little channels to hold my fingers and Fiore reset my nose with a break and a twist.

It was a little like being tortured again.

Every time I surfaced to consciousness, it was to realise that d'Herblay would get to Emile ahead of me. Was already there. Emile must be dead ...

I find I have spoken too much of pain, and you gentlemen are appalled.

Very well.

Sabraham got me across the Lombardy plain. He didn't do it in one go, but in little sprints and legs that I remember as days of pain and nights of cold ache. We went as pilgrims and sometimes I was a plague victim. Usually I was unconscious when we were on the road.

Bless Nicolas Sabraham. He took me all the way to Venice where Father Pierre sent me to the monks. And then I had doctors and drugs, opium, good wine, and broth. Warmth, and no movement, and a warm bed, deep and white, or so I remember it.

I really remember very little.

And one day there was the sun, and I was awake, looking out over the lagoon, and it was beautiful. And the beauty made me cry.

And crying hurt my nose, if you must know.

And Emile said, 'Oh, William!' or something equally lovely.

I looked at her. I considered whether I should tell her ...

Bah! When I look at Emile, I do not think well. 'Your husband ... I thought you were dead,' I managed. Probably the first words I had said in months. I croaked them.

She ran a finger down my hip. I suspect because the doctors had told her it was the only place that didn't hurt.

'Hush,' she said.

Days of Emile, and I was unable to speak. She would sing, or play with her children. Her two girls came with her, and she led one of them about – he was learning to toddle. She had wet nurses for both, and they would come and go, and after a while I decided that I was on the same island as she.

Little by little, I recovered my head. It was scattered at first, and seeing Emile was somehow a blow. Perhaps I lost my wits. Perhaps in all the blows I received, something in my head was broken.

But she was there.

And at some point, I can't remember when, she brought the King of Jerusalem. He spoke about the crusade. I can't remember anything he said. Instead, I thought of what d'Herblay had said about Emile ...

It was dark, inside my head.

Despite the darkness, I am not utterly a fool. D'Herblay had once told me that his wife had died in childbirth when she had not. He was, perhaps, too weak to torture a man physically, but he was the sort of bastard who enjoyed planting the needle inside, the torment of doubt.

She was there by my bed every day.

Why did I doubt her?

When I had been a month in that bed, I was able to walk. And move my arms. My hands hurt all the time. And everything was stiff – so stiff that I thought at one point I'd never be able to swing my arms again. And then the old monk came.

He didn't say anything for the first two days.

I was just learning to speak again. My mouth hurt, and my teeth hurt – everything hurt, really, and something in my head was just beginning to heal.

I looked over, hoping it was Emile breathing, and it was the old monk. 'Who are you?' I asked.

He smiled toothlessly.

He was perhaps the most devoted torturer I have ever known.

He worked for the abbey, and he trained men and women to go back to their lives. He was a man of few words; not from vows, I think, but inclination, and at some point, when he swore at me in frustration, I knew he'd been a knight. He knew a great deal about pain, and about the way muscles worked.

And at some later point, he appeared with Fiore.

I burst into tears. I was ruined, as a knight. I had no hands, no muscles. My hands were splayed claws with no grip – indeed, I could not close the left at all, the right would not make a fist. Neither hand could hold a sword.

No armour, and no spurs and no horse.

But Fiore, who often missed social cues, held me in his arms for as long as I moaned, and then put me back on my feet.

And the next time he came, he brought two wooden wasters.

The first time, I couldn't hold one. But the old monk kept it and made me bend my stiff, painful hands around it – some days he dipped my hands in hot wax, some days he nearly boiled them in water: he had a thousand ways to torment me, but he got my right hand closed on the waster's hilt.

So the second time Fiore came, I could just barely hold one. And as soon as I did, which took another few visits, we stood on guard, Fiore swung – and I flinched.

Fiore pursed his lips, as he did sometimes. 'Um-hmm,' he said.

I had learned physical fear in a way that I had never learned it as a boy. I cringed when a hand was raised, and I turned my head away instead of covering a blow. I would break my posture to back away rather than swinging. Fiore would purse his lips and continue, with endless, damningly gentle patience. Often he would talk with the monk.

Sometimes he would speak to Emile.

And this went on for a month. The sun began to grow warmer. There was a hint of green outside the window and my friends came. They came one at a time; later I heard that this was the stricture of the abbess and Fra Andreo. Nerio came and I was happy, for a little while, but his sanguine good humour, his handsome profile and his vanity in his own appearance – a fine velvet gown embroidered with his arms, an embroidered purse to match and a pair of gloves that I recognised with a pang as my own, borrowed, no doubt, from my portmanteau – all conspired to make me feel the more my own lacks.

Miles came. He brought a chess set. Miles didn't have a great deal of conversation at the best of times – he was younger than any of the rest of us, and less … experienced. He knelt by my bed and prayed, and held my hand. He, too, made me feel worse. His concern and his piety only made me feel fragile.

Fiore came. His visits were in some ways the worst of all. He'd memorised two subjects to discuss, both foolish, and he stared out the window and muttered to himself. Then he sat and fidgeted. After half an hour, Emile, dressed in almost clerical black, came with her embroidery and sat with us. She had all three of her children with her. They *always* made me feel better. Edouard, the eldest, was not yet old enough to notice that I was badly injured or even out of sorts, and he would make me laugh by bringing in a frog or a butterfly. The girls, Magdalene and Isabelle, would curtsey, or at least attempt to do so – Isabelle was adept at falling plop on her bottom while assaying the curtsey.

At any rate, Fiore spoke neither to Emile nor to her children. He stared at his sword hilt, looked at me, and said a cursory prayer.

Please don't imagine I couldn't speak. By that time, I could talk, with some difficulty. It took time for my voice to recover because the ligaments that control speech had been damaged. So mostly I would smile and wave, trying to encourage people to speak. This worked on some adults, and was marvellous to children – what adult gives a child unlimited license to speak? But for Fiore, it was torture.

After ten more minutes of his fidgeting Emile raised an eyebrow.

'Have you no conversation, Ser Fiore?' she asked, a little too bluntly, I fear.

Fiore recoiled in fear. He stammered, and retreated, a man who was unbeatable with a sword, worsted in moments by a beautiful woman.

The last visitor in the rotation was Juan.

Seeing Juan was somehow very like seeing Emile – or like wearing your best old shirt, the one that fits perfectly and is worn to uniform comfort. He did not hem or haw, he did not stammer, nor preen.

'Your lady is very beautiful,' he said, sitting on my bed. His Catalan accent made his French charming.

Emile flushed, which made me love Juan for ever.

He leaned over me. 'I have prepared a complete chronicle of our lives without you,' he said with the tone, the exact tone, of the old priest who read to us during meals in the commanderie of Avignon.

Emile smiled. 'I must feed Isabelle,' she said. 'Please excuse me, gentlemen.' She curtseyed, and Juan bowed graciously. Emile reached out and touched my hand, and departed.

Juan watched her go. '*Par dieu*,' he said and grinned at me. 'Let me see ... where was I? Ah, Nerio Acciaioli has taken a new mistress! And she, defying convention, is young and beautiful!'

I must have snorted.

'He has also managed to forget her name only once,' Juan went on, 'and – well, no more should be said.' He pretended to roll up a scroll and toss it over his shoulder. 'We leave aside the hunts, the ridings abroad, the secret visits, and the new clothes as of no interest.' He mimed the opening of a second scroll. 'Ser Fiore has stunned the company by spending his days, not in frivolous conversation, but in the practice of arms. Suddenly this appears to be his consuming passion.' He went on until I was convulsed with laughter, the knitting bones of my ribs grating together until tears came to my eyes and suddenly he was holding both my hands.

'Oh, my friend, I'm so sorry!' He shook his head. 'In truth, I'm bored to death without you. Hurry and get well – we'll ride abroad, slaughter your enemies and ...' he laughed, 'and doubtless borrow money from Nerio. Is it true? That it was the fine lady's husband?'

I wheezed. But some secrets were not mine. I shook my head.

He shook his. 'I think you are a liar. Listen, if you die, we will rip off his balls and make him eat them. We have sworn it.' He leaned close. 'They say he is at Mestre, with the army. We'll kill him, yes?'

This from one of my brothers in the order. Juan was always my favourite.

I wish I had told him so.

A beautiful pair of galleys were fitting out across a narrow arm of the lagoon. Because I watched them every day, I learned a great deal.

Listen, much of the rest of this story is tied up in ships. I grew to manhood in London, with one foot in the sea, and yet I knew almost nothing of its ways. I had been to sea; I've crossed the channel a hundred times in everything from the royal flagship to various fishing busses and smugglers with a pair of oars and six sticks that float.

But life as animate cargo does not a sailor make.

Thanks, however, to the old monk Fra Andrea, I learned much of the terminology from the comfort of my bed. I learned that the two low, sleek predators fitting out across the lagoon from my window at St Katerina's were *galia sottil* or 'light' galleys. Fra Andrea pointed out that if I rose from my bed and hobbled as far as his rose garden, I could see the massive elegance of a *galia grossa* towering over the narrow streets of Mazzorbo, the small town on the back side of our island.

The *galia sottil* was not like any ship I had seen in England. We have galleys – King Edward had a dozen – but they are simpler vessels and built smaller. Even the ordinary galley had twenty 'banks' of oars a side. Each bank is in fact a bench, set slightly diagonal to the keel of the ship, where the rowers sit. In a Venetian galley, there are three rowers on a bench, and all of them have oars, but save in the direst emergencies, only two men row at any time, which allows a constant rotation of manpower.

English galleys also lack the apostis, which is a shelf, an outrigger that extends the width of the deck and the corresponding bulwark or fence to allow the oars to sit well out and pivot at just the right distance for the weight and length of the oar. In English galleys, without an apostis, the rower can never balance his oar, and has to use his main strength at all times just to support the weight. Fra Andrea told me that the apostis was a new invention. Fra Peter told me later that it had been well known in antiquity and was rediscovered by Petrarch, cementing the *serenissima*'s love of that difficult gentleman.

I say difficult, because as I improved, he came to visit me, not once but several times. Each time he would sit and read to me, which was a delight – but he would cast Emile out of the room. He was, apparently, no lover of children, or bright sunlight, or strong red wine, or Ser Fiore, with whom he had a quarrel, *sotto voce*, down the hall from my cell.

He read to me from an *Historia* he was composing, which was quite brilliant, called, I think, *De Viris Illustribus*. It cheered me to hear tales of heroism from the past; nor were his tales of patience rewarded lost on me. And who does not take pleasure from having one of the lights of the age wait upon you? He must have come ten times, and when he came with Philippe de Mézzières, I discovered that it was the Cypriote chancellor who had arranged for him to come. When spring made the lagoon easier to navigate, de Mézzières came with an equerry.

De Mézzières sat stiffly; the sun was shining on a Venetian April, and the nuns were singing and I was allowed to sit in the garden. His equerry looked familiar – a strikingly handsome man in a plain dark jupon.

'I have heard a great deal about you since Krakow,' he said carefully.

Emile was sitting by me, doing embroidery. We had not so much as touched, except perhaps as she adjusted a pillow, in three months, and yet we knew each other better, I think, than we ever had. One of our jokes was that she, who had spurned embroidery utterly in her youth for the pleasures of flirtation, was now growing quite accomplished at it while other women walked the same path in the opposite direction.

At any rate, I looked at her, and met her eye as she bit a thread. She glanced at the equerry, looked back at me, and winked.

'I confess to having taken a deep dislike to you, and having been mistaken,' de Mézzières said. I was still smiling at Emile's wink, and de Mézzières' words wiped the smile off my face.

But I had managed five minutes with a waster that day, and had not flinched even when Fiore struck my hand. I had Emile to watch and smile with and all was right with the world. So I rose – I was much stronger by April – and bowed. 'I suppose it was the manner of my knighting,' I said. I could remember clearly his face when I related my battlefield dubbing.

He frowned. 'Not at all, far from it. I was made knight on the battlefield myself, at Smyrna.' He shrugged. 'My father could never have afforded to have me knighted.'

He smiled, his eyes on some event far in the past. Then they focused on me.

'You killed de Charny,' he said. 'He was my friend – my mentor.' His eyes were like daggers, like the blows of my tormentors. 'He made me a knight.'

Well.

Emile shifted, put her work aside, and stood. 'Gentlemen ...' she said. She was a noblewomen and she'd had a lifetime of listening to men start the dance that leads to blood. She knew exactly how the opening notes sounded.

'He was a great knight,' I said. 'I met him in London during the peace, when he was a prisoner.'

De Mézzières shrugged. 'I would have been in the Holy Land, I fear.'

'He was kind to me when I was a shop boy. In fact, he encouraged me to – to be a knight.' Just thinking of it made my voice tremble.

I know men who flinch from steel, and others from memories of steel. I am not one to carry the bad dreams, I have not been so cursed. But that day, in the spring sun in the rose garden, speaking of the great Sieur de Charny conjured him, and there he was, killing my knight, Sir Edward, with a single blow of his spear. Every muscle in my neck and back tensed.

'Tell me of his end,' de Mézzières said.

I told it simply. 'There were many of us, squires, mostly. The Gascons and some English knights were trying to take the king – King John of France.' I frowned. 'The English were all fighting to take the richest ransoms, and the French ...' I shrugged.

Emile looked away.

She was a Frenchwoman to her finger's ends. Janet is, too – talk of Poitiers and they bridle. But to be fair, Emile lost a brother in the red-washed mud, and Janet lost two uncles.

'Monsieur de Charny had the Oriflamme.' Well, I told it as I've told you: I got him around the knees and helped bring him down.

De Mézzières locked his eyes in mine. 'Is that how you would want to die?' he asked.

Now I took a breath. 'On a stricken field, with my sovereign's banner in my fist, feared by every foe and loved by every knight? Taking twenty men with me?' I grinned, and for a moment, I was not a man who had been beaten to a pulp by brigands. I was Sir William Gold. 'By God, sir, give me such a death and I will embrace it.'

De Mézzières rose and bowed. 'I mistook you for another kind of man entirely. The king, who is your admirer – and I – pray daily for your recovery.' He glanced at his squire, who grinned.

Now we were all standing. 'I would rather not have killed him,' I said. 'I can only say that he would not let himself be taken.'

De Mézzières looked away. 'No. He would not.'

Emile put a hand on his arm, her face still full of concern. 'Please, the waiting has gone on so long. What of the crusade?'

De Mézzières frowned.

Emile smiled at me. 'I think we could all sit,' she said. The squire, a bold rascal, smiled with her.

We sat again. De Mézzières had so much dignity that he found sitting difficult. His back was so straight it never touched the back of the wooden chair that had been brought for him.

But he sighed, looked at Emile, and shook his head. 'Genoa has done everything in their power to block this expedition,' he said. 'Nor has the Pope been forward, precisely, with the promised money.'

Emile nodded. 'My chamberlain in Geneva says that the money collected in Savoy will not come here, and that the Green Count and the Savoyards will mount their own crusade.'

De Mézzières shrugged. 'The worldly vanity of the great lords is past anything I could ever have imagined. Sometimes I must admire the Turks and the Sultan in Egypt. Islam is not divided as we are. Nevertheless, the issue is money. Genoa has demanded enormous reparations for our supposed faults, and Venice will not loan the king money that will go directly into her rivals coffers for the war we all know is coming.'

'What war?' I asked.

De Mézzières sighed. 'The war between Venice and Genoa. Next to which, this crusade is but a sideshow.' He nodded. 'Few enough of the men-at-arms we raised managed to hang on through the winter and those that did ate their leathers and sold their armour. We will not sail before June, at best. We need money. We need Venice to settle their revolt on Crete. We need to have our own warships repaired, and we need Venice to complete her fleet.' He waved a hand at the two *galia sottil* hulls fitting out.

'June!' Emile said. 'I will be a pauper!'

De Mézzières bowed in his seat. 'My esteemed lady, the king is already a pauper. This crusade has cost him three years of the complete revenue of his kingdom.'

The equerry sat back, his attitude anything but servile. 'I didn't want the job in the first place,' he said.

I'd guessed, somewhere in the muddle of telling them of de Charny, that the equerry was King Peter incognito. He didn't have the posture of a squire, and he was too old. But I might have known him – and I didn't.

Emile had known all along. What did her wink mean?

But King Peter stood and began to walk among the rose bushes. 'I wanted the Pope to confirm me in my kingdom so that I would not have to deal with Hugh and his claims for the rest of my life.' He looked at me. 'And now look – I will be allowed to ruin my kingdom and I'll involve my subjects in a war they cannot win with the Sultan *and* his ally Genoa.'

When the king stands, you stand. We were all up again. He looked back. 'Please sit. I am not really here. Please do not listen, either. I am full of poison today.'

De Mézzières raised a hand and stepped towards the king. 'Sire,' he began.

The king frowned. 'I know that you desire this thing,' he said. 'If I were allowed, I would board the first ship that could float, take my household, and sail for Cyprus, where on arrival I would kiss the ground and would never leave again. Let the Pope and Venice and Genoa have their own wars without me.'

He looked at me. 'I liked what you said,' he admitted. 'I too would die that death.'

'You are willing enough to fight the Turks, your Grace!' de Mézzières said, with an intensity that sounded to me like the remnants of an old argument, often rehashed.

'The Turks!' the king said. 'Not Egypt! Not the Sultan!'

Emile looked confused. 'Are they different?'

You must remember that most of us in England and in France called the Saracens 'Turks' and 'Hagarenes' and made little distinction among them.

The king smiled at her. 'Sweet Emile,' he said, 'the Egyptians have the richest port in our ocean, and trade. The Turks are pirates and scoundrels and slavers – the very Genoese of the Moslem world.'

'Are not all the *paynim* equally our enemy?' Emile asked. She glanced at me. I was very glad, just then, to receive her glance. The king's attitude toward her told me that, at the very least, I had a rival. His visit here, incognito – what was I to think? There are men who can share a woman and other men are happy to share a woman with a king. And perhaps you might say I shared her with her husband, but *par dieu*, gentles, she hated him as much as I. She did not hate King Peter.

De Mézzières began to speak, and the king spoke over him. 'No!' he said. 'Only the fools west of Italy think so.' He frowned. Then he shook his head. 'I am not myself today. Sir William, are you enjoying Messire Petrarch?'

I bowed. 'With all my heart, sire,' I said. 'But not half as much as I enjoy the company of this lady.'

Just for a moment, I was eye to eye with the King of Cyprus.

So. And so.

I saw him, and I saw her – in one glance.

What I saw filled me with joy.

He frowned, then managed a smile. 'How fortunate, that you may see her every day!' he said, with forced chivalry. 'And how fortunate for us all that her husband keeps his distance. What a fool he must be,' the king said.

She looked away.

Thanks to the intercession of the Blessed Virgin, it was then that the bells rang for Mass.

The knowledge that the King of Jerusalem was my rival for Emile put something into me that had been beaten out. And perhaps to the power of adulterous love might be added some excitement for the crusade. I had been sure, until de Mézzières came, that the ships would sail without me. Easter saw me just able to go to Mass and return to my room without fainting, to swagger blunt swords with Fiore for a few minutes.

But after de Mézzières' visit – and the king's, of course – I began to gain ground.

Fra Andrea must have granted some permission or other, too, because suddenly all my friends were there. Miles Stapleton came and taught me to play chess – which is to say that I had played chess, but

Miles taught me to play well. And he taught Emile as well. No man I ever met did aught but enjoy her company, and she was full of life that spring.

Ser Nerio came so often that I suspected him of a liaison with a novice or a nun; nor was I alone in my suspicions.

Juan came with Fiore. In fact, they all came together after a few scouting missions. They would sit in the nun's parlour, and they would join Emile's men-at-arms behind the convent where the novices and the servants hung the laundry, and we would fence. As I grew stronger, I would wrestle, box, try a spear or a staff.

I remember one golden day, late April, I think, perhaps the fourth Sunday after Easter. I hit Fiore with a spear thrust after a cavazione – a feint. He laughed, although he'd have a bruise. He thrust back at me, and I made my cover – and he pushed it aside and ran the pole-end into my gut.

As I picked myself up, I whined.

'I suppose I'll never be the knight I was,' I said. I was cursedly weak.

Fiore grinned. 'You will be my thesis,' he said.

Perhaps it was that night, or the next. The Abbess of St Katherine had delivered an ultimatum and an offer, and we took dinner together with the handful of monks who had their own dormitory.

The Abbess had offered my friends free passage into her kingdom, in exchange for nothing but their words of honour that they would not outrage, seduce, charm, or even flirt with her charges.

Ser Nerio drank off a glass of a local wine and raised an eyebrow. 'I would be giving up a great deal,' he said.

Miles Stapleton raised his eyes and sighed. 'We are soldiers of Christ, not seducers.'

Nerio ruffled Stapleton's hair, which the younger man hated. 'No one seduces a novice,' he said. 'You lie back and let them seduce you.'

Juan blushed. 'I would very much like to – to help Guillermo to make his recovery.'

Nerio sighed theatrically. 'Well, I will prove that I'm the best knight among us by making my knee bend to the Tigress. Although I suspect I'm the only one making any real sacrifice.' He leaned over. 'You don't suppose she just needs a good fuck herself?'

Fra Andrea laughed aloud. 'You are brave,' he said. 'Listen, young pup. Go suggest it to her. I will stand here and take wagers on how long you live.'

Nerio's sense of his own place in the world did not accept much derision. 'I'm sure I can outlast the old witch.'

Fra Andrea shrugged. 'I've never seen anyone slain by raw scorn, but I imagine that it desiccates the corpse.' The other monks were laughing. Nerio frowned.

Nerio did not like to be told 'no'.

I think it was that same evening that Juan was complimenting me on how well I was recovering. I shrugged off the praise: I did not want their pity and Fiore laughed.

'I am making you anew,' he said.

'How so?' I asked. 'Teaching me not to flinch?'

'Teaching you everything. Listen, every swordsman is a blob, a sticky mass of all his own flaws and all the bad teaching of his masters and the injuries he has and all the errors of thought and decision and control. Even I am riddled with these flaws.'

'Even you?' Nerio quipped. 'I can't imagine that you have any flaws.'

'Yes, I admit it is difficult to imagine,' Fiore said without so much as a smile. 'Yet I have them. Nerio leans forward when he is excited, Juan stamps his foot like a small boy, Miles bears the marks of a noble upbringing, and has a tell which guarantees that he will never, ever hit me until he rids himself of that foul error. I could name others, gentlemen. Dozens. In the end, we are a bundle of flaws.'

'Man is but a fleshy doll packed full of sin,' Fra Andrea said.

Fiore shrugged. 'Sin is not my business,' he said. 'But with William, his misfortune will be his fortune. The men who broke him changed his body. Fra Andrea and I have brought him back from the dead like Lazarus, with better training.'

'Jesus Christ,' Nerio said. 'You mean to say Sir William will be without sin?' He grinned at me.

'I would like to be stronger than Emile's daughter, however,' I said. 'Right now, I would lose a tug-of-war with a kitten.'

Fiore just looked smug. 'I am making of you my thesis,' he said again. 'And tomorrow we start in earnest.'

*

By Saint George, the Friulian meant what he said.

Every day except the Sabbath, the nun's laundry yard rang with the sound of blades. We ran around the island; we fought with sticks and clubs and blades; we fenced with sharp blades. I swung at a pell and boxed with my shadow and sometimes I did this while Fiore lay full length on the wall. Once, I remember that he went to sleep while I was jumping like some antic mime.

I would like to say that he, as the master of the blade, never took his eyes off me, but he was human. And the novices began to congregate in the laundry yard. They would wash their hair and dry it in the new sun; they would wash laundry outside, and they would raise their hands above their heads and stretch to the heavens – I swear there is something in what Nerio said.

I have known many worthy women with a deep passion for the calling, and a real profession. But in Venice, many a penniless younger daughter was forced into the order at Saint Katherine; many a wayward young thing was sent to the island until her scandal was no longer a nine-day wonder among the canals. Or to have her baby.

At any rate, I was not allowed to pause and wonder at the lilies of the field, nor to appreciate the cleanliness of their linen. I was driven until I could not hold myself up. I couldn't have managed fornication if Aphrodite had risen from the waves at my feet or if Emile had pulled her gown over her head and leapt upon me. I was exercised all day – my hands, my feet, the placement of my feet, my shoulders, my posture. It was endless, like some sort of torment in hell.

And as endlessly corrected – my posture, my feet, the way in which I stepped, the distance I stepped, and angle of my toes. Nay! I am not enlarging! Fiore was insistent on the way in which my feet pointed, and for five long days I wore a rope between my feet to limit my stride to a particular length.

I didn't argue.

Because I assumed that Emile was watching.

Perhaps she was and perhaps she wasn't. But I assumed that she was, and I know she did, from time to time. I knew, too, that I was in a struggle for her esteem – at least – with the King of Jerusalem. Rumour had it that he loved his wife, and that she was less than faithful to him and that he, too, was a lovesome man and had lovers in revenge.

He was a king, and not used to being gainsaid. He came at least once a week, and each time he would work to be alone with Emile.

Each time, she would thwart him, usually with me.

And despite this or, by God, because of it, I came to admire him. He was a fine man, and he accepted his lot as commander of the crusade with a humility that I admired. He loved Father Pierre as much as any of us and he admired Emile.

Perhaps you gentlemen would have me hate him as my rival, but is that the way of a knight? We admired the same woman, because she was made to be admired. In beauty and in courage she had no peer and it would have been as unjust to hate the king because he loved Father Pierre.

At any rate, it is because of our unspoken rivalry for the Countess d'Herblay that I began to be included in the king's private council.

At the end of April, we had word from Genoa that they had agreed to the stipulations signed by Father Pierre in January and that the indemnity, a grotesque payment from Cyprus to Genoa for alleged injuries, had been paid.

The king, in concert with Father Pierre, set a sailing date and a rendezvous off Rhodes, where the Order had its headquarters.

As the Venetians made their final preparations, so I was stronger and stronger, and so I had to face my poverty.

I had neither horse nor arms. In fact, I didn't even own a sword. The crusade was a month from making sail, and I lacked the tools of my trade.

My first rescuer was my Bohemian armourer. I went to him and he fitted me for another complete harness; not, I am saddened to say, as pretty as the first one, now broken up among thugs. But pretty enough.

I wrote him a bill, promising payment even in the event of my death, but after a few days, I took the note to Nerio, sat him down with wine in his hand, and asked for a loan.

He read my note of hand to Master Jiri and sneered. 'You are a fool, Sir Knight. How often have I told you that I can loan you money?' He shrugged.

'If I die on crusade—' I said.

'Pah! I've taken worse risks with dice. Here is a note on our house for a thousand ducats – let us hear no more!' He waved at me airily.

A thousand ducats!

'Could you purchase us a ship?' I asked.

Ser Nerio leaned back. His eyes were already on a fetching young woman with carmine lips who wore the red dress of her profession very tight indeed. We were in the wine-arcade by the Grand Canal.

'Oh, brother in arms, I have done better. The Corner family has built and manned a warship-a new *galia grossa*. They intend to put her in the pilgrim trade after we take Jerusalem.' He shrugged. 'Whether we take Jerusalem or not, I suspect.' His eyes flashed, and the scarlet girl began to make her way towards us.

Now that he had her, Nerio turned back to me. 'We will be aboard that ship, and not stacked in the hold, either. The Corners almost worship you. And they are fond of money.'

The scarlet girl came and put her hands on his shoulders. I smiled at him. 'Have you ever been in love?' I asked.

Nerio smiled. 'Every hour, brother.'

I paid Jiri in full. He loaned me a sword and a dagger – good plain work from Germany.

Fra Ricardo – less close-mouthed about the sins of others then Fra Peter – had let me know that it was King Peter who was keeping the Count d'Herblay ten miles from his wife. 'He has libelled the Count to the Doge,' Fra Ricardo said with a disapproving frown, 'so that to the sin of adultery he adds the sin of bearing false witness.' He raised an eyebrow. 'Gossip links your name with hers as well. No good will come of your attachment to such a woman.'

'I hold the Countess d'Herblay in the highest esteem as a true lady.' I met his eye. The beating had changed more than just my face. 'The Count d'Herblay is a coward, a poltroon, and an enemy of Father Pierre and the crusade.'

Fra Ricardo was not a worldly man, but he was no fool and he fair worshipped Father Pierre. 'Ah!' he said. 'Is he so?'

'The lady brought us six knights and is eager to go to Jerusalem,' I said.

'Going to Jerusalem ...' mused Fra Ricardo. In Venice, the phrase 'going to Jerusalem' suggested the accomplishment of an impossible task – or perhaps living in a dream world.

'The count had me beaten,' I said.

Fra Ricardo pursed his lips. 'Very well, William,' he said. 'The legate wishes to see you.'

Tired in spirit and injured in body, I went to see the legate. He was sitting in his own scriptorium, at a table covered in scrolls. Sister Marie sat by him on a stool.

He looked up and smiled warmly. 'My son,' he said. He rose and I knelt, and he blessed me.

Then he scared me by sending Sister Marie from the room.

'William,' he said. 'For as long as I have known you, your name has been paired with this woman's. This Emile d'Herblay.'

I looked away.

'Fra Peter has told me about the count.' Father Pierre's eyes were kind. But not deceived. 'I forbid you to avenge yourself on him.'

I might have choked.

'You, my son, have sinned against him – and his marriage.' His eyes bored into mine. 'I'm told he is a bad man. Does that justify your actions?'

'He serves your enemy!' I said.

Father Pierre shook his head impatiently. 'I have no enemies,' he said. 'I serve only Christ. I am not important enough to have enemies.'

'Robert of Geneva seeks to destroy you and d'Herblay is his tool!' I said, with some heat.

'His death would suit you very well,' Father Pierre said. 'It is easy to rationalise sin, is it not? I tell you, my well-beloved William – if you kill this man, I will send you away.'

I looked at the floor, the magnificent parquetry floor.

'I will obey,' I said.

He nodded. 'Yes. And now,' he took my hand, 'I must give my thanks for saving us in Genoa.'

'Sabraham saved us,' I said with some asperity. Nothing is worse than to have one's sins known.

'Sabraham says that, but for you, we would all have died. I have thanked him anyway. William, saving you from the tree was one of the best days work I've ever done.' He met my eye again, and though he smiled, his eyes were as hard as any killers. 'Don't make me send you away.'

*

236

A few days after, when the Hungarian horse dealers came to the camp at Mestre to sell warhorses to the men who'd wintered over, I took a barge to the mainland with my friends. I was past needing the convent, but I was utterly unwilling to leave Emile, and I loved it there, to be honest. I played chess with the abbess, who had less use for men than any woman I ever met but seemed nonetheless to like me, and I was swimming with Fra Andrea, and swimming better than I ever had before. And I was learning to enjoy children. I will not fill this annal with tales of parenting, but I spent any time that was allowed with the three of them, and as the spring improved, that became hours every day. Nor did I confine myself to Edouard. Emile's other children were, I discovered, no less entertaining, nor could the three be separated easily, and as I played with them, I thought of d'Herblay. He was at Mestre, and I was not to kill him.

What a tangle.

At any rate, we went to the camp at Mestre, and after a day with the horse thieves, I chose a fine big bay of indeterminate ancestry. He had been well trained, and that was his greatest selling point. He lacked Jacques' great heart – and I admit, I walked the lines the first morning, hoping against hope that Jacques had come to Mestre. After all, we had the greatest accumulation of men-at-arms in Europe that spring. Hawkwood, defeated at Cascina, had nonetheless held Pisa together. Pisa had a new tyrant, Lord Agnello, who sounded at least as brutal as the della Scala lord of Verona. All over the rest of Tuscany and Lombardy, the Pope's Italian war with Milan dwindled away and contracts ended, and the market was flooded with out-of-work men-at-arms and soldiers. Many turned brigand and many came trudging across the late spring roads to the terra firma of Venice, looking for work.

I hoped to catch my enemies there.

But that bastard who took Jacques was not there, and I bought my bay and called him Gawain for my favourite knight of romance. He was a better horse than he looked. In fact, I suspect he was Jacques' rival. But at the time I saw him as a poor second for he had none of Jacques' beauty.

I missed Jacques. I purchased Gawain.

Having spent an entire day prowling the camp for my foes, on the second day I was off my guard. I had collected Gawain and needed a saddle, preferably used. I was counting my ducats and florins, walking towards the horse market, when I looked up and found the Emperor's sword, walking along, the scabbard considerably the worse for wear. It hung from a belt a few men in front of me, and the scrofulous fellow wearing it was the same who'd taken it from the pile by the road. I didn't know him at first – I confess, I wouldn't have known any of them by sight.

But when he turned to talk to his mate, I knew his voice and the odd, sing-song Gascon-Catalan. I motioned to Marc-Antonio and chased them.

I suppose that I might have gone to the master of the camp, but I had something to prove to myself. Nor could I bear to let them from my sight.

I followed them into the tent lines and pressed closer as they slowed. The shorter man had de Charny's dagger in his belt. Just beyond him, and to my joy, I saw Juan with Marc-Antonio.

Thank God, I thought about what I was doing. A knight has the right of justice, but justice is not the same as revenge. I knew the one man but not the other; his voice was not the voice of the brigand who took the dagger.

'Messieurs!' I called out.

Heads turned for fifty yards, and both men turned to face me.

The man with the sword knew me in an instant.

The other frowned. He had a heavy moustache – an Easterner, I thought. He had a riding whip in his hand, and he pointed it at me and said something.

I didn't slow. 'That's my sword and my dagger,' I said. Juan was coming from the other direction.

The man with the sword smiled. He didn't have many teeth. He was old, forty or more, and he had on a worn, padded jupon with the stuffing leaking out. It didn't go with the Emperor's sword, although six months of bad care had helped the scabbard to match his style better.

His Hungarian mate was shouting for his friends. Hungarians are easy to spot in a crowd – long hair, sometimes in braids, and nobles wear pearls in their hair.

Every Hungarian in the tent row came at us at a run.

That didn't slow me, either.

I think my lust for that sword – the completeness of my desire – shut out fear. I should have been afraid. A beating can break a man, and if I wasn't broken, I was surely bent a long way.

But I saw nothing beyond my gap-toothed adversary. I walked towards him, and he drew his sword and stood there in the sunshine.

Everything seemed to still. Perhaps this is only memory playing tricks on me, but I think the crowd fell silent and the running Hungarians slowed and stopped.

Far off, one woman was singing.

Gap-tooth raised his sword in a poor imitation of the middle guard, *posta breva*.

The woman's voice rose.

Three paces away, I drew. My sword swept up from the scabbard even as his fell. Up and up, covering me, and back along the same line, and he fell, dead. I'd slammed his sword out of line, up into the air with my rising stroke and then cut about two inches into his head and ripped the point all the way from his temple to his jaw with my descent, and then continued down into my first guard.

He fell without a cry.

The Hungarian stepped away from the body.

Gap-tooth's hand twitched and I put my point through his neck into the ground, knelt, and retrieved the Emperor's sword from his not-quite-dead hand.

At my back, Nerio, Juan, Marc-Antonio, Davide, Miles and Fiore all stood with their blades in their hands. Despite the blood and the flies that began to gather immediately, it is one of my favourite memories: I knew we could not be beaten, not all together.

And I knew I had never been so good.

And I admit, a little revenge can be like a drug.

I pointed the Emperor's sword at the Hungarian. 'Monsieur has my dagger,' I said. 'I am Sir William Gold, and I can prove my ownership if required.'

My Hungarian untied the dagger from his belt without outward fear or flourish. He bowed and handed it to me. 'I believe I have just had all the proof any gentleman requires,' he said in good French. 'A pity. A fine weapon. I wondered why I had it so cheap.'

I offered to cover his purchase, and he grinned and shouted something in Hungarian, and twenty longhairs faded back into the camp.

'Perhaps we can discuss a price if we meet again,' he said.

He walked away, unruffled.

I bent and began to retrieve the scabbard from the dead man's belt. I know he'd ruined it, but it had a bye knife and a pricker in the scabbard and pretty furniture, and I was sure that Bernard and I could run up a new scabbard on the old wooden core.

So naturally, I was kneeling in the spring mud robbing a corpse when I saw d'Herblay.

Well – the Bourc thought he'd killed me, and now d'Herblay had the same experience.

He recovered well. 'Satan had given you more lives than a cat,' he said. He had a dozen of his blue and white men-at-arms with him, and I knew one of them immediately. He was a Gascon and I knew him from my days as a routier, but his name wouldn't come.

I had the belt undone. The dead man had tied it in a lose knot rather than take the time to buckle it. I rose to my feet.

'You would know Satan better than I,' I said. I had the sword in my hand again. And Father Pierre was a long way away.

I'm only human.

The man-at-arms was one of the de Badefols. That's how I knew him. He took his master's shoulder.

At my back, I had six of the best swords in the world. And our weapons were all drawn.

D'Herblay's men closed around him.

'Now who will be the first to reach Hell, Monsieur le Comte?' I asked. I began to walk towards them, and all my friends and our squires walked forward with the nonchalance of bloody-minded young men.

The count's Savoyards and Gascons were not wilting flowers. They were knights. They drew – half a dozen of them – while the others pulled at their master.

He turned and allowed himself to be led away, even as the camp's marshal appeared.

'Sheath!' he roared. 'Sheath or I'll fine the lot of you.'

That's how you control routiers. With fines and money.

Nerio ripped his purse off the hooks on his belt and tossed it at the marshal's feet.

'That will cover our fines,' he said.

It was a fine flourish, but none of us needed to kill Savoyards or

Gascons. I wanted d'Herblay, and he was already a bowshot away.

'Your master has a fine notion of courage,' I taunted.

Nerio – really, he would have made anyone a bad enemy, leaned past me. 'Is he a difficult man to follow?' he called. 'He moves so fast.'

But the marshal's men were in half-armour, and had poleaxes. They took up positions between us.

'Aren't you the legate's officer?' the marshal said to me, incredulous.

I sighed. I had a cooling corpse at my feet and a dead man's sword in my hand. I bowed. 'I'm sure this is all a misunderstanding,' I said.

Nerio laughed. 'You could be a banker,' he said.

Sabraham told me later that I should have caught Gap-tooth and held him, put him to the question and handed him to the Venetian authorities. I suppose that might have helped me in my struggle with d'Herblay, with the Bourc, with the Bishop of Geneva.

Sabraham asked me many questions about the Hungarian, too.

Perhaps. But that day, our one blow duel helped me a great deal. And God have mercy on his unshriven soul.

I began to consider what action I might take against d'Herblay. Or rather, I began to consider how exactly I would reach him to kill him.

June. We went to Mestre and practiced unloading the galleys on the beach over the sterns and we practiced fighting from the galleys, and a young Provençal knight fell into the sea and drowned, a warning to us all. If d'Herblay was there, I never saw him.

I went to Mass with my brethren, and I confessed to Father Pierre, who was obviously delighted that I had so little to confess. I was perhaps less delighted; I might pretend that a chaste love for Emile was enough for me, but as my body returned to health, it expressed itself more forcefully than I might have liked. And there is some terrible urge on me, I admit, that after killing the brigand who had my sword, I would have lain with any woman available. It is always thus with me. But a barge from Mestre to a convent is not full of tools of Satan. And an evening chess game with the abbess was surprisingly free of temptation, as well.

At any rate, it can't have been three days before I was on my knees in the legate's office at the Doge's palace, confessing my desire to kill d'Herblay.

After confession, I had a private interview with the legate. It may seem antic that I could go from my knees to a comfortable stool with my confessor, but he was the best priest I ever knew, and even the act of contrition was a shared thing, almost pleasant, despite the shame. At any rate, I sat with him while he wrote out orders, mostly to do with money and the accumulation of supplies for the summer. I learned from him that we still did not have a particular target for the crusade.

'How do we make a war whose intention is the triumph of the Prince of Peace?' he asked.

I confess that I had no answer to that.

When the business of my interview – the ordering of the volunteers – was done, the legate took off his spectacles. These were round, horn rimmed devices of ground glass that allowed him to read documents more quickly and gave him a look of slightly comic, owl-eyed wisdom. He polished them on the sleeve of his robe.

'And what of you, William?' he asked.

I suppose I said something about being healed and eager for duty. What one says to a superior in such situations.

He nodded. His eyes were elsewhere, on, I think, the crucifix at my back that dominated the room he used as his office. But then his eyes focused on me. 'You are giving thought to revenge,' he said.

Remember that I had just confessed; remember, too, that revenge is not one of the sacraments of the church. Nevertheless, I did not lie to Father Pierre if I could help it. 'I will, in time, avenge myself on the Count d'Herblay,' I admitted.

'I might tell you that wrath is a sin, and that the future is in God's hands.' Father Pierre smiled without cynicism. 'But I will instead tell you that by my order, the count has been taken at Mestre and is to be tried in an ecclesiastical court for a blatant assault on a crusader.' He held up a hand. 'It occurred to me that no matter what I might say, your first act on reaching full recovery would be to ride to Mestre and find d'Herblay. And that you will kill him, in time. I need you, Sir Knight. The church needs you, and further, has first call on your time and life. You have been valiant in changing your actions, in penance and in contrition. Despite which, you owe the Order for your salvation – not just in heaven, but from a noose and a shameful death.' He raised an eye brow. 'I hope I'm making myself clear.'

He leaned forward. 'I'm sure that every soul is of value to God. But my son, I hold him worth less than a fig seed compared to you, and I beg you to treat him with the same indifference. Let him go. Such men punish themselves.'

From that moment I subordinated any consideration of revenge. He was right; he usually was. Beyond religion, piety, faith, I owed Father Pierre and Fra Peter a debt of honour. I was not going to desert them to kill d'Herblay.

I nodded. I think I said something foolish about changing my mind.

The legate laughed. 'Listen, Sir William. The crusade's various enemies have made a number of attempts to kill me while you were dallying in bed. And agents of various powers have spent a small fortune luring away the bands of cut-throats that form the bulk of our crusaders.' He shrugged. 'Now I must woo them back. And remain alive to do it. May I trust that you will be at my back, William?'

I bowed my deepest bow. By Christ, I loved that man, even when he reminded me of my sin. Or perhaps because of it.

Mind you, after Father Pierre was done with me, I went to Fra Peter – out of the frying pan and into the fire. Fra Peter sat me down and filled me with dread about the legate. From him I learned the truth: that there had been two serious attempts on Father Pierre's life over the winter. One had come from a hired assassin in the street who had been cut down by one of the Order's brother-knights, Fra Robert de Juillac. The other had been a poison so strong that it killed a page named Clemento Balbi, a young noble of Venice who was waiting on the high table at a dinner given by the Ten for the Genoese ambassadors. As far as Fra Peter could make out, the boy, like pages the world over, drank a few sips from Father Pierre's cup and died in agony.

I mention this because all of us, the thirty Knights of the Order gathered in Venice and the dozen or so volunteers who served with them, all practiced together in June; we practiced defending the legate on foot and on horseback, in streets and in fields and on the deck of a ship. It was a very different kind of fighting, and I was but a single oarsman, if you will, on a very well-coordinated ship. I think we trained together twenty or thirty times, which was more group fighting than I think I had ever trained for since I was first a man-at-arms. We all tried different weapons – spears, mostly, and poleaxes, although Lord de Grey seemed to fancy a heavy mace and one of the

Provençal brother-knights fought with an axe, and I came to know the spear all over again.

Fra Peter was our captain. He worked us hard, and then served us wine with his own hands and it was during those evenings in the Venetian Baillie's house that we discussed the threat to the legate, the Genoese, the various factions at Avignon ...

In many ways, Europe was a cesspool and I was not the only man who longed for a good fight against an enemy I could see.

I have perhaps given you the impression that we were a band of brothers; indeed, in my memory, we are always those seven swordsmen standing in the spring air, facing down the Hungarians at the horse fair. But it was not always like that. I loved Miles Stapleton like the younger brother I didn't have, but he could be a stick. His piety was greater even than Juan's: he talked no bawdy, he didn't look at women, much less ride them in alleys, he was slow to anger and quick to forgive; his conversation was almost entirely about religion and weapons; he was dull at the best of times, and his relentless good cheer could increase the burdens of an early morning and a hard head.

One evening, while I was still living at St Katherine's, I remember preparing to leave my friends to go back to the island. There was wine on the table, and Nerio's latest conquest was serving it. I rose, gave them all a half-smile, and bowed. 'Friends, I must leave you,' I said, or something equally witty.

'To go back to your private nunnery,' Nerio said. In Italian, as among us nunnery can be used to mean brothel.

I bridled. Nerio's casual blasphemy and arch misogyny could pall.

He laughed in my face. 'I suppose it frees you from sin that it isn't a novice you're tupping,' he said with a superior smile.

I may even have reached for my sword.

Nerio put his hands on his hips and laughed derisively. 'You know why it is so valuable to all of us to keep young Miles about us?' he asked the room.

Miles blushed, as usual.

'Because without him, Sir William would seem a prude,' he went on.

So ... Miles was holy. He was also more than a little superior about his holiness, which could at times be grating.

244

Nerio's abiding sin was arrogance. His endless venery was more comic than tragic, and his success, while legendary, was itself so fraught with complications as to render him more human. The evening he met his former mistress, the grocer's daughter, on the street while strolling with a courtesan he'd hired remains indelibly printed on my thoughts. The courtesan, terrified for her looks, proved a coward, and the grocer's daughter proved to have a full Venetian command of the language as well as a fast right hand. She was the victor of the encounter, leaving her rival stretched full length in the street, and Nerio was so inconstant and so obliging that he instantly restored the grocer's daughter to her former position – and so charming that she accepted his blandishments.

He did these things because he believed that he could escape the consequences. And he usually could; good birth, brilliant good looks, skill at arms, classical education and vast riches gave him every advantage. His riches made him insensitive, and he could be the worst friend imaginable.

Gloves were a constant issue among us. In Venice, no gentleman could be seen without gloves. And good gloves were expensive; they take hours to make, the makers are expert, and the materials themselves are costly. To make matters worse, gentlemen's gloves were expected to be clean.

And yet, as swordsmen who trained each day, we wore good gloves, chamois, or stag skin, for fencing. And wearing gloves for such work stretches and discolours them.

Now, we were poor. Or rather, Fiore was very poor, but cared little about dress; Miles had an allowance; I had no money at all but good credit, and Juan seemed to have money all the time, but seldom spent any. Only Nerio had all the money he required. And his money was always at our service – he would buy us whatever we asked, and never request repayment. And yet, this paragon of generosity never seemed to own a pair of his own gloves. He wouldn't get fitted for them, or purchase them.

And it happened that he and Fiore had hands exactly of a size. Now Fiore was not a pillar of courtly dress – in fact, he cared very little for his appearance. But two things he fancied, because he felt they contributed to his Art; shoes, and gloves. He would spend half a day being fitted for the plainest shoes, fine slippers with minimal toes at a time when all of us sported poulaines with toes outrageously endowed; and he would linger like a lover in a glove-makers.

He was poor as a dock rat, though, and he hated to borrow money – any money. He never borrowed from Nerio. Instead, he would scrape together a few ducats and resort to a brothel that had cards and dice, from which, sometimes, he would emerge as poor as a *shaved* dock rat, but at other times, he would be as rich as Croesus. One evening he went with Juan, of all people, and returned laughing. He had lost all his throws but the last, and his fool of an opponent had accused him of cheating. The two of them had retreated to the alley, where Fiore had relieved the man of his life, and then his purse – such things were thought perfectly honourable.

And he used his winnings – by the sword or the dice cup – to buy his gloves. He always kept one pair inviolate: virgin, as we all called them. One pair of perfect chamois gloves sat on top of his portmanteaux, and he would wear them in his belt, clean, uncreased, unstretched.

Nerio, who never purchased gloves, had a tendency to pick up Fiore's virgin pair as if by right. He would lift them off the Friulian's trunk and put his hands into them before poor Fiore could speak.

Fiore would scrunch up his face in rage.

This happened several times, until it threatened to return them to the state of enmity from which they had begun. And Nerio never did understand why because he could replace Fiore's gloves and his horse, sword, purse, and all his clothes if he wanted. Every time, he'd say 'For Christ's sake, I'll pay for them!'

And Fiore would shriek, 'Buy your own gloves, you whoremaster!'

The story had a happier ending that shows, perhaps, the utility of having your friends in fives. We were sitting in our tower – it might have been May or June – and I was reading a bit of Petrarch from a manuscript I had borrowed from de Mézzières. Juan was reading the gospels, and Miles was sharpening a dagger, and Fiore was staring off into space. I think it was the day we met the Vernonese artist Altichiero and he had sketched Fiore in some of his postures of fence; anyway, Nerio was going out to church with the grocer's daughter and he snapped up Fiore's gloves. He didn't even think about it; he took them and thrust his left hand deep into the virgin chamois, and Fiore screamed and lunged at him.

Nerio had his dagger in his hand – without thinking, I expect. Fiore grappled for the dagger hand and made his cover, of course.

Miles leapt between them. That was a braver action than it sounds and Miles did it without a thought. He smothered the dagger. When he rolled away, Juan had Nerio, and I had Fiore.

'Whoremaster!' Fiore roared. 'Sodomite! Banker!'

Nerio was white and red with anger. He struggled. 'You *idiot*,' he said. 'They're only gloves! I'll buy you a pair!'

The bell was ringing for Mass.

'I want my *own* gloves,' Fiore bellowed.

Of course it makes no sense.

Juan stepped between them. 'Gentlemen,' he said, 'it is time to go to church. But I propose, to solve this problem, that Ser Nerio give Ser Fiore one hundred ducats, and Ser Fiore, of his courtesy, take him to the glovers and get him ten or fifteen pairs of these gloves. And that he takes half for himself, for a penalty of Nerio's poaching. And that Ser Nerio take the other pairs for his own, stack them in a drawer, and use them, and not Ser Fiore's.'

I laughed. Nerio and Fiore were still full of fight, but we got them to agree to Juan's plan. Indeed, Nerio eventually referred to it as 'The judgment of Solomon'.

My point is that Nerio had little respect for the possessions of others. He could be a bad friend, but by God, he was a worse enemy, as I discovered. He would use the full power of his father's house against any rival, however pitiful and he would not stint to bribe or threaten. After I began to recover, he informed me one evening of the steps he'd taken to ruin d'Herblay.

He laughed. 'You'll be pleased at one of my little stratagems,' he said. 'Do you remember forming a society for sharing ransoms?'

'After Brignais? In sixty-two?' I asked. He nodded, and I said something like 'Of course. I've told you—'

'And you recall that my father bought your account from the Bardi,' he went on.

I struggled not to feel a little humiliated, but they were bankers. 'Yes,' I said.

'With that purchase came the documents on your unpaid shares of the society and your share was collected by Sir John Creswell, an Englishman. He in turn divided the money with the Count d'Herblay and the Bourc Camus – I have a witness statement, signed.' Nerio smiled.

I writhed. I had known it, and yet at another level, to hear it this way ...

'So I'm suing them in a French court, and again in a Savoyard court, and again in a Genoese court.' Nerio laughed. 'I have a suit against the Bourc and d'Herblay in Avignon that's making him smart as if he'd been stung. The irony is that Father Pierre had d'Herblay taken up for attacking a man on vow of crusade – that's you. And because he's held at Mestre, he cannot escape my suit for debt!' Nerio roared. This pleased him inordinately.

I wanted d'Herblay's neck between my hands and I said so.

But Nerio said I was a barbarian. 'Or do you want the rich widow?' he asked.

I put my hand on my dagger, but I bowed.

'Bless you, your account was worth two thousand ducats when I bought it, and I'll make five thousand off your court cases. You can borrow all you like from me. And I can punish your enemies. Isn't it droll?' He smiled. 'I'll break d'Herblay financially.'

I shook my head. 'He's very rich. I don't think five thousand ducats will break him.'

Nerio played with a rich ruby on his finger. 'It will cost him three times that to fight the case, and he's enough a fool to fight.' He shrugged. 'Pater owns the college of cardinals, or at least, he should. He's paid them enough. Perhaps not enough to get *everything* the Queen of Naples wants, but certainly enough to ruin a little French nobleman.'

It was a little like kissing a beautiful maid and finding that she had the eyes of a serpent. Nerio was too fond of money and power.

And Juan – Juan was more nearly the perfect knight than any. He was a perfect jouster, a cool swordsman, a deadly hand. He rode better than any of us, and he had the eye for horses that makes a great rider even better. He, too, had riches, but he had a childish temper that too often got the better of him, especially when there was wine involved. With three cups of wine inside him, he could suddenly turn to a waspish pedant given to telling the rest of us about our failings. And he hated to be compared to Miles Stapleton. Just as Nerio detested, or affected to detest, Fiore.

And Fiore? Petty, self-aggrandising, foolhardy and miserly. He hated poverty and dreamed and schemed for worldly fame and fortune in a way that Juan and Nerio found tiresome, even infantile, the more especially as they sometimes paid his bills in secret. He resented their money and breeding, and as his fame as a master of arms spread and more men came to him for lessons, he used his money to buy clothes and cheap jewels. But – and I hate to say this of a friend, but it still makes me laugh: his taste was on a level with his talent for wooing, and just as he could ignore a comely girl to discourse on a lance blow, so he could wear a jupon of the most virulent orange with hose of a deep scarlet, simply because each individually had been expensive and fashionable.

And second-hand. He never bought anything new. He and Nerio almost came to a fight one night when Nerio accused him of following coffins to get dead men's clothes.

They were not perfect, and none of us *always* loved the others. But taken all together-brawling, playing dice, praying, going to Mass, in the street or in the Doge's palace or going into action by sea or land, they were my comrades. For every display of rancour or selfishness, I can name ten of selfless friendship.

Which was all to the good, because we were to be sorely tested.

It was a good time. I have seldom known a better. And about that time, I had a meeting with Nicolas Sabraham.

He was a strange man: an Englishman who spoke ten languages, a well-travelled man who seemed to know everyone and yet often passed unnoticed. He often served the legate as a courier, and he was often away.

Some men disliked him. He could be very slippery – he was often guilty of agreeing with other men merely to escape controversy or debate, which bored him. He once pulled me away from a fight and told me that I could not kill everyone I disliked. I never had better advice.

But in June, he sat across a chessboard and a pitcher of wine from me. He was dressed for riding, in thigh-high boots and a deerskin doublet. He'd been away, all the way to Avignon, or so Fra Peter said.

'So, is the Countess d'Herblay your lover?' he asked.

What do you say?

He leaned forward. 'It's palpably obvious, to those who can read faces. Listen, my friend, I took note when d'Herblay acted against you. Even if no one else did. Eh? I had a look at some letters – best not to ask. And I had the briefest of discussions with one of the lads who had *taken* you. If you *take* my meaning.'

I suppose I looked away. I knew I couldn't meet his eyes.

He grabbed my hand. 'Listen, Sir William, you love life, and the state of your mortal soul is nothing to me. Have her every day – on the altar, for all I care. But this is crossed with the legate, and that makes it my business.'

I was speechless, filled with anger, shame, panic, rage.

'D'Herblay was supposed to take and kill the legate at Genoa, yes?' Sabraham nodded. 'I wondered how on earth we escaped. I begged the legate not to go. I find that we escaped because d'Herblay put all his energy into taking and killing *you*.' Sabraham leaned forward. 'D'Herblay is out of the game for a while. Off the board.' He lifted a knight – a red knight – and took him off the board.

'Camus hates you, you know this?' he asked. He smiled a nasty smile. 'Quite the piece of work, the Bourc. Fra di Heredia sends his regards, Sir William, and says that Camus is toothless, for the moment.' He took another red knight off the board.

'Do you know who the king is, Sir William?' he asked.

I nodded. 'Robert of Geneva,' I said.

'Soon to be Archbishop of Geneva. His brother, the Count of Turenne, is coming on crusade with us.' He picked up a red knight. 'I want you to imagine this piece transformed to have all the powers of a queen. But appearing only to be a humble knight.'

'Turenne?' I asked.

'Turenne is a fool. Possibly a coward.' Sabraham shrugged. He put the red knight back on the board. 'But in his retinue is d'Herblay. And a Hungarian.' Sabraham smiled. 'A man like me. Do you understand?'

I thought of the Hungarian with the pearls in his hair, standing coolly over the corpse of the man who'd stolen the Emperor's sword. 'I think I've met him.'

'He has been paid to kill the legate,' Sabraham said. 'And you, of course.'

My friendships with men were not the only relationships being strained.

One evening I returned to the convent and Fra Andrea let me in the wicket. He led me silently through the rose garden and then walked silently away.

Emile was there. She was with the King of Jerusalem and he was on one knee, kissing her hand. She was looking out over the lagoon.

She turned and saw me. She didn't start or flinch, but merely smiled and gently tugged at her hand.

The king would not release it. 'How long will you make me wait?' he asked.

She stepped back, and he rose suddenly and collected her in his arms.

I allowed my spurs to ring on the stone steps.

The king turned but did not see me. 'Begone! This is not for you, Mézzières,' he spat over his shoulder.

I cleared my throat. There was plenty of light left in the sky to see Emile's relief.

'Your Grace,' I said.

'You may *walk on*,' he said without turning.

'Your Grace, I live here,' I said.

'Your presence is not wanted,' he said quietly. He looked at me, then. An expression crossed his face, an indignation annexed by a secret amusement.

'Countess?' I asked. Of course I was pray to rage and jealousy, but also to good sense. Was she the king's lover? I would have to fight for him, either way. And her look ...

'Sir Knight,' she said. 'I would be most pleased ... if you joined us.'

The king backed away as if I had struck him.

But I'll give him this, he did not lack grace. 'Ah ... my lady countess, I had mistaken you,' he said. 'And truly wish you every happiness.' He bowed to her, touching his knee to the ground.

She turned her head away, obviously mortified.

The king glanced at me.

I shrugged – a very small shrug.

He shook his head, a slow smile crossing his face. 'I suppose,' he allowed, 'that I will have wine with the abbess as a consolation.'

He walked away and in that moment, he reminded me of Nerio. He was not defeated. And he turned his own disappointment to amusement, as Nerio did on the infrequent occasions he was balked.

Emile slumped back against the brick wall. 'Oh, my God,' she said.

I watched the king. 'Shall I go?' I said.

She put a hand to her face. 'Do as you like,' she said.

Then she burst into tears. They weren't the loud tears women and children use to get their way, nor the sobs you hear with heartbreak. They were quiet tears, and they sparkled in the last light, which is the only way I knew for sure she was weeping.

I summoned my courage. Let me tell you, I can stand the charge of cavalry better than face a woman in tears, and I knew what I had to do without apparently being able to will my limbs to move.

Step by step I walked to her.

If I tried and failed ...

I saw, in a levin-flash of the mind, that I had enjoyed my spring with her because it had no tension. Because I didn't have to engage or risk her good opinion, or discover what she really thought, or what, or whom, she loved.

One more step.

It is one of the hardest moments in the Art of Arms, to make yourself step forward into a blow. Every sinew cries out for a retreat, with its guarantee of safety – a pass back, and the opponent's sword whistles harmlessly through the air.

But you will seldom win a passage of arms by retreating.

If you pass forward and make your cover, you have your adversary at *abrazare*, the wrestling distance. The close distance.

I suppose it is risible to you gentleman that I saw that last step as a combat pass, but I drove forward on to my left leg with the same effort of will that I would make to face Fiore's sword. I felt the tension in the muscles, and I raised my arms, and I put them around her shoulders, enveloping her.

She raised her eyes. Took a breath. And her head snapped round, so that she was looking, not at me, but out over the lagoon. 'If you hadn't come,' she said with bitter self-knowledge, 'I would now be in *his* arms.'

By the suffering of Christ, she was soft. Hard and soft against me.

For some time, we only breathed.

I was supposed to say something. As a knight, it was my duty to avenge my honour. But I was unmoved. I wasn't without jealousy, but ... she was in my arms.

Bah! I was not unmoved. I was uninterested in her life with the king.

'Do you understand me, William?' she asked.

I shrugged.

I tried to kiss her, and her lips brushed mine, but then they were gone. And yet her hands crossed behind my head and she leaned back to look at me.

'When I was young, I was quite the wanton,' she said.

'So you have said,' I put in, which may have been ungallant and was certainly unnecessary. She frowned.

'No, listen, if you wish to kiss me. Listen.' She stepped back, out of my arms. 'I would kiss any boy who put his lips on mine. Any one of them who wanted me. It was enough ... merely to be wanted.'

In a way, it was like the blows in the village square. Not because it should have hurt me, but only because it hurt *her*. She hated saying these things.

'I had the reputation of a slut, and I was almost proud of it, or pretended so.' She laughed, but the laugh was wild. 'But my father was rich, and powerful, and made me a good marriage. To a man who held me in contempt, because I came as soiled goods to his bed.' Now I had her eyes on me in the dying light, and now I could feel every blow as she stuck herself with words. 'His contempt spurred me to *greater efforts.*'

I wish I might have thought of something clever to say.

'And then I met you,' she said. She bit her lip. Slowly, she said, 'William, I would like to say that after you ... but no. I have had other lovers.' She looked me in the eye. 'I did not come to constancy in a single leap,' she said with her old humour. She narrowed her eyes. 'I find it ... difficult,' she said.

She turned away. 'You know what would be easy? It would be easy to be your mistress. Or the king's! *Par dieu*, I've never climbed such heights.' She turned. 'Perhaps both of you at once.'

Oh, I writhed. Women were not allowed to speak this way of love. But she was angry. I think now – but no. I will take some secrets with me.

At any rate, she smiled. 'But at some point I had babies. And babies make changes. Do you know?'

'Know what?' I asked.

'Edouard – my son.' She smiled. 'He is yours. D'Herblay has no idea.' She laughed and she leaned back against the brick wall, and I didn't care about any of it. She was the most beautiful woman I had ever known.

I had, in fact, counted months and seen a certain hint of freckles in Edouard.

'So?' I asked.

In a fight, there's a moment when you throw the blow. *The* blow. And long before it hits, you savour it. When your opponent's sword reaches for it and fails to find it, you have time, long indivisible aeons of not-time to savour the blow.

Mind you, sometimes your opponent makes his parry, and you are shocked to have such a perfect blow stolen from you.

But my studied nonchalance was the equal of her self-anger.

She turned. Slapped me playfully. 'I'm pouring out my soul!' she said.

I looked out over the waters. 'Just tell me when I can kiss you,' I said. 'I'll listen until then.'

She choked. I can't say whether she sobbed or laughed. Perhaps both.

Then she shook her head. 'I think that I am asking you not to kiss me,' she said. 'I believe my choices resolve down to none, or many. I choose none.' She looked at me under her lashes. 'Why are you not disgusted? The king would be disgusted.'

'Only after he was finished,' I said. I smiled. 'At least, if he's like Nerio.'

'Yes,' Emile said. She smiled slowly. 'You understand? Truly?'

I shrugged. 'I have been some dark places. All I hear you say is that you, too, have been to them.'

She shuddered. 'And you?'

I frowned. 'Emile, I have killed men for money.' I turned, getting my back to the wall. As if it was a fight. Perhaps it was. 'You know what I have gained from Father Pierre? A sense of my own sin.' I smiled. 'And I'm mortally certain that if you put the bastard who took my horse in front of me tomorrow, I'd cut his throat.'

Her mouth twitched.

'So what penance shall I assign myself, when I know the next sin is just at the end of my sword?' I asked and took a chance. I put my lips on hers, left them long enough to be sure, and then stepped back. 'I love you. Would you prefer to wait for marriage?'

'You'll kill my husband so that you might marry me?' she asked. She met my eye with her head half turned, and I think her amusement was genuine. 'I don't think we will be able to count on Father Pierre for that wedding.'

She made me laugh. Christ as my Saviour.

Because the answer was – *yes*.

The next day, after training with the Order, I was summoned by de Mézzières. As I expected, I was left alone with the king.

He motioned to me to rise from my deep bow. 'Is a certain lady under your protection?' he asked.

I think I laughed. 'I doubt that she needs my protection,' I said.

The king grinned. '*Par dieu*, monsieur, you are a man after my own heart. When this is done, come to Cyprus. I will give you lands and men, and you can one of my lords.'

You still won't get Emile in your bed, I thought.

ALEXANDRIA

1365

We sailed in early July. My body was healed, and I left behind me my revenge on d'Herblay, my fears for the Bishop of Geneva, my new-found love of Venice, and my hatred of Genoa. I had had this experience before, leaving London to go to France. War is always a sea voyage – if you return, everything is changed. Even you.

We had perhaps four thousand men-at-arms, the cream and the riff-raff of all the men-at-arms in Europe that summer. We had the best of the Italian knights and many of the best French professionals; there was a rumour, right until we sailed, that du Guesclin would join us, and I wished for him. We had some very good English knights, as I have said before, and a surprising number of Scots and Irish – not that I can always tell the two apart. But the Leslies had brought men from the isles west of Scotland. They were, every one of them, as good as Kenneth MacDonald and his brother and Colin Campbell.

Mostly, we had the scrapings of Poitou and Gascony, desperate men in armour whose outward rust belied the state of their souls, their purses, and their general discipline. Yet these same men were as tough as old saddle leather and as careless of danger and pain – vicious old mongrels who would bite any hand if paid. What the masters seemed to ignore is how they behaved when *not* paid.

But just then, between Venice, Cyprus, the Pope and the Accaioulo, we had gold.

Sabraham used some of the gold to buy informers within the brigands, so that we might work out any plots against the legate. He was thorough, and he trusted no one. Even me. Later, as you will hear, he shared some information with me, when he had no choice.

Ah, Chaucer. You know Sabraham, eh?

Later, in June, I heard that there had been a mysterious riot among the Gascons, and three men had died – with crossbow shafts in their heads. An odd sort of riot; Sabraham's sort.

We left the lagoon, and loaded the ships, and I relaxed.

After all, we only had to fight the Saracens.

After a day at sea, it became clear to me that our hosts, the Venetians, had very different goals than the Pope, the legate, or the king. This didn't surprise me unduly; I was a professional soldier, and I was aware that employers were often at odds with their own soldiers over strategy – but having Nerio in the next hammock on board the *Saint Niccolò* gave me direct access to his Florentine perspective on the Venetians and the Genoese, the Pope and the French. He knew more of Venetian policy than Ser Matteo Corner, who commanded our magnificent galley. Every night, whether we were in one of the small ports of the Adriatic or nestled stern first on a beach cooking on the hard-packed gravel, we'd debate the possible targets of the crusade.

Miles Stapleton assumed we'd go directly from the rendezvous at Rhodes to assault Jaffa, the port for Jerusalem. He described this one night, and Fra Peter laughed aloud. He was sitting on a folding stool, checking the leather straps on his harness and rubbing oil into them to protect them against the salt air.

'Jaffa isn't so much a port as an open beach,' he said. 'It's unprotected in bad weather.'

Miles nodded. 'Ah, but God will provide us good weather. And it is the closest port to Jerusalem.'

Fra Peter shook his head. 'We need a good port where we can take water and food; a port that can be defended from the Egyptian fleet.'

One of the French Hospitallers looked up from his own armour. 'Acre?' he asked.

The older men debated Acre and Tyre, both ports that had been held by Christians, almost within living memory. Acre had fallen almost eighty years before, to the Mamluks. Tyre had been lost through infighting and sheer foolishness.

I had never even seen a map of the Holy Land. I suppose that I thought of the world as a vast plate with Jerusalem at its centre, and I assumed that, like any great city, it would be easy to reach.

Fra Peter scratched his chin and went back to his leather. But another night, in a waterfront taverna on Corfu, he sat tapping his teeth with his thumb, clearly impatient at my poor geography. He took the hulls of pistachios for cities and used wine to draw coastlines.

'Look,' he said, as much to me as to Miles or Lord Grey. We were all shockingly ignorant of the Levant. 'This is Anatolia, which juts like a sore thumb out of Asia. Two hundred years ago it was all in the hands of the Greeks and many Greeks live there yet. Here's Greece and Romania ... here's Venice.' He drew the coastlines in broad sweeps. 'Under Anatolia's thumb, the coast of Syria runs almost straight south.' He placed pistachios. 'Here is Venice, up in the armpit of the Adriatic. Here's old Athens, out at the end of Greece. Here's Constantinople, where Asia and Europe meet. The Dardanelles, the Pontic Sea, the Bosporus, the Euxine, which is ruled by Genoa and the Bulgarians, these days. Here to the south of the Dardanelles are a mess of Greek islands, some held by the schismatic Greeks, some by the Genoese, and a few by our Order – Lesvos, Chios, Rhodos. South on the coast of Asia-Syria is Tyre. South of Tyre is Acre. South of Acre is the open beach of Jaffa near Jerusalem.' Fra Peter clicked down the last city, and a silence fell.

Matteo Corner was nodding along. There were twenty of us sitting in the July heat, most of us the legate's men. Corner put a finger on the pistachio hull for Jerusalem. 'You have been?' Corner asked.

'I've made a dozen caravans,' Fra Peter said. 'It is the ultimate duty of our Order, to escort pilgrims to Jerusalem.'

Corner smiled cynically. 'I have been as well.' He shrugged.

His shrug was dismissive, and I was as shocked as if he'd blasphemed. 'Surely, messire, it is a fine city?'

Fra Peter sighed. 'Do not confuse the earthly Jerusalem with the Heavenly, young William. The earthly city is neither very large nor very holy. And it's only trade is the pilgrim trade.'

But Fiore leaned forward. 'And then comes Africa?' he asked, tracing the outline of the Syrian coast in red wine on the table.

Matteo Corner nodded. 'Yes. This triangle is the Sinai.'

I had a pleasant shock. To hear the names of places from the Bible as real landmarks!

Corner kept sketching. 'This is the Nile delta. The delta is enormous – a hundred leagues across, with several cities and three or four navigable branches. This is Cairo, where the Sultan lives, here at the base of the delta. Here is Alexandria.' He placed another pistachio.

'Here is Damietta, where Saint Louis met defeat.'

Alexandria. If Jerusalem was the holiest city in the world, Alexandria was the greatest, founded by the mighty conqueror himself on the burning sands of Africa. I had grown to manhood listening to the Romance of Alexander; indeed, there were men singing verses from it in the fleet. And in Sienna, in Genoa, in Venice and in Verona we heard constantly from merchants who had sailed there of it's fine harbour and magnificent waterfront, of the power of the Sultan, the ancient library and lighthouse, the early Christian churches now used by heretics.

Matteo Corner shook his head. 'When I first saw Alexandria, I thought I was seeing the heavenly Jerusalem,' he said. 'It must be ten times the size of Venice.'

Fra Peter nodded. 'You could fit London in it over and over,' he said. 'The whole of the new city is walled, and the walls have forty great gates, and every one of them as well-fortified as the gate castles of London, or better.'

Sabraham nodded. 'Their customs take is greater than the whole income of the order,' he said. 'I know.'

Nerio leaned back. 'Have you gentlemen read any of the crusading manuals?'

It turned out that most of the Knights of the Order had, although I had not. I had read Llull, though.

Fra Jean, a Provençal knight, nodded, and leaned forward eagerly. 'Saint Louis thought the same as the author, that the Holy Land could only be conquered by way of Egypt.'

Fra Peter said nothing, but tapped his teeth with his thumb and stared at the candle on the table.

Nerio smiled his careful smile. He flicked a look at me and when he spoke his voice dripped with an entirely false adolescent innocence. 'Is it possible we will attack Alexandria?' he asked.

I thought Fra Peter might break his teeth, he tapped them so hard.

Fra Jean shrugged. 'We do not have the men, even if we had God's fortune and the best knights in the world, to take Alexandria.'

Lord Grey, who was usually the most reticent of English gentlemen, leaned forward with enthusiasm. 'I believe, gentlemen, that with such a legate and such a king to lead us, we might accomplish something.'

Fra Ricardo Caracciolo joined us and added his weight to the

260

argument. 'The best crusade launched in a hundred years – and we will fall like a lightning bolt wherever we land,' he said.

Fra Peter glanced at me. 'What happened when you attacked Florence last year, Sir William?' he asked.

I was knighted. But I knew where his thoughts lay. 'We had fewer than four thousand men-at-arms, and we assaulted the barricades,' I said.

Every head turned.

'We seized the barricades of one gate, and held them for a time,' I went on. 'But Florence is a city with fifty thousand men in her, and so great that we could not be serious about a siege; we could not surround her walls, nor seriously threaten her. Had her population sallied, we might all have been taken or killed.' I smiled at Ser Nerio, because I knew the Florentine had been present.

He laughed. 'Indeed, unless one was told that the English were at the gates, it was hard to know. Farmers brought their goods, the wine was cheap, and the money markets almost unaffected.' He shrugged and smiled at me. 'I mean no offence.'

'None taken,' I said.

Fra Peter nodded. 'But this is what I meant. Six thousand men do not even offer a threat .. city of a hundred thousand or more. I suspect even Acre is out of our reach. We might do better seizing a city or two on the Asian shore to secure the Order's islands.'

Nerio smiled cynically. 'The king would like that,' he said.

Fra Peter narrowed his eyes.

Nerio shrugged. 'The King of Cyprus has made his reputation seizing small Turkish ports in Cilician Armenia and the Levant,' he said. 'It is good for Cyprus, good for *trade*.' He sighed, blowing out his cheeks theatrically. 'You needn't worry – Alexandria is safe from the force of our arms. Genoa is sending a contingent, and Genoa is the Sultan's ally. The Genoese would never allow us to attack Egypt.'

Indeed, the Genoese contingent did not meet us at Corfu, as they had promised, but sailed for the Peloponnesus and thence to the Genoese possessions on the coast of Asia. We discovered this while lying in a small port on the west coast of the Morea, my first visit to Greece.

It was fine country, with rich farms and splendid weather, if hotter than a blacksmith's shop, yet dry and with a breeze. And Nerio took us all to see the ruins of an ancient temple close by the beach where out ships floated.

When we returned to the beach, several of the Venetian ships were like beehives for their activity. Venetian oarsmen are citizens, and they camp on shore under awnings when they can, and it takes time to unrig these awnings.

I found Fra Peter with the legate and the king. He waved me to him, and I approached them, made my bows, and received Father Pierre's warm smile as a reward.

'The very man,' Fra Peter said.

Lord Contarini was one of the two Venetian admirals in charge of the ships. He was remarkably old for a knight, with one eye milk white, a long brown scar across his forehead and wispy white hair. He was sixty-five years old. He turned his good eye on me.

Father Pierre caught my hand. 'Listen, Sir William. The Turks are at sea – indeed, they have taken a series of towns facing Negroponte. A Venetian colony.'

Contarini laughed. 'Not a colony, or I'd have more authority there. An ally.'

Fra Peter nodded. 'Be that as it may, the Venetians feel that they need to—'

Father Pierre shook his head gently. 'Venice, the Emperor of the East and the Pope have a treaty for the mutual protection of Christians in the East,' Father Pierre said. 'I helped to negotiate this treaty, and now, I'm afraid, we need to give it some ...' he paused.

'Teeth,' snapped the King of Cyprus and Jerusalem. He grinned at me. 'The Venetians would like to take their galley fleet and sweep for the Turks. They swear they will still make the rendezvous at Rhodes.'

'What of the pilgrims? And the soldiers?' I asked. In fact, I cared little for the mercenaries in the holds of the great Venetian round ships, packed like armoured cordwood. But I was worried about Emile, who was aboard one of the two ships that carried non-combatants, most of whom were wives of the crusaders.

King Peter nodded. 'They should go the shortest route to Rhodes, my lords.' He glanced at me. 'The Venetians don't want to pay the routiers. So they won't take them to relieve Negroponte.'

Ah, Christendom. We had an army of excellent professional soldiers under our hatches, but Venice didn't want to pay. Venice wanted the Pope to pay.

I bowed to Fra Peter. Very softly, I said, 'I can't see how this involves me, Sir Peter.'

He scratched under his chin, thought the better of it in such august company, and looked at Father Pierre. And tapped his teeth with his thumb.

The legate nodded his head to Lord Contarini.

The elderly Venetian sighed. '*Misericordia!* You *gentilhommes* would like the Serenissima to pay your mercenaries, and I, too, would like such an army, but I have not been given a ducat. I am commanding the largest fleet that Venice has one the seas, and if you gentlemen,' he nodded to me, 'would *volunteer*, I believe that I could run the Turks out of the Ionian. At least for long enough to cover the rendezvous of the allied fleet at Rhodes.' He shrugged. 'If they are left uncontested, surely it is to the disadvantage of all of us?'

'There is the Roman fleet at Constantinople,' the legate put in.

'Six *galia sottil*,' Contarini said with something like contempt. 'In bad repair. They will cower inside the Golden Horn until their brothers, the Genoese, come to rescue them.'

Father Pierre showed some of the strain he was feeling by shrugging. He rarely indulged in displays of temper or even impatience, but the near-defection of the Genoese contingent, sailing its own route to the rendezvous with an unknown number of French and Imperial men-at-arms, and now the possible desertion of the Venetian military fleet, was sapping even his boundless good humour.

I bowed to Lord Contarini. 'May I have leave to consult with my friends?' I asked. I looked pointedly at Fra Peter, who followed me out of the meeting. To my surprise, so did the king.

I found Fiore, Miles, and Juan at a fire, cooking bacon on sticks. Nerio's squire was doing it for him – Nerio was watching a woman bathe.

There was some consternation when my friends discovered that they had the king and Philip de Mézzières in attendance. We provided wine as well we could. In the background, our *galia grossa* was repacking her stores at a great rate, surrounded by a fleet of small craft who were loading bulk cargo over the side. The oarsmen were assembled on the beach in neat rows, every man with his javelins and his sword and coat of mail. Venetian oarsmen are excellent soldiers as well as providing the motive force for their fleet.

'The Venetians are mounting a subordinate expedition to chastise the Turks who are attacking Christian shipping,' I said.

'Where?' asked Nerio, suddenly interested.

I probably showed the depth of my ignorance on my face, having little idea where Negroponte was. But the king came to my aid.

We recreated the wine-shop map with sand and pebbles. 'East of Attica is an island that is rich and well-castled,' he said. 'It is allied to Venice.'

Nerio whistled. 'My father has manors there,' he said. 'By the devil, gentlemen, *I* have a manor there, on the coast of Thebes facing Euboea.'

'Kindly do not swear by the devil while you wear the cross of Saint John,' Fra Peter said.

Nerio flashed an eyebrow. 'But of course, and I was foolish to speak so,' he said in a tone that robbed his words of any conviction.

I looked at the king.

Mind you, you must imagine my friends all bowing or kneeling in the sand.

He glanced at Nerio. I think he was amused by the young Florentine's bluster. Perhaps it was like calling to like. His mouth wrinkled in a wry smile, almost like a sneer.

'I would like you gentlemen to stay with the Venetians as volunteers,' he said. 'I would esteem is as a great favour – the more especially if, having chastised the Turks, you ensured that Lord Contarini continued to Rhodes. Without these galleys, I lack the strength at sea to accomplish anything of this *empris.*'

I snuck a glance at Fra Peter, but there was no help coming from that quarter. Fra Peter didn't have to worry about King Peter's attempts to woo Emile; on the other hand, he was charged with protecting the legate, which was probably a more worthy concern.

'Your Grace,' I said. 'Yet I am a mere knight, and not a great magnate of France or England. I have not power to keep a lord of Venice to his promise.'

Fra Peter allowed himself a smile. 'You are, however, the officer of all my volunteers, and if I send you – or rather, if the legate sends you, and the other volunteers of the order, it seems to me unlikely that the admiral will maroon you or strand you far from the crusade.' He nodded to me. 'Sir William, you have a famous name. Contarini asked for you.'

Well. There's fame for you.

Nerio nodded vehemently. 'Is this a council of war? Sir William, are you asking my humble opinion?'

The king and Fra Peter frowned at Nerio's open derision. But I nodded.

Nerio bowed. 'I, for one, would be delighted.'

Fiore made an Italianate motion of his head, one that had as much pitch and toll as a ship in a storm. 'If there is fighting?' he said, as if that summed up all that needed to be said.

Miles Stapleton grinned. 'Against the Turks?' he said.

Juan beamed. 'I will fight the Turks,' he said.

In fact, we had twenty more donats, knights and men-at-arms. But their enthusiasm was unanimous.

Nerio and Fiore went to the great ships, the round ships, to see if we couldn't find a few 'volunteers' from among the so-called 'crusaders', the routiers and mercenaries in the holds of the great ships. Men like me. Or like the man I had been.

I returned to Contarini and swore to follow his orders. We brought him almost forty armoured men, stiffening his marines. They were a mixed bag of crusaders, routiers and volunteers, and included some famous men – we had the Baron Roslynn from Scotland, who is today the Earl of Orkney.

I didn't see the king again. As you can imagine, I had some thought that I had been used as Uriah by King Peter. I tried to get aboard the pilgrim ship to see Emile, but there wasn't time. Lord Contarini ordered me aboard his flag, the *Christ the King*, a *galia grossa* of magnificent size, with the broadest top deck of any galley I had ever seen. Her hull was scarlet, and she had enough gold-work on her sides to support every gilder in London for a year. He took all five of us and our squires and pages to augment his marines.

As an aside, a Venetian usually ships noble 'marines' from Venice; gentlemen-marines are allowed cargo space and decent living quarters. But to press more of the crusaders aboard, Lord Contarini had left all but three of his gentleman-marine berths open.

He put to sea with fourteen *galia sottil* and two more *galia grossa* stretching away behind us down the coast of the Morea. I saw Emile and waved.

She blew me a kiss. She said something, and I couldn't hear it, and we were past. I watched her for as long as I could, but our deep rudder turned us out of the line and I lost her behind Turenne's *galia sottil*. And there on the bow was the Hungarian from Mestre, with his long hair wrapped in pearls. I would not have seen him except that I was staring after Emile. And then he too was gone.

I had thought the admiral a quiet, dignified old gentleman, but on board his flagship he was a tartar. He was always on deck; often, he would take the helm of his ship and steer her personally. Of course, as I knew, it was *his* ship – he owned the vessel, her cargo, and most of the standing rigging, the arms, and tools. It was from watching him, and talking to him, when the mood was on him, that I learned how little he relished taking the Venetian squadron to sea in pursuit of the Turks.

'They sprout ships like mushrooms in a rainy winter,' he said. 'If we beat them, they will be back directly. If we lose?' He looked up from the rail. 'I'm ruined, and so is every man who outfitted a ship.'

I learned a great deal from him, and from listening to him discourse to Nerio. He often forgot we were not Venetians and he freely discussed his orders and his reasoning. Not, I suspect, because he sought our opinions: in terms of naval tactics, none of us had anything useful to offer. But as I have found since, it is often useful to speak to intelligent men – ay, and women! – if only to clarify your own point of view.

I had little experience of the sea, beyond, as I have said, crossing the channel, running up and down the Thames, and the recent voyage out to Greece from Venice. Yet now that the Venetians had left the king and the crusade behind, I discovered a whole new level of hurry, of hard-pressed sail, and hard-pressed mariners.

Admiral Contarini might have been hesitant about meeting the Turks in battle, but he was in a great hurry to reach the point where the decision would have to be made, and he pressed us hard. We had the great lateen sails rigged on both the foremast and the mainmast. When the wind was right, on her quarter, we could rig a lateen to the stubby stern mast. When the wind was dead astern, we'd rig 'gull winged' with one great lateen out over each side. The great galleys were odd cross-breeds, with heavy masts and a sail rig, yet the long hulls and oar banks of a galley, and I lacked the knowledge of ships that would allow me to know if they were good ships or not. The passage of time has made me a better sailor, aye, and a better judge of ships, and now, of course, I know that the great galleys of Venice are one of the handiest and most dangerous warships afloat, but they looked so little like the King of England's warships that I had my doubts.

You may imagine that I did not express those doubts. Instead, I accepted orders and instructions and listened to the irascible old man scold his subordinates, curse his sailors and woo his oarsmen through two long weeks of Ionian summer. During that time we learned that on a Venetian galley, in a long row, the gentlemen are expected to put in their time at the great oars, and we rowed almost every day. It was excellent exercise, and the hard bellies and heavily muscled arms of the Venetian courtiers I knew were explained.

Often, Venetian gentlemen-marines are also men in training to command galleys, and as the admiral tended to forget that we were foreigners, we received instruction every day on the rudiments of navigation and operations at sea. I learned a little about taking the helm and steering the ship, enough to know that it would require a lifetime of practice to be proficient. Still, in two weeks, the group of us learned a fair amount, all except Fiore, who had at last found an element that was not his own. The sea defeated him, and he didn't stir from his hammock except to lose his latest attempt at a meal over the side.

During these lessons I got to know Contarini's Venetian gentlemen better. His captain was Messire Vettor Pisani, a famous sailor and merchant. Pisani had a great name as a fighting sailor, and we heard tales from the sailors about his exploits against the Turks, the Egyptians, and most especially against the Genoese. He was in his forties, tall and weather-beaten, with a great nose like the prow of a ship and cheekbones so high and sharp he might have been a Tartar. He had a vast dignity, for a man of his age; he seldom spoke unless he had something to say, and his silence was sometimes more effective than Contarini's diatribes.

I learned about him and his history from Carlo Zeno, one of the Venetian gentlemen. Zeno didn't like me when I came aboard, and I heard him, at meals, make slighting reference to my poor Italian. I might have bridled, but I was working very hard on my temper, and Pisani gave me yet another example of a dignified chivalry. So I smiled at Zeno whenever we met, and refused to accept his ill humour. When the officers began my sea education, he mocked my ignorance.

I was, I confess, angry. I'm sure I showed it, and his mockery continued. I bit my lips and tried to listen when Messire Pisani showed me how best to grasp the tiller and taught me some of the Italian words of command. A galley is strange animal, which is a country of its own. It speaks Italian, but does so with both Greek and Arabic words thrown atop the Italian.

I walked about the ship after exercise each day, chanting my new words to myself. I'd say them to Marc-Antonio when we wrestled, or to Fiore when we fenced. Zeno would walk along the *corsia*, the central gangway, with his hands behind his back, saying the same words – aping me, in other words, while the oarsmen laughed.

I bit the insides of my cheeks.

Nerio laughed at me. 'Smack him,' he said. 'He's a Venetian – he'll resent it the rest of his life, but that will be the end of this.' Nerio grinned. 'Venetians are good haters.'

Fiore was no use; he was virtually prostrate with seasickness.

Use, however, made him master, and by the time we reached Piraeus under the magnificent hill of ancient Athens, Fiore was at least able to keep his feet at sea and could engage in some practice of arms. The Venetian gentlemen, Carlo Zeno and Gianni di Testa, were both young men, but they had each served in a sea fight, and had participated in many drills and exercises at sea, and with their help we practiced clearing the central gangway, repelling boarders, clearing the little poop behind the ram – the spur – and protecting the helmsman's station.

The Venetian marines both used spears in sea fights. We practiced with spears and with longswords. As far as we could tell, each weapons offered some advantages. The spear gave you reach, and offered no threat to your oarsmen – remember, in a fight on a galley, your own motive power is sitting in vulnerable rows not more than a few inches on either side of where you set your feet. On the *Christ the King* the rowers were set low, so that the benches were below the height of the gangway and the rowers' heads came up to the marines' knees or slightly higher. This required a man using a longsword to be judicious in wielding his sword from the lower guards.

I know this, as I clipped a rower in the head with a wooden waster one afternoon off the Hand, south of the Peloponnesus. He was quite kind about it when he came to, but the incident made me more wary of heavy blows from low guards. And of course, Messire Zeno mimed my bad sword cut and made the rowers laugh.

It was not all bad. Several times Zeno held forth, very intelligently, on matters of navigation, or on history, ancient or modern. He knew the Levant well, having served all over for Venice or as a mercenary for the Turks, who he rather admired. He'd been an exile for some time. I had a hard time hating him, even when he was mocking me.

It was also during this voyage that I fell in love with the stars. At sea, you can see them all, thousands and thousands of them. It is not like watching the stars on land. It is, instead, like communing with God. At first I dreaded night watches, but I fell in love with stars, and then the watches passed in learning their names.

At Athens we paused to take on water and dried food, and the admiral had most of the Venetian ships sell off their heavy cargo, if indeed they had shipped any. We were told to take a few days to rest.

Nerio explained that the Duke of Athens – also the King of Sicily – was not always a Venetian ally, but that summer, with the crusade at sea and the Venetian fleet supporting the Achaean lords in their attempts to stem the Turkish tide, the Duke of Athens was very friendly to Venice indeed.

We had the pleasure of riding up to the great and ancient citadel of the Acropolis, which some men call 'the castle of Athens'. Many of the antiquities are in ruins, of course, but the magnificent church of Saint Mary is in the ancient temple of the Virgin Goddess of the Greeks, and part of it is now the ducal palace.

I had never seen anything so moving in my life. I have seen Rome, and Paris, and Constantinople and my beloved London, Venice and Baghdad and Vienna and Krakow and Prague, and to me, none of them have the ancient majesty of the citadel of Athens, which seems to me to be as ancient as man's presence on the world of sin. And it makes me feel odd … small, and somehow weak, to imagine that this was built by men like me, so long ago that we have lost the crafts by which it was made.

Bah! My views on ancient architecture bore you. So be it. The King of Sicily was, at that time, the Duke of Athens, and the city was held by the bishop – an Italian. He was, to all intents, at war with the Duke of Thebes, who was French: Roger de Luria, of whom I might say more later. Suffice it to say that this man, the Marshal of Achaea, was, despite his high-sounding title, a routier, and was in league with the Turks. Nerio seemed to know everything about Greece and I learned from him many a curious fact, not least of which was that his father already owned land all over Romania (as we call it) or Greece.

He gave his lopsided smile. 'I am myself the Baron of Vostitza,' he said, waving a hand airily toward the Morea.

I wanted to ride farther afield. Greece is rich; the farms on the plain behind Athens are magnificent and well-tilled, yet a third of them stood fallow and the castle at the edge of the plain was burned.

Nerio shrugged. 'Romania is falling apart,' he said. 'Bad government, greed – mostly our own greed.' He looked at me. 'My father has strong views on how Greece should be ruled. You should ask him.' He looked out over the plains. 'For myself, I love it,' he said.

I was falling in love myself. The air was so clear, and the overwhelming sense of the ancient was very beautiful to me.

It must have been that night – I suppose we were only in Piraeus three days – when we went up to the town of Athens that nestles under the castle. Everywhere you can see the ancient city, like bones of soldiers long dead on an old battlefield. Some bones were well preserved – a Greek priest told us that the temple with a church that we admired had once been dedicated to Hephaestus, the smith god of the ancients. But the town was very small, with fewer than five thousand people. Nerio said it was so small for the same reason that the castle on the plain was burned – the constant state of war.

'The Frankish lords fight each other,' he said. 'And the Franks fight the Despot at Mistra. And the Greeks fight among themselves, and fight the Vlachs and the Albanians. The Genoese fight the Venetians. The Turks attack everyone, but no one fights them.' He spread his hands. He might have said more, but we were climbing in the last light into the occupied parts of the town on the slope of the acropolis, and he saw a girl leaning over the door of her house, and he smiled at her, and she probably smiled back and I lost him.

I might not even remember that evening, except that Fiore felt better and my friends ordered a dinner from a big taverna, perhaps the only taverna, almost directly under the walls. It was a pleasant building and had tables out on the roof of the next building down the steep slope, and we seemed to be sitting among the stars while we ate lamb and rice. The local wine was good, but Nerio was anxious to be away; we all knew him by then, and Miles smiled at me.

'He wants to get to church,' I said.

There was, in fact, a pretty little church, a Greek church, but we were not so choosy in those days, and the Greek priest rang the bell himself and welcomed us to compline. Nerio had chosen the taverna and seemed very eager to be at Mass.

I had never been in a Greek church before. Everyone calls them schismatics and heretics – I once asked Father Pierre to explain how they were heretics, and he laughed.

'My son, it is all too possible, that it is we who are the heretics. Peter wrote letters to the Corinthians and the Thessalians, but none whatsoever to the French, the Italians, or the English.' He laughed his lovely laugh and then looked directly at me. 'Don't tell the Pope,' he said. And changed the subject.

At any rate, we all had dispensations, from Father Pierre as legate, to hear Mass under the Greek rite, and I had never done so, so we went to Mass. The singing was very different from our own, but beautiful, and Fiore said it was like masses he had heard in Venice.

We were in the church just long enough to admire the lamp, a magnificent hanging lamp of silver, when Nerio's sudden burst of religious enthusiasm was explained by the arrival of the girl from the doorway down the hill, wearing a veil. I didn't know her, but Nerio beamed at her – oh, that man!

At any rate, immediately after Mass, all the Greeks went out into the tiny square and drank wine, and Nerio sat with his lady. He had a little Greek and she had a little Latin, and they conversed with long looks that smoked and smouldered.

We heard the shouts and did nothing, because we were a little drunk and the Greeks were being very friendly, but when one of the shouts became a scream, Fiore was on his feet, sword in hand. I suppose I should say that, in Romania, men openly wore swords, even longswords, and all of us had ours by our sides.

I followed Fiore when he ran past the church and plunged into the darkness. The streets were narrow, wound like a tangled skein of yarn, and were as steep as a mountain. As we ran, we heard shouting again.

This time, we could clearly perceive that the shouting was Italian and the screaming was from a woman. We cut down another street and came out above a round tower and found four men fighting one while another fumbled at a screaming woman's clothes. He had her on her back.

There was another man down, but in the darkness, it was very difficult to make out who was who.

The single man fighting four had his back to the tower – they call it the 'Tower of the Winds' – and he would charge out into them, swing wildly, and then back away. The four were cowards: they would not close with him.

I became convinced that the single man was Carlo Zeno. Some combination of movement and the tone of the shouts.

Zeno – if it was he – was trying to cut his way through to the woman. She, in turn, was resisting her would-be rapist with spirit. She kicked him in the head, and when he tried to raise her skirts, she got them over his head and stabbed him with a knife. I know this, because by then I was upon them, running full tilt. I gave him the pommel of my sword in the back of his head and left him to his tender victim.

I passed them and pressed into the back of Zeno's *mêlée*. He was beside himself, and he used his sword two-handed, sweeping it back and forth, trying to make a hole in the four men facing him.

I kicked one in the back of the knee. He went down and I stamped on him while thrusting at a second man, and Fiore passed his blade over the head of a third and threw the man into the wall of the tower so hard that he died.

The fourth man fell to his knees. He wept and begged – attacker to victim in a matter of moments.

Zeno stabbed him through the mouth as he begged. It was a pretty thrust.

The failed rapist was thrashing his heels on the ground in his death throes. His intended victim had cut his throat.

Miles Stapleton ran up behind us, but it was done.

Gianni di Testa was lying at the foot of the tower, his head broken by an iron club. We carried him to the priest's house and then bought wine for the woman. She was Greek, and possibly a prostitute. The men were foreign scum, waterfront workers from Piraeus. If anyone knew them, no one claimed their corpses.

The rest of the evening was not very pleasant.

The next day, we received further news of the presence of the Turkish fleet, which had raided Negroponte for twenty days, so that the smoke of the Turkish fires could be seen in the north. The Venetian lords in the area and their feudal subordinates, as well as the bishop of Athens and his allies, had rallied a dozen galleys of the smaller size, and there were two Greek galleys in Piraeus. Syr Giannis Lascarus Calopherus and Syr Giorgos Angelus had accompanied us from Corfu, aboard the Corner galley, and they came aboard to inform us that these were Katakouzenos galleys from Mistra and not to be trusted.

The politics of the schismatic are as depressingly convolute as our own, and it transpired that the current Emperor had been ruled as a child by a regent, John Kantakouzenos, who had as so often happens, taken the throne for himself. When he abdicated in favour of his lawful charge, he had granted to his own children the Despotate of the Morea, a string of Greek states carved out of the Latin dominions in western Greece. Despite which, Lord Contarini was delighted to accept their service: the two Greek galleys were large and well-built, and well-crewed.

I watched Lord Contarini spend all his effort on food and water, and I learned much. War at sea is like war on land, except more so. A general can allow himself to believe that his men can live off the land, and most armies can do so for a few days at least, although the results can be catastrophic for discipline. But an admiral cannot believe any such thing – there is neither food nor fresh water at sea, and an admiral must carry every scrap of food and water his men will consume; and he can count the number of days his men will be able to maintain the campaign before a single arrow is loosed or his ships have even left the beach.

Any road, by the end of three days we put to sea with thirty-one galleys. The Venetians were the core of the alliance, but provided slightly fewer than half the ships.

At the south end of the strait between Negroponte and the mainland, we found, not the Turks – though we spent the better part of a day creeping over the ocean to reach them as stealthily as possible – but a pair of galleys belonging to my own order. They were part of the Christian League squadron that covered Smyrna, and they had shadowed the Turkish squadron for twenty days, doing what damage they could.

The commander of the galleys was an Italian, Fra Daniele Caretto. I sent my respects to him by a note when the admiral sent Messire Zeno aboard his ship, but he didn't send a response. He knew, of course, that the crusade was at sea. He said the Turks were equally aware, and that their campaign on Negroponte was probably an attempt to pre-empt our attack and force us on the defensive.

Contarini laughed. 'They imagine we are all allies,' the old man said bitterly.

'As we imagine of them,' Pisani added.

With thirty-three warships, Contarini was, if not eager to engage, at least far more willing to seek out the enemy. We cruised up the channel between the great island and the mainland of green Boeotia practicing all of his fleet manoeuvres, most of which consisted of making various half-circle formations of ships and the vital art of backing water. Because the rowing was endless, all of us took part, day after day.

I confess that I hated it. It was as hot as my image of hell, with burning winds blowing along the Greek coast and the smell of thyme in the air with animal manure and sea salt. I had a touch of something, from Athens, bad food or bad air, and I was as weak as Fiore had been. But rowing every day in the sun made me better, and stronger, and eventually I began to feel something of the strength I had had before the beating.

We took our ease the third night on the beaches of northern Negroponte. And there our Greeks – and especially Giorgos Angelus – entertained us with stories of the days of greatness in Greece. They told us of a great sea battle fought for four straight days between the fleets of all the Greek cities and the Persians, right there, at the bend in the strait. After dinner we took our cups of wine and climbed the headlands to see the columns and collapsing roof of the temple to the Greek goddess Diana.

'In our tongue, Artemis,' Syr Giorgos said. 'And this headland, Artemesium.'

His companion nodded. 'It was one of the greatest battles of the ancient world,' Syr Giannis said.

'Who won?' Miles asked.

Syr Giannis shook his head, the wide head shake of the Greek. 'No one,' he said. He pointed to the south and west. 'The King of

Sparta died over there, at Thermopylae. When he died, the Greek fleet retreated.' He smiled. 'It is a famous place, to Greeks. I wish to go to Thermopylae someday.'

I had heard of the death of the Spartan king – there was a romance about the Persian Wars making the rounds in Venice. The current fashion for aping the ancient world was just in its infancy then; men like Petrarch and Boccaccio were reading the ancients and even translating them. So I was enthusiastic.

'Perhaps we could arrange a passage of arms!' I said enthusiastically.

The idea caught everyone's imagination, and we drank a toast to the notion.

But first we had to fight the Turks.

Dawn brought us a fair wind and the labour of getting our ships off the beach. But as soon as we were underway – and we were moving before the red disk of the sun was free of the eastern horizon – we could see the Turks moving toward us under bare poles. I'm going to guess that the admiral had received scouting reports the night before – why share them with me? – because he seemed unsurprised.

We stayed with the wind under our quarters while we armed. Most of us had squires by then, but what I remember about that morning, my first sea fight, is Nerio, the proud, buckling the armour for Marc-Antonio, perhaps the humblest squire. We all served each other.

I had commanded men before, and yet that morning, when we formed in two dense and iron-clad ranks, knights in the front, squires in the back, it made my heart soar with joy.

I had never seen a sea fight before. I had some idea, from all the order's drills and the Venetian drills, too, but I hadn't experienced how different it was from a land fight. Perhaps the most difficult difference – hard to explain, and hard to endure – is the waiting and the interludes. The ships determine the pace of combat, not the knights. A battle is usually a single long grind of action and terror and amidst the terror, most men fight using nothing but their training and their fear. The grind of battle makes men tired; their armour makes them tired, their fear makes them tired, and their fatigue makes them afraid, until they conquer or die.

At sea, it is different. At sea, battle is episodic. You face an enemy, ship to ship, and when you conquer one, you have time to breathe, to rest – and to be afraid all over again; too much time to think before the next foe. Sea battles can go on for hours, where a land battle would have been resolved at the first encounter.

Perhaps I can sum it up like this. At sea, you have nowhere to run. And neither, under the pitiless Mediterranean sun, does your foe. There you are, locked together in a close embrace of timber and hemp, and you fight until one side is massacred.

At any rate, the Turks came at us. I thought there were too many of them, but I was officer enough by then to mind my tongue.

I clanked my way back to the command deck. On a *galia grossa*, the command deck was in the stern, raised three steps above the catwalk over the rowers, and covered by a screen of leather against archery. Even as I mounted the steps, the admiral was ordering the screen cleared away.

He glanced at me. 'I'd rather be able to see,' he said. 'You know why old men are sent to command fleets?'

That's one of those questions you shouldn't answer.

Marc-Antonio was arming him. He wore full harness, despite his years, but he winced as the chain haubergeon went over his head.

'Because our bodies hurt so much we don't care whether we live or die – curse you, boy! I only have six hairs left – no need to pull them out.' He cuffed Marc-Antonio, but the Chioggian boy seemed to take it in good part.

His own slave, a Circassian, handed him a spear so beautiful that I still remember it, with the Virgin rendered in carved steel on the head, and a verse of the Bible inlaid in gold. He glanced at me with an eye undimmed and full of humour.

'See that I don't have to use this, Sir William! I'm not quite the deadly hand I once was.' He looked grimly under the leather screen and called to the helmsman, 'Get this fucking thing sheeted away or I'll have your hide, timoneer!'

'We'll fight, then?' I asked.

The admiral didn't savage me for my temerity. Instead, he looked under his hand at the Turks, still a league downwind.

'I have every advantage but numbers. Their ships are full of loot and they've been at sea too long and I have the wind.' He raised an eyebrow. His left eye trembled – sheer age – but his right eye was merciless. 'With the wind, I can swoop on them like a hawk, and they lie there-rowing into the wind's eye, wasting their men.' He looked aft, looked at the sun, and looked at the Turks. 'They have almost twice our numbers, ship for ship. We'll need to be very careful.'

I never did learn what he meant by careful, because despite being over eighty, an age at which in most men, daring is dead, and timorousness is its own form of stubborn accomplishment, he swept down on our foes like the falcon he had himself named. A quarter league from the foe, the Venetian ships furled their lateens; the great yards came down on every deck, covering the rowers with canvas as the first Turkish arrows fell.

I had never faced a barrage of arrows. In the first heartbeats of our combat, I got a taste of what our English archers send to the French, and I confess I did not like it. The Turks mix screaming arrows with their deadlier brethren, and I, the veteran of ten battles, was afraid of the harsh screaming.

I was struck five times in the first three breaths of the action. Each arrow struck like a punch. None of them touched me, but they brought with them a wave of fear that cancelled much of my exhilaration at entering battle.

Marc-Antonio took an arrow all the way through his bicep – it went under his spaulder and right through his maille.

Juan caught him, cut the head, and extracted the arrow. Marc-Antonio's face was tracked with tears of pain, but he blinked furiously and insisted he was well enough to fight.

The rowers were protected for a hundred heartbeats by the sails on deck, but even as the oars went in and dipped in response to the oar master's rhythm, the sailors were clearing the sails off the yards and the yards were rotated amidships and laid along the edges of the catwalk.

One of our advantages was our three great galleys. The Turks had nothing like them. Even our ordinary galleys were bigger and often longer than the Turks, but our great galleys towered over them.

Even as the third and fourth volleys of Turkish arrows flashed in the sun, our centre was again gathering speed. I was no sailor then, but even I could see that we had not lost way as we'd coasted during the brief transition from sails to oars, and now the oars were sweeping like wings, or the legs of a mechanical centipede.

The Turkish centre attempted to back water, but their flanks carried forward, sweeping like arms to surround us. In a few moments, we could see Turks on almost every hand, and the sky was full of arrows.

My heart almost failed me. On land, to be surrounded is to be defeated.

I didn't know much about the sea.

The master mariners at the steering oars gave us a slight turn to starboard, the oars frothed the sea in a massive effort, and we shot forward like a gargantuan crossbow bolt. We struck a Turkish galley and trod him down entire – our vast weight pushed his ship down into the water, the near gunwale went under, the lighter galley filled with water instantly and went down, so that as we swept over the wreck we could see men drowning under our feet, and her mast caught in our steering oars for a moment.

I looked aft, and the admiral was pointing at something aloft, a flag out of place, perhaps.

We turned again. I saw that the dying enemy had ripped away our starboard steering oar, and that limited our ability to turn. And a small cloud of Turkish galleys came at us.

Now, every ship carried a ram – not under water, like the ancients, but a spur above the water for breaking oars and fouling the enemy cathead and his rowing benches. Nonetheless, such was my experience that I assumed that the ram was the principle weapon and could sink us.

Even as I watched, two Turkish galleys turned nimbly out of their crescent formation and charged us. Their archers loosed and loosed, so that there seemed to be a continuous stream of silver-lit shafts in the early morning sun dazzle. But it is very different to shoot *up* than to shoot a bow *down*. Our rowers were not directly exposed, and at first we took few losses.

But we could not steer and I prepared for death.

The oar-master roared a command I didn't know, and then all the great oars began to fly inboard. Under my very feet, the big oarsmen were crossing the shafts of their oars, wedging the handles under the opposite bench so that the oars stood proud of the water like cocked wings. This brought the outboard portion of the oars above the ram of the enemy, so that they struck – when they struck – only Dalmatian oak.

The hull rang, and I was knocked from my feet. I was praying to the Virgin.

I got to my knees and the second blow knocked me flat – again.

Practically at the end of my nose, three oarsmen on a bench were grinning like savages as they pulled maille haubergeons over their canvas rowing shirts.

The nearest one, a gap-toothed giant with a gold earring, grinned as he pulled a wicked axe from under his bench. 'Eh, messire!' he shouted to me. 'Easier to fight on your feet!'

The benches were emptying.

I got my feet under me to find the rest of my marines similarly employed. And forward of us, every Turk ever birthed was pouring over the rails from both sides into the waist of our ship.

Sometimes, when you fight, you are in command of the army that is your body. You parry and snap blows, you deceive and you thrust and you counter as if on the practice field.

Whatever men say, such encounters are rare.

The Turks who got aboard didn't pause to sweep the benches. They came straight up the companionway, aiming to kill the admiral and sweep the helms clear and take the ship.

I have a memory of the moment *before* the wave of Turks broke on my line. I had a spear in my hand, held underhand, blade up, as Fiore recommended if one was fighting in line with companions. And I had the man himself on my right and Nerio on my left, and Marc-Antonio pressed so hard at my back that he was pushing me forward.

I remember a man in plate and maille and a pointed helm, with a sword as long as mine and curved like the Crescent of Islam. He was grinning.

And then I was panting like the bellows in a forge, and I hurt: my arms would scarce obey my command. The great scimitar was on the deck at my feet, and my spear was shattered, and the end with the sharp point was reversed in my hand like a thick dagger and sticky and red.

Fiore's spear was red from iron to point.

Nerio had a dagger in each hand, one his own, one Miles's.

Miles stood with his longsword upright between his hands.

Juan was on one knee, panting, and he, too, had his sword in his hand.

We had held.

I was just letting thoughts filter into my head – really, there was nothing there. Men call it 'the black' or 'the darkness' but for me it was just an emptiness, a void that was suddenly filled with noise and light.

The admiral was pounding my backplate with his armoured fist.

'If you're done resting, take their fucking ship!' he screamed. 'Or do I have to do it myself?'

The last Turks were scrambling over the side, and their sailors were trying to pole off, but our oarsmen were having none of it. I was lucky to be a marine on a veteran ship: I should have led the boarders, and instead I was perhaps the tenth man on to the enemy deck.

And friends, I had to make myself leap.

Perhaps the beating ruined me as a knight. Or perhaps time, training, and a better life gave me more reason to live. But I hesitated at the rail.

Bah! Then I leaped over the sea – instant death for a man in harness should he fall in.

I injured men just by falling among them. I went down, and the Turks piled on me, but they were unarmoured sailors, not armoured marines.

A steel harness is a cruel weapon.

A steel gauntlet can do ten times the damage of a fist, and mine had heavy brass studs on every knuckle. The knees and elbows were hardened steel and had sharp ridges and protective flanges that themselves could flay a man's unguarded flesh. I lost the remnants of my spear and by the time I was on my feet with my dagger in my right fist, the deck around the mainmast was a slaughterhouse and the Venetian oarsmen were killing the survivors with a ruthlessness that would have been a crime on land, even among brigands. Teams of men, bench mates, would grab a Turk, stretch his neck and cut his throat while the third man rifled his body for gold and coins before they all three lobbed him, dead and robbed, over the side.

They took no prisoners. Neither did the Turks take any.

I have hear men speak of decks slick with blood, and that is a lie. The decks were *sticky* with blood. My harness was coated with the stuff, and my sabatons jammed with it.

And that was one ship.

We took three.

By the second ship, I could not really breathe. At some point, I drew the Emperor's sword. And used it in clearing the third ship. The pretty grip, which even the brigand who stole it hadn't fouled, became a clotted mass of brown gore in my fist.

And then we were done.

But we were not. The Turkish fleet broke, though still two-thirds intact, and ran. But the old admiral knew his business; had known it, indeed, from the moment he looked at the sun. By the wounds of Christ, messires, he was a great knight, the old devil. He fought the Turks with all of us as his weapon. Not for him the void and passion of combat, although his beautiful Virgin spear was red. But he fought more like Miles played chess – with his head and not his heart.

And he didn't intend to have a partial victory. I hobbled aft – I had a wound in the sole of my left foot, nothing glorious, I do assure you, but the product of stepping on a Turk's axe. I remember that my left arm harness had taken so many blows that Marc-Antonio, who'd lost the use of his right arm altogether as the fights pressed on and on, had to cut the straps and drop the harness in among the row benches.

Contarini glanced at me and went back to shouting orders at his helmsman. His voice was thin, but he never lost his force all that long summer's day.

He helped me get my bassinet off and his slave gave me water.

'Give you the honour of a noble victory,' I said.

He raised an eyebrow. His trembling eye moved so violently I feared it might fall out. His face was red and a great vein beat against his temple.

'Not even a skirmish, yet, Sir William,' he said. He pointed forward and I followed his hand.

The Turks were trying to raise their sails as they rowed away from us.

He turned to the second helmsman, who was finally getting a new oar in the water. 'Master Foccario, when you have that fixed to your liking, get the banner of the Virgin aloft and dip it thrice to signal 'General Chase.' He frowned at me. 'Now we pay for weeks of soft living,' he said.

We ran the Turks into the surf of Thessaly. One of their ships, shallow as she was, staved herself on the rocks, and two more weathered the long headland which was like a stony finger pointing into the sea and were away, flying to safety.

We came alongside another, and our crossbowmen, who must have been shooting steadily throughout the action, finally came to my notice. They were able to use the rail to aim, and to shoot down into the lower Turkish ship. Our crossbowmen cleared their quarterdeck before we grappled, and we took the fourth Turk entire. Her rowers were mostly slaves, Christians and Jews and Syrian Moslems.

I could barely walk, I was so tired.

But we were not done.

The admiral recalled his boarding party and we were away, the oars beating the sea. The last remnants of the Turks, the ships not lucky enough to have weathered the cape in the strong wind, were running themselves ashore on the beach, not stern first, either, but bow in.

The admiral called me aft.

'I'll place you ashore between those two Turkish galleys,' he said. 'And you hold the beach. I want *all* these ships. If I can't drag 'em off, I'll burn them here.'

Just then, it seemed to me impossible that ten Christian men-at-arms, all exhausted, could hold a beach that was *alive* like a disturbed anthill.

And as we turned end for end, the great sweeps reversed on one side so that the port side oarsmen rowed facing forward while the starboard side rowed facing aft, my friends and I watched the beach.

Nerio raised a blood-flecked eyebrow. 'Even for me, this is insane,' he said.

Marc-Antonio, right arm strapped to his side, brought us wine. It was uncut malmsey, thick and dark and sweet and we drank it like water.

The Turkish arrows began to fall among us.

Alessandro began to lace our helmets. The third men on the benches began to come aft with javelins and axes and arming swords. Some were now armed with Turkish weapons.

'Oh,' Fiore said. 'I though he was only sending the five of us.'

Somehow, that seemed the greatest jest ever told, and we hooted.

'Last man on the beach buys wine,' I roared, and jumped into the surf.

This is what a harness of plate is for. I only had to jump ten feet, and the water and the sand took the shock of my leap – but I fell forward, my foot catching on a rock, and my helmet filled with seawater. And then I was up, with no memory of rising. Arrows struck my helm and my breastplate, but thanks be to God not a one struck my unarmoured left arm or shoulder, and I was moving up the beach with seawater pouring out of my harness like milk from a leaky farm bucket.

Perhaps it was the wine, or perhaps the freedom of having space to swing, to engage one opponent and sidestep another, but I remember that fight much better than the four before it. I remember catching the Emperor's longsword at the *mezza spada*, the middle of the blade, to face a Turk with a heavy axe, and using the quillons of my sword to gouge his eyes before running the point over his hands and severing the tendons while my armoured knee slammed into his balls. And I stepped through him to plunge my point like a dagger into the unprotected back of Juan's adversary as they wrestled, and as another Turk tried to put an arrow into my back, Fiore beheaded him.

Behind us, the oarsmen roared 'Saint Mark! Saint Mark!'

More Venetians were landing all along the beach, and then, finally, it was over.

Sometimes our finest moments are lost in the black and the fatigue. It may be the best fight we all had together.

Well, the fighting was over.

War at sea is the hell of squires. My harness had been drenched in seawater and covered in blood, scorched with fire – I have no idea where the fire happened, but I had burns and scorch marks and all the straps on my left cuisse had to be replaced. Oh, and then I rolled in wet sand.

Marc-Antonio, with the best will in the world, was hurt far worse than I. His right arm was all bandages and they were red with blood, and he'd stayed on his feet and used a sword left-handed – a truly knightly act. But there on the beach, when the Turks broke and ran – to the tender mercies of the local Greek peasants, a tough bunch if ever I saw one – when we'd slumped to our knees, breathed like bellows, and gradually dropped most of our priceless harness in the blood-soaked strand, Marc-Antonio shook his head.

'You'd better clean that and get some oil on it,' he said. He grinned, so I didn't kill him. And I knew he was right.

This is what you are trained for, in the order. Not just so that you can triumph on the day of battle, but to have the will to conquer your own body and the listlessness that comes with survival. Oarsmen were sitting among the dead, passing bottles of wine and water. Crossbowmen were coming ashore to loot.

My four brothers and I began to clean our armour. The Venetian marines knew tricks we didn't – that one stain could clean another. Under their instruction we waded into the sea and cleaned our sabatons and our greaves of the ordure stuck to them, and while Fiore and I washed the pieces of harness, Miles and Juan dried them and oiled them with sheepskin and whale oil.

Nerio drank wine while Alessandro worked, and then he shook himself like a dog and handed his wine to Marc-Antonio. 'Sometimes I'm an arse,' he admitted, and set to work.

The two Venetians joined us, and one by one the looters stopped and fell in, too, washing their maille in seawater before scrubbing it with oiled lambswool and wrapping the dried shirt in a dry fleece full of old lanolin.

Eventually I was clean from wading in and out of the sea, my shoes ruined, my cut foot a burning anvil of pain only then beginning to intrude on me.

'By Saint Mark, if you and your friends hadn't made such a slaughterhouse of the beach, we could get our cook fires lit,' said the admiral at my back. But his smile belied his tone. 'Sit! You've earned it, and so have I.'

Slaves and oarsmen cleared most of the dead off the beach, though the rocks were full of corpses and leaving the fire for a piss could raise a ghost, I can tell you, but there was a wind rising, and the admiral refused to leave the site of his victory.

'I won't lose one hull,' he said. 'We're in for a two-day blow. And not a man of us will be worth a shit in the morning.'

There was one more incident. Alessandro and Marc-Antonio did their best to prepare a meal, but firewood became the last crisis of the day, and suddenly every man on the beach was so utterly tired that many let their fires die rather than walk up the headland for wood. Nor were the local peasants especially gracious, but I forgive them. They had daughters and coins and unburned farms and they probably feared us as much as they feared the Turks.

At any rate, Juan and I managed to get to our feet and walk up the beach, and then, after some desultory searching, we found a whole tree that had floated ashore as driftwood, dry as a bone and ready to be three fires. I managed to walk back down the beach to get the dead Turk's axe, and then back to limb the tree. The wood was strong and hard and well-seasoned, and it took all my strength, hobbling on a badly cut foot, let me add.

You might think I'd have been too tired, and perhaps I was, but those of you who have stood the blows of the enemy know that something to do – something, *anything* to occupy your mind is preferable to nothing. Or perhaps to considering how close one was to nothing.

As I cleared branches, Juan – Spanish aristocrat – piled them and used dead men's belts to make bundles. The belts came from the corpses that the slaves and servants and junior oarsmen had tossed in behind the driftwood. They didn't smell rank, yet, but they had the copper-shit smell of dead men, the battlefield smell that northerners call 'Raven's call'.

At any rate, I was halfway up the trunk of the tree when one of the corpses opened his eyes. I lifted the axe automatically. His eyes met mine. He groaned.

In a fight, I can kill without a thought. But by the gentle Jesus, on that windswept beach that smelled of death, I'd had enough of it. I knelt and looked him over, fetched him water – hobbling to the fire and back, damn it! And in the end, Juan and I carried him to our fire. The oarsmen had stripped him naked for his clothes, and left him to die.

He should have died. He had a spear wound in his gut – a ticket to a nasty, week-long bout with delirium before death, but God and Saint Barbara had other plans for my Turk.

The admiral's prediction was as accurate as a sorcerer or an astrologer's. The next day we had the first rain of autumn, and a heavy wind blew all day. Men huddled by the fires in silent misery; muscles ached, and wounds seemed worse.

Some were, but they weren't mine.

The second day wasn't much better, and our old admiral lay in his blankets all day under a makeshift tent.

But the third day dawned bright and clear, and trumpets called us to our duty.

'Mutton and cheese in Piraeus,' the admiral promised. 'And wine enough for every man to forget.'

'And then on to Rhodes,' Nerio said.

The admiral glared. 'I've just won the greatest naval victory of these last twenty years,' he said. 'More than any Venetian expected of this "crusade".'

Sometimes it is best to be silent.

We were.

Piraeus was delighted to receive us. The Turks were a constant threat in Attica and Thrace, and I found the attitude of the Greek soldiers and peasants very different east of Corinth from that west of Corinth. I had a good chance to learn about Greeks in Athens and Piraeus.

Thanks to Giannis and Giorgos, I had translators and Greek friends, and my friends and I were the heroes of the hour: all the Greeks in the two Peloponnesian vessels had seen us break the Turks on the beach. They were eager to buy us wine, even though we were Latins and schismatics; that is, heretics to their church.

'You were magnificent!' said an older man with a beautiful white beard. He wore scale armour plated in gold, with enamelled scales and fine Italian elbows and leg armour. We were parading our prisoners and captured ships for the people of Athens, Latin and Greek alike. The older man turned his dark eyes on me and grinned. 'For a brazen-haired heretic, I mean.'

His Italian was better than mine and I wasn't sure what to say, so I bowed.

'You are from Thule? That is what I hear, yes? Far away over the sea, where the Emperor's guard is from – Hyperborea. Yes?' He looked at me as if I was a rare heraldic animal. 'The Axe-bearing guard, yes? You know?'

I had Giorgos Angelus at my back. I turned and looked at him.

'One of the Kantakouzenoi,' he said.

The old man smiled thinly. He spat something in Greek, and Angelus stiffened.

Giannis Lascarus shook his head on my left-we were lining the pier for the Duke of Athens and his friends. 'Kantakouzenos calls Giorgos a traitor and a heretic. Giorgos chooses to say nothing, but the Kantakouzenoi betrayed the empire.'

The old man offered me his hand. 'Iannis,' he said. 'I am Navarch aboard this ship.' He pointed at one of the long Greek ships.

I bowed. 'Sir William Gold,' I said.

The ceremony passed without further incident, and evening found us filling a street of waterfront tavernas that allowed us to have several hundred men all sitting at what seemed like on long table.

John Kantakouzenos sat opposite me. 'Fighting the Turks is a waste of time,' he announced. 'They are good soldiers, and the empire needs soldiers.'

Angelus grunted. 'They will take the empire and break it up among themselves,' he said.

Kantakouzenos shook his head. 'No, it is we who will break them up. Look at the Patzinaks and the Cumans and all the other nomadic peoples – they come to us and we make them Romans! We used the Huns to break the Goths, and the Patzinaks to break the Bulgars. Perhaps with the Turks we will rid ourselves of the Latins. Yes?' He laughed.

'You seemed willing enough to fight yesterday,' I said.

The old man shrugged and drank. 'My brother says fight. I fought. The despot has an agreement with your knights, the Duke of Athens, the Emperor, and Venice.' He smiled with half his mouth. 'It will only last as long as it is convenient for you Latins, and then you will stab us or sell us. As always.'

Father Pierre had maintained that the Greeks would be strong allies of the crusade once they saw that we were serious and friendly. An evening drinking wine with Syr Iannis made my head spin. He had a different story for everything I knew, not least, of course, that we were the heretics and he was the practitioner of the true religion. He reminded us of the perfidy of the Venetians in attacking the empire a hundred and fifty years before, and he referred to the Latin lords of the Morea as pirates and brigands. It was an eye-opening conversation.

And when Giorgos Angelus accused him of treason again, he just smiled. 'My brother was the best hope the empire had,' he said. 'We need to be done with gentle men who know the ceremonial and love to debate in church. We need soldiers and statesmen and even merchants.' He shrugged. 'The empire has no tradition of primogeniture like you Latins and your barbaric ways. Here, if a man takes the empire, it is his. It is nothing but the will of God.'

'Your brother is a friend of the Turks!' Angelus spat.

'Better than Turks than the Franks,' Kantakouzenos said. 'The Turks are honest and decent. The Venetians would sell their mothers as whores for a few ducats.'

Nerio might have been expected to take part, given his father's record in Greece, but he had found a girl, a beautiful girl. Juan was befriended by a Greek priest and they had a conversation about theology and Juan followed him to his little Athenian church to see his icons. Fiore spent two hours debating the Roman origins of our martial tradition with Giannis and one of Kantakouzenos's officers. Miles basked in the admiration of twenty knights and sat with the two Hospitallers, drinking in their praise.

I listened to Syr Iannis Kantakouzenos, and I worried.

Carlo Zeno never explained what he had been doing at the Tower of Winds. But he never mocked me again – well, any more than Nerio or Juan. Despite that, for one evening, Greeks and Venetians and Hospitallers were all on the same side.

And later we danced. Nerio had become the centre of attention: his name had got out among the men-at-arms, and his father was a famous figure among the Latins of Greece. People came out of their houses to see him, and the atmosphere became less constrained.

I had no idea how famous our little victory was. It was my first sea fight, and if I've told it well, that owes as much to hearing the old admiral tell me what had happened as anything I remember. I know that the wind changed at some point and that seemed of great moment to the sailors; of course I understand better now. And I know that the Greeks and Latins shared this – they were starved for victory. The Turks, the Serbs and the Bulgarians had beaten them over and over for twenty years, not by skill in arms but by sheer numbers. And why? For the most part, as far as I could see and by the relation of Giannis, Giorgos, Nerio and Lord Contarini, the lords of Achaea and the Morea were beaten because they were divided among themselves. I have heard it said many times that the knights of Romania, as we called it, were the best in the world, and *par dieu*, gentlemen, those I met were hardy, cruel men of *preux* and cunning, , but they had not the gift of loyalty, and so they were easily bested by lesser men.

Or so I see it.

Regardless, that Sabbath eve in Piraeus and Athens, we had won a victory that gave them heart-heretics and schismatics together, so to speak.

The next day we gathered cargoes on the waterfront. I had a hard head; I had drunk too late, I think, and I was in a foul mood. I was worried for Marc-Antonio, whose wound was festering, and inclined to find my Turk, who I expected to die despite the treatment of the brothers of the Hospital. In short, my view of the world was as black as it can be for a man four days out of battle. My own wounds hurt, my head hurt, and life seemed ... empty.

Usually I filled this feeling with a woman. There, 'tis said. Taken like a drug. But chastity, and chivalric love – a terrible pair to yoke together – left me alone with my thoughts instead of abed with a soft friend. Alone, a man in dark mood can see many things ... differently ... and I walked the docks, tormenting myself with Emile's words, her lack of love for me, her inclination (as I saw it in my darkness) for the king.

A man can use any tool to justify himself to sin and I was busy using my blackness to work myself to hate Emile so that I might find myself a pretty Greek. But Miles saved me from this, with a sort of deadly cheerfulness that made me vent my spleen on him. He gave me the sele of the day and enquired after my wound.

'It pains me,' I said. 'I can scarcely walk.'

He dared to smile. 'And yet you go up and down these piers as if searching for our Saviour,' he said with gentle derision.

'I have much on which to think!' I said.

He laughed. 'I am younger than you,' he said, 'but it seems to me a man can think while sitting down, if his foot is cut.'

'Are you wandering about explaining to men the errors of their ways, or do you have some errand?' I asked. I may have been even more direct. Perhaps I said, 'What business is it of yours?'

Miles smiled. 'In truth, the senior knight of our order was asking for you this morning, and Milord Contarini is sitting under his awning just there, awaiting your good pleasure.'

I was being mocked; knights await the good pleasure of lords, and not the other way about.

I realised that I had been pacing up and down in full view of the command structure of the fleet and no man likes to look a fool.

'And how long have you known that I was wanted?' I asked. In my mood, I saw him laughing at my pain and watching me pace the docks.

Miles bowed, refusing to be drawn to temper. 'About as long as it took me to walk from the poop to this spot,' he said.

Something in his restraint finally cracked my bad composure. 'Miles, my apologies,' I began.

He shook his head. 'None needed.' Really, he was too good to be believed. He didn't seem to need a wench *or* a confessor and he had fought quite brilliantly.

I sighed, and hobbled to the gangway of the great galley. What inconsistency of the mind allowed me to walk back and forth, cursing Emile's imagined faithlessness, without so much as a twinge from my foot-but the moment I returned to my duty, it hurt with every step?

Bah! I see both of you gentlemen are familiar with this sort of thing.

At any rate, as I limped, I watched the deck crew using the foremast's yard as a crane to lift a bale of hides inboard. Something turned over in my head. Hides wouldn't go outbound to Rhodes – Rhodes might have a leatherworker or two, but hides were a homebound cargo for Venice. I *had* been listening to Nerio and to Lord Contarini when they spoke about merchanting.

I looked down the main deck to the stern, where the command deck rose a few steps above the main deck. Lord Contarini was sitting, just as Miles had said, in a low chair. The leather battle curtains were brailed up for the breeze. He was watching the loading of the great galleys shallow hold. He saw me and his demeanour changed.

I am no fool. I had the evidence, and I assembled it. He was loading us for Venice, not Rhodes.

Let me tell you, I prefer a fight to a debate. But I had promised the legate.

I had perhaps thirty slow steps in which to marshal my arguments and make a case. And the first choice was whether to allow myself to be mastered by anger, or to be all sweet reason. The anger was right there, boiling together with the injustice of Emile's behaviour, the perfidy of the king, d'Herblay's cowardice, my fear of Cambrai's long arm, my own fatigue and black mood. Anger was easy.

There are moments in life that are as definite as battle. As stark. There are moments when you see things as if they were outlined in scarlet, when truth is illuminated, when a man's character changes because he understands something heretofore hidden, for good or ill. We remember with pleasure those moments that are achievements of some goal: the wife, the treasure, the golden spurs, the Emperor's sword. But in our secret mind we know that some of the red letters that mark our days were not achievements but discoveries. I have known a good woman ruined by another woman's perfidy, ruined to dissipation by a relentless cynicism. I have seen one man turned faithless by another man's bad faith, accidentally discovered.

In one brilliant flash as I stepped aboard and crossed myself to the crucifix at the stern, I saw that anger would serve no purpose whatever in this debate. And that, further, my anger was a bent, nicked sword in any debate. I can't tell you by what train I arrived at this conclusion, but I saw it. This was one conversation in which I must not be governed by my black mood.

Like a man approaching a fight in the lists, I examined my opponent and tried to find an attack that would carry his conviction. That he had given his word? That our victory needed to be known on Rhodes?

Like many young men entering unequal combats, I had not prepared my attack when I entered his distance. But at least I knew the manner of my own defence, and had my first feint, as it were, prepared.

I bowed, touching my knee to the deck. 'My lord summoned me?' I said.

Lord Contarini inclined his head. I knew he liked me. 'I need to talk to you on a serious matter,' he said, a little too portentously.

In a fight, you can read an opponent in a hundred little things. A man may lean back slightly when you present your blade at his eyes – that little flinch reveals everything. Lord Contarini's voice and his first words told me that he was not happy in his own mind with the choice he had made. And that was an opening.

'I see we are loading for Venice,' I said bluntly. I neither smiled nor frowned – my voice was steady.

He broke his eyes away from mine. 'Yes,' he said. 'It is necessary.'

I neither nodded nor frowned. 'It is my duty, my lord, to tell you that your action will force the cancellation of the crusade.'

His head snapped around. Had it been a fight, I had just landed a blow.

I admired him, and one of his most admirable qualities was that his age rendered him immune from the petty ambitions that ruled the rest of us. But I had him. Having won a great victory, he was chained to the good opinion of the world.

He glared at me. 'Venice must be informed immediately if this victory is to be followed up. And perhaps this sea fight is as great a victory as the crusade was ever expected to win.'

'The crusade is intended to take Jerusalem,' I said.

'With six thousand men?' asked the admiral. 'Spare me your pious crap, Sir Knight.'

I bowed and clamped down on my temper. 'My lord, I gave my solemn word to the legate that I would return to him at Rhodes – and I believe you did the same.'

'My duty to Venice outweighs my word to the Patriarch, however worthy that gentleman.' He said it, and yet I could see that it rankled.

'Can we not send a galley or two, or even an overland messenger?' I asked. But my mind was running on, and I thought I had it. I was too young to fully appreciate the impact of a great victory won in old age, but I understood that Lord Contarini wanted to live to enjoy his fame. It was something in his face when I said the word *messenger*. He wanted to be his own messenger, to enjoy the worship of the crowd, the *Te Deum* at Saint Mark's.

It was an uncomfortable wisdom, because I fully comprehended his desire. I, too, want to live to tell my stories. There is little value to fame after you are dead, whatever the ancients may say.

He shook his head. 'I need ...' he began. He paused.

'My lord, if you support the crusade to the end, your fame will be *greater*,' I said quietly. 'If you return now, some will smear your victory with terms like desertion.'

He stood suddenly, overturning his seat. 'You *dare*?' he spat.

This is a form of confrontation I dislike. I dislike enduring the anger of a man I admire. But I had given my word, and my sudden wisdom flowered in a hundred ways as I saw – better – how to command myself and other men.

I bowed. 'I must dare,' I said. 'My lord, I am only doing my duty to my lord the legate. And, my lord, to *you*.'

'Betake yourself out of my sight,' he said. 'It is too late. We have a cargo engaged, as do most of the ships in the fleet.'

I bowed again. 'A set of cargoes that can be unloaded in as many hours as they were loaded – and warehoused until we return.'

'Now you will advise me on merchanting, Sir William?' he asked.

I bowed and left him, but I was shaking inwardly. And yet I thought the balance had shifted. I had caused him some doubt.

I limped down the gangway and turned my halting steps for the Hospitaller galleys. I did not dread the summons of the senior knight – or perhaps I didn't dread it enough. I had come under the orders of different knights at Avignon, but I had little notion of my own subordinate position.

Fra Daniele del Caretto soon enlightened me.

'I am surprised that you did not repair aboard immediately,' he said, 'To pay your respects to your senior officer. I have waited in surprise for some days, and now I find you wanting utterly in either respect or humility. And where is your surcoat? Are you too proud of your earthly riches to wear the Order's cross? The cross of Christ?'

This from a man whose own surcoat was so thickly embroidered in gold and silk thread as to constitute another layer of armour. He wore his over a short gown of linen and silk. His hose were silk – he wore a small fortune on his back.

He continued, 'I was utterly against the inclusion of your kind in our great *empris*. I expect that you were shocked to find that there was nothing to loot aboard the Turkish vessels.'

Righteous indignation is a useful tool, to be sure. But sometimes, if one is lucky, a conversational adversary makes a claim so ludicrous that it allows you to smile. Remember, too, that I had just had my road to Damascus about temper; not, as you'll hear, that my conversion was perfect or durable. But in that hour I was a different man.

He leaned forward. 'Speak, man. Have you nothing to say for yourself?'

I looked at him straight and again, neither smiled nor frowned. 'Lord Contarini intends to sail for Venice and leave the crusade in the lurch,' I said. 'I was just with him.' I bowed my head. 'I am very sorry if I have seemed wanting in respect, Fra Daniele.'

'The admiral spoke of you *commanding* the volunteers when in fact such a thing is impossible – no volunteer can *command* anything.' He looked at me down his long patrician nose.

I might have shrugged, two hours before, and earned his ire. But I did not. 'Fra Daniele, might I move you to address Lord Contarini?' I asked.

He sat back. 'Lord Contarini is a merchant adventurer of Venice and is in no way under my authority. You are. I find you insubordinate.'

He seemed very satisfied with his little sphere of power. I have known such men all my life, and the church attracts its fair share. Yet this man had fought his ship with spirit – even with skill – during the battle.

'Fra Daniele …' I considered my words. I was a knight. I was his equal in every way, except within the insular world of the order. Yet the order had given me much, not least my life.

His eyes narrowed. 'You may address me as "my lord",' he said.

I met his eye. 'No, sir. You are not my lord. The papal legate is my lord. I am here on his express authority – I have his orders to command the other volunteers for the greater glory of Christ, and to return them, and the Venetians, to their duty at Rhodes.' It was a mistake. His face hardened as I spoke. But I enjoyed it.

He shook his head. He was honestly baffled. 'You may not speak to me that way, sir. I am the Lord Preceptor of Cyprus, a Cross of Grace, a veteran knight of your Order. I am your lord in every way. If you will not submit …'

I was finally learning how to do something other than fight.

I bowed. 'My lord, I spoke in haste.'

We regarded each other across his stern cabin table. I let my eyes inform him that my surrender was *pro forma*.

'Well—' he began.

'My lord, the Venetians are proposing to desert the crusade and sail for home. I believe that you have it in your power to convince Lord Contarini to stay true to his vows.' I put a hand on the table.

'You speak well, for a mercenary,' he said.

'My lord, I was a routier, a brigand. I was saved from that life – and from death itself – by the legate. I owe him everything, and I will do anything in my power to see his orders obeyed and his wishes complied with.' I held his eyes.

He looked away. 'What a strange, insistent fellow you are, to be sure,' he said with irritation. 'Very well, I'll go chivvy Lord Contarini. But these Venetians are not gentlemen – mere merchants.'

The next morning, we rowed down the harbour in a dead calm so flat that the smell of dead fish seemed to cling to the rigging, and the ocean was like a badly polished mirror stretching away to the island of Salamis across the strait. But we weathered the cape, rowing like sweating heroes, and altered course to port and not to starboard. At noon we were seeing the great temple to Poseidon at Sounion, which Nerio pointed out and described in great detail. As great detail, in fact, as the charms of his Athenian mistress, whose lush breasts and insatiable appetite for him he was describing with the kind of relish that—

I beg your pardon. But my new found evenness of temper was not, in fact, accompanied by a whole change of temperament. Listening to Nerio did not incline me to chastity. Nothing did.

At any rate, the admiral was reserved but courteous. He was in his chair on the command deck until the sails went up after we passed Sounion, and then he went below. The next day, and the next, he remained aloof, and I was sorry to lose his regard.

We ran north and east on an empty sea in light airs. Word of our victory had sent every ship into the nearest safe port. The captains of the Ionian felt about our fleet exactly as the peasants of Thessaly had felt about our landing – they feared us as much as they feared the Turks. We didn't site a fishing boat until we were on the Aeolian shore, or at least what Nerio assured me was Aeolia. I was receiving a second-hand classical education, combined with an endless volley of erotica, from every conversation.

And what of my Turk? As I have mentioned, the Hospitaller knights had taken him aboard their galleys. We were on the beaches of Lesvos, the isle, I am assured, of a brilliant and beautiful poetess whose descendants Nerio was pursuing closely, when I had time to go visit my Turk. The Hospitallers were drawn up close to us on the long golden beach under a tall and equally golden headland. They had a number of brothers who were very good doctors, and Fra Jacob, an older German doctor, had taken him in hand. He spoke to my man for some time and then turned to me.

'He's not a Turk – did you know that? He says he is a Kipchak. Do you know the word? The Genoese sell them to the Egyptians as slave soldiers. Superb archers.' He rolled back the sleeve on the man's linen shirt to show me a host of tribal tattoos.

'Moslem?' I asked.

They talked in low tones. Eventually Fra Jacob shrugged. 'More Moslem than anything else, though I think his notions of spirits would puzzle the Caliph.'

I told him of meeting the Kipchaks – the ambassador – at the court of the Emperor at Krakow.

Fra Jacob raised an eyebrow, said a few words to my captive, and the man groaned and then laughed. He was not dead, and that was something, but he could not be troubled long. I sent him fruit from the town, and a chicken, and some wine – which I should have known no Moslem would drink.

The town was crowned with a fortress so ancient that the peasants claimed it featured in *The Iliad*, and the hill was called 'Watchful' in the local tongue. The fortress at the top was commanded by an English knight who had served at Poitiers, and we had good cheer for three days while the fleet scraped their hulls and loaded water and food. I was surprised to find an Englishman on the coast of Asia – I began to think that we were everywhere.

Sir John laughed. 'The Gattelussi – you know them? Lord Francis is prince of this island and a good friend of the Emperor.' He nodded, enjoying his master's reflected glory. 'He hires us in Italy.'

Indeed, Sir John Partner had as many Genoese and Pisans and Bretons as he did Britons, but for all that his little garrison had an English air. There were men there I knew, at least by sight, and it was pleasant to speak English, although less so to climb to the fortress.

The last day in Lesvos, Fra Jacob led me to the man again. 'He's making a good recovery,' Fra Jacob said. 'Which I attribute to sea air and divine intervention. There should have been the usual sepsis followed by death, but in this case, a week on, and with the original lesion closing? I have to believe he may recover.' Fra Jacob paused. 'He has indicated to me that if he recovers, he will convert.'

I grinned. A soul saved is a soul saved, and it is always a benison to have a good deed rewarded.

'Will you keep him?' Fra Jacob asked.

I shrugged. 'I assume he knows horses. I could use a page. So yes. I won't make him a slave – I'm not a Genoese.' I laughed.

Jacob spoke to the Turk – I thought of him as a Turk, and they were speaking Turkish. The man grinned and nodded at me.

'He offers you two years and two days of his life as ransom,' Fra Jacob said.

I gripped his hand.

Fra Jacob nodded. 'I'll keep him in this hammock until we reach Rhodos. We'll baptise him if he lives, and by the time we raise the island, I'll have taught him a little Italian.' He nodded. 'You are one of our volunteers?' he asked.

I bowed and agreed that I was.

He smiled. 'Enjoy Rhodes,' he said. 'You've had an encounter with Fra Daniele?' he asked carefully.

I nodded.

'His kind is not rare,' Fra Jacob said. 'Listen, I am a doctor, trained in Italy. I have been a brother of this Order since my wife died in the Black Death.' He took a cold cloth and ran it over my Turk's face. He met my eyes. His were mild; in the low orlop of a Hospitaller galley, his eyes seemed very dark. He smiled, apparently without malice. 'My father is a nobleman and my birth perfectly decent. But I have never been allowed to dine with the knights, nor offered accommodation, despite the Order's vows or my own skills.' He shrugged. 'I am less resentful than perhaps I sound, but your reputation is as a man of blood.'

It was my turn to shrug. 'I serve the legate,' I said.

He nodded and his brow wrinkled. 'You may find that there are many in the Order who have little respect for your legate.' He paused. 'Or none. He was born a serf – a peasant.'

I laughed. 'I am warned. But I grew to manhood being excluded by the English court – I won't be broken by aristocratic airs.'

While I was speaking, he got a Greek lamp, lit with olive oil, which smelled so much better than the whale oil you find in the north. By its light I could see my man. 'What is his name?' I asked.

We went back and forth, and the best I could reckon, his name was something like Kili Salmud.

He tried to bow, lying in a hammock with his hands together. He flinched as the movement reached his stomach muscles.

'Let's get him baptised with a Christian name,' I said.

Fra Jacob frowned. 'You might feel differently, were your situations reversed,' he said.

I think I grinned. 'But they are not,' I said, or something equally glib.

South of Chios, we spread our line wide, a dragnet fishing for Turkish vessels, and we snapped a dozen of them up – fishing smacks, a lateen-rigged merchant, a three-masted tub that proved to be a pirate-taken Genoese. We ran her down ourselves in light airs, with the whole crew rowing triple banked, and Fiore and I led the boarders – Nerio was down with the flux. The crew fought to the last; the last being a man that Fiore beheaded with his false edge strategy, the showy bastard. Their resistance was pointless, as my friends and I were in full harness despite the heat, and with the two Venetian men-at-arms, all the dying was done by the crew of the round ship. In the hold we found the rotting bodies of the Italian crew, and saw why the Turks – really, as it proved, the merest Levantine pirates of no race whatsoever – had fought to the end, as the cargo was worth a pile of gold, being all silk, and the crew had been ill-used to the point of horror: tortured and humiliated before being killed like sheep with their throats opened, youngest to oldest.

The old admiral, who had scarcely spoken a word to me since our argument on his quarterdeck, came below when summoned by his marines. He didn't avert his eyes, but merely shook his head.

'You killed the bastards too quickly,' he said. But he flashed me a smile. 'Pirates – animals. They prey on Christian and Moslem alike, and are the enemies of all men.' He nodded at one young man. 'That's a bad way to die, eh?'

And later, he had malmsey served to all of us, and he said, 'It is easy to prate of the foul religion of the infidel and all that, but when you look at what those pirates did – to Genoese, my natural enemies – you know that it is *those* bastards who are the enemy. And they live in the seams and fissures between the rivals and ply their horrid trade because the lawful powers are busy fighting.' He looked at me. 'I'm sure I'll go to hell for saying it, Sir Knight, but I'd rather clear the fucking pirates off the sea than conquer Jerusalem. I can go to Jerusalem any time I want, just for paying a fee to the Sultan in Cairo, who is a lawful man with normal appetites. And when we take Tyre, or Jaffa, or whatever unlucky town we storm ...' He shrugged. 'I've said too much.'

You see these horrors at the fringe of war. Routiers rob and rape, and worse, and I've known men who eventually go dead inside, and rouse themselves by inflicting horror. I've heard Camus say that raped nuns make the best whores, and the Levantine pirates were of the same breed – men dead to anything but the false feeling of power. But when I looked around that afternoon, the dead Italians very fresh in my head, I saw that Nerio and Juan agreed with the admiral, whatever they might say. They did not believe in the crusade.

Perhaps no one did.

We raised Rhodos at the first breath of autumn. I didn't know the Mediterranean then as I do now, but I knew a storm when it came, and we rowed, sailed under a scrap of brailed-up lateen on a short yard, and rowed again until our hold was awash with waves breaking over bulwarks amidships and the rowers were sitting in water and every man not rowing was bailing or manning the pumps. We were three days and two nights somewhere north and west of Rhodos, and when the oarsmen were exhausted and the water was gone, the admiral conned the ship himself, got into the lee of an islet and rested us in calm water until we were strong enough to beach stern first on a beach of gravel.

The Venetians are superb seamen. We didn't lose a ship. I will spare you my thoughts, except to say I feared death more every moment during that storm than I ever had in mortal combat. I think that is because we fear that with is foreign, and not that which is familiar. The storm terrified me, so that when the sky was black and rent with fire, the timoneer struck me with his rope and pushed me to an oar. And I went.

Nor did I hold it against him.

At any rate, we raised Rhodos, and entered the ancient harbour – everything east of Venice is ancient. Rhodes had a great navy when Rome ruled the world, and now she does again: the ships of the Hospital are few, but well feared.

The harbour was packed with shipping the way a Bristol keg is packed with mackerel. Or perhaps the way Sherwood Forest is packed with trees – aye, that's more apt, because their masts stood like a forest. There were more than a hundred ships in the harbour or on the beaches outside. There were forty fighting ships: from the Order, from Cyprus, from Genoa, from the Gattelussi. There were even two from the Emperor at Constantinople. With the Venetian galleys, there were almost sixty fighting sail, and another hundred round ships to carry the army and their horses.

And the horses! All Rhodos was covered in a carpet of warhorses. We had almost five thousand knights and men-at-arms, and most of them were mounted. The Order's chancellor told me one night after Mass that he was feeding near four thousand chargers out of the Order's farms and byres.

I didn't see the horses at once, because as soon as we beached I went with my friends to see the legate. Marc-Antonio waited on me; his inflammation had gone down at sea, and the storm had, of all things, cured his fever. We found the legate in the English *langue*, the tavern devoted to the needs of English knights and squires within the Order.

I haven't said as much as I might about the Order. When they found me, I was as uncritical as a man can be. I loved everything about the Order: the sense of community, the brotherhood, the religious devotion, the discipline, the training in arms. When I came to the Order, they seemed to me the very antithesis of the routiers, who had no spirit, no driving purpose beyond greed, no training, and no discipline. Who sold their own members for money.

By the crusade summer, I was more critical. Juan di Heredia's combination of competence, intense ambition, lax morals and amoral piety had, despite my respect for the man, cost me something of my idealism. The realities of preparing the crusade – even my beloved Father Pierre's open questioning of the uses of violence – all made me look more deeply at the Order. Fra Daniele didn't shock me – his ilk existed in Avignon – but he helped insure that I would look at Rhodes with a careful eye.

At any rate, the Order – on Rhodes, and in any commanderie with multiple 'nations' or 'languages' – had inns to house and support them. In the earliest days in Jerusalem, I suspect this had been to comfort new knights, so that they could hear their own language spoken. By the crusade summer, some of the languages no longer had as many adherents, and other, new divisions had grown to divide *langues* and inns that formerly had been pillars of the Order. The French *langue* was deeply divided between French and Burgundian and Hainault; the Italian *langue* was bitterly divided between the knights of Genoa and the knights of Venice, with the Florentine and Neapolitan and Sianese and Veronese knights as a sort of third 'side'. There was a German *langue*, and an English *langue* that included Scottish and Irish knights – two groups who did not view themselves as English any more than a Provençal knight was French or a Catalan knight was 'Spanish'.

Despite these divisions, --perhaps even because of them, the Order was a solid fabric. The Order could be petty and bureaucratic; it had whole slaughterhouses of parchment scrolls dedicated to knight's's' genealogies and land holdings and registered rents and leases, but the Order provided inns, hospital care, and in some cases, transportation for pilgrims travelling to the Holy Land from all of Europe. From your front door in London or Aix-la-Chappelle or Nijmegen or Nuremberg or Prague or Verona or Barcelona or Nájera or Paris or Bordeaux you could travel all the way to Jerusalem guarded, supported, and cared for by the Order.

The decision to guard the pilgrim routes and to provide care for the sick, whether pilgrims or not, had been one of the earliest, defining moment in the Order's history. Unlike the rival Templars, the Hospitallers had not defined themselves solely as warriors. With the fall of the Holy Land, about a hundred years before my time there, the Templars had lost their purpose, but the Order continued to provide caravans to Jerusalem.

I mention this because on arriving at Rhodes, the capital and fortress of my Order, I saw for the first time how few the Knights of the Order were. In truth, in times of peace, the Order maintained only about three hundred brother-knights at Rhodes, and another few hundred serving brothers. Some serving brothers were professed soldiers: that is, professional soldiers who had taken all the vows of the Order, but were of insufficient birth to rank as knights. They were called brother-sergeants. There were very few in the commanderies in Europe – just two in Avignon, a few retired old men in England helping to raise warhorses – but there were hundreds at Rhodes, where they provided the expert leadership and technical skills in siege work and ship handling to the knights. But most of the serving brothers were doctors, apothecaries, nurses and herbalists, carpenters and blacksmiths and other skilled men. They were not warriors except in the direst emergency.

All this is by way of explaining that Rhodes was a military base, a great fortress in the very face of the Turkish enemy, but also a small state, like Vicenza in Italy or Strasbourg. It had a small but expert army, a set of skilled craftsmen, a subject populace of free peasants most of whom were Greek schismatics, and a handful of feudal lords – mostly Latin, but a few Greek. It had a government and ambassadors and the Grand Master was as powerful as many princes. Rhodes had an excellent fleet of six *galia sottil* and one *galia grossa* and two dozen lesser craft, small galleys with fewer than a hundred oarsmen, fast and shallow in draft, that could cover shipping, transport pilgrims, or raid the enemy coast. The navy drove most of the Order's military preparations. Rhodes was a naval power. She contributed two full-time galleys to the defence of Smyrna, a city on the coast of Turkey . that the last crusade had seized in Crecy year.

Yet this small fleet, and the garrisons of the dozen castles the Hospitallers manned in Outremer and the Ionian islands, and the armed caravans that took pilgrims to the Holy Land – these small operations required almost all of the Order's manpower. Rhodes always had to be prepared for siege, still does. At any moment an enemy fleet might descend like the Assyrian wolves to try to snap up the port or lay siege to the city. And every mark of the revenue of the islands, the tolls paid by pilgrims, the revenues of all the Order's estates in Europe and Cyprus – all that money was already spent and on the same castles, ships and caravans I've mentioned.

We always imagined the Order as a great Roman legion of knights, ready to march at a moment's notice against the Saracen foe. But the truth was that for a *Passagium Generale* the Order had to summon in all the knights and brother-sergeants and donats and other volunteers from all over Europe, which cost money and took ships. And then they had to feed and house all those men, see to their equipment, put them in the field, feed and maintain them and their horses. All that, while continuing to serve pilgrims, heal the sick, and defend their own fortresses. So, they were a legion, but most of the legion was tied down in routine duties.

We arrived – that is, the *legate* arrived – with fifty brother-knights from the commanderies, men like Fra Peter Mortimer. And there were a hundred more come with the Genoese or making their way in private ships. Rhodes was packed to the gunwales with knights.

And every one of them had precedence over me.

The inn of the English *langue* was so much like home that I blinked in the great stone doorway and imagined, for a few heartbeats, that the

Thames was two streets away. The English *langue* was located below our bastion, the section of walls for which the English are responsible during attacks. The building is tall, like a London house, and broad, taking up the space that two or three houses would occupy, with a glittering facade of mullioned windows. The ground floor is stone, and rubble-filled timber soars away, whitewashed over stucco over brick, four tall stories of London shining in the Mediterranean sun. Deep stone basements protect the ale and they go down so deep in the soil that you can see the ancient street from the time of Alexander and there is a marvellous bust in one of the cellars, a bearded man's head that some say is Saint John and Nerio says is Messire Plato, the philosopher.

It might be the best inn in London, save for the omnipresent smell of garlic and the presence of oil lamps on every table and olive oil in the food. But it is a noble building with many rooms and many places for private conversation; unlike any other inn I know it has a chapel and a chaplain. The courtyard has a line of pells where men may practice the art of arms, and the archery range and tiltyard are close.

By ancient custom, the commander of the English *langue* is the turcopolier, or the officer in charge of mercenaries. I'm not sure what this says about the English, but in the crusade year, the turcopolier was the captain of the Order's cavalry and scouts; a senior military officer. His name was Fra William de Midleton, and he was a tall man of enormous girth, and no amount of exercise seemed to reduce his size.

I learned all this on arrival, because the turcopolier was sitting in a snug with the legate.

He rose, his great belly pushing at the table that Father Pierre was using as a desk, and extended a massive hand. 'Sir William de Midleton – I am delighted at your coming, sir, and the more so as the manner of your arrival reflects so much credit on our nation in the Order.'

In the next few minutes I learned that our battle with the Turks was the talk of the waterfront and indeed of the whole town, where it was fairly reckoned as the first fruits of the crusade, since the whole coalition fleet was composed of men committed, at least on paper, to the attack.

'How did you find your first brush with the enemy?' Fra William asked.

I was flushed by his praise, but I bowed and thanked him. 'I found them to be good soldiers and wonderful archers. Brave and very dangerous. But poorly armoured.'

Fra William nodded. 'Those are Turks. Brave and reckless. Wonderful archers! When we get a few to convert, we recruit them instantly, I promise you. But when you face the Egyptians, the true Mamluks, you will see that courage and archery united with the industry and discipline of Egypt. The Ghulami are fully armed – and twice as dangerous.' He smiled. 'Luckily, we have ... arrangements ... with the Sultan.' He smiled at Father Pierre.

The legate did not smile. 'No Christian should have an arrangement with the infidel,' he said.

Fra William raised both eyebrows. His face was broad and flat with a large nose and wide, childlike eyes – he looked more like a favourite uncle than a commander of mercenaries. 'Excellency, when you have lived here as long as I—' he began.

Father Pierre looked at me, and not the turcopolier. 'I have been in the East since the year of Poitiers,' he said. 'I have lived in Constantinople and Famagusta. I know the Latin sees of Outremer. I know that Venice and Genoa and Pisa and Florence have made their own pacts with the devil – but I do not expect such rhetoric from the Knights of Christ.'

Fra William showed his dismay and anger. He leaned against the cool stone wall and shook his head.

I thought of the admiral and his statement about pirates. But, quite wisely, I think, I didn't say what came to mind.

In the difficult silence, Fra William bowed stiffly – or perhaps, roundly – and squeezed past me. 'I'm sure the legate would like to brief you alone,' he said. 'When he has finished with you, perhaps you would be as kind as to come to my closet and I will assign you a cell.'

He was perfectly pleasant, although I could see his irritation. He walked out of the oak door and closed it behind him.

Father Pierre rested his head in his hands. 'Why does the Pope want a crusade – an armed attack – on men half the Inner Sea view as allies?'

Sometimes men ask rhetorical questions. They don't want answers. But in this case, I felt that it was worth a try. 'The Pope has declared crusades against Milan and even Naples,' I said.

Father Pierre sat back. 'I do not like my role here. Enough of that – you are too young to share my burdens, and it is unfair of me even to mention them. You have won a great victory.'

I shrugged. 'My lord, we all won a victory.'

He nodded. 'And the Venetians? They came willingly?'

I shrugged again. 'My lord, they are here.'

He laughed. 'Sir William, you sound more like an Italian every day. Your friends – *my* friends – they prosper?'

I nodded. 'None of us took a bad wound,' I said.

'By the grace of God,' added the priest, and I bowed my head.

Then I told him most of the expedition, leaving out almost everything Admiral Contarini had said. He nodded.

'The Venetians are the best sailors on the face of the inner sea,' he said. 'But they turn their God-given talents to the service of greed and not God. The Genoese beat them here.'

'The Genoese were not present when we faced the Turks,' I said.

Father Pierre nodded. 'The Genoese say that by fighting the Turks, we provoke a naval reaction that may threaten the entire Crusade,' he said. He raised a hand as I began to protest. 'Spare me, spare me! I know. The Genoese serve only their own city.'

I leaned forward. 'Have you chosen our ... goal?' I asked softly.

For the first time in my life, I saw Father Pierre be evasive. He was a very poor liar. 'No,' he said.

I knelt and confessed myself of my amorous thoughts. My confessor laughed. 'Chastity sits heavily on you, my son,' he said. 'Be careful. Be ... wise.'

'Wise?' I asked.

He shook his head. 'I have said too much. For your penance, you may find all your friends billets in this city and then join me for dinner. Lord Grey celebrates his birthday and he is eager to see his nephew. How was Master Stapleton?'

'He was brilliant in arms and a good man throughout.' I waved towards the closed door. 'He is the last man among us unknighted.'

'You would recommend him for knighthood?' Father Pierre asked, his hands steepled in his accustomed way.

'Without hesitation. He will be a better knight than I am.' I bowed.

Father Pierre shook his head. 'I doubt that,' he said, the best compliment he ever paid me. His praise was given sparingly, and often to third parties so this was very sweet, despite being so brief. He waved me away in dismissal. 'I'll speak to Lord Grey,' he said.

As I closed the oak door – it might have been imported from England, it was that heavy – I thought that in the past few months, my beloved Father Pierre had begun to act more like a prince of the church. He was not spoiled. It was merely that his new dignity shrouded his enthusiasm and his genuine friendliness.

I missed Father Pierre. He was there when his eyes laughed at my petty sins, when he knelt with me on the floor to pray, when he embraced me. But the cautious *strategos* who lied about the goal of the expedition ...

At any rate, I went up a floor and along a hallway so narrow that a man in full harness would have had to go sideways like a crab. I asked the servants – some English, some Greek, some Arabs – the way until I found the open door at the end of a hall that should have been straight but was not. Later I learned that the English *langue* was one of the richest, and was built in four stages that did not perfectly align, so that the main hall of the second floor was neither straight nor flat.

Fra William filled the room he called his 'closet.' It had a pigeon roost (as we call it) for scrolls, and the whole shelf was packed with them, hundreds of scrolls, and there were more around the room in baskets. In among the scrolls was a table no bigger than the sideboards on which squires cut meat and mix wine, and it, too, was covered in scrolls, and the bulk of the man was wedged between the pigeon roosts and the writing table. By his side was another tall man, this one as thin as Sir William was round.

'Sir Robert Hales – Sir William Gold.' He waved at us.

Sir Robert Hales rose and took my hand. 'I have heard of you, in France and in Italy.'

I bowed. 'Indeed, my lord, we were introduced at Clerkenwell.' I smiled. 'I was with Juan di Heredia's nephew.'

Sir Robert flushed. 'Sir William ... indeed. I swear you were younger then. Or perhaps smaller.'

We all laughed. I had been a squire of no account whatsoever. Now I was a knight of moderate fame.

Sir Robert sat. 'Of course, I know your sister, who shares your high courage.'

My turn to flush. I had scarcely thought of my sister in six months.

Fra William looked up from his writing. 'Sit, Sir William. By our lady, clear him a space. There's nowhere for a man to sit.'

I stood against the far wall and hoped that nothing fell on me. Very gradually, I leaned against a set of shelves weighted down with scrolls and books and tall stacks of parchments being led to their dooms by their heavy seals, slipping gradually but inevitably towards the floor.

'You had a quarrel with Fra Daniele,' Fra William stated. He did not ask.

I said nothing.

'Senior Knights of the Order are commanders,' he said. He was still writing quickly. His big hand was perfectly well-trained, and his writing was as neat as a professional scribe's hand. He was writing Latin. 'Many of my paid soldiers are commanders in their own right, and I have to explain to them that here, on Rhodes, their authority is nothing, and only the brother-knights have the power to giver orders.'

He looked up at me. 'In Outremer, mercenaries sold themselves to the enemy. We have become careful.'

I nodded.

Fra William pursed his lips. 'You further informed Fra Daniele that the legate is your lord.'

I suppose I sighed. I was trying to control my temper, and not doing a perfect job.

Fra William frowned. 'He is a great man, perhaps a saint. But you, as a volunteer in the Order, must obey your superiors. You swore an oath to obey.'

'Any reasonable order,' I said.

'No,' Fra William said. 'There is no such stipulation. You swore to obey. Kindly keep that in mind. I have no doubt – no doubt at all – that you are a brilliant soldier. The dockside tales of your daring are worthy of Roland or Oliver or Gawain. But if you wear the red coat, you must obey.' He raised both eyebrows in his most cherubic look, one I would come to understand better. 'Even Fra Daniele.'

'Yes, Sir Knight.' I bowed carefully, given the limited space.

He smiled, and the room seemed to fill with his glow. 'Good. As an Englishman, you fall to me, and I am proud to have you. I'm sorry I had to start with discipline. But we take it seriously. And you will see why if we come to battle. Knights – gentlemen – are used to doing just as they please, even on the battlefield.'

Fra Robert smiled. His smile was as thin as Fra Williams was beaming. He didn't strike me as a man who had much time for humour.

I nodded. 'I have some experience of this,' I said.

He handed me a set of keys. 'Perhaps the greatest advantage of being English,' he said, 'Is that we have the richest inn except for the Italians, but the smallest *langue* in numbers. So while there are men camped in the streets, I can give all of you cells, good cells with beds. Enjoy them – they may be the only beds you see for a year. The food here is excellent, though I do say so myself,' he added, patting his belly. 'We will pretend that your friends are English. Fra Daniele thought they were.' He went back to writing, and I was not sure whether I was dismissed or not. After some time, he looked up. 'You know John Hawkwood. How is the bastard?'

I shrugged. Italy had made me the master of many shrugs – shrugs for knowing too much, or nothing at all. 'I wrote to him twice last winter and had no reply. He was badly defeated last autumn, but he rescued much of his army.'

'There a rumour that he and the Visconti are threatening Genoa,' Fra William said. 'That the Pope used Hawkwood to put pressure on the Genoese to participate in the crusade.'

I shook my head. 'It may be, but he was nowhere near Genoa when we undertook the last round of negotiations. That success belongs entirely to the legate.'

'I knew him as a boy.' The turcopolier frowned. 'Our lives have taken very different paths.' He met my eye. 'How many men have you commanded?' he asked suddenly.

'I was a corporal last year against Florence, with fifty lances,' I said.

Fra Robert smiled his thin-lipped smile again. He murmured something I did not catch.

Fra William raised an eyebrow. 'Most of the volunteers who came out with the legate have declared a desire to serve together.' He signed his name, took hot wax and sealed his document. 'If circumstances align, I might like to see you command them. It would be unprecedented for a man not of the highest birth – commands of volunteers and donats usually go to princes and kings.' He grinned sourly. '*I* don't have one, this fight. Did the Emperor really gird you with that sword?' he asked.

I smiled. I drew the longsword carefully and handed it to him, and he regarded the Emperor's sword with something like lust.

It is worth saying that the sword was almost unmarked by a dozen combats. There was not a nick in her blade, not a mar on the surface of the metal between her fullers, except where I had covered myself against the sweep of the Turk's axe – I had not allowed his weapon anything like a direct cross, and yet his edge had left a cut on her forte.

'You fought in a tournament,' he said.

'Yes,' I admitted.

'While wearing the surcoat of the order,' he added. Then he shook himself; indeed, he quivered. 'Never mind. But please understand that you have flouted some rules that young knights are punished for disobeying.'

'Are these rules written down somewhere? I asked.

He laughed. 'Every baillie has his own. Every *langue* has some few. It's only ten years ago that we were allowed to keep a copy in English – until then we had to read the rule in Provençal. But I'll find you a copy of the rule. You won't find any mention of tournaments.'

Sir Robert leaned forward. 'Sir William, do you know anything of the – the factions within the order?'

I shook my head. 'No,' I said.

Sir Robert had the look of a man all too well versed in politics. Certes, he was – and is – a great man at the court of the English king. He played with his beard. 'Men may join the order and yet remain loyal to their former lords. We are still English. The French are still French.'

I suppose I smiled.

'What I mean is that there are, no doubt, those within the order who do not relish your legate or his crusade,' he said.

'Or his evident partiality for Englishmen,' Fra William laughed.

Sir Robert nodded. 'Do you see how this can affect all of us?'

'Of course he doesn't,' Fra William said. 'Let him breathe, Robert. He'll come to know us soon enough.' He waved his hand. 'Go find your friends and I'll see you for Lord Grey's birthday.'

Lord Grey's dinner was a gathering of all the English on Rhodes, and I was surprised – and deeply pleased – to see how many of us there were. The English Grand Prior, Fra John Pavely, had led a goodly body of knights and men-at-arms out to Rhodes for the *Passagium Generale*. There was Nicolas Sabraham; there was Steven Scrope, who, like Miles Stapleton, was a squire ready for knighting. Fra William Midleton sat with his friend Fra Robert Hales, who was holding forth of the current state of finance in the English priory. Sabraham whispered to me that I could expect Hales to be Prior of England. We had the Scottish knights, Sir Walter Lindsay and his brothers Kenneth and Norman. We also had Sister Marie who I had not seen in months. She had accompanied Marcus, the legate's archdeacon, on an errand to Naples and joined us late. There were two other women present in a very masculine party, both sisters of the order. One was Fra William's sister Katherine. She, too, was nearly perfectly round, and her eyes also had the bright twinkle of intelligence. She was by me during the speeches, and her undertone of comment on her brother was so funny as to be a danger to all around her. And always by her side was young Sister Mary Langland, who I mention only because she was perhaps the most beautiful nun any of us had ever seen, and yet so utterly pious and chaste as to prevent untoward advances, even from Nerio. It was a splendid evening, with fine food and a flow of talk – and ten thousand compliments for our part in the Venetian victory off Negroponte.

I enjoyed Rhodes. By the time we'd been there a few days, it seemed as if we'd been there forever, and by the end of the second week, it was as if it was the only life I'd ever known. We lived, with our squires, in the English *langue*; we served all the offices from matins to compline. Nerio sang so well – the bastard, he did everything well! – that he was taken to sing in the choir.

I was privileged to be a reader. Fra Peter had known me in London and knew that I was in the most minor order, as a reader of the Gospel. He didn't seem to know that I had been accorded that status to save me from branding. I confess to you that standing in the great church of St John by the harbour of Rhodes and reading from the Gospel to the knights, brothers, and volunteers – and mercenaries – of the order was a great pleasure, not unmixed with fear. I found reading to be much like fighting in the lists: the attention of hundreds of eyes can confuse or even terrify.

One pair of eyes especially. Emile had a dispensation to hear Mass with the knights. It was not an uncommon dispensation for pilgrims to obtain, but it made Mass all the more important to me – see what a sinner I am – that Emile was there. When I read the Gospel, I was all too aware that she stood very close to me, on the other side of the choir stalls, with the Order's sisters.

Otherwise I had virtually no opportunity to see her. I had imagined that we would lie in each other's arms every night of the crusade (how complex a set of sins that is) and of course, when the reality presented itself, she was sealed away among the women. I took consolation, though; without the post-battle darkness of spirit I was not nearly as jealous and the king could no more come to her than I could.

I tried to arrange opportunities to be with her. The one I remember was a ride in the countryside, hawking. The children came, but the duenna I had arranged, the wife of one of the Order's standing officers, was unable to ride, being sick, and that forced Emile to remain with the nuns. We did manage to smile at each other a great deal in the gate house. And I had a lovely day riding along dusty lanes with the nurse and the three children, as well as Marc-Antonio and Miles, both of who proved far better hawkers than I.

Edouard was five or six, and I had found him a pony – really, an island horse. He rode beautifully. In fact, he rode better than I did, and he was polite, attentive, and very excited to be out in the country with a real knight.

'You don't have your big sword,' he said accusingly.

'No,' I admitted.

'What if the Saracens attack us?' he asked.

I pointed over the great blue horizon. 'The sea protects us. Before the Saracens could come here they would have to assemble a fleet.'

'You would kill them all anyway,' he said. 'Maman says so.'

There is something disagreeable in the flattery of a child, second-hand. 'Eduard, being a knight is not all killing,' I said.

'Is it not?' he asked with the terrible disinterest of the young child. 'When I grow up, I will kill anyone I don't like.'

I had not spent enough time with children to know how to handle this.

Miles, on the other hand, had a variety of brothers. 'Even the ones who surrender?' he asked. He smiled as he said it.

Eduard looked pained. Here I had been at the point of imagining him a violent recreant. When I knew children better, I learned that they merely experiment with ideas, and look to adults for encouragement. Some children are encouraged even when adults do not mean them to be.

Miles cut across that. 'Think about the word "gentil",' he said.

The boy pointed at me. 'But Sieur Guillaume is a great knight, and he kills everyone! This is what Maman said.'

'Look!' cried Marc-Antonio. He'd found us a target for our birds, and he halloo'ed at the flock of birds. His intervention couldn't have been more timely.

I resolved to spare someone as soon as possible.

The time passed pleasantly. I suspect it was made better for the five of us that we arrived on the wings of a famous victory, and that we had, apparently, been seen to be important in it. I say this with some amusement. It was a hot fight, and a desperate one, one of the harshest I had seen until that moment, and I had no way to judge the importance of my own role, or my friends'. I had been in fights where I knew I had turned the tide – the bridge at Meux comes to mind – but at the sea fight off Euboea, I fought, and that's all I know.

After the dinner for Lord Grey, I knew most of the English knights and squires, whether they were donats, brothers, or crusaders. Through Nerio, I quickly came to know the Italians in the Order; Fra Ferlino di Airasca was a Savoyard. He was the Order's admiral, as senior as Fra William Midleton, and as easy to know. He had the beautiful manners of the Savoyard court, and his family were friends of Emile's father's family. He was a fine swordsman, and he and Fiore made an immediate and close acquaintance. Fra Palamedo di Giovanni was commanding one of the Order's galleys, and Nerio visited him frequently.

Each day on Rhodes, after matins, we'd eat a light meal – hard bread and cider, perhaps a little cheese, some sausage, whatever was left in the kitchens – and then we'd debouch into the yard and train. We'd stand at the pell with Fiore yelling at us, and we'd engage each other. The Order believed in the English game of sword and buckler, with sharps, and we'd swagger our good swords, first left- and then right-handed. And then spend hours taking out the nicks. I was careful of the Emperor's longsword, and used my spare.

By the summer of the crusade year, Ser Fiore had begun to codify many of his notions of sword and spear play. He had a theory, much like the way the theologians with whom we discoursed had theories on the divinity of Christ, or the Virgin Birth, or the nature of the Host, or the nature of blessings administered by priests. If I dwell on the profession of arms, it is because I was not a priest, but on Rhodes, as in Avignon, we were surrounded by the profession of Christ, so to speak, and we would have had to be far more ignorant men then we were not to imbibe some of their wisdom and their style.

So with Fiore's theory. One of them was that the forming of the first cross in a fight determined all the actions that followed until the two combatants broke apart, or one was hit. And the process by which the combatants came together – in a fight, you never think of these things, but Ser Fiore did, all the time. He would stand watching us, purse his lips, shake his head, and I'd think *what am I doing wrong?* And it would prove later that he was thinking of making us fight to music.

Because fighting has a rhythm to be exploited, of course.

In the yard and in the squares and on the parade of the fortress we trained and trained. Fra Peter led my company, in which, to all effects, I was a corporal. It was the only time I saw him, except occasionally at dinner. When not training, Fra Peter attended constantly on the legate and sometimes on the Grand Master. I missed him.

We formed lines and squares, we formed wedges on foot and mounted, we fought alone, as pairs, as teams of five and as units of fifty, and we practised with spears and swords. A few men had axes or poleaxes – a difficult weapon with which to train, believe me. A good man can ruin a pell with an axe cut. Fiore installed a line of springy saplings – very different from our heavy oak pells – to give us a more rapid, more flowing 'opponent'. But the axe men could lop them to pieces, and sometimes did.

Fra William used a very small axe on a long handle, a weapon he'd taken from a Turk. With a mischievous gleam on his face, he appeared one afternoon and worked his way down our saplings, turning them into kindling with his little axe.

Fiore watched him and then picked up a victim, a thin branch, no thicker than my thumb. It was cut through and almost polished. The cut ran straight.

Fiore nodded and looked at the turcopolier. 'He is very good,' Fiore admitted.

I was amazed that a man so big was so capable, but the man was amazing.

My Turk was also amazing. We baptised him on the feast of Saint John, and he took the name John. Everyone called him John the Turk – Iannis Turkos, in the local tongue. By the time the hospital released him, his Italian was acceptable, although he was not good at tense or time and his idea of the agreement of numbers could be very difficult.

'I am very honoured to being so many knight,' he said with a bow to my friends. 'All with Christ now.'

It is easy to make a man sound like a fool with bad speech and John the Turk was no fool. He could ride anything, and he was impossibly generous – his understanding of Christ's word shamed the rest of us. I gave him some coins to drink my health one day, and watched him the next day give all of it to a beggar.

'Does He not say, give all you have and follow Me?' John asked.

Nerio slapped him on the shoulder. 'He didn't mean a horse or arms,' he said.

John laughed. 'Of course not!' he said. 'Christ no fool.'

John also thought I was a priest because, at his baptism, I read the Gospel. From John I learned that an imam, a Moslem priest, was a reader first and foremost. I discovered that imams are not disbarred from being warriors or having wives, which led me to suspect that the Saracens might have certain advantages.

Be that as it may, John was the first real servant I ever had. He was both a wonderful and terrible servant. He had no notion of subservience: that is, he had respect for my rank, and my friends, but he, too, was a professional warrior, and he didn't expect to be treated any differently. He was happy to lay out my kit, polish my armour, sharpen my weapons, and especially care for my horse but he refused to have anything to do with the serving of food or the cleaning or maintenance of clothes, all of which he described with withering contempt as 'women's work'. He handed all of them to Marc-Antonio.

One day they appeared before me, Marc-Antonio with two black eyes and a long gash on the back of his right hand, and John virtually unmarked – but whatever was settled between them, Marc-Antonio was no longer referred to as the 'woman'.

It is odd, to me, that some men have such opinions of women. Women, to me, are brave, careful, smart, and delightful. I would cheerfully do laundry to have an hour with a woman, and I'd think nothing of sewing clothes for anyone I like. And the Blessed Virgin was a woman. I defy any gentleman anywhere to offer her insult, and I offer that cartel without restriction to any defamer of women.

But my Turk, my Kipchak, saw the roles of women and men as separate streams. If we are held here long enough, perhaps I'll tell you how John came to change his spots. But as the weeks passed, and we trained and trained, and our horses fattened and recovered their muscle, so John became one of us. And one day we watched him shoot his bow.

First, he was given a bow by Fra William. He thanked the turco-polier profusely – and then, when the man's back was turned, he fumed. He ridiculed the bow as too weak, badly made, with a cast. He strung it and unstrung it.

He took the quiver of arrows he'd been given and went through them one by one.

'A bow for slaves. And arrows to match,' he all but spat. He up-ended the quiver, an English arrow bag, really, and in it was a mixed bag – literally – with arrows of every colour and nine or ten different fletching styles: round vanes, elliptical vanes, and pointed vanes like our own arrows. He fetched a stool (we were in the yard) and began sorting them into piles, staring down the length, holding them to the sun, and running his thumb down the vanes.

One of our crossbowmen, the Order's, I mean, came out with an English ale in his fist. 'I hate to see them apes given arms,' he said in Genoese-Italian. 'But they're born to bows like little centaurs.' He watched the Turk. 'Almost intelligent, eh? Good bow, eh?' he said to the Turk.'

'Bow is craps. Arrows are turd every one,' John said. 'Made in Genoa.'

The crossbowman flushed and went back inside.

John smiled a grim little smile, and went back to sorting arrows. In the end he chose five – of forty. Another ten he set aside, and after he'd taken the steel or iron heads off all the rest and thrown the shafts on the inn's pile of kindling, he straightened the ten he'd chosen over a little fire. A few days later, when the garrison was shooting at the butts, John appeared with his English quiver at his belt – on the wrong side. When I tried to correct this, he laughed at me.

The garrison archers and crossbowmen were loosing at about seventy paces. We stood and watched them, about thirty paces further up-range. John strung his bow, and then, without drawing a breath, loosed an arrow over one of the Genoese.

It struck the distant target.

Every man on the line turned and the Genoese crossbowman began to yell insults.

John raised his bow and loosed the other four arrows in his fingers as fast as I can tell this, the last arrow leaping high into the sun before the first one struck.

When they hit the target a hundred paces distant, they struck *one, two, three, four*.

I looked at Juan. 'Why didn't they kill us all on the beach?' I asked.

John laughed. 'I am out arrow.' He turned his back on the Genoese in contempt. 'Get I good bow, fight better.' He shrugged. 'Sword, horse.'

Juan looked down range at the target and the angry archers. 'May Saint George and all the saints preserve us,' he said.

'Amen,' I agreed. 'John, do all the Turks shoot like you?'

He shook his head in disgust. 'Turks, no.' He said. 'Turks and Turcoman not all good archer. Some fall off horse. Horses. Yes? But Kipchak and Mon-ghul ride, shoot, always win.' He shrugged. 'Not always. Yes? But many.'

Juan pursed his lips. 'Yes, John,' he said.

John was not the only Christian Turk, not by a long chalk. As I later found, the Greek Emperor had a whole regiment of them, and so did some of the lords of Achaea and Romania. But his archery was superb and the tales of his prowess circulated rapidly. Some of our crusaders came to see him shoot and to wager on him. I confess I made a fair packet on him one afternoon, wagering with a dozen former brigands as the marks were moved farther and farther away.

A new shipload – a great round ship – of crusaders had come from Venice. It had aboard a number of Gascons and some other French and German knights. I hadn't met them yet, but they all came to watch the archery and complain of the heat.

One of crusader knights was d'Herblay. With him as a full retinue of men I knew – some well, like young Chretien d'Albret, who remembered me as a routier only slightly less barbaric than Camus, and many Gascons, Bretons, and Savoyards men-at-arms who clearly viewed me as their lord did, as an enemy. Gascons are the touchiest people on the face of the world. They hate each other, and everyone else, in equal parts, and when one of them achieves a measure of fame, they expect to be treated like Charlemagne and Lancelot all rolled into one. The Bretons were hard men who said little and scowled much. The Savoyards were veteran men-at-arms.

And they were with the Comte d'Herblay. Young d'Albret wore his colours, so that I had some warning that the man was present.

I wanted d'Herblay dead – humiliated and dead. But there was more to it than that. Even while John the Turk took their money with his archery, I was watching them. They swore, they blasphemed, and perhaps more important, their clothing was slovenly and their jupons were all spattered with the rust of their maille, which they probably didn't trouble to clean over much. The Order drilled its knights and volunteers every day; these crusaders never seemed to practice at all. They ate, they drank, they gambled, and they fornicated. Their state pressed through my hatred of d'Herblay.

These were bad men.

Very like the man I'd once been.

D'Herblay paid over his debt on his wager with a poor grace. 'And when did you become a little priest, Gold?' he asked. 'Have you discovered little boys? Are you pimping for the Pope?' He nodded and smiled his ironic smile. 'Of course you are not dead. Of course. When a gentleman wants something done right—'

'He needs to have the courage to do it himself,' I said.

I was curious to find that his taunts had very little impact. In a camp in Provençe in fifty-seven or fifty-eight, those words would have sent me into a rage. Here, I looked at Juan, who was hard by, and he rolled his eyes. You must imagine us, in our sober brown gowns, neat and clean as new-made pins, and these rust-stained brigands. D'Herblay was himself well dressed, in incongruous and sweat-matted fur and wool. But his men looked like the scrapings of a particularly rancid barrel.

'You used to have the name of being a fighter, Gold,' d'Herblay said.

'I would be delighted,' I said carefully, 'to fight you at any time.'

He flashed his fake smile.

'Daggers, right now?' I offered.

Juan put his hand on my arm. 'The order would cast you out. And perhaps excommunicate you.'

'I don't give a *fuck*,' I said. Ten minute with them, and I was becoming one of them again.

D'Herblay stepped back among his men-at-arms. 'And be knifed in the back by your thugs?' he said.

I didn't even trouble to reply. Just for a moment, I considered drawing my basilard and killing my way through to him.

To the ruin of my career.

And the death of my soul, perhaps. Or perhaps I'd be making the world a better place.

He tried to whip the Gascons into a fury against me, but they didn't think highly of him, and he left us with a trail of imprecations that might have earned immediate heavenly retribution and made him sound weak – and I found that Fiore's hand was heavy on my shoulder and Nerio was pressed against my side.

'Wine,' Nerio said.

Of all people, Chretien d'Albret came and stood by me when d'Herblay was gone. He was older, heavier, and had a scar on his left arm that ran down on to his hand, a bad wound. He approached me with reserve.

I bowed and then reached out and embraced him. We had, in fact, survived some hard times together. His face brightened as I embraced him.

I introduced him to Juan, and to Fiore, and Nerio, who greeted him with no warmth at all.

Fiore hadn't met him, but by happenstance had heard me speak of the youngest d'Albret.

'Ah!' Fiore said. 'Sir William speaks of you often.'

As a method of warming an old friend, this line cannot be beaten, and Fiore's sincerity was indubitable. When we had collected all of John's winnings we took him back to the English inn, and gave Chretien d'Albret and his friend Henri – I cannot remember his style – at any rate, we gave them some wine and were treated to a long dissertation on the state of politics in the Duchy of Aquitaine, which was of interest only to me. Fiore shuffled in his seat, eager to be back in the yard, and Juan took to peering out the mullioned windows, and eventually I let them go.

D'Albret shook his head when Fiore made his excuses. 'You are so ... mild,' he said. 'I remember you, you and Richard, running the inn in that little town we held all winter when you were fighting Camus. When you took me. You remember?'

I laughed. 'Of course I remember.'

He shook his head. 'You don't swear. You are dressed like a monk. D'Herblay says you fucked his wife. Is that true? Or are you really a monk?'

'He is a coward and a bad lord,' I said. 'You should not serve him.'

D'Albret fingered his beard. He had a louse crawling out of his collar, headed for his hair. I remembered living in clothes full of lice.

It seemed a long time ago.

'You think you could kill d'Herblay?' he asked, and he cocked an eyebrow.

I didn't say *in a single blow*. I shrugged. 'Any time. But I will spare you my boasts,' I said.

'You ran a brothel,' d'Albret said. He said it in accusation, but the accusation was not hypocrisy. The accusation was *You used to be one of us.*

The truth of it was that by changing my spots, I accused him. And he knew it. He was uncomfortable. Even as we sat in the inn, brothers and knights would come in from exercise, or divine office, or mounting guard, with many a pleasant word, or the benison, or a saint's name on their lips. I had grown used to the company of men who used courtesy at all hours – d'Albret still lived in the world from which I had come. Even when he swore, he did so only to try me.

I shrugged. Again. D'Albret seemed to be trying to say something; he kept rising to it, and then slipping away. 'I enjoy serving the Order,' I said. 'Have another cup of wine.'

'What do they pay?' he sneered.

'Your family is rich enough,' I said. 'Why don't you pay the fee and become a volunteer?'

He looked at me as if I'd just made a lewd suggestion and he was a nun. 'I fight for *gold*,' he said. 'What can your Order do for me?'

'Why are you come on crusade, then?' I asked.

He laughed, leaning his stool back on two of its legs and stretching

319

his booted feet towards the unnecessary fire. 'To be rich!' he said.

'Not to travel to Jerusalem?' I asked.

'Not unless the streets are actually paved with gold,' he laughed.

Despite my new-found maturity, he was beginning to get to me. He meant to, and when they set themselves to it, Gascons can be the most offensive men in the world. Perhaps even when they do not set themselves to it.

'This crusade is just a chevauchée?' I asked.

D'Albret grinned. 'There's no war in France and not much in Italy since Hawkwood got beaten. They paid us to leave Provençe, and then they paid us to winter at Venice, and now we'll take a few Saracen cities and despoil them and go home rich as bankers. It was this or Spain.' He looked into the distance. 'Or perhaps when this is done, I'll go to Spain. There's to be fighting there. I hadn't expected this misbegotten expedition to take so long.'

I started to speak, but he rode over me.

'It's the fucking peasant the Pope sent. He knows nothing of war – a total fool. Can you imagine? An actual serf off Talleyrand's estates, pretending to command men. The Pope *wanted* this expedition to fail.'

I had finally understood that he meant Father Pierre. 'The legate?' I said. 'Without him, there would be no crusade. Don't be a fool, d'Albret. Whatever his birth, he's no peasant.'

D'Albret laughed his older brother's nasty laugh. 'Once a serf, always a serf. They flinch when you snap your fingers.'

I could imagine what Father Pierre would say if I fought a duel for his good name. So I took a deep breath, looked elsewhere, and finally rose. 'We will have to agree to disagree,' I said. 'I see him as a great man, a living saint.'

D'Albret spat. 'Well, the problem will be solved for us soon enough, or that's what I hear. The Serf – that's what we call him – has given offence to certain parties, eh?'

'Who do you mean? And how will the problem be solved?' I asked. I had been about to slap money on the table and walk away, but I knew a threat to my lord when I heard it.

D'Albret looked both smug and superior. 'I just know the Serf will be gone soon. And then we will have a good war, and booty. That's what everyone says.' He shook his head. 'When you killed that French bastard who stole your sword in the spring? I told everyone I knew you. I was proud to know you, eh? What happened? Priests take your stones? I heard d'Herblay beat the crap out of you. He says you are a coward.'

Before I knew it, my hand was on my hilt.

He laughed. 'So you are still alive,' he said.

'You serve d'Herblay,' I said. It was obvious. He wore the blue and white arms.

'He's not so bad. Better than the Bourc. The money's good.' He shrugged. 'He'll kill you, William. When the legate's gone you had best hide.'

It was a busy day. D'Albret wasn't gone a heartbeat before Nicolas Sabraham occupied his stool. From his look at d'Albret's departing arrogance, I immediately understood his interest.

'He claims there's a threat to the legate,' I said.

Sabraham laughed. He didn't laugh often, and his contempt was obvious. 'The French have ten plots going to kill the legate,' he said. 'All talk. They are the most hopeless conspirators, and the most pompous.'

'D'Herblay is here,' I said.

Sabraham knew that. 'What I came to tell you,' he said. 'You show promise in this role, Sir William.'

'Why do they hate him so much?' I asked.

Sabraham sighed. 'His birth. Their fears. They were raised to hate peasants, now a peasant will be Pope.'

'I find I am not as close to young d'Albret as I once was,' I said. 'But I might be able to learn more – perhaps to turn him. He was a good man once.'

Sabraham put out a hand to stop me. 'No. I know all I need to know about the Gascons and the French. Although, if we take Jerusalem with those men, it will, I promise you, be entirely due to the will of God.'

I winced. 'They are good men-at-arms,' I said.

Sabraham shrugged. 'They are thugs in armour. I'd prefer to use the Mamluks to exterminate *them*. In fact, I sometimes suspect that was the Holy Father's intention all along. No, I am not here for your Gascons. I'm here for your Turk. May I meet him? Fra William says he is quite the marvel.'

I summoned John – more arrow repair in the yard – and bought him a cup of wine. He never made any fuss about wine, and I find that many easterners will drink it. But that is beside the point.

Sabraham spoke to him in Turkish. In minutes, they were speaking quickly, a veritable barrage of words, guttural and liquid.

Sabraham dismissed my servant back to his 'work' and leaned back. 'What a treasure,' he said. 'A fine man. You are very lucky. His people take death-debt very seriously. And he thinks you are a priest of Christ. His theology is a little weak, but you won't suffer for it. I must go ... I hear he's a famous archer?'

'He is, too,' I admitted.

Sabraham nodded. 'Soon, Sir William, we'll get to see what this crusade is made of. An archer who speaks good Kipchak may be the best asset we have.'

A few days later, early in September, I believe, Miles stood the vigil before knighthood. We had a fine ceremony, and after vigil in the knights' chapel of the Order, we heard Mass. Vigil in armour is a complex form of penance; the armour both supports and fatigues you, and as you tire, the plates of your knees begin to press harder into your kneecaps, and if I'd had a little less wine, I'd make a moral of that. But I won't. Emile came. We touched hands at the holy-water font – I dipped my hand for water, and she put her hand in atop mine, taking her water from the backs of my fingers.

Oh, it sounds like nothing, but I still flush to tell it.

'When you sail,' she said softly, 'I must stay here. The comte is here.'

There was no time to question her. We moved apart. But Father Pierre told me that the non-military pilgrims and the women would stay at Rhodes while the crusade attacked, and when we had seized Jerusalem, we would send for them.

I wanted to see her again. Her face was before me all the time, and she was only six streets away. Finally, I summoned my courage and sent Marc-Antonio to the nuns with a note. He had a way with nuns – it was his innocent countenance.

Thanks to that note, we began to plot our meeting. Emile suggested a church – Rhodes is full of churches, and some nearly deserted, especially after compline. We sent back and forth a date, a time, a place. It was delicious to correspond every day. I would fly home from the drill field, strip my armour and look for a note. Sometimes Marc-Antonio would put it into my gauntleted hand while I was still mounted. Some days there was no note at all.

One day she sent 'Be careful – you have more to lose than I.'

That seemed odd.

But her notes seemed to promise everything, and I became less inclined to secrecy and more to romance.

Fiore hit me in the head a great many times that week.

We chose the Monday night as the most private, the most secret. By Friday, I had fine castile soap and a little Hungary water and my clothes were cleaned and brushed. Repeatedly. Marc-Antonio was beginning to show his irritation with my new level of personal beauty.

On Saturday evening, we had two tables of piquet at the inn. The knights did not forbid gambling: with wine, it was an 'allowed' vice. I was playing with Fra William when the legate came in. We all rose.

He glanced at the cards with unhidden disapproval. 'We are so close to Jerusalem that a man might reach out and touch her,' he said. 'The centurions diced at the foot of the cross, I suppose.' He looked at me. 'I need you.'

I bowed. 'My lord.'

He took me to one of the snugs, where Marcus, his archdeacon and sometimes his secretary, served us wine.

'Sabraham will sail tomorrow,' he said.

That didn't surprise me. Many of the ships had water aboard and all had their full compliments of sailors and oarsmen. We, that is, Nerio and Juan and I, thought that the expedition might load on Friday and sail on Saturday week.

'He desires you to support him,' the legate said.

I had no choice but to agree. I owed Sabraham my life, and I owed it to the legate as well.

'You hesitate,' he said.

I shrugged.

'You may tell me anything!' he said.

May I tell you that I have an amorous meeting in a church with the woman I love, where I hope to woo and win her, to make love among the pillars of the nave? May I tell you that, Father?

'I'll be ready,' I said.

'You go to scout beaches for the crusade,' he said.

I confess, I was proud to have been chosen by Sabraham.

Proud … and devastated.

I sent Marc-Antonio with one last note.

> *My dear,*
> *I sail in the morning. Only the orders of God's Vicar could keep*
> *me from you. Pray for me, and know that you have all my love.*
> *Your knight*

He came back an hour later. 'No note,' he said. He sounded puzzled and angry and handed me a packet.

It was no packet. It was a piece of blue silk, and on it was picked out a passage of the Gospels, in pearls. It took me a long time, too long, to realise that it was a favour, meant to replace the old one.

A slow, strong smile filled my face – and my heart.

On Sunday morning, just about the time we were leaving Mass, the Cypriote fleet entered the harbour – almost eighty sail. The king's brother was there, and all the rest of his nobles and officers who had not seen him in two years. I understood from what I heard in Venice and on Rhodes that the king feared that if he went home to Cyprus, he would never leave. As it proved, I think he knew his people well. I never saw him on Rhodes – later I learned why – but the coming of the Cypriotes doubled our army and our fleet, and made the whole *empris* seem possible. With eight thousand men-at-arms and almost two hundred ships we might actually take Jerusalem. Surely it was the largest Christian host in a hundred years.

In fact, the last two weeks we were at Rhodes the Turkish emirs of the coast hastened to send submissions and surrenders to the King of Cyprus and even to the Order. Fra Ricardo was heard to joke that the Order should gather a hundred ships every autumn because we had them scared. The naval victory in the north had paralysed the two largest Turkish emirs, and now the smaller fish were wriggling.

I went back to my friends and embraced them, one by one.

'Leave some Turks for us,' Fiore said.

I carried my harness down to the seaport in a state of inner confusion. I had not seen Emile. I was not taking my friends.

At the pier, Sabraham looked at the wicker hamper containing my harness and smiled, his teeth bright in the torch lit dark. 'You won't need that,' he said. 'I'll see that it gets loaded onto the correct ship with your horse and the rest of your equipment.' He nodded at Marc-Antonio. 'Better yet, send your squire with your war gear. All you need is a dagger.'

We sailed in one of the Order's own ships, a galliot or light galley commanded by a Brother Sergeant. She was a fine ship, and we had beautiful weather. We were two days at sea while Sabraham explained to me just how we would choose the beaches where we would land. I had John and no one else – my friends would sail with the main fleet.

We had no warhorses, no armour, no surcoats.

'We will swim ashore,' Sabraham said.

In private, he asked me if I trusted John.

'No,' I answered.

Sabraham smiled. 'Then you can take him. Don't trust him – never let him be more than an arm's length away. You *can* swim?' he asked again.

We swam by the ship while she rowed until Sabraham was satisfied and he taught me a few words of Arabic.

Six days at sea. We sighted Cyprus. My geography is stronger now than it was then, but I could see through a brick wall in time. I watched the coast of Cyprus growing larger for two days and then slipping astern as we weathered Cape Salamis.

My navigation was non-existent then, although Sabraham, who seemed to teach rather than talk, was showing me the rudiments of open water navigation, and I had begun to stand all of Brother Robert's watches with him. Brother Robert had been a small English merchant until his wife died on pilgrimage. He was a fine seaman and my first real teacher about the sea – I suppose that Lord Contarini should have pride of place here, but Brother Robert was patient. He taught me well enough that a day after Cyprus went under the rim of the world, I turned to Sabraham at the edge of dark.

'Where are we going?' I asked. It had taken me two days to ask.

He looked forward to where Brother Robert was teaching John better Italian with the aid of a book of Psalms.

Then he frowned. 'Alexandria,' he said.

Alexandria. Founded by the conqueror. Some men said it was the greatest city in the world and Fra Peter said it had forty gates.

I had guessed the answer, and yet my breath caught in my throat. Alexandria.

Alexandria is said to be the largest city in the world. Now, I have been to Baghdad and Constantinople, and Barcelona and London and Paris and Prague and a few other cities. Baghdad, they say, was much larger before the Mongols sacked it. Constantinople is perhaps the largest of all these cities, but it is almost empty – fifty thousand people inside walls that have held twenty times as many. Rome is a ruin of a ruin.

But Alexandria is mighty. It stretches all along the shore of the sea on a set of sand spits and islands, much like Venice, or I think it was when first laid down. Alexandria has a great double wall like Constantinople's, pierced with more than forty drum-shaped gated towers, and each pair of towers at a gate was like a small fortress with a garrison, able to be locked away from the city and held. The city has two great harbours, which some men call the old and the new but we called Porto Vecchio and Porto Pharos, after the ancient lighthouse. Porto Pharos was defended by two superb castles, both so new that you could smell the mortar from a mile away – the Casteleto, the little castle, was on the eastern arm of the spit that defended the great harbour, and the Pharos Castle, which has an Egyptian name I never learned, guards the western spit and overawes the city which had more than a hundred mosques as well as twenty Christian churches for the various schismatics there – Nestorians and Gnostics and Greeks. The Porto Vecchio was full of ships, including Genoese and Cypriote ships while the Pharos harbour held privileged visitors and the Sultan's navy.

'Egypt has a weak Sultan, very young,' Sabraham said. 'Al-Ashraf Sha'ban. The regent rules him. He is a Mamluk and holds the title *atabak al-'asakir* or as we say, Constable. Commander. He is called Yalbugha. Repeat the name.'

'The Mamluks are a kind of Turk, yes?' I asked. I probably massacred the name, as he made me repeat it and the title that accompanied it. That was part of my lessons, too. I also learned to say *'Allahu Akbar'* or 'God is Great'.

'The Mamluks are Kipchaks and Circassians,' Sabraham said, 'taken as slaves – sometimes as war captures, but sometimes sold by their own parents. The Genoese bring them by the hundred, and the Egyptians buy them as soldiers. Sometimes they are called "Ghulami" or "slaves".'

'If they are slaves, why do they fight at all?' I asked. 'Why don't the Egyptians do their own fighting?'

Sabraham nodded. 'Warfare demands horsemen, and Egypt is rich, but it is terrible country for horses – too hot, and too many insects. The rainy season kills horses by rotting their hooves and the dry season kills their forage and robs them of water. But the troubles in raising horses don't effect the army horses – it is that there are not enough horses to raise a boy to riding from infancy. You cannot create a horse-archer overnight.'

I nodded my agreement. I knew how much effort it took to remain capable with a lance, or a longsword.

'So they buy boys who were raised from birth with horses. Most of them are Kipchaks like your John. Some few are Turks, but they are not trusted with senior commands.' He shrugged. 'A Kipchak boy can rise to rule. All of them have fine armour, beautiful horses, superb weapons, any woman they want, and they live well.' He shrugged. 'I'm told that Kipchak boys have been known to compete to go to the slavers.' He paused. 'Do you know who Baybars was?'

It was like being asked who Satan was. 'Yes!' I exclaimed.

'He was a Kipchak. You understand?'

I supposed that I did. I certainly understood why Sabraham was so pleased by John the Turk.

At any rate, Sabraham watched the shoreline as we approached; it was as flat as the fens around Boston and green as spring, even in early autumn. We made a rendezvous of which I had not been informed – Sabraham was very close with information about our meetings. Off a village to the west of Alexandria, we transferred, by prior arrangement, from the Order's galliot to a Cypriote merchant of less than a hundred tonnes, a stubby, round-hulled ship with a crew of six men and holds that stank of fish guts.

Brother Robert saluted us and slipped away to the north, and Theodore, the captain of our new vessel, a Cypriote Greek, welcomed us aboard. It was immediately clear to me that he was in the pay of the Order or perhaps the king, but Sabraham insisted that the six of us – his own servant or squire, whose name was Abdul, his two silent soldiers, whose Christian names I had never learned, as well as John the Turk, Sabraham himself and I – stay well separate from the crew of the fishing smack. By his order we all wore our hoods at all times, and we bespoke no man.

In the last light of day, beautifully timed, I must say, Theodore entered the outer harbour under a shivering lateen very close-hauled. The broad harbour had four rows of ships anchored well off shore, but for some reason no vessel was anchored closer than a bowshot from the beach.

Our captain called to Sabraham and they had a brief conference.

Sabraham returned to me and shook his head. 'He says the Porto Vecchio is so silted up that he cannot approach the shore. Why did he not tell me this earlier?'

'I thought you had been here before?' I asked.

'Always from the land, with caravans,' Sabraham said. He frowned.

Theodore made a signal and the ship turned south, deeper into the harbour. He appeared to mistake his anchorage, and passed the pilot boat. As we ran down wind, with the Arabic anger of the pilot boat in our ears, Sabraham gathered us in the stern. 'The water under the keel will be less than two men deep,' he said. 'Swim up the beach and strip your clothes. We will be met.'

I touched the dagger at my belt. 'If we are not met?' I asked.

He frowned. 'We improvise,' he said.

He himself wore only a cheap wool gown over his braes, with a heavy basilard in his rope belt. I emulated him.

But the pilot boat had changed tack, and her rig was lighter and faster than ours.

Master Sabraham watched her in the dying light. 'Too bad,' he said. 'We will have a long swim.'

Just then, the tubby fishing boat's hull skidded on the sea's bottom. We were a long way from shore; the city seemed close enough, with the lights of the taller buildings reflected in the still water of the Porto Vecchio, but those waters were still several hundred cloth yards wide.

Captain Theodore shouted commands in Greek and the helm was put up. Sabraham swore.

'Look, we improvise,' he said.

I was looking over the side. As we turned, I could see the bottom as clear in the failing light as I can see the floor of this room. It was right under our keel. Even as I looked, we touched, and Sabraham and I were thrown flat on the deck.

'Shit,' Sabraham said. Without any further imprecations, he rolled over the side into the water as the pilot boat came alongside with a swarm of Arabic imprecations.

The side at the waist was only three feet above the water, and the water was as warm as blood. But it stank of human excrement and dead fish. My hand brushed a dead cat floating like a bloated, matted fur hat, stinking of decay and I was all but paralysed with a kind of disgusted panic.

Fortunately, the water was shallow. It was so shallow that we were touching bottom before we were at a safe distance from our smack. Twice I had to force my face under the foul water to avoid detection, and by the time I was halfway to shore, I was only waist deep.

Despite that, I made it ashore. We all did. John spat and spat – I think that Kipchaks are very clean people – and two Alexandrines appeared out of the darkness. There was a muttered exchange of passwords and they provided us with gowns of linen and cotton.

Sabraham had spent the days of the passage briefing us, and I knew my role. It fitted my inclination and my training, so John and I left Sabraham almost immediately and walked along the beach front for more than an English mile, gazing with fascination at the sea wall above us. It was magnificent, as fine as the wall of Constantinople, tall, built of layers of pale stone that glowed like fine chamois in the dark and the sally gates we passed had marble lintels with Arabic inscriptions that neither John nor I could read.

The night was full of noise and foreign, intoxicating smells: smells of alien cookery, of plants, and spices, and garbage. The thin sounds of music, elfin, silvery and magical in the moonlight, slipped over the sea wall. Women laughed. Men laughed, too.

Over the walls towered the stele that marked the tomb of Alexander, and as we made our way west and south around the walls, we saw the twin pillars that Sabraham had pointed out from the sea – the columns of Pompey. We crossed the river at the great stone bridge, which was unguarded, to my astonishment, and made our way to the Cairo Gate, where Sabraham had ordered us.

It took us the better part of the night to walk around the city, and by the time we reached our first destination, I was drunk on the foreignness and the wonder of Alexandria. It was gargantuan – thrice the size of Florence, or so it seemed in the darkness.

Eventually, we reached the gate that Sabraham had described and we lay down in a *caravanserai* with pilgrims and merchants and slept. I slept – I was young.

In the morning, we rose with the others. We made no pretence of being Moslems, which, if you consider, is odd, as John might easily have passed as one. But no one paid us any attention, and after their morning prayers, we purchased horses. They were the fine-headed Arab breed, and impossibly cheap; that is, in Italy I had never been able to afford an Arab, and in Egypt, despite the difficulty in raising them, they cost little more than a palfrey cost in France.

If dawn revealed a superb world of gilded minarets, veiled women and handsome, bearded men in all the colours of the rainbow – *par dieu*, the Egyptians were rich! – but as I say, if the sun revealed their riches in all their startling adornment and magnificence, it also revealed a level of horrifying poverty that was the more shocking compared to the opulence. Outside our *caravanserai*, there were two beggars, dead. They lay where they had died, and no one seemed to care. Beyond the market's horse lines – we were outside the great customs gates of the city, and there was a market – a line of beggars sat in the dust. There were lepers, and men with their hands cut off: criminals, my Turk assured me. But there was a single leper woman with seven children, and every one of them was a leper; most of them were naked, so that every touch of the disease on their poor little bodies was on display. The leper woman and her seven children had much the same effect on me as the floating cat's corpse.

Moments after we purchased our horses, John suddenly grabbed my arm.

'Sit down,' he said. 'Don't stare.'

A troop of horse, perhaps a hundred men-at-arms, came out the gate at a canter. The leader was mounted on the finest horse I had ever seen, a bright gold horse like Jack, years ago in France, with bronze mane and tail and dark legs and muzzle – I had never seen such markings. The horse's caparison and tack was all of green and silver, there were jewels on his bridle, and his rider was in green silk. His helmet was a tall, peaked spiral with an open face and a superb aventail of tiny links. His green gown seemed to cover more armour, and he carried a golden axe in his hand.

The guard at the gate turned out and saluted, more than two hundred men in maille and plate, with heavy bows of horn and sinew and heavy, curved sabres.

I noted that John's advice had been exact – almost every man and woman in front of the gate was sitting. Most were silent, and all wore attitudes of respect.

I watched the men-at-arms, as they were the first Mamluks I had seen. They were well mounted. Most of them had light lances, like our boar spears, and all had a case carrying at least one bow, although some had two, and one big man had three bows. They all carried one bow strung.

I noted at once that they rode a different saddle from us. Of course I had heard this from Sabraham and indeed from Fra Peter, but their saddles were very small and had no back, and their caparisons, where worn, were only silk, with no mail underneath, though their armour and helmets were heavy enough, by Saint George.

An old woman sitting next to me in the dust spoke to me and cackled.

'Say nothing,' John enjoined me. He spoke low.

The woman's eyes widened and she shuffled away.

'I told she you are sick,' he said.

The Mamluks waited in front of the gate through their lord's inspection of the garrison. The troopers began to be bored, like soldiers the world over, and the men in the front rank began to examine the crowd.

The rightmost Saracen in the front rank was a big, heavy man with a henna-dyed red beard. His horse was the biggest there, almost as big as my warhorse and his eyes roved the beggars, and then the merchants.

I tried to make myself very small.

His eyes went right over me.

So did the eyes of the younger man to his left.

Their lord received the salute of the gate's garrison, and returned it imperiously with his axe, then he turned and made his horse rear a little, and the crowd almost cheered. It was a curious sound, almost like a whisper.

He raised his whip – his axe was hung by his saddle bow – and called something in his tongue, and all the mounted men shouted.

The gates began to open, and the Mamluks began to form in a column with perfect discipline, all except the younger man, one file to the left of the old bastard with the dyed beard. The younger man put his heels to his mount and seemed to fly across the packed dirt. For a few horrifying beats of my heart I thought that he had chosen me, or John, but he went past us, almost over us.

I turned and saw a group of pilgrims. As it proved, they were a wedding party.

The young Mamluk rode in among them. He reached down and raised the veil of the bride and came riding back with her over his saddle. She was screaming and reaching for her husband but the young man lay face down in a pool of blood.

It had happened very quickly, as such things do. I'd seen it done in France.

I started to rise, and John struck me with his fist. I went down.

I rose on one knee, as Fiore taught, and John caught me. He wasn't attacking me – so much for trust – he was restraining me.

'Calm!' he said. 'Or we have been dead. All of us.'

Henna-beard shouted something, and the young man with the bride over his saddle laughed and waved his riding whip. Henna-beard shook his head in disgust and rode through the open gate. About half of the cavalry followed the Green Lord out of the gate and down the road to Cairo, and the rest formed by fours – a beautiful spectacle – and rode back in the gates.

Well. In those moments, I learned everything about the Mamluks.

The anger in the market was palpable. The Egyptians were not cowards, whatever my Italian friends said. But they had no weapons; no one I could see had more than an eating knife. There were men shouting, suddenly, and the wedding party was paralysed until one of the women burst into a wailing cry, and instantly it was taken up.

The garrison had begun to march inside when someone threw a paving stone, and a Mamluk soldier was hit and went down.

The garrison halted and began to reform. They were in some confusion about whether to reform inside the gate or outside.

The people in the market were working themselves up to a riot. I had seen it in London and Paris and Verona, and I found it fascinating, in a detached way, how much an Arab mob resembled a good English mob.

'Run!' John said.

We caught the bridles of our new horses and ran. The mob was solidifying around us; men were running up from the low shops and stalls along the market, and a farmer bringing produce to sell jumped down from his cart, seized his stick and ran to join the crowd. Men and women – even children – joined the crowd.

A hail of stones hit the soldiers.

They drew their bows.

And loosed. By the wounds of Christ, they killed fifty people in their first discharge, and they nocked and drew again, and the arrows flew. More died.

Arrows found their way past the front rank. We were fifty paces beyond the front of the mob, and an arrow went over my right shoulder and over my horse's rump to kill a Jew standing by his stall. He crumpled, a look of consternation on his face. His son stared at me, face white. The boy was ten or eleven and he had no idea what to do with his father suddenly dead.

They were a horse-length away. Before I had gone another step, two Fellahin, the local Arab peasants, grabbed the Jew's stall table and overturned it and began to rob it.

'Run!' said John.

Men looked at John. He had shouted in Italian. But another flight of arrows came in, and more of the onlookers fell.

At the forefront of the riot, a woman was screaming in Arabic. She had an arrow in her gut, and she pointed at the Ghulami and shrieked.

A tide of rioters rolled forward at the thin line of archers, and they shot hurriedly. Most of their arrows carried over the rioters and struck in the market where I was. My horse took an arrow in the muscle above her right front leg but by the grace of God, it went all the way through, and it was a moment's work to cut the head and extract the shaft while she bit at me the while.

By the time I had her calm, John was in the saddle.

There was a cloud of dust where the Ghulami had stood with their bows. And no more arrows.

They were bad men, and had shot into a crowd of their own people, but they died horribly, and God have mercy on their infidel souls.

I got a leg over my wounded horse, and we were away. We rode in a long, curving path out and away from the Cairo Gate and back along the shore of the inner harbour.

I looked back in time to see the mounted Mamluks re-emerge from within the gate to charge the crowd. The roar of the rioters rose to become a scream.

The Mamluks had sabres in their fists, and they were killing every rioter they caught.

I didn't look back again.

Like most other cities, Alexandria is surrounded by suburbs and some of these are small towns or villages of their own. We entered one, watered our horses, and purchased food; bland food, with no meat or even chicken. And we had an odd bread that seemed to be made of chickpeas that was highly spiced. There was no wine, and heavily sugared hot water with spice was the only beverage.

We had outrun the news of the riot, but John returned to me after some discussion and shook his head. 'The man who cook the food say the Mamluk Ghulami they do bad thing every days,' he said.

It occurred to me that under other circumstances, with some gold, I could make trouble for the Sultan here. I resolved to say as much to Sabraham.

I was also learning that I needed to learn to speak Arabic. I endangered us every moment by my failure to understand what beggars and street people and grandmothers and tea-sellers shouted at me. The combination of being mounted – and thus rich or powerful – and not understanding the language should have led to our instant unmasking, except that the city and its environs couldn't imagine that they had a foe at all, so rich and powerful were they; and further, although I didn't know it, many people imagined I was a Mamluk. There were 'Franks' among them, Italians and Gascons. Conversion to Islam was not a serious matter to men who had already turned their backs on God and his angels. Nor did the Mamluks make many demands on their soldiers as to religion: so long as a man professed Islam, all was allowed.

Be that as it may, we rode unharmed out of the riot, broke our fast under palm trees in a small taverna, and then rode along the beach east of the great city.

After all our trouble, my actual mission took less than three hours. We found the sand of the beaches firm and wide enough to form our army. John found a path that broke the line of dunes and we went inland – to find an open space of mudflats and dry gravel that was large enough to make a camp for the Hosts of the Phalanx of Archangels and all the Company of Heaven, much less our little force.

We were thorough. This was a task I knew from serving Sir John in Italy, and I knew that a good camp with secure access to the ships would make the siege possible. We found a line of wells, each with a small farm about it, and I confess to some pity for the unbelievers who were about to be driven from their farms or killed so that my crusaders could have water. But not much.

What I did not see was firewood, nor was I confident that our wells could water an army of ten thousand men and as many animals. So no firewood, and no wood to construct siege engines.

I didn't mention any of this to John. He was on edge, but then, why should he not be? I was mostly concerned because I'd noted, as Sabraham had said, that most of the Mamluks were men like John. Kipchaks have a well-deserved reputation for honesty, but I wondered how great the temptation might be to abjure his new religion and go riding in among men of his own kind, men with obvious riches and power.

For whatever reason, he did not.

We slept under the stars. Then the stars vanished, it rained, and we were miserable, although I was pleased to see that my chosen camp shrugged off the water easily. Then the moon rose on the world and we were cold – cotton holds no heat when damp. It was a long night, and the first grey light of morning was cheering.

Meeting Sabraham at the appointed rendezvous, a wrecked ship pulled high up the beach to the west, was even more cheering.

He looked out to sea. 'We have missed our day,' he said. 'The governor was away visiting Cairo with his bodyguard. Now he is back.' He looked at me.

I pointed at John. 'You should ask John, but I think the governor rode out again this morning.'

Sabraham turned and spoke in Turkish. They both spoke at once, then John spoke, pointed at me, and smiled.

'The governor is marching to Mecca!' Sabraham said. 'Well done, Sir William.'

I laughed. 'He might be going to the moon for all I'd know. I need to learn Arabic. I'm as helpless as a babe here.'

Sabraham asked another question in Turkish. John answered in Arabic. They both looked at me.

'You like it here?' Sabraham asked.

It was an odd question. I must have shown this in my face. Sabraham put a hand on my shoulder. 'Some men can't stand the foreign. Sights and smells they don't know seem to anger them, or terrify them. To do this task, you must like the people with whom you mix.'

I smiled. 'Oh, as to that,' I said. In fact, I'd liked what I saw, except the dead beggars. You could walk London from one side to another, and you'd only see a dead man in the gutter on a bad day. That's what alms and hospitals are for, in London. When rich men die, they endow so many beds for the poor. And the same in Venice.

'Did you learn aught else?' Sabraham asked.

I pointed east. 'We can land anywhere here,' I said, 'Except right off the long point, which is all mud and soft sand. There's good ground for a camp to the south and west. There's water.' I was tired, that's what I remember best about that morning. 'But no wood.'

Sabraham laughed. 'Welcome to Egypt,' he said. 'There's no wood here. Well done. You did well to avoid the riot. I was afraid you were caught in it.'

I explained how narrowly we had escaped.

Sabraham didn't seem to be listening. When I was done, he waved at the walls of the city, a mile distant. 'Do you think we can take it, with your friends the crusaders?' he asked.

'How many in the garrison?' I asked.

He smiled. 'Two hundred per gate. Forty-three gates. A thousand superb cavalry in reserve.'

'Ten thousand men,' I calculated. 'We're attacking a walled city with a garrison almost twice the size of our whole army.'

Sabraham smiled thinly. 'Yes.'

Over the next hour, we built a small fire on the beach from driftwood. The wreck of the ship was stripped, and nothing was left but the heavy timbers of the bow and even they had been hacked at inexpertly. Wood was of utmost value.

When our fire had been going for a bit, a man on a donkey came to the edge of the beach and watched us.

Sabraham frowned. 'Our horses are too good,' he said.

John nodded.

'I am keeping mine,' I said.

Sabraham looked at me as if I was a fool, but John grinned. 'Good horse,' he said. 'Mine, too.'

So when Theodore's round ship came up to the beach, we wasted an hour – with Sabraham cursing us – taking the horses. John was the master at this; he swam each horse out to the ship in a few feet of water and with the help of the master and the yard, he got them over the side into the waist of the ship where he lay them down. The Turks and the Mongols move horses around all the time, even by water, and John seemed much better at it than anyone I had seen.

At any rate, despite Sabraham's curses and Theodore's remonstrations, we saved all four horses, and we were away in the last light, wallowing across the wind. But after an hour the wind came straight off Africa, full of dust – bad for our eyes, but very good for our speed.

I slept a long, long time, awoke and swam, and slept again. When I awoke, it was to see the whole of the crusade fleet stretched away in the dawn.

The crusader fleet lay off Crambusa, a tiny islet on the southern coast of Turkey. As soon as we hove in sight, trumpets sounded from the *galia grossa* that King Peter used as his flagship. Before Sabraham and I scrambled aboard, I had the pleasure of seeing the Venetian admiral wave from his command deck, and agree to take our new horses aboard at the beach. My little Arab had survived two days at sea without showing any temper, and John was smugly triumphant.

We were rowed over to the flagship in a small boat, and as we approached the stern ladder we found quite a crowd of Venetians and Genoese sailors thumping each other's boats with bargepoles. But our Cypriote oarsmen made their way through the press and got us up the stern. The king received us, reclining in the stern cabin. He was lying on cushions like a Turk, and de Mézzières sat to his right with two of the king's other officers, the marshal, Lord Simon, who I had last seen at the Emperor's banquet, and the admiral, Jean of Tyre. Cramped along the low, carpeted wall was a man I didn't know at all, but he was introduced as Sieur Percival, a knight of Coulanges who was deeply knowledgeable about Alexandria and served the king. The Hospitaller admiral, Fra Ferlino, was crouched like a servant on a stool. He waved courteously. Wedged in by him and taking up a third of the space in the cabin was the turcopolier, Fra William de Midleton.

A servant brought me wine.

Fra William indicated Sabraham. 'Your Grace, Master Sabraham is a volunteer with the Order, as his Sir William. Together they have visited Alexandria in secrecy.'

'That is a fine deed of arms,' King Peter said to me. He smiled. 'I will not forget you, when I come into my kingdom.'

Sabraham bowed – as much as the low overhead beams and situation permitted. 'Your Grace, we found the city well-armed, but the governor has just left for Mecca. He took many of his guard with him on his pilgrimage.'

King Peter nodded, and propped himself up on his elbow. 'That is good news. What of the garrison?'

Sabraham let go a breath. 'Well-armed and well provided. I visited at least twenty of the towers and found them all manned.' He looked at me. 'I expect that I saw enough to count ten thousand men.'

Every man in the cabin twitched. The king glanced at me.

I nodded. 'At least, your Grace. The garrison I saw was well-armed in good harness and carried bows as good as John the Turk's bow.'

King Peter sighed. 'Ghulami,' he said. 'We have faced them before now.'

'They're all cowards,' Sieur Percival said. He shrugged in contempt. 'I was a prisoner, a slave, in Alexandria. The town wall is enormous – the circuit is almost ten miles. They cannot hold the whole length, not event with ten thousand men. And they will not stand and fight like men.'

Sabraham raised his eyebrows. 'They don't need to stand and fight,' he said, 'when they are mounted. They shoot and run, shoot and run.'

'Like cowards!' insisted Sieur Percival.

'And yet they took you prisoner,' de Mézzières said.

Men laughed, and Sieur Percival flushed.

'Come, Percival, I know you and I know your mettle.' King Peter waved a hand. 'Where would *you* land?'

'In the Porto Vecchio, where the foreign vessels wait for entry into the New Harbour,' he said. 'There is a fine expanse of white sand and gravel that runs right up to the walls. We can land an army there, aye, and encamp it, as well.'

Sabraham looked at me. I bowed. 'Your Grace, we landed on that beach. It is foul with garbage, and the old harbour is very shallow. The ships anchored there could foul the manoeuvres of the fleet. And any camp would be immediately under the walls of the city—'

'Where they must be to conduct a siege,' Sieur Percival insisted.

'Where there is no water or cover of any kind,' Sabraham said.

'There is no other place,' Sieur Percival insisted.

I leaned forward. 'Your Grace, there *is* another place, about a mile to the east along the coast, with nine good wells—'

'He is lying,' Sieur Percival said. 'There is no other place.'

Some men resent any disagreement. I cannot account for Sieur Percival's instant rage, but it was remarkable, and he did himself no favours.

'You are a fool,' he said. 'A mere boy. A veteran soldier would not make this mistake. East of the city is a wood of palms—'

'Only inland,' I said. 'On the coast, there are farms behind the dunes, and—'

'Be quiet!' Sieur Percival shouted. 'You know nothing.'

De Mézzières put out a hand and physically restrained Sieur Percival. 'My lord,' he said gently, 'the king has asked for this young knight's report.'

'It is worthless. This is what you sent on your reconnaissance? A Jew and a boy?' Sieur Percival spat. He actually spat on the king's cabin floor.

The king lay back and fanned himself for a few breaths. He sighed heavily. 'Very well, my lord de Coulanges. You think the town is possible?'

Sieur Percival crossed his arms. 'We will take it with ease,' he said.

The king looked at the Hospitaller admiral. 'Fra Ferlino?' he asked.

'Tell me of the fortifications on Pharos,' the old Italian asked.

Sabraham ignored de Coulanges. 'My lord, they are new, very new. There is a main castle, as tall as a mountain with heavy machines on its corner towers. It is surrounded by a new curtain wall that has eight towers, all with artillery. There is no ground from which to lay siege to it.'

The king glanced at de Coulanges. 'You have never mentioned this,' he said.

De Coulanges stamped his foot. 'A lie! They seek to make the place sound stronger than it is. Perhaps they are in league with the infidels. Make the Jew eat a piece of pork.'

Sabraham was growing red under his dark skin and I could see the tension in his shoulders.

'The old harbour is deep enough for any ship, and we will have an easy landing there, right in the face of the enemy,' de Coulanges insisted. 'The state of this great castle is of no importance.'

Fra William stroked his beard and fingered the beads at his belt. 'May I speak, your Grace? It seems to me unlikely that this man, your chamberlain, no matter how worthy, knows more of Alexandria than these two who were there but two days ago. Sabraham, how often have you been at Alexandria?'

'Not more than twenty times,' Master Sabraham said. 'I believe that the worthy gentleman is exaggerating the weakness of the place because he desires his revenge against it – a worthy desire, but not one to generate an accurate report.'

De Coulanges opened his mouth to speak and de Mézzières put a hand over his mouth. 'You have said enough,' he snapped.

Silence reigned.

'Do you think we can take Alexandria, Master Sabraham?' the king asked from one elbow.

Sabraham sighed. 'Only with the grace of God and a miracle, your Grace.'

King Peter swung his legs to the floor. 'They have ten thousand men and a double-walled city of forty-three towers. We have half their numbers, but by God, messieurs, we have the best knights in the world, and I say it is better to stumble in a great *empris* then to take some village in Asia of which no one has heard.'

That morning, after he heard Mass aboard his flagship, the king announced to all the captains that the target of our expedition was Alexandria. He waited until we were all together, and he announced that no ship would be allowed to quit the fleet. He was open in his concern that the Genoese or the Venetians might betray the expedition.

I saw Admiral Contarini's face when the king made this remark.

The king gave orders.

We were to follow him straight south. We would rally the fleet in the Porto Vecchio, the old harbour, and when the king sounded his trumpets, we would attack.

We crossed the sea in two days, and it would have been better if we'd taken three. By good fortune and ill, we raised the great castle of Pharos and the spire of Alexander's tomb well before the sun had set after a perfect passage on the blue water without a sight of land and we descended on them like a bolt from the blue.

Unfortunately, the sun would not stay in the sky for our attack. As the sun set, we were coming up into the roadstead and the king was unwilling to try the anchorage in the dark. So the Alexandrines saw us, and all chance of surprise was lost.

At last light, King Peter summoned all the admirals to him. While they were meeting, I received word from Fra William that I was wanted on the Hospitaller galley, and the Venetians rowed me across to the turcopolier with great willingness.

The sun was going down in the west, a great red ball, and the temperature was perfect, neither too warm nor too cold. The stars were just coming out, and the muezzein's calls filled the air – alongside alarm bells and gongs and the cries of soldiers which carried across the water as if they were on the next ship.

I climbed the ladder and was taken on to the command deck.

Father Pierre stood with Fra William and Fra Peter – and Sabraham.

I bowed, knelt, and kissed my lord's ring. He hugged me. 'So far away!' he said.

'We can't all ride the same galley,' I said.

Fra William was leaning his great bulk against the stern rail. He pointed over the water at Pharos Castle. 'I see Sabraham was not lying about that pile of stone,' he said.

Sabraham shrugged. 'I wish I was,' he said.

Father Pierre looked at the great sweep of the city. Alexandria is almost flat; there are two low hills in the middle, rocks, really, and it is almost three Italian miles across – honestly, it takes your breath away, it is so huge. He was shaking his head.

'Every time I look, it terrifies me,' he said. 'It is bigger than Rome.'

We all looked.

Father Pierre shook his head again. 'We are committed to this attack. The crusaders cannot remain in the boats.'

I bowed again. 'My lord, it is not too late to land east of the city.'

Fra William shook his head. 'The problem is not laying a siege. We lack the men, the artillery and the provisions to lay a siege. Let us be frank. For six months this expedition has been patched together and patched together again, one patch on top of another until the whole is like a frayed old garment and we have never met the enemy.'

Fra Peter smiled, but to me, in the red light, he looked old, tired, and angry. 'It is no fault of ours. It is a miracle that we are here at all.'

Fra Robert frowned. 'It might be better if we were not here. There are a hundred Knights of the Order in these ships. We have not set a hundred of our brethren ashore in Outremer for twenty years, to say nothing of the soldiers and turcopoles. The cost is staggering, and it will hurt us for another twenty years.'

Father Pierre shook his head. '*Mes amis*, let us pray,' he said. And we knelt on the deck and prayed. When we were done, he rose, and blessed us. 'That is my contribution,' he said. 'The king is determined to land in the Old Port and attempt the gate of the old castle. His reports make it the weakest.' He looked at us. 'I leave it to you gentlemen to see if there is another path to victory.'

And then he left us.

It was, perhaps, an odd performance, but he was not a soldier; in fact, he wore no armour and he never meddled in our councils except to aid us. He was, as I have said a thousand times, an exceptional man.

When his head vanished into the stern cabin, the turcopolier nodded to Sabraham. 'I'm eager to hear any ideas you may have.'

Fra Peter looked at me. 'Or you. You have seen a great deal of war, Sir William.'

I shook my head. 'It's Florence all over again, isn't it, my lords? We have a tiny army, and even if we could defeat the enemy ...'

Fra Peter nodded. 'Perhaps that makes you our expert, then,' he said.

We discussed and discarded various plans. I stopped suggesting that we make our landing up the coast where I had reconnoitred a camp. The turcopolier's statement was too true to deny – we lacked the men to lay a proper siege. There was no point to making a camp so far from the walls that men would wear themselves out walking back and forth.

Of course, in Italy, we did just that, but we rode everywhere. And our 'sieges' were mostly raids.

The sun set, and the warm red light stayed only on the towers of the city and the fortress of Pharos.

'They're winding a machine on the fortress,' Sabraham said.

We watched them wind it. It was three-quarters of a mile way, and the last light showed it plainly.

'The machines are new,' I guessed. 'The captain of the fortress wants to test his range.'

While we watched, the gate of the fortress opened and a column of cavalry appeared like a black worm spitting out of the fortress mouth and it wound and uncurled along the road over the neck of land from the main walls. The men must have been on horseback for they moved fast.

'He's ready to cast,' Sabraham said. 'Watch for the fall of the shot.'

It was almost dead calm. The fall of the stone from the machine vanished into the water, and we didn't see it. Three-quarters of a mile is just too far.

I pointed at the column of cavalry. 'That must be a goodly portion of the Pharos garrison,' I said.

The turcopolier nodded. 'You think we could take the fortress by escalade?' he asked.

I shrugged. 'I've known it done.'

When the admiral returned, we had the beginning of a plan. Which is to say we had an idea.

The old Savoyard pursed his lips and stared at our model of the shore and our fortress and it's outpost, the Casteleto on the opposite spit. He looked very serious indeed, but he kept his council and allowed us to take Brother Robert and his galliot.

By moonlight, we were rowed across the entrance to the new harbour. We stayed well out of bowshot, but Brother Robert was willing to risk the machines in the citadel.

'In the dark?' he asked. 'No. God is not going to let my poor ship take a stone from heathens in the dark.'

When we reached a certain point, our rowers were ordered by whispers to cease rowing. We rocked in the very gentle swell. There was almost no wind, almost no waves, and we could hear everything.

We listened and listened. We heard very little besides gulls and two women having an argument. Sabraham translated some of the choicer moments.

'It can be done,' I said.

Sabraham, for once, looked unsure.

'Now,' I said.

'And this is your idea,' Nerio said.

'All mine,' I muttered.

All of the Order's volunteers, as well as a dozen of the English crusaders who were in the turcopolier's galley and another dozen Gascons from the admiral's galley were with me. To top it all, I had Chretien d'Albret and his retinue of French and Gascons and Savoyards. I should have wondered why he was following me, but at the time I was merely delighted to have some crusaders to add to my assault.

And most of them, especially the Gascons, had done this before.

We stripped all of the Order's galleys of their stern ladders and the carpenters pegged them together.

None of us wore any harness.

Nor did we carry any weapons but our swords and daggers. I put the Emperor's sword naked through my belt and left the scabbard for another day.

It is difficult to prepare for a fight in full darkness. At least we didn't have to arm, or get at our horses. We had eighty men-at-arms – a pitiful number against the city of Alexandria.

The admiral brought us all the lanterns of the galley, and we used them to prepare, and then we swiped lamp-black off the insides and used it and the lids from the small cook pots to blacken our faces.

'Go with God, messires,' he said. 'If you succeed, it will be a great deed.'

'And you may save the crusade,' Sir Robert Hales breathed.

'The king's attack goes in at first light,' the admiral continued.

The legate came on deck and blessed us. We gathered with our blackened faces and all our fears on the *corsia*, the gangway amidships, and Father Pierre passed along, blessing every man. Many he confessed. It took time I didn't feel we had, and my heart was in my mouth, so much so that I couldn't breathe, and when Father Pierre reached me, I could barely speak.

But I knelt, confessed, and was absolved.

'*Deus Vult!*' the legate whispered.

'*Deus Vult!*' we growled.

We went down the stern on ropes, our ladders being already stowed in the *galia grossa's* longboat. We packed eighty men into five ship's boats and, with muffled oars, we pulled for shore.

Ahead, a city woke. It was not yet dawn, but we could hear shouts and marching.

In the stern of the lead boat, Sabraham turned to me. I could see nothing but his nose and his teeth. 'They're alert,' he said.

'No,' I said, with far more confidence than I felt. But I had a career of taking castles by *coup de main*. In this, at least, I was the old hand.

We rowed to the east, putting the spit of land on which the smaller castle stood between us and the city, and then we turned back south and west.

'Lay out!' I growled at the rowers. They were free oarsmen, and most of them had helmets and maille shirts, javelins and axes. It says something about the importance of volunteers to the Order that we were to go first, and only call for the oarsmen if we were successful.

Now the low boats moved like dolphins across the mirror of the water, so still it reflected stars and moon. We shot into the moon shadow of the Casteleto, and then slowed. We were under the very walls of the castle. Our oars were muffled and yet we seemed to make more sound than I could bear: the drip of water, and the Gascons would whisper – oh, sweet Christ, in that hour I almost put my basilard into one bastard from Poitou just to silence him, and all my newfound strategies of calm maturity were tried. And then we could see the low pier of the Casteleto's dock before us.

Brother Robert brought us alongside the dock without touching.

I leapt on to the stone pier and ran for the stairs, my shoulder blades tense for an arrow, my ears cocked for a sudden sound. Up and up ... I believe there were but twenty steps to the sally port, but I thought it took me half my life ... up and up, my feet pounding on the stone, the soles of my leather shoes slapping too loud, too loud ...

Dawn was close. I could smell the change in the air, and hear the birds.

Fiore was by me, and then Nerio and Miles and Juan. Right behind them were our Greeks, Giannis and Giorgos. And then another six men with our ladder, which struck the walls of the stone stairs like the sound of a trebuchet loosing its payload, and we all flinched. And then they did it again, so loudly that the sound echoed off the city walls, and the men, English and Gascon, carrying the ladder, cursed in shame.

Sometimes, the worst part of an escalade is that you cannot shout 'Shut up!' at your troops.

Somewhere inside the Casteleto, a door slammed.

'Now or never,' I whispered.

Thirty pairs of hands raised the ladder. We had one. *One.*

The moment the feet of the ladder were braced, I was on my way up.

I hate ladders. I hate heights, have no head for them, and when a sailor goes out on the yard of a ship to brail up a sail, it makes me queasy on the deck.

But there are things you must do yourself. You cannot lead an assault from the back.

I went up and up, and as I climbed, I was going from night into day. Our ladder was just the height of the wall – and I only *knew* that ten feet from the top. And as I climbed the last few feet, winded, and terrified by the creaking and cracking sounds the ladder made as my weight bore on the whole length, a sentry on the Pharos Castle across the harbour entrance saw us.

Up until that moment – despite my terror, the burning in the back of my throat, the feeling of lassitude that threatened me from fatigue and fear, the spike of pain at the base of my guts, and the annoyance of finding that my unscabbarded sword was cutting into my hose – despite all of that, time had passed very slowly.

After the sentry across the water sounded his gong, everything seemed to break apart like a dropped glass, and my memory of the rest is fragments.

I got a leg over the wall and jumped. It was farther than I expected, a man's height or more, to the catwalk and I landed hard.

There were no enemies on the walls. Instead, a dozen men were blinking in the grey light, standing in muslin shirts and skullcaps on the pavement of the courtyard, and they saw me about the time I saw them.

They had bows.

I remember running down the inner face of the wall – there were steps, and by God's mercy they ran the right way, so that I was shielded from their archery.

One of them paused to point up where I had come. I assumed Nerio had made the wall. I was in the courtyard, among hen-houses and a pile of wood that in daylight turned out to be the castle's palings and hoardings. I moved behind it.

Arrows were loosed.

I found that there was a crawl space behind the palings. And I moved along it.

I suppose I charged the archers. My next memory is fighting. I do not know if I fought well or badly; somehow, the archers had lost track of me, or never knew I came down the wall. Or, like soldiers the world over, they engaged the enemy they could see, the men coming up the ladders.

But the grace of Our Lady was with us, and none of my friends took a hit, and then the archers were dead and Fiore was by me, and Nerio and Sabraham and Juan and Miles and Marc-Antonio and John the Turk and we were clearing the galleries at either end. Men came out of doorways and died, or leaned out of towers and loosed one arrow before the men on other catwalks ran them down.

The only moment in the fight that I remember is when Fiore killed an archer by throwing his sword. It was incredible.

Then it was over.

We moved through the castle like an ill wind. The last watch in their barracks were waking, and we slaughtered them at the doors and by their pallets. We gave no quarter. There is no other way, in a storming action.

It was a military castle and had, thank God, neither women nor children. Fiore had the admiral's great banner, and he carried it to the top of the central donjon.

From there, we could see the morning.

I would have said that it had taken us an hour to land and storm the Casteleto, but when we looked, the sun was still low in the pink and gold sky. Over to the west of us, we could clearly see the white and red sails of the crusader fleet, many marked with crosses as big as whole ships, as they entered the Old Harbour in two lines. Closer, almost at our feet, lay the magnificent tower of Pharos just across the mouth of the New Harbour, perhaps a long bowshot away.

To our right, out to sea, lay the Order's fleet – four galleys and ten transports as well as a few of the smaller galliots and round ships.

More than a hundred crusader ships were trying to make enter the Old Harbour. The great lines stretched like frayed rope out to sea, and there were gaps – the galleys needed no wind, and made better time, and many ships had left their place in the line and proceeded, so that there were collisions. But that was not the worst of it: even as we watched, ships attempting to go into the beach struck the shallows. A Venetian galley rolled her mainmast overboard.

Still the king's great red galley crept closer and closer to the land. Aboard the king's ship, someone was conning them through the deepest channel.

But ahead of them waited the army of Alexandria.

Perhaps if we had landed as soon as we arrived, we might have surprised them, but by the morning after our sails were sighted, every soldier that the governor's lieutenant could spare was standing in close array on that beach.

Why didn't they man their walls?

Perhaps it was a day in which Christian and Moslem sought to rival each the other in bravery – or in foolishness. Or perhaps the governor's lieutenant felt, as our king did, that they could not garrison the whole of a ten mile circuit.

Perhaps they were as eager to slay us as we were to slay them.

They were too far from me to see their quality, but they filled the beach from east to west, and even as we watched, a troop of horse that glittered in the rosy light emerged from the great towered gate at the Egyptian army's back. They looked like ants, but they sparkled with steel.

The crusader fleet was running aground more than a bowshot from the shore.

Nicolas Sabraham made it to the top of the tower, his sword red-brown and his hands sticky on the hilt. He looked out over the battle of Alexandria.

'Oh, sweet Christ,' he said.

A little less than a mile away, tiny figures were leaping off the king's galley – into the sea.

Nerio emerged on to the roof of the Casteleto just as we saw the Hagarenes on the other tower begin to wind their engine.

'Get the sailors,' I shouted. 'Find men who know how to make these machines shoot!'

Nerio nodded. 'I think we have them all. The castle is ours.'

I ran across the tower to look at the city at its nearest point. The gate was shut. So there was no counter-attack coming. Nor would it be difficult to resist any attack; it could only come along a single stone road two horsemen wide.

'They're not loosing at us at all,' Fiore said.

The engines on the Pharos castle had begun to hurl their rocks the other way, at the immobile crusader fleet.

Even as we watched, a Venetian cog took a direct hit. Timber flew into the air, and in a moment, the little ship sank. She went down in less water than there was to cover her hull, but her armoured men drowned in water not much over their heads.

'Sweet Christ,' moaned Sabraham.

Let me explain again. The harbours of Alexandria are like a gothic letter E. Two harbours, separated by the long spit with the Pharos fortification between them. That fortress could batter the crusader fleet, and looked to me to be impregnable. We'd just taken the Casteleto, at the bottom of the E, if you like, and the crusader fleet was trying to get into the old harbour, between the Pharos spit and the top of the E.

Huffing, Brother Robert and a dozen sailors came up the ladder to the top of the Casteleto's donjon. Brother Robert had to stop at the top and breathe, despite my urgency. His face was so red I feared he would explode.

Miles stood by him. 'Can I tell you something that will make you laugh?' he asked.

I was watching the destruction of the crusade. 'I doubt it,' I said.

'The sally port door was unlocked,' Miles said. 'I just pushed it open and walked in.'

I didn't laugh, but I do now. That's war, friends. All the terror on the ladder – and I might have tried the door!

The engines on the far tower were coming back again.

I pointed to them. 'Brother Robert? Can you do anything?'

His head bobbed. 'I'll do what I can,' he said, and began to issue crisp orders. The Casteleto had a pair of machines, both mangonels, mounted high.

'They're higher than we,' Brother Robert said. 'I don't think I could strike them save by the will of God.'

Sabraham shook his head. 'You don't need to strike home,' he said. 'Those aren't hardened men. They rush their shots and they miss. If you come close, they will turn their fire on us.'

Fiore had by this time found a half-pike. He fixed the admiral's flag to it and looked at me.

I nodded. 'As secure as we'll ever be!' I said.

Fiore dei Liberi planted the order's flag on the walls of the Casteleto, the first lodgement the crusader army made in Alexandria.

Out on the water, there was no immediate change in the Order's ships.

The great bows of our two mangonels began to bend back. I went to the winches with the sailors and my friends and two Gascons who'd ended in the tower.

We got the bows back, and the great cogs of the mechanisms clicked into place. With heavy pry bars, Brother Robert and two sailors began to move the engines, levering them a few inches at a time.

The far tower loosed its deadly hail at the crusader fleet.

I was panting from winding the great bows. But out to sea, the oars were out on the whole of the Order's squadron, and they gave way all together, a magnificent sight. Caught by my attention, other men came to look.

The Order's ships formed a line behind the *galia grossa*.

'Here they come,' whispered Juan. He fell to his knees and began to pray. Most of us who were not actively aiming the engines knelt and prayed.

'Let's try that,' Brother Robert said. 'With God's grace,' he muttered, and pulled the lever.

The bows stunned the air, and the great engine slammed back in recoil, jumping a hand's breath and slamming back down to the stone roof so that dust rose up.

Brother Robert's first missile was visible at the top of its arc. And then it fell too far and slammed into the Pharos castle, about halfway up its tower. Dust and stone fragments flew.

We all cheered.

Every man in the enemy tower ran to the wall facing us to look. Until then, despite the alarm sounded by one of theirs, I suppose they had assumed themselves safe. Truly, I have no notion what they thought.

We started winding the engine and Brother Robert moved the second one into firing position.

Nerio was grunting along with me on the torsion. 'Think – that – whoever – designed – this tower—' he grunted.

Brother Robert loosed his second dart. It went higher, and struck the enemy tower just a hand's breadth below the top of the crenellation. There was a little dust, but there were screams. They carried, because it was a silent dawn, and we could not hear what was happening on the other side of the Pharos spit, where the crusaders and the king were landing. And dying.

It was just luck. In four more shots we didn't come close to hitting the top: one went over, and two slammed into the flank of the tower and one vanished into the sea because we hadn't tightened the torsion all the way.

Then the first rock came back at us. It was well-aimed and struck our tower close to the top, and men were cut with stone chips. The whole tower moved the way your breastplate moves when a heavy arrows strikes it true. I wished for my armour.

Brother Robert loosed another engine. His dart struck well up, and knocked in a merlon. I knew from what I'd just experienced that a hail of stone chips had just flayed an engine's crew – nothing mortal, probably, but a healthy dose of fear.

'Don't touch this one!' Brother Robert shouted. 'Wind her gently, I pray you!'

A stone the size of a helmet struck him, and tore him to gobbets like a doll worried by a dog. He seemed to explode.

I shook myself – I still see him. Bah! We wound that engine like demons. And perhaps his dead hands held the engine steady. Fiore pulled the handle and the beast leaped. For the first time, our dart *just* cleared the far wall and vanished into their tower.

Marc-Antonio handed me a scrap of cotton. I used it to wipe my face and it came away bloodied.

Now, I could hear the sound of combat. On the far beach, men were fighting. And dying.

At my feet, the fleet of the Order stood in, due south, under oars. It was too late for them to turn, and now they were going to run the gauntlet of the Pharos fortress's plummeting stone and make for the beach of the Pharos Harbour.

Our tower took two more hits and some of our sailors began to flinch. And some of us began to take cover under the stone of the curtain wall. Men are only men and flesh and blood cannot stand against stone.

'Again!' I shouted. 'Wind it again!' I was on one drum, with Nerio, and Fiore and Miles were on the other. Juan had two Gascons and a Catalan winding the second machine.

I can't tell you where the next stone hit us – only that we were all lacerated, one of the Gascons was messily dead and Juan had a gash from eyeball to ear and was stretched full length on the roof.

My handle came up to the stop.

So did Miles'.

Fiore moved the engine. No hesitation – he'd watched the Englishman serve the machine and he knew his mathematics. He stepped back – no expression on his face, and pulled the handle.

The iron dart leaped away, and the machine slammed back to the roof.

Miles ran to the other machine. He and one of the Gascons and another sailor worked to clear the corpses away from the base.

Fiore stepped across our dead and used his crowbar again, and pulled the lever, uncaring that the leaping monster crushed a dead man's skull.

Men were cheering in the courtyard.

We were struck twice – *slam, slam!*

The Casteleto tower rocked.

Now there was a crack all the way along the middle of the roof.

I leaned out and saw the Order's fleet standing in for the New Harbour beach. They were not going for the Porto Vecchio, where the king and the crusaders were mired in shallow water. They were running the gauntlet of the Pharos tower, using the gap we'd made by taking the Casteleto. Going to the New Beach.

Which was empty of enemy.

The galliot was nosing into the Casteleto dock. I didn't need new orders to know what that meant.

The cheering in the courtyard went on. Fiore, with Miles and Nerio and the sailors, had the leftmost engine loaded just as a big rock – I swear, as God is my saviour that I saw it in the air a moment before it struck – crushed the engine that they had just abandoned. Pieces of wood as big as my arm flew, jagged splinters that were as sharp as swords, yet not a man was killed.

The crack in the tower's roof widened and the whole building shook like a beaten drum.

Before I could shout a warning, Fiore pulled the handle on his machine and the dart soared away. I never saw what any of our last shots accomplished.

'Down!' I roared – or perhaps I squeaked it. Standing on a damaged stone tower while a heavy machine pounds your friends to pudding is not at all like fighting in harness, friends. I was so afraid I wanted to shit myself.

But we got Juan through the trap door. Miles got him to me and I threw caution to the winds because the steps were cracking and jumped to the second storey floor, cradling his head. I dropped him, but we were down.

A piece of the roof fell, a corbel.

'Down!' I yelled. 'All the way out of the tower!'

In fact, we might have taken our time. The roof didn't fall in for three days. But the next rock split the tower the way an axe splits a big billet of wood.

Juan recovered his wits in the galliot. He threw up twice, drank some water, and shook himself. For as long as it took us to reach the beach, he could only speak his native Catalan. The ways of the mind are strange.

Behind us, the Admiral's banner continued to fly from the Casteleto, and the machine on the tower of the Pharos threw great stones at it. But most of them fell short, and they loosed very slowly.

We left the oarsmen and sailors as a garrison, with Fra Ricardo as castellan. My part in that battle was done.

I landed almost dry shod, and I had had the whole run down the harbour to don my harness with Marc-Antonio working like an automaton at my side. As soon as my breast and back were closed, he went to the others. Juan armed last, when the stern of the galliot was drawn well up the beach and the horses were going over the sides on the transports.

Oh, yes. The horses.

There was my Gawain, shining in the sun of Outremer.

There seemed no hurry at all. Men came and shook my hand, and the legate embraced me and Saracens came to the walls of their town, just half a bowshot away. Guillaume Machaut says we were showered with arrows, and Nerio was hit, so I suppose that this must be true, but I have no memory of darts or arrows. I only remember the feeling of calm, of confidence, that Father Pierre inspired in that hour. He wore no harness, only a fine gold and silk stole over one of his Carmelite robes. He had no weapon in his hand, but held a simple wooden cross. The only order he gave was to demand that the Knights of the Order would maintain the sanctuary of churches in the event we broke into the city, that we kill no women or children, that we behave as soldiers of God.

And then the Knights of the Order were mounted – a hundred of them, a block of scarlet. I'm not sure when the world had seen a hundred Knights of the Order all together on their chargers – perhaps not since the fall of Acre. The sight was so noble as to steal my breath.

I got up on Gawain. Marc-Antonio got me a lance, and I began to form the donats and the volunteers. We had lost a good number of men at the Casteleto. Their ranks were filled by d'Albret and his Gascons and Savoyards, who were, strictly speaking, crusaders and not volunteers or Donats, but they were there and had their mounts. I still did not question what they were doing with us.

I had formed my volunteers in a wedge at Fra Peter's command and D'Albret came up behind me. He pushed right in, his visor open. 'I like this better,' he said. 'Ah, monsieur, now perhaps we will see some fighting.'

He was grinning ear to ear.

It was not at all like being pounded by stone balls.

Ser Nerio brought his destrier up so that his right knee tucked behind my left. Ser Fiore brought his charger to where his left knee was behind my right. In the next rank, d'Albret was pinned between Miles and Juan. And so on, until our last rank was ten wide.

Off to my right, by the water's edge, the men-at-arms and turcopoles, the Order's light horsemen, were arming as fast as they could.

354

John and Marc-Antonio, having got us into our armour, were now pulling maille shirts over their own heads and trying to find their own mounts in the herd of horses now swimming or walking on to the beach. There seemed to be horses everywhere.

Miles' uncle advanced the papal standard.

Fra William got his turcopoles formed. He had about a hundred squires and 'light' cavalrymen and they did not form a wedge, but instead cantered out to form an open line to our front.

Fra Peter rode out of the central wedge and rode along our front.

'Christians!' he called. 'For this you have trained. For this you have endured the penance of your harness and the taste of your own blood. Now is your hour!'

Four hundred voices roared. And were silent.

Four hundred men.

The legate was in the centre of Fra Peter's wedge. As safe as the knights could make him, and our three squadrons began to ride along the foreshore, toward the keening sounds of combat.

The sun was high.

It was just noon.

Fra William took the turcopoles up the beach, formed at an order so open that there was twenty yards between horsemen, but that meant that his hundred covered almost the whole width of the beach and the sandy plain below the city walls. I had seen them practice this 'screen' on Rhodes, and I had assumed it was a matter of deception because even a very thin line of horses raises enough dust to cover most movements.

But the screen covered more than movement. Because the men in the screen had bows and crossbows, they could deter enemy light cavalry. They could also see and scout obstacles and could react far more quickly than we armoured knights to changes in the field or sudden sallies. Best of all, they were themselves very difficult to hit; at twenty yards apart, each horseman was an individual target. A single horseman can slow or speed, angle left or right, and if he knows his business, he can tie down a good amount of archery. You might argue that the archers could simply shoot over him or past him at the serried ranks of knights behind, but that is not the way of men in war. Men in war shoot at the target closest to them and most immediately dangerous.

At any rate, the confidence and calm of the Order was so great, and I think that Father Pierre's presence had something to do with it, that I had time to admire the precision of our formations, and the advance of the line of light horse was splendid.

As we moved west along the beach, the sounds of fighting grew louder. When we came to the spit of land on which the Pharos castle stood, well out in the bay, the line of rocks that supported the spit made a wall. In fact, I have learned since that it *is* a wall, built in ancient times by Great Alexander and has since silted over to form dry land.

But along this wall came part of the garrison of Pharos.

Our turcopoles changed direction like a flock of starlings in the air. One moment they were a line across the beach, and then they changed front to the north, and formed to our right flank, facing the new threat from the garrison.

It was one of the day's most important fights, and I missed it. I saw a little of it and it gave me a taste of how warfare in the Levant must be conducted – utterly different from the protracted armoured mêlées of Italy and France. The garrison of the Pharos Castle was part mounted Mamluks and part infantry archers. They moved very quickly along the top of the rock wall, seeming to walk on the sea. Our turcopoles changed front to meet them, as I have said, and both sides ended up on the sand at the sea's edge, loosing a cloud of arrows as they closed.

The end of the Saracen line was only a hundred paces from me, and I gathered my reins and looked at Fra Peter.

He rode to me from his wedge. 'Absolutely not,' he said. 'You will *not* charge until I command you. Do not betray my trust in you, William.'

Well.

I saw Marc-Antonio go down under his horse, and I saw John's horse leap my downed squire even as John loosed his bow with perfect control, leaning well back, head thrown back. He feathered a Mamluk at a range of perhaps one pace, and his horse reared, at his command, I think, and he had *another* arrow on his bow and loosed it *down* into a man close enough to have been struck by his sword. He shot and shot and I couldn't take my eyes off him.

And the whole time, we were moving. We passed *behind* the mêlée, or shot-stour, or call it what you will. We left our turcopoles to hold the garrison, and we rode west.

And now we could see the battle.

In the centre, King Peter's *galia grossa* had made it close in to shore. I was told later that there was a single channel, the width of a ship, that came within half a bowshot of the beach, and the king's ship was piloted to the end of the channel, bow first, and not stern first. So the king and his knights had to go into the water over the bow, and they leaped into the waves in three feet of dirty seawater.

The army of the city loosed thousands of bolts, shafts, arrows, and stone at them. This I saw with my own eyes and the gentle surf carried shafts ashore for days, but even more wondrous was the forest of fletchings that rose out of the flat waters where arrows had buried themselves in the shallow bottom.

When the arrows had minimal effect, when, in fact, the king's galley disgorged most of his retinue, the king and his knights began to wade ashore. Guillaume of Turenne, Sieur Percival, Simon de Thinoli, Brémond de la Voulte, Guy la Beveux and Sir John de Morphou all formed close by the king and followed him as he waded, heavily armoured, through the sea.

They began to fight their way ashore – surely, messieurs, one of the greatest feet of arms ever by Christian knights, as there were fewer than seventy of them, and they fought their way to the water's edge against ten thousand men.

Other ships tried to emulate the king's feat. But, as we had seen from our tower, they ran aground too far from the king's ship to succour it, and their men-at-arms had to wade neck deep towards the shore, exhausting in armour – and a misstep could mean death. Then the king's brother, the Prince of Antioch, hit on the notion of running the stern of his galley against the stern of the king's galley, and making a bridge.

By this time, the king was surrounded by Bedouin and Berber auxiliaries. Jean de Rheims told me that the king killed fifty men before he fell, and I can well believe it, having seen the dead. Percival de Coulanges, who is, believe me, no friend of mine, was yet a very pillar of valour, and his sword was like that of an avenging angel. Brémonde de la Voulte had a poleaxe, and with it he cut a tunnel through the infidels.

For an hour, the sixty or seventy knights held a section of beach against ten thousand men. Finally, the Prince of Antioch's retainers boarded the king's galley and ran the length of it, using it as a sort of pier, and other ships began to follow suit. Ships full of crusaders laid alongside the king's galley, or crossed her stern, or grappled themselves to the Prince of Antioch's galley.

Imagine, then, as the whole of the crusader fleet roped itself into a great floating dock from which to land men, how it would have fared had the machines on the Pharos Castle still been able to engage them!

Truly, it was all God's will. It certainly was *not* good planning or brilliant tactics.

By noon, Prince Hugh was ashore with six hundred more men. The king was still fighting, and would not retreat. Nor were six hundred knights, however brave, enough to defeat the whole number of Alexandrines.

The rest of the army, the crusaders, either hung back or could not get ashore. I mean no dishonour to those who tried – men *drowned* leaping over the sides of ships in frustration, into water just over their heads. But many ships hung back, the Genoese, and, I confess it, the Venetians, much as I love them. I was not aboard Contarini's flagship when he was finally informed that the target of the fleet was Alexandria, but I have been told he swore to sink the King of Cyprus's ship himself.

He did not. But neither did he land.

The city garrison began to close in on the knights on the beach. Now, the annals of chivalry are full of tales of one man defeating ten, or a hundred, and that with God's help. But any man trained to arms knows that if ten untrained peasants are brave and have sharp sticks and do not fear death, they can bring down an armoured knight, aye, and kill or take him. Perhaps it would take twenty to bring down a de Charny or the Black Prince. But the odds of ten thousand against six hundred could only be held so long.

The circle of Cypriote knights was wavering when de Mézzières got his round ship in close and leaped into the surf. The water came up to his neck – I have heard this from a hundred witnesses – and he had the banner of the King of Jerusalem in his fist, which had not flown in Outremer in a hundred years. And he walked slowly out of the waves, the white banner of Jerusalem trailing on the dirty water behind him, and twenty knights followed him. De Mézzières raised the banner of Jerusalem, and the knights of Cyprus and the handful of crusaders ashore shouted.

And the admirals of Genoa and of Venice, cursing, no doubt, began to manoeuvre to land their knights.

They were half an hour behind the action.

The king was doomed.

When we passed the sea wall, it was, as I have said, noon. The Egyptian sun, even in autumn, was impossibly brilliant, and the air was as warm as an English day in high summer. The dazzle of the noontide sun on the water of the bay was like a thousand-thousand points of light, so bright they burned the air like daggers.

The army of Alexandria lay before us on the dirty white sand. Now, I have heard men say that Alexandria was undefended, and they lie. This is the foolish jealousy of men who, having missed a great battle, seek to deride all those who were there.

They had a great army, and the governor's lieutenant had the whole garrison of the Pharos Castle, and there was another lord under the walls with a strong force of cavalry.

But the very impetus that was about to win the battle for Islam, the sheer force of ten thousand against six hundred, had drawn them out of all formation into a great clump, a heaving, desperate mass at the centre of the bay of the old harbour's arc. They had no formation, and the Mamluk bowmen, the Al-Halqua, non-Mamluk, troops of the garrison (as Sabraham later identified them) and the Sudanese spearmen – good troops, as I would have reason to know – were packed in like glasses in woodchips.

When the lord under the walls saw the Order, he led his cavalry at us. He had more horse than we, but not many more, and their horses, while beautiful, were small. Nor were they in wedges. He led his Mamluks forward, and again I gathered my reins short, and Fra Peter turned; his visor was still up.

'Abide!' he called.

I was too eager.

We walked along the sands. In my memory, our formation was perfect.

To my right front, where the king was, the banner of Jerusalem wavered. And fell.

The hosts of Alexandria let out a great roar that rang from the walls, and the people of the city echoed their cheer.

Fra Peter leaned back. He was speaking to the legate.

Chretien d'Albret cursed. 'The fucking serf! He's going to let the king die. Charge, Gold! Lead us!'

He began to push his mount forward.

We were formed very close. I turned and thumped the butt of my lance against his chest. 'Abide!' I shouted.

Fra Peter made a set of hand signals with his bridle hand – to the southernmost wedge. To me, he held up his hand – flat.

Halt.

I could not imagine why we should halt.

But Fra Peter and Fra William had been very clear about obedience, and despite d'Albret shouting that I was a coward, I raised my lance and reined in. My whole command halted. Horse shuffled – somewhere close at hand, a horse let out a long fart.

The southernmost wedge plodded along the sand.

The Mamluks let their horses have their heads, took up their bows, and loosed their first arrows. They were at long bowshot, perhaps three hundred yards. A light cane arrow fell from the sky and hit me in the helmet.

Oh, armour!

There was a sharp *ping*.

Fra Peter's gauntleted hand closed on air and pumped, once.

'Walk!' I called. I put my weight forward.

'Now what? Gold, for the love of the Virgin! The king is down!' D'Albret's voice had an odd ring. He'd been an excitable boy and he'd spent too long with Camus, who imagined himself Hell's emissary on earth.

As if Hell needs an emissary.

I looked, and the circle of the crusaders on the beach had been broken.

The three bodies of the Order were now in echelon, the southernmost slightly ahead, then the centre body with the legate, and then mine. Our angled line of three wedges was like a barbed scythe.

And Fra Peter's fist pumped, once.

I heard the change in the hoofbeats as the arrows screamed in. I touched Gawain with my spurs – and he leapt forward.

The Knights of St John have been fighting in the Holy Land for two hundred years. One of their many tricks is this change of speed as the first serious arrow volley is launched. In three strides, Gawain and I were at a gallop, still with Nerio and Fiore leaning into me, their armoured knees behind mine. We were an arrowhead, a battering ram of horses and steel.

The Mamluks rode in close, trying to break our formation. By Christ, gentles, they were brave! They came right in, almost to our lance tips, to loose their arrows, and it seemed to me that in one beat of my heart they were impossibly far away and the next they were right atop us.

Deus Veult!

One shout, like a crack of thunder. This, too, we had practiced since Venice.

Our lances came down.

And they turned away. They had neither the formation nor the horseflesh for mêlée and they turned and shot over the backs of their saddles.

One man down – one at the front of the wedge – and the whole force would be dissipated into a wreck of falling horses and broken men.

God did not will that.

I do not remember closing my visor. But my whole world was limited to a single man, his beard dyed red, his armour gold and silver in the brilliant sun, his horse's rump shining with sweat and the back of his saddle just two horse-lengths from me.

His arrows struck me. The first slammed into my breastplate like an axe blow, thrusting me back in my saddle like a good hit in a joust, and the second hit my visor – and penetrated it. I felt my death slide across my cheek.

But as I was not dead, I rode on.

Then everything changed.

The Saracen's Mamluks charged us from under the walls, and moved diagonally to cross our front. But when they failed to break our formations, they evaded straight away instead of galloping lightly away from our impotent lances – and slammed into the rear of their own infantry.

In my memory, I pursued my hennaed Mamluk for hours across an infinite plain of sand. But then, in one beat of my heart, I caught him, and my lance struck him in the back. I imagine I killed him instantly – his coat of plates and mail failed against the force of my charge. My point went in, and the whole of my lance penetrated him: his horse had balked.

I lost my lance.

In two more heart beats I was deep in the Saracen army. Gawain was killing more effectively than I; he danced, his iron-shod feet like four iron maces. Weapons struck me – and it is in moments like this that you discover your training. I drew the Emperor's sword without a conscious thought; it flowed into my hand, and I cut. I do not remember fighting men, only cutting at a mob. Gawain was still moving forward.

I had one thought, then, to cut my way to the king. If I raised my head at all, I could see the last of the crusaders on the beach, perhaps three hundred, now, the brilliance of their armour showing where they stood through the press of foes.

And next to me was Fiore, his arm rising and falling like an executioner's axe, and on the other side of me, Nerio and his superb horse left a wake of red ruin. Miles was at Fiore's left knee and Juan at Nerio's right, and the five of us were the point of the Christian spear thrusting for the king.

And yet, as we slowed, I had time to be afraid.

Usually, in combat, there is no time to be afraid. Fear comes earlier, when you prepare, and wait, and later, when you consider, and shake. But on the beach at Alexandria, we took their foot so completely by surprise that we were at their backs, and I saw bearded, shouting faces suddenly turning to me. I had time to consider whether my four friends and I could, by ourselves, best the greatest city in the world.

I had no idea what was happening elsewhere. I spared no thoughts for the legate, unarmoured, in the midst of the press, or for Fra Peter or Fra William or any of the other knights. They were off to my left and they might have been in other spheres.

Ahead, I saw the flash of armour.

Now I was using my sword two-handed in fatigue, and desperation. The danger is hitting your own horse. As the horse moves its head – and horses move their heads often – you can catch the back of the neck above the mane, killing your own mount.

Fiore had no wasted his time.

At some point – hours? Days? We struck the Naffatun. They were veteran Mamluks armed with grenadoes of naphtha, a sticky stuff like tar that ignited on contact and burned armour and human skin, the very stuff of hell brought to earth. They had pressed far down the beach and burned two galleys that they'd caught aground, and now they hurled their bombs at us and charged with their swords.

Imagine that you see this through the narrow slits of your visor while your lungs struggle to pull in enough air through the tiny holes in your helmet. Imagine the stink of your own sweat on a sweltering day, wearing eighty pounds of armour, fighting for your life.

Something caught me from behind. I was taken by surprise, and in a moment, I was unhorsed. You always imagine that this will take time – but by Saint George, one moment I was horrified by the Naffatun and the next I was off my near side, down in the sand.

Men caught fire, and died horribly. Horses panicked close by me – hooves were everywhere as our dense formation exploded in a rout of burning men and terrified horses.

But as we were surrounded by the Army of Egypt, our own near destruction only served to thrust us again at our foes. Panicked horses exploded into the serried ranks of the foe.

Truly, God willed it.

Not that I was aware, particularly. I was more aware of the hooves, everywhere, and the ranks of enemy infantry.

The Naffatun were well armoured and had shields of some horrible beast with a knobby hide. I got to one knee and hammered one with my sword one-handed and failed to penetrate it, and my adversary slashed at me with a heavy sabre from the shelter of his buckler and his sabre had no more effect on my harness than the Emperor's sword on his shield.

On the third or fourth exchange I remembered a play of Fiore's and, as my weapons struck the face of his hide buckler, I rotated my hand up and leaned forward. My point slipped past his shield and *down* into his face, and he fell backwards, my sword deep in his guts.

And I went with it. By luck or practice, I used the collapse of his body to drag me off my knee and to my feet.

Gawain was close; I knew him, and was sure he wouldn't leave me. I needed a few seconds in the press to get him.

That was the time of the longsword.

The men around me were mostly Bedouin – unarmoured men

with small shields, daggers and spears. Interspersed with them were Sudanese Ghulami, men as black as Richard Musard, or blacker, with heavy spears like the ones we'd use for a foot combat or a passage of arms. I cut hard, a long, flat cut from right to left, clearing a little space and severing a man's fingers. He fell back, and I killed another with a flick of my point: I was spending my spirit the way Nerio spent ducats.

But by God, I was fighting well.

Fiore reached me first, angling into the enemy from my right and killing his way like a ship under sail cuts the water. His charger dropped a big spearman whose heavy shaft was absorbing my blows. I caught his stirrup and his good horse hauled me ten paces through the press and I was hit twenty times. I was bruised, and I took a wound in the back of my right bicep under the spaulder, but when the pain forced me to relinquish the stirrup leather, I was close enough to the crusaders to see their crests and their coat armour.

I could see Mézzières, forty feet away. He had one foot on either side of the king, who was lying flat in the sand.

I thought of de Charny.

I prayed.

I was hit. And I stumbled.

And then Juan was there – Juan, who'd been knocked unconscious in the first action. He was tall in his saddle, his seat firm, his back straight, and his arm rose and fell like a man threshing wheat, and Saracens died. Because of him, I finally had a moment to gather Gawain, who should have followed me like a loyal dog.

My horse was nowhere to be seen.

I believe that I cursed.

Miles had our banner, and now he was close to me, and behind him I could see Nerio and the scarlet coat armour of my volunteers. The Saracens were screaming – the keening came through my helmet – and the dying were screaming a different tune and the cry 'On, on!' thundered out, grunted from the mounted knights.

The world balanced and the balance held, like two combatants when both make a strong pass and their blades lock. We were locked. Mézzières, Nerio, Fra Peter. Somewhere out on the bay, Carlo Zeno leapt into the water. A ship full of Genoese discharged a heavy volley of arbalest bolts into the flank of the Naffatun.

I saw none of this, you understand. Nor had I seen d'Albret un-horsing me, or trying to kill me and being driven off by Juan. In the helmet, you just don't see.

Where I was, there was only the grit in between my teeth, the heaving of my sides as my lungs begged for air that my breastplate denied, the sweat that wept into my eyes from my hairline and the soggy padding of my cervelliere, and the sword I held in both hands.

Listen, then.

I got my sword up into a high guard – rare enough, on the battle-field – but something came to me, in the locked moment, some grace, whether from God or Fiore I leave you to guess. But I took up the guard called Window with my hands crossed, and my adversary was an armoured Saracen in light mail. He had a scimitar and a buckler with five bosses and verses of the Koran inscribed in gold.

I cut. I rotated my hands and cut between the bucker and the scimitar, rotating forward on my hips.

Like many men against whom I trained, the space between his sword and his shield was less guarded than it ought to have been. My sword touched both his sword and his shield. And continued through his helmet and into his head. My hand was so fell, so heavy, that the blade went through helm and head, down and down.

He fell, and I pressed forward one full step, cutting the reverse line *up*. I felt as if the very power of God had filled me. By Christ, all my life I have heard men claim to have cut through a helmet, but I have seen it done with a sword only three times, and that was one.

My rising cut broke a man's wrists and half severed them and I threw him to the ground with my knee and my left hand and finished him with my knee while I cut flat and low against an unarmoured spearman. His spear thrust was weak and skidded on my breastplate and I cut into his leg and probably fractured it with the same blow and he too was down.

And then I was face to face with Mézzières, across a horse-length of beach. My friends were clearing away the front of the Cypriotes, and they had their ring of steel reformed.

The army of the Alexandrines shrieked their dismay. And then, like fools, they turned and ran.

The 'crusaders' were finally landing, all along the beach, many in boats provided by their ships, and some captains had run their small craft ashore. The Venetians and Genoese knew the harbour and came in close, well away to the right, and their landing cut many of the fugitives off from the open gate.

I saw none of that. I leaned on my sword and panted, and my breath was all I could breathe inside my helmet, and somehow I got my visor up.

De Mézzières stood there in the sun with the banner of Jerusalem in his hand. Then he raised his visor. He had a ring of dead at his feet.

Our eyes met.

What can I say? You know what we both thought.

The man at his feet coughed, and coughed again, and in a moment we were on him the way the pursuers were on the Saracen fugitives. I had assumed the king to be dead, but we got his bassinet off his head and his blue eyes fluttered open.

He rolled to his hands and knees and spat blood into the sand.

'Ah,' he growled. 'Ah, Mézzières. I gather we are not in heaven?'

Most of the men who won that day will tell you that the charge of the Order won the day. Listen, Chaucer, you've heard Hales tell it, have you not? Fifty years those men had waited for their day, and when they charged, their lances were tipped with fire.

The Alexandrines had no idea we had a second force, and the Order showed them what a few mounted knights could do. And Fortuna – or God's will – gave us everything: the Casteleto, the error of the Mamluk's charge.

But by Saint George, it was a glorious day, as great a day as any I have seen.

The crusaders – no, the routiers, let us call them – slaughtered the Saracens. And the pity of it is that they did not just slaughter their army. Thousands of Alexandrines, including women and children, Jewish street vendors and Christians who had come out to see their brothers rescue them – they were by the gates – and our army killed them. This is the monster that is war, a monster that devours everything in its path.

And still the men of Alexandria got the gates closed. They left brothers and sons to die and slammed the gates in their faces to keep us out. And the routiers who had played no part in the victory roamed the beach, killing unarmed men.

Fra Peter gathered us again under the legate's banner, but not before King Peter made Steven Scrope, one of the blood-covered figures at de Mézzières' shoulder, and Miles Stapleton kneel and the sand, and he knighted them both. He knighted a dozen other men.

He took his own collar, a magnificent thing of silver gilt and jewels made of swords and roses from around his neck and he broke it with his sword, and gave half to de Mézzières.

He gave half to me.

He made me one of his Order of the Sword while our army of mercenaries murdered the innocents who had come to watch the battle.

I am a knight, and the business of my Order is war.

Do peasants sicken of the plough? Do priests tire of saying Mass?

I was twenty-five years old, and Alexandria was my sixth great battle. In the fighting, each was different, as one lover is from another. In the aftermath, there is a sameness that defies description – foul, cruel, evil.

The king never regained control of the host of mercenaries we'd brought from Italy and I will not lie: what follows is dark and there's little chivalry in it.

The routiers ranged along the walls. To them were added most of the marines and many of the sailors. The captains brought their ships off the shoals and sands of the Old Harbour and rowed or sailed around Pharos Castle into the Pharos Harbour and the Venetians attempted an escalade on the Pharos castle before sun set. The governor's lieutenant resisted manfully, and threw them back with losses.

I was sitting on an upturned boat at the end of the sea wall while a Venetian surgeon probed my shoulder with a knife fouled from cutting ten other wounded men. Then he sewed the flap of separated skin back down. I promise you that it hurt!

Marc-Antonio had three arrows in him. Carlo Zeno pushed the surgeon aside and cut them out with his own hands. Of our army of five thousand, only a thousand had been engaged, but that thousand had enough wounds for ten. Yet we had very few dead. Our harnesses were so good that most men lived at least to see the dawn, and many are still with us.

It was growing dark when Nerio found Chretien d'Albret. Nerio's squire Davide fetched me, and we rode across the sand. John the Turk had found Gawain and restored him, and had landed our little Arab horses, who shied at blood but nonetheless were firm footed and well-rested; Gawain had ten cuts, one so broad that his red muscles showed like a gap in a curtain. John gave him opium and then sewed him up like the doctors were doing to men.

Much later, perhaps a year or more, when I was telling the Count of Savoy about the fight – his nephew was there, but the Green Count was not, of course – John was fletching arrows by the fire, and I saw him grunt and shake his head while I told this story.

Later that night, I went to him. By then we were old friends and I asked him why he had sneered at my story. He laughed mirthlessly, in his Tartar way. 'All battle the same,' he said. 'Young men sing. Old man grunt.'

I thought he was posturing. 'John, you were a hero – you *saved us*. I saw you save Marc-Antonio. You earned glory—'

His Tartar eyes burned with sudden anger. John is seldom angry, but he stepped forward at me although I am a head and more taller. And I suspect I stepped back.

'I save friend!' he spat. He reached his left hand behind him and wiped his arse elaborately and then brought the hand up to my face. 'Worth more than glory, is my shit,' he said.

I tell you gentles this, because not everyone agrees on what we saw and did at Alexandria.

We rode to Chretien d'Albret.

He was dying. Listen, in paintings, saints die with serene faces, whether on the rack, or full of arrows, or like Christ on the cross. But men do not go that way, and most especially when they have been burned across most of their upper body with naptha.

The fire had done something to d'Albret. He thought he was going to hell. In fact, he thought he was already in hell, burning alive.

Well.

The poor bastard.

Flesh came away whenever he moved, charred strips like bad meat. And he screamed and screamed until you'd think he'd have had no voice left. His eyes were gone.

Christ, I can't tell this ...

*

He raved.

To most men on the beach, his raving sounded like the last words of a man in torment. But I knew what he was saying. He was saying that d'Herblay had paid him to kill me.

I stood and listened.

Nerio was better than me. He made a little sound like *pfft* and killed d'Albret, drawing, thrusting, wiping his blade and returning it to the scabbard so fast that it was as if his hands were full of silver fire in the moonlight.

'I hope one of you will do the same for me, if my turn is like that,' Nerio said.

But we had all heard what we had heard. It wasn't just me d'Albret was after. D'Albret had died screaming that he had been paid to kill the serf. The Serf.

A man in agony cannot be interrogated or questioned or threatened or begged. He screamed d'Herblay's name. He screamed his repentance at the sky, and was killed.

God have mercy on his soul, and the souls of all those who died in the sand.

We went back and slept on pallets of straw in a rough camp that the sergeants and lay brothers of the Order had prepared. But before we lay down our horses were groomed and fed, their wounds tended, their tack stripped away and cleaned. It took me, I swear, half the night.

Marc-Antonio's habit of getting wounded when there was work to be done was remarkable! But with John's expert help and my friends and their squires, we got it all done. We made the Gascons d'Albret had brought do the same, though they complained and complained. I might have raged at them – you could see Fra Robert Hales and Fra Ricardo and a dozen other older knights patiently currying horses in the moonlight while a handful of young Gascons proclaimed themselves too nobly born for such work, but I was too tired for rage. And I wanted them where I could see them.

The legate was tireless. He went from wounded man to wounded man, and late, when the moon was high, he came to us. We prayed, and I told him about d'Albret.

He shrugged. 'My life is worth nothing,' he said. He smiled his simple smile and went off to find other men worse off than we. Later, he spent an hour protecting a huddle of Moslem survivors from the routiers.

I was asleep.

We rose to pain. I was under my military cloak – Egypt's nights can be cold – with Nerio pressed close to me on one side and my wounded squire pressed close to the other. He had the fever we all dreaded, and he was so hot I thought he was done. All three of his wounds were red.

So was my shoulder.

I have little memory of that day. Fra Peter ordered us to horse, and we tacked and bridled and we were mounted in the dawn, and our horses were as stiff as we were ourselves. But not an arrow did we receive from the walls. The king awoke late, mounted, and rode the whole circuit of the walls before noon with the Order as his body-guards. Two hundred knights, and the greatest city on earth.

They might have laughed us to scorn, but they had their own troubles.

King Peter sent them a cartel, summoning the city to surrender. Their commander returned a defiance.

We rode from point to point, and everywhere I looked for d'Herblay and asked me if they had seen him.

He was nowhere to be found. Most 'crusaders' rose late and began to prowl around the walls like dogs searching for food. They were not an army. I know, because the king stopped many times, trying to reason with men. He stopped Sir Walter Leslie, who was with his brothers and some other Scottish knights and asked them to rejoin the army.

Sir Walter bowed deeply. He was in his harness, as were his brothers and all their men, and they were stripping some houses in the suburbs by the Pepper Gate.

'You Grace, we came here to be rich, and if we cannot take the city, at least we can loot these towns,' Sir Walter said.

Gascons, French, Scots – they ran riot over the countryside, looted a caravan they caught coming in, killing the animals where they stood. The Venetians stormed the Pharos again, and found it empty. The town's lieutenant had stripped it of men and valuables and slipped away after the attack the night before, convinced he could not hold it.

As I say, the Saracens had troubles of their own. One was that the lieutenant was himself shattered by defeat. I have seen this in other places; he had a larger army and a magnificent defensive position, but defeat robbed him of his will to resist.

And we had neglected the most simple precautions, and so the Alexandrines were able to send messengers to Cairo. On the other hand, with all the harbour castles in our hands, the Venetians and Genoese were suddenly sanguine. Their ships were safe, and any ships that remained in the old harbour were rowed around to the New.

By mid-afternoon, the king had perhaps two thousand men-at-arms under his hand. He had all the English – perhaps the habit of obedience was better among the English, but I think it is that there were more lords and fewer routiers. At any rate, the English stayed together as a body, and the Scots, despite Leslie's comments in the late morning, came back to the beach and remained part of the 'army'. But the French, the Gascons, the Bretons, the Savoyards and the sailors were uncontrollable.

Nor were they the only ones uncontrolled. In the town, a riot set the Christian quarter afire and the heads of a dozen Christian men appeared on spikes over the Sea Gate that the locals called Bab al-Bahr. The French routiers got barrels of pitch from the Venetians and tried to burn the gate and the garrison drove them off with heavy losses.

No one knows what happened in those hours. But we saw the smoke rising in the town, and as the French threw themselves against the Sea Gate, we covered their flanks. Parties of Saracens would emerge from the sally ports along the waterfront to kill the attackers, and we – mounted – would trap them against the walls. In fact, mostly we trapped air and sand because they were too quick for us.

Late in the afternoon, the Scots had a go at the Sea Gate. Sir Walter Leslie led them forward, and they rolled barrels of flammables to the base of the gate. But the Naffatun had come, and they rained fire on the earth. Sir Norman Leslie died in his harness, so burned that the plates buckled, and many another Scot died with him. But they got the gates afire, or possibly the naptha that killed the Scots also caught the gate.

The infidels made a mounted sortie, trying to clear the gate so that they could put out the fire and we charged them, and for the first time we were sword to sword with Mamluks. I was by the king for he did me the honour of riding with my contingent of volunteers, and we had a sharp fight, but the Mamluks didn't linger. We pressed them hard into their sally port, but they got away.

Mostly I remember being tired, hot, and miserable.

Sunset was close when the king summoned all his counsellors.

'Well, my lords,' he said. 'Here we are at the walls of Alexandria.' The smell of smoke was everywhere. There was a fire inside the city, still burning. We didn't know that Janghara, the cowardly lieutenant, had ordered the Christians killed and then snuck out of the city. We had no idea that there were more Alexandrines fighting the fire than fighting our armies.

King Peter was never greater than that hour. Tall and slim even in harness, he seemed fired by the same energy that animated Father Pierre, who stood by his side. 'Now is the time to take the city, my lords,' the king insisted. 'Advise me.'

Percival de Coulanges, the same who had called Sabraham and me liars, stepped forward without hesitation. 'I know the right gate to attack. This one is too obvious because it is close to our camp. Let's take ladder and try the Bab al-Diwan. The customs house gate.'

The king had a heavy gold link-belt on his hips, and his hands rested on it. 'My lord, you are a good and loyal vassal,' he said. 'But your advice on the Old Harbour left something to be desired, and we all almost bleached our bones on your beach.' He laughed. 'Are you sure?'

Percival shook his head. 'No, my lord,' he admitted. 'But when I was a slave here, the Lord of the Customs cast the army forth and said that his gate was his alone, and only his own men could be there. He was such a corrupt bastard that he couldn't have the Sultan's men watching him.'

Fra Robert Hales laughed aloud. 'I'm glad the Saracens suffer from all the same sins as we,' he said.

Raymond Bérenger, the new Master of the Order, nodded. 'Let us have a go at this gate.'

Father Pierre sighed. 'I mislike the – the fractures. Many of our men are wandering like sheep without shepherds.'

'Like wolves without older wolves,' muttered Fra William Midleton.

The Count of Turenne, the greatest nobleman present, had fought brilliantly the day before. Now he shook his head. 'My lords, we have won a great battle and surely shown these Saracen dogs our worth. Should we not withdraw?'

Up until that moment, no one had suggested withdrawal.

The king looked up at his banner. 'My lord, for myself, I go to Jerusalem.'

Turenne nodded. 'As you say, your Grace.' He was not sincere.

Percival de Coulanges had been utterly wrong about the Old Harbour and the landing, but he had the Customs Gate dead to rights. We rode widdershins round the city until we came to the point where the pillars of Pompey could most clearly be seen, and there was a small gate and an empty market in front of it. Yet behind the gate were two immense towers and a set of walls.

I have said that the king was not in command of our 'army,' but many of the wolves followed us when we moved. The Scots came with us, and some of the French under Turenne and others with de la Voulte. The king had the Order and the legate had all the English under Lord Grey. And hundreds of Venetian sailors and oarsmen came with us, scenting something.

The king made an excellent plan. He brought up two small scorpions and men who could use them from the Casteleto, and flammables – pitch and naphtha taken at the Pharos. That was, I think, the first time I saw the black powder that men use in cannons. We had had it with the king's army in the year of Black April, but while I had smelled its hellish scent I had never used it. But the king ordered the captured powder brought forward, and while Cypriote pioneers and Venetian oarsmen wrestled with the barrels and the machines, the king gave us orders.

'The Scots and the English will assault the gate,' he said. 'The mounted men will make two bodies, one with me, and one with the Grand Master. We will keep any Saracens from taking the assault to the flanks.' He looked back and forth among us. 'If we get the gate open, then summon the army. But in that case, all the mounted men – on me. We will fight our way through the city to the bridge at the Cairo Gate.'

'I know it,' I said.

'Ah, Sir William! So you will help get us there.' He watched the gate for as long as it takes to say a Paternoster. 'And we will use the powder to knock the bridge down. I have seen this done. Eh?'

I had my doubts. I had seen the bridge, and it was big and broad and beautifully built. But dark was an hour or two away and the light was failing. And I didn't imagine we'd win through, anyway.

But God, as Father Pierre likes to say, moves in mysterious ways. Sir Walter, determined to avenge the death of his brother, and supported by a dozen Scottish knights, with some wild Irish among them for good measure, assaulted the gate. They were brave, and for some time, while they tried to kindle fire against the wooden doors of the outer sally port, we thought that the gate might be un-garrisoned. But after about ten minutes, there was a sally from the next gate, and we charged them. They were no match for our armour or our horses, and they ran. I began to wonder if the garrison was already having problems of spirit – it seemed to me that only their leader had shown any courage, and he was lying face down in the sand, dead by the hand of King Peter.

When we got back to the gate, the towers above it were manned, and arrows and javelins rained on our Scottish knights. Sir Walter was wounded, and so was Lord St Clair, and one of the Irish knights took a blow to the helmet that knocked him unconscious. But the other men stayed at their task.

By that time we had quite a crowd of sailors and routiers about us, and they were prowling the walls. A few were killed – the garrison of the customs house leaned right out over the wall to shoot them. But they had no hoardings, and so the Italian arbalest men and the handful of English and Scottish bowmen began to pick them off.

John asked my permission to join the archers and I sent him off with my blessing. The loot of the battlefield the day before had yielded him not one but three Mamluk bows, a fine sabre with verses of the Koran in gold on the blade, and a hundred arrows. He was as eager to employ them as a new-dubbed knight is to wear his armour.

I can't imagine that there were more than a dozen archers, all told, but they swept the walls. One of the differences I noted between the crossbow and the self bow is that John and the English archers had to draw and loose as a target was revealed, but the Italians could watch a particular crenellation, weapon aimed, waiting for the unlucky Saracen to expose himself.

Nonetheless, John scored the spectacular success of the afternoon, hitting an officer as he passed between merlons so that he fell with his head over the battlements. After that, the Saracens dared not show themselves, and again I thought they showed a want of spirit. They could have flooded the walls with archers and buried our men in shafts, and instead they allowed a dozen men to clear their walls.

One of the Italians, a veteran of fifty actions, I'll wager you, moved forward. He had a light crossbow, the sort lords use for hunting-still a puissant weapon. He moved forward with the crossbow sweeping the walls, and moved all the way to the base of the wall. From there he moved to the gateway, from where he covered the knights, shooting his bolts almost straight up. Two more of the Italians joined him.

The three Englishman and one Scot of Ettrick – all brilliant archers – grew bored at the paucity of targets and they joined the sailors at the base of the wall. One of the Englishmen found the outlet of a jakes, a shithole so old that it was merely a mound of greenery. He was up on his mate's shoulders in a moment and I saw this.

He was too broad to make it in,

I looked at Fra Peter; he gave me a nod and I rode down to the archers and sailors.

The archer wrinkled his nose. 'Old shit, my lord.' He grinned. 'I been and used a few shitholes and your pardon in France, if you take my meaning.'

I laughed. 'I used an apple tree once,' I said.

He nodded. 'I know, me lord. I won there. Afore Poitiers, where we took King John.'

I dismounted and clasped his hand, old shit and all.

'Ned Cooper,' he said. 'I was with the Prince at Poitiers. These criminals is Ewen, a barbarous fuckin' Scot, and Rob Stone.' He spoke slowly, and blinked a great deal, and I think he'd been hit a little too often in the head. Which is an odd thing for me to say, I admit, having received a few blows myself.

'Which the thing is,' Ned went on as if we were old comrades … and I suppose we were. He certainly knew me. 'Which the thing is, that a small man, a really small man or a boy, would go through that hole as slick as …' He looked around, and came to the unavoidable conclusion, 'shit.'

Ewen, the Scot, and obviously not a candidate, shook his head. 'I 'ate the smell,' he said.

Rob Stone stretched his arms. 'I'd rather roll in the stuff than go up a ladder,' he said. 'Methinks I'm too big in the arse, but I'll have a go.'

But even as he tried – and failed – John the Turk appeared. He watched Stone struggle to get his shoulders through the hole and frowned. He walked away and I thought that was the end of it.

By this time the entire garrison of the customs house was in the towers, safe from our archery, lobbing red-hot sand and boiling tar and naphtha and all the weapons of hell on Sir William Leslie and his people.

The Scots were not getting in the gate. The two highlanders were hacking at the wooden door with axes, but it had been built for such attempts, although perhaps not from two northern giants.

John the Turk came back with a small boy perched on his saddle.

Ned Cooper nodded. 'Now you're thinkin', mate. Now you're usin' yer noggin. Let the boy ha' a go.' He turned and pulled Stone's ankle. 'Get thy fat arse out there, Rob Stone.'

Stone grunted, sneezed, and dropped heavily to the ground. 'Too bloody big,' he said.

John showed the boy two gold ducats and the boy grabbed one, grinned, and stripped naked. John ran, flat footed and ungainly when off his horse, to the Italians. One of the bowmen had a grapple and rope, and John took it. The sailors came trotting back with my Tartar, and they looked up at the hole and did what soldiers do in such situations – they began wagering.

The boy stared at the rope, and John tied an end to the boy's ankle. Ewen the Scot boosted the naked boy as if he was weightless and he vanished into the hole like a sword going into a scabbard.

And the line started to flow up the wall.

One of the Venetian sailors was a very small man. He stripped to his hose and hung his dagger round his neck and went up the rope. He got a shoulder through, there was a streak of curses and blasphemy utterly unbecoming a crusader, and a chunk of ordure-encrusted masonry fell, and he was in.

And then ... nothing.

The Scots finally had the sally port alight. The axes of the two highlanders had gouged the surface enough for the fire to take hold, or so it appeared, and I rode back to the king.

He was eating a sausage. He looked at the sun, two fingers above the horizon, and back at the inferno the Scots had made. They had piled every scrap of wood they could find against the gate, and added some hellish stuff from the Pharos Castle. It burned fast.

By my estimation, the enemy had had the time to build a defensive ditch and rampart behind the sally port. If we were unlucky, they had a blank wall and false turn to trap a dozen men and drop naphtha on them.

I would have.

But the Mamluks were just men, neither better nor worse than ourselves.

'It is now or never,' the king said, finishing his sausage. He looked at Fra Peter. 'You heard Sabraham's report.'

Fra Peter nodded. He glanced at me. 'Sir William hasn't heard. The Sultan in Cairo is marching an army to the relief of his city. Probably here tomorrow. It marched before we came off our ships.'

I whistled.

The king smiled at de Mézzières. 'You know, gentlemen, this was never my choice. But now we are here, I think we should try and make our mark. Let us do something worthy, that our names may live forever.'

De Mézzières nodded. 'I am with you, your Grace.'

The king dismounted.

To the Grand Master, he said, 'Give me the volunteers – they are the younger knights. If I have you and the Order at my back and a horse, I will fear no sally.'

The Grand Master nodded. 'You are determined to assay this, your Grace?'

'I will take this gate or die in the attempt,' King Peter said gravely. Then he called forth his squire and knighted him.

The fire was burning down and the gate was a blackened tunnel.

'One rush, my lords. No one hesitates, and the first man in the city will deserve something precious of me.' He reached out to de Mézzières and took the great banner of Jerusalem.

We dismounted and went forward at a trot. You can run in full harness, but we had been on shipboard for a week and we were not at the height of our conditioning. I hurt in a hundred places, and my breastplate rubbed the top of my hipbones because Marc-Antonio was wounded and John didn't know what holes to use on the straps. My arms ached from fighting the day before and I had a wound that was fevered.

I was in fine shape compared to some of the volunteers. Juan was pale under his dark skin and Nerio had circles under his eyes.

Fiore burned with puissance. And so did Miles Stapleton: just knighted, he was ready to take the city on his own.

We jogged forward.

Seeing us, the Saracens launched a barrage of arrows and darts. Our Italians shot back, trying to angle their bolts into the slits in the towers. I can't tell you whether they succeeded or not because my visor was closed and I was breathing the hot air of Egypt in my stifling faceplate.

We had about four hundred paces to cross. Halfway there I saw the Scots coming in from the side – they'd been huddled under the wall with the archers and the sailors and they were angry at their wounds and their dead.

I passed the king. In a storm, it is every man for himself, and I was lengthening my stride as I took hits. A heavy spear stuck in the sand in front of me.

My breath came in gasps, and I hadn't fought anyone.

Nerio appeared at my shoulder and Miles began to pass me.

I was hit again.

And then I ran into the wall of heat. Even inside my visor, I could not breathe that air. It was appalling. I thought my eyes would burn and I was in armour. I tripped over a fallen beam and stumbled; my shoulder hit a wall and I bounced, shoulder burning. I caught myself left-handed and the stone burned the heavy deerskin off the palm of my hand.

Sweet Christ, it was hell! The tunnel behind the burned door had caught fire – something had been stored there, perhaps. But the stone was hot, and part of the passage was still burning. It occurred to me that this was the stupidest thing I had ever done.

I got past the fire. The heat had finally got through my heavy fighting shoes to my feet and then I was in the sun. There were men there, but only twenty or thirty. Not a hundred or a thousand.

I'm not sure I actually thought anything, then.

I had the Emperor's longsword in my hand, and I used it.

I suppose this is the moment to tell you of my epic duel with the Captain of the tower, my longsword against his spear – and oh, my friends, I'd love to tell you such a tale. But I remember little of it, and mostly they were unarmoured, desperate men. Let no man ever tell me they were cowards. Those men, Alexandrines and not Mamluks at all, hurled themselves at me the way we had thrown ourselves at de Charny.

Why were there not more of them? Where were the armoured men? The engineers? The burning oil?

I knew none of these things, and neither did the terrified men facing me.

I know that I spared no one. I know that I used every weapon and every limb. My sword stabbed and cut, and I used my arms and legs, my elbows, my knees, the pointed steel tips of my sabatons.

I would say that I was alone against them for an hour, save that Fiore has sworn to me that he was never more than three steps behind me in the tunnel.

That's how it is, sometimes.

But then I knew when Fiore was next to me, because the pressure eased suddenly. Ever play with a child, and she sits on your chest? And then she rolls off ... It was like that. And then there was even less pressure as Miles thrust forward, and then Nerio, and then Juan, and we were pushing forward, step after step.

Juan died there. He'd taken a wound the day before, and worse, been knocked unconscious, and he was slow and pale, as I've said. He got a spear under his aventail and down he went. Fiore stood over him, and his sword *flew* and he killed men the way a housewife kills flies.

And then the king was with us, the banner of Jerusalem charred in his fist, and de Mézzières and de Coulanges and a dozen other of the king's knights, and we burst out of the gate house and into a courtyard. I realised we were between the walls and had it all to do again, but ... the far gate was *open* and there were no more than forty Saracens between us and the city and not a Mamluk in sight.

There was no time to mourn Juan. I knew he was dead – I'd seen the spear and the sheer amount of blood.

The Saracens charged us, trying to put the djinn back in the bottle as they might say themselves. And there was a flurry of archery from the inner towers and we were like rats in a trap, surrounded by towers full of enemy archers.

But the far gate was open and Alexandria, the richest, biggest city in the world, beckoned.

I suppose I killed my share, but I only remember the late afternoon sun slanting down on the street beyond the gate. That site filled my visor.

Something was happening beyond my helmet. It took me time, perhaps three exhausted, desperate blows with my longsword, before I realised that the enemy archery had stopped. Had I looked up, I would have seen the cross of St George, the banner of England, flying from the outer towers of the Customs Gate.

The boy and the thin Italian had got a line over the wall, and the Venetians and the English had taken the towers even as we cleared the yard and occupied the attention of the defenders. John said that they cleared the first tower by running in an open door and all the garrison were shooting down at us, their backs to the door, and John and Ewen stood in the doorway and killed them with arrows.

About that time, the last men in the yard threw down their scimitars and their spears. And died. We gave no quarter. Chaucer, you have been in a storm. There is no quarter. Sir Walter Leslie killed the kneeling men.

The archers were more merciful, and took a tower full of soldiers alive. It is from those terrified prisoners that John learned why we had succeeded. The captain of the Customs Gate was not a soldier, but a customs official, as Coulanges had said. He had refused to allow the Mamluks to augment his garrison.

He paid with his life. Thus perish all corrupt officials.

In less time than it takes to say Matins, we had the gate itself open. Then Fra Peter led our horses in, and the banner of Jerusalem joined the banner of England on the gate.

The Venetians poured in right behind the Cypriotes, and then the 'crusaders' came up, the mercenaries and routiers. They wouldn't obey the king, they wouldn't fight for him – but now they came like jackals when we had done all the fighting.

I was kneeling by Juan, with my friends, and Fra Peter.

What can I say? Juan was dead. I had lost people over the years, starting, I suppose, with my parents. I am a hard man. But I had been with Juan almost three years. He was my first friend in the Order. He was my brother in redemption, if you will. At an inn outside Avignon, we had wrestled naked to amuse our girls, and that evening we'd drunk wine with our heads pillowed in their laps and talked about God and women and wine and swords. I'd held his head when he wept after his girl died of the plague in Italy and he'd covered my back when d'Albret tried to kill me.

He was dead. He seemed too small for his harness, and his smooth olive skin seemed impossibly alive. His body held the usual amount of blood, and it was on our feet, mixed with that of all the other poor bastards who'd died in the yard.

The king was already mounted. He leaned down; Fiore was weeping.

'Let women weep. It is for men to avenge,' he said.

Perhaps those words seem bold to you. To me, they rang empty. Revenge? I wanted *Juan*.

And he was dead.

We mounted and followed the king. It was not my finest hour. I was supposed to be a leader, and I couldn't get much past Juan's death. I don't let people get too close – except a handful who take me by surprise. I like men, and women more, though I don't want them under my skin. But Juan was under my skin, and his loss – Christ, gentles, I'm sure I didn't pay him enough attention which he was alive, and that burns me now as it burned me in the streets of Alexandria. Fiore was the better swordsman, Nerio was far wittier, Miles was more holy.

Juan was merely the one I liked best, but he had to die for me to know it. He was like my left hand – I don't think about my left hand much, but by God, cut it off and I'd mourn it.

We rode across Alexandria. We were the news of our arrival, herald and hammer both.

Coulanges knew his way about. After a time, I was able to navigate by Pompey's pillars to the west and Alexander's obelisk to the east, but I would never have made my way through that web of streets. Coulanges, for all he was a fool – and that he was – was a good guide.

We had two or three fights, sharp fights, with terrified men. We passed down a street, an avenue as broad as an English town and long enough that the whole stretch of the thing seemed supernatural.

By Saint George and Saint Maurice, Alexandria was staggeringly big. It was growing dark by the time we were all the way across.

Then we dismounted, and stormed the Cairo Gate from behind.

It sounds noble that way, and there was some fighting, but nothing worth making a song of. Mostly, we were killing men trapped in their towers without hope of survival. They didn't fight well and we were not giving any quarter. And I killed my share. I take no joy in it: when you are climbing a winding stair and the man ahead of you is burned with hot sand and you get some in your harness, too, then the virtue of mercy is a far country, and prowess is a word without meaning.

We cleared the towers of the Cairo Gate. But the Breton knights misunderstood the king and set the gates themselves afire.

The king was beside himself, and tired enough to vent his rage on de la Voulte. 'Are you a fool, messire? Or do you crave glory so much that you wish to fight the Sultan's army now? By Christ's heavenly kingdom, by burning these gates you have cost us this town!'

De la Voulte was contrite, but the Count of Turenne, who, as I hear it, actually ordered the gates burned, replied with equal heat, 'Perhaps *you* are the fool!'

He sounded like a man in the grip of a tremendous fear, his voice pitched high and wild. His knights took him and dragged him – I mean that exactly – away.

And then we mounted again. The king was determined to break the bridge.

Darkness had fallen. It was not an unkind darkness; the sky was still ruddy, and the stars were out, and there was still moonlight and when we rode out of the Cairo Gate, I could see enough to know that we had fewer than half the knights we'd had back at the Customs Gate.

It may make you laugh to hear it, but I, the veteran mercenary, hadn't even thought of loot. We were in the richest city in the world, and I was still following my king and Fra Peter. That is how far I had come in my life from serving Mammon.

We had about eighty knights and men-at-arms; our horses were tired, and every man in that column had fought the day before, some for hours, then we had stormed the Customs Gate, crossed the city, and taken the Cairo Gate, too. We had faced fire and brimstone, burning sand, Saracen arrows, poison and naphtha.

We rode along the Cairo road rode for less than a mile before we came to the river.

There was an army there, and we struck the outposts in the dark before we knew what had happened. The entire ride, we had ridden through and over refugees, and the transition from terrified refugees to surprised Mamluks was too sudden. They were well mounted and suddenly we were in a tangle and I took a hard blow to the head before I had my sword out of its scabbard.

Night is a terrible time to fight in armour. A night mêlée on horseback is one of the most desperate encounters a man can have. And in an ambush, when you are nigh dead with fatigue – that is when you have nothing but your training.

I have lightning flashes of memory. I remember a Mamluk on Fiore's back, straddling his horse, searching his armour for a weak place with a dagger, and I got my longsword around his neck and threw him to the ground. I remember cutting over and over at one man who parried and parried until Nerio killed him with a spear, and God only knows from whence that spear came.

I remember the banner of Cyprus going down in the light of the city afire and Miles Stapleton raising it.

I remember being knee to knee with de Mézzières, fighting in opposite directions.

Someone won and someone lost, no doubt. We extricated ourselves. There were three Mamluks on the king, and Nerio and I cut them off the way you clear a swimmer of leeches and they rode away into the darkness, and so did we.

We didn't make it to the bridge.

The king rallied us in the darkness and begged us to attack the Mamluks again.

That was when I realised that Fra Peter was not with us. I made Gawain, who was badly knocked up, trot all the way around the huddle of Latin knights, but Fra Peter was gone. We had two dozen Hospitaller knights with us; Fra Robert Hales was there. And he, too, had lost Fra Peter.

De Mézzières was begging the king to go back into the city.

I found Nerio by his crest, a spray of peacock plumes as thick as a man's wrist, and a coronet of gold. It's amusing: he'd been censured for it on Rhodes, and Fra Peter told him to keep it, told him we'd all be able to find him.

'Fra Peter,' I said, or something equally fluid.

We were only four. But we went back into the darkness and the Mamluks.

*

I remember once, while hunting a stag in the east, I ran headlong onto a bear. The bear was as surprised as I, and instead of exchanging blows, we each fled as fast as our panic could carry us.

I'm going to assume that this is what happened with our Mamluks. At least, when we reached the ground of the ambush, the mutual ambush, I suspect, there were horses wandering and men on the ground and the only enemies were dead or wounded.

Fra Peter was easily found. His horse was dead. He was not, and we passed some anxious minutes freeing him. The ever-practical Fiore retrieved his saddle and bridle.

We got him over a Mamluk charger that did not think much of his smell or his weight. Nerio attended him with Miles.

Fiore and I determined that we would scout ahead. We were already most of the way to the bridge, so we picked our way along the road, riding into the palms on the east side of the Cairo road. But the road remained empty, and our stealth was wasted. We rode all the way to the great stone bridge.

It was empty.

There was a great army on the other side of the bridge, but they were in motion – away. Abandoning their fires and their hasty camp, they were in full retreat.

It was a miracle, if you like. If we had had fifty more men and a wagon of flammables – or some kegs of the alchemical powder that men call 'black', we might have accomplished something.

If Turenne had not burned the gate . . .

I am glad I went with the king that night. Glad I rode all the way to the bridge, and that we found Fra Peter. I only wish I'd stayed out of the city longer.

Did I say that the tunnel behind the Customs Gate was hell?

It was nothing but pain and terror.

The city of Alexandria the night of the sack – that was hell.

A city taken by storm is sacked. Those are the laws of war, the rules. Who, one might ask, makes these rules?

When we attacked the barricades of the city of Florence with six thousand Englishmen and Germans, it was an article of faith to us that we could not do the city any great injury. I think, perhaps, we underestimated the criminal savagery of man.

We had about seven thousand when we took Alexandria. Perhaps another two thousand in sailors and oarsmen. Perhaps yet another two thousand in armed servants. But I don't think so. I think we were far fewer than ten thousand men.

I will make no excuses. Machaut sings that we left not a man alive of the infidel.

Perhaps. We certainly tried.

Fiore and I found Nerio and Miles and Fra Peter waiting in the darkness outside the Cairo Gate. The darkness was full of refugees, screams and imprecations – and the sounds of combat and murder. Nerio wanted to go through the city, and Miles, rarely insistent, was demanding that they ride around the city over the broken ground to the north and east.

I agreed with Nerio. Perhaps we were wrong, but we had drunk all our water and our horses were done, and I didn't think we'd last for the ride around the city.

We re-entered the burned Cairo Gate at midnight, I'm guessing, because the city was afire and there were no bells. Men were looting; men were raping; men were killing. The city was an orgy of destruction, a phrase used by chroniclers but now brought to horrific life. Fiore asked the guard on the gate – men of the Order – where we might find the king. They didn't know.

De Midleton had taken command of the gate. He was rallying all the Order's men. We found Fra Peter, whose breathing was very difficult, a place to lie full length and we put him there as gently as we could manage. Miles and I were just looking at his wound when John the Turk appeared at the door – we were in one of the gate house towers, and it smelled like a charnel house. The smoke caught at our dry throats and made our stomachs burn, too – you know that feeling? When it feels like the smoke is in your gut?

'Syr Midleton asks you!' he shouted. But he had water – blessedly fresh water.

We drank before we ran back into the yard. Sabraham's squire was speaking urgently to de Midleton, who turned as soon as he heard our sabatons on the cobbles.

'It's the legate,' he said. 'I can't spare a man. Will you go?'

Marc-Antonio was still back at the ships. Or dead. Alessandro was with Nerio, and Juan's squire, Ferdinando, was with his master's corpse.

On the other hand, I could lay hands on three veteran archers, and John the Turk.

'I'll go,' I said. We had the Cairo Gate's stables by us and in less time than it takes a man to get armed, we had beautiful local horses for all the archers, and we were mounted in the yard. Ned Cooper and his mates had all strung their bows, and John had a panoply of looted Mamluk equipment.

We followed George.

We had heard fighting in the quarter behind the gate, and the cry of the Order; on horses, with George guiding us, we were there as quickly as we'd got mounted. I was amazed that we reached the place at all – I was so tired that when my horse stopped, I almost fell asleep inside my helmet and I was sure I couldn't have lifted my sword.

We found a church, a Coptic church, a small, round church, un-mistakably Christian. It was packed full. And on the steps outside stood the legate and Lord Grey and Sabraham and the two Greek knights, Giannis and Giorgos.

At the bottom of the broad steps stood twenty 'crusaders'. They were English and Breton, Gascon and French. Or they might have been.

Two of the routiers were dead.

Even as we rode up by a street, another rout of brigands appeared out the alleys.

'Burn it! Burn it!' shouted the crusaders. 'Death to the infidels!'

I saw d'Herblay and the Hungarian almost immediately. They were together, near the back of the crowd, and thus invisible to Sabraham, but the Hungarian's long hair and the ribbon of pearls that confined it gave me my clues. And I knew d'Herblay. I would have known him anywhere, I think. And he was so arrogant he was wearing his surcoat.

But Fortuna was against me, and no sooner had my fatigue-addled head slowly produced their identities than d'Herblay turned, as if warned by Satan. He elbowed the Hungarian and the man looked back at me. He had a steel crossbow in his hand, the weapon the Italians call a Balestrino.

Three horse-lengths beyond the Hungarian, backlit by the lamps burning inside the church, the legate stood unarmed and unarmoured on the steps, with a wooden cross in his hand. He was shouting that these were Christians. In fact, I could see Moors and Moslems and

Jews and Christians all huddled together on the portico, and more in the church behind.

'Kill them all!' roared the routiers. They pulled a man past the knights on the steps and butchered him, laughing.

Leering crusaders killed a teenage girl.

All this in two beats of my tired heart. The Hungarian raised his crossbow one-handed, but my horse was moving and he whirled – and shot.

Fortuna is a fickle mistress at the best of times. I was leaning forward on Gawain's neck, my longsword reaching for the Hungarian's neck, when he shot. His bolt struck the blade of my sword – and glanced away.

He parried my blow, which I confess was greatly weakened by the bolt, with the steel of his crossbow, and rolled off to my right, away from my horse.

The legate, either unaware that I was at hand, or believing that we were more routiers, suddenly plunged into the crowd. Giorgos endeavoured to cover him with his sword but the legate strode down into the mercenaries.

One of the bastards struck him with his spear haft – and he went down.

That was it for Sabraham, and for Fiore, and for Lord Grey. The men on the steps began to use force and Fiore led our party right into the backs of the routiers, the so-called crusaders.

They drove them from the square. I would not have imagined that I had more to give, that I could raise my sword. But I wanted d'Herblay.

I lost him. I was exhausted, and thirsty, and I can make other excuses, but I lost him as smoke swept over the little square in front of the church. Fighting caused men with torches to drop them, and Fiore was like an angel of the Lord, glowing in the flames. He tried to cut his way to the legate's side.

Of course, we were killing crusaders, to save infidels and heretics.

I suppose we saved a hundred Greeks, and a handful of Jews and Moors. Many of them spat at me.

I wanted d'Herblay, but in that dark and smoky place, with the inferno all around us as Alexandria burned, what I got was Father Pierre. I can't say I cut my way to him. I can't even claim that I bravely decided to save my commander instead of getting my own revenge on the man who nearly broke my body.

I stumbled over him. All I can claim is that, God having given me this sign, I didn't step over Father Pierre and try to shed d'Herblay's blood. Instead, I looked down. But I knew – it's hard to say why, with the smoke, the visor of my dented helmet, my fatigue – but I knew I had him. There was a flurry of violence – a man with a spear, and all I did was beat it away.

And then I sheathed my sword, raised Father Pierre in my arms and carried him into the church. He was crying.

I had seldom seen him cry. He had taken a bad blow, and his scalp was torn. But his face held more than suffering – I had *never* seen him without hope. His small face always beamed with something from inside, some special benison he brought to the world. But, that night in hell, it was gone.

He knelt before the altar and spread his arms and fell face forward, saying, 'Forgive them Father, they know not what they do.'

Perhaps. But I had been one of them, and I knew *exactly* what they were doing.

They were raping, looting, and killing. They were very good at these things.

And d'Herblay and the Hungarian and *his* men were out there in the darkness, still probably looking to kill the legate, even though it was now too late. The crusade was victorious. We'd taken the greatest city in the world.

The man lying full length before a ruined altar would be Pope.

If I could get him home alive.

Such is the life of arms. Or rather, such is one path on the life of arms.

We got the legate back to the Cairo Gate on a horse. The church to which the legate had gone to save its congregation was only six turnings from the gate, and yet those six streets seemed full of menace. And getting there seemed to take half the night.

I reported to Sabraham. He was wounded, and he shook his head. 'I wish you'd got him,' he said. He was watching the rooftops. 'I want the legate out of here.'

As it proved, the legate wanted to be quit of the city, too. He was slow to recover, but when his eyes were open, he demanded – begged – to be taken to the king. He had decided that he could convince the king to stop the 'crusaders' from raping the city.

Our men had a small fire in the courtyard, and torches. Tired men were at least taking the corpses out of the towers, and a dozen captured slaves were washing the blood off the tower steps.

'I thought that I was done,' I said, a little bitterly.

The legate blessed me. 'You sleep, my son. I will ride back to the ships.'

Sabraham shook his head. 'I'll take him,' he said. To me, he said, 'D'Herblay is out there. Waiting for us to move him.'

When you imagine yourself as a knight, what you imagine – if you are like I was as a boy – is that moment when the Knights of St John charged the infidel. A windswept beach. Three hundred brave men in brilliant scarlet and steel. That seems to you what knighthood will be.

But this, my friends, is where I think we find chivalry – when our throats are so parched we cannot swallow, when the smoke from a thousand fires cuts our lungs, when our armour seems to hurt us more than an enemy can, when our jupons are heavy with our sweat and our blood, and our hands won't close properly on our swords. When all we want is sleep. Or death.

That is when we find what makes us knights, I think.

I looked around in the firelight at my friends. None of us had even dismounted. Sabraham had blood flowing over his cuisses – he'd taken a wound in his armpit. A real wound.

'You stay,' I said. I didn't want to. I wanted to sleep. But: 'We'll take him to the ships.'

Miles leaned out across his horse's neck, hands crossed in fatigue. 'We should go *out* the gate and ride around,' he said for the second time that night.

But de Midleton wouldn't hear of it. 'There's Sudanese Ghulams out there, and Mamluks,' he said. He pointed to where a dozen of the Order's brother-sergeants were improvising a barricade. 'I expect an attack at dawn. I'm not sending the legate out into that.' He took me aside. 'Let me put some food and water into him. And your poor horses, gentles. But I agree he shouldn't stay here. If this tower falls ...'

I could just about think. 'We won't have Coulanges,' I said. 'I'm worried about losing my way.'

Sabraham was being helped from his horse by a trio of serving brothers. He could scarcely stand. 'Take George and Maurice,' he said. 'They know how to get around.'

He beckoned me to him. When the brothers put him down, he went all the way to the ground. And lay there.

I had to crouch by him.

'I've lost a lot of blood,' he muttered in a tiny voice. 'Move fast. He can't stay here. One attack – tower is lost. Get him to the ships. Please, Will!'

'I'll do it,' I said. In fact, I was ready to fall asleep with my head on his chest.

One of the serving brothers pushed me aside. They were cutting Abraham's clothes off even as he spoke. A man came up with an iron rod glowing red.

I smelled the burning flesh. For good or ill, Sabraham could offer no more advice – he was out.

I stumbled back to my horse. Poor Gawain had taken ten wounds the day before and now had been ridden all day. Oats and water kept him alive – but they didn't make him well.

I looked over my people.

'Friends,' I said. 'I need every one of you. There are men in the streets who mean to kill the legate. I have promised to get him to the ships.'

Ned Cooper turned his face to one side. 'Kill the legate?' he asked. 'He's like a fuckin' saint, beggin' yer pardon.'

Ewan the Scot put a finger alongside his nose. 'I know,' he said.

'What do you know?' Nerio asked.

Ewan shrugged. 'Men come round, offering us silver for some fancy shooting.' He laughed. 'Guess they didn't think you was up to it, Ned!'

'There's a Savoyard. D'Herblay. Anyone met him?' I asked.

No one had. Except, of course, my friends.

We all ate. I decided, having set a few ambushes myself, that it would not hurt us to make the Hungarian wait and we all slept for an hour. We had no real way of knowing the time: no cocks crowed, there were no bells, but the Order's men knew the hours well. Men fed and watered our horses and I had to be wakened roughly, even though I had slept in my harness.

We all had. And I ached, and so did the rest of them. But we drank hot wine with spices, which the Order's people had going in the yard, and we chewed cloves – by Saint George, spices were all but free in Alexandria. I looked at the Emperor's sword by firelight, and there was no dent in the blade, no kink, where the crossbow bolt had struck it. Instead, there was a scratch about as long as my little finger, as if an inexpert engraver had started to make a line. I got a stone from Davide and touched up the edge.

It was obvious to a soldier that the legate had a head wound – the kind that makes men fey and strange for days. The brothers had kept him awake, on principle, but he was having trouble speaking. I placed him with Miles. Lord Grey could not ride – a deep thrust to his right thigh.

I gathered my friends, and indeed, my whole little command. 'Here's my plan,' I said. 'I'm happy to hear it bettered. We cut across the city and go out through the same Customs Gate where we entered. It is the only way I know – and besides, we don't know if the other gates have fallen, or are still in enemy hands.'

Maurice blew out his cheeks, but said nothing.

'Outside the walls, we gallop. We'll be west of the city, and I can't see any enemy making for there in the dark, with a tide of refugees around them. We make our way *past* the crusader fleet and take the legate to the Order.'

Stapleton narrowed his eyes. 'He *asked* to be taken to the king.'

I nodded. 'So he did,' I agreed. 'Any other questions?'

Maurice frowned. 'We will move quickly? What about prickers? Outriders?'

I shrugged. 'I was hoping the archers would agree to lead the way.'

Ewan laughed. 'Is there any money in this?' he asked. 'I see you're all soldiers of God, an' all. But everyone else is looting, and we're here working an' getting killed.' He looked around and spat. 'Not yet, mind. But this here's a mad trick, ridin' across a city gettin' sacked.'

Ned Cooper looked at me like a shy maiden – a particularly old and ill-favoured shy maiden. 'True knights is generous' he said. 'The Black Prince used to offer us a douceur when we was missin' out on the loot.'

Miles all but spat. I'm glad he didn't. 'The legate is every man's friend, and has held this expedition together,' he insisted. 'He trusts the English more than any!'

'More fool he,' Ewan said. 'Fuckin' English. Present company, eh, Ned?'

I glanced at Nerio. Nerio laughed. He had lines on his face like an old man, and the firelight made him look older and more dissipated than his father. But his laugh was his old laugh. You might have thought there was a wench in the offing.

He nodded. 'Twenty ducats a man when we reach the ships,' he said.

Ewan raised his eyebrows and frowned at the same time. '*Eh bien,*' he said.

Rob Stone, hitherto silent, said, 'Amen.'

Ewan spat on his hands. 'Let's ride,' he said.

John the Turk looked at Nerio. 'Me, too?' he asked.

Nerio laughed. He turned to me. 'Jesus had it all wrong, brother,' he said. 'He should have offered to pay men to behave well.'

Fiore laughed. 'I could use twenty ducats, too,' he said, which was as close to making a joke as I ever heard the Friulian come.

About ten more minutes passed while the legate was prepared. We tied him to a borrowed warhorse. I rubbed Gawain down, gave him a little water, and he seemed spirited. He was a far better horse than I had thought, back at Mestre.

It was fully three hours after vespers, the very dark of the night, when William de Midleton opened the sally port for us. 'God speed,' he said.

I confess I almost expected a crossbow bolt to take John the Turk, the first man out the sally port. But he slipped out of the gate, low on his horse's neck, bow strung but in the case at his side. He rode with George and Maurice and, after a minute of rapid heartbeats, I sent the archers after them. Rob Stone winked as he kneed his rouncey through the gate.

I went with Nerio, and then Miles and the legate's deacon, Michael, supporting him on his horse, and then Fiore with Davide at the rear.

By my estimation, the ambush had to come right away. If d'Herblay and the Hungarian really planned to kill the legate – or me – they would know we were in the Cairo Gate. By waiting, I hoped to bore him into assuming we'd spend the night. He'd post men on the gates, and they'd tell their master when we moved.

By the time we reached the great avenue in the middle of Alexandria, lined with palaces – I had all but forgotten the Hungarian. Instead, my senses, tired to the point of failure, and then overwhelmed with noise and light, were bruised. Buildings were afire everywhere. By the ruddy light, we were treated to a carpet of corpses on every major thoroughfare. The sheer numbers of the dead staggered us all, even men who had seen fighting in France.

And further scenes from the inferno played out around us. A dozen soldiers chased a woman who ran screaming, half naked. She might have been beautiful if her lower jaw had not been cut away. Against the background of burning building, her agony was an insane vision of man's wretched state in a world of sin.

A horse wandered, walking, trotting, screaming in agony, and it's guts uncoiled behind it, leaving a hideous ribbon to glisten in the dark.

Laughing looters sat on cooling corpses and diced for the stolen goods. A dozen brigands lay in an alcoholic haze, apparently unconcerned that they lay among their victims.

And everywhere, little furtive packs crept, and struck. Many of the victims must have joined the sack – it was always thus in France – so that the numbers of the murderers and rapists were always increased. I saw men in local dress killing and burning. The poor of Alexandria joined the scum of Europe.

Through this, we rode.

We were, by my estimation, almost half way along the avenue when John rode back out of the chaos. He shouted – and I'm ashamed to say his shout woke me. I had fallen asleep in Hell. He shouted again.

I slammed my arm into Nerio's backplate. He was also asleep. I turned, but Miles was doing his duty, and the legate's eyes were open; glazed, but open.

John reined in at my side. 'Rider – two.' He pointed beyond the nearest palazzo, a squat and inelegant building with two minarets that rose like horns on a toad. 'I think they watch. I kill one.' He grinned. 'Now they no watch.'

Nerio backed his horse. 'How long have they been with us?' he asked.

That was too much for John, who shrugged. 'Two men,' he said. 'Now one.'

I rode ahead to the archers, whose horses were just visible in the next firelight.

'We're being followed,' I shouted. 'Stay—'

Ewan ducked and the stone hit me, not in the head, but in the back. I assume it was thrown with a sling, and it was a big stone. It left a dent.

Luckily for me, the Bohemian had left me room in the upper back to flex my shoulders. That became the space for the armour to absorb the blow.

It still knocked me straight down, off my horse and into the street.

I rolled. I'll stop this litany, but only the hardest training will get you to roll off your horse when you are taken in an ambush and near dead from fatigue.

I don't remember any of this. What I do remember is coming to my feet in the fire-shot darkness with the Emperor's sword in my hand. Ewan was off his horse and running. Ned Cooper was at my back with an arrow to his bow. He was unashamedly using me as cover.

It was as well he did. A bolt tested the quality of my breastplate. It penetrated, but only about half an inch.

That, too, was luck, because my visor was up.

Ned loosed. I felt the heavy shaft whisper away through the air and I heard hoofbeats.

Nerio was three horse lengths away, sword out. He was riding at something – his gaze was fixed. Behind him came Miles and the legate – right into the heart of the ambush.

Sometimes, in war, you must take the dice as they roll.

'Ride through!' I croaked. My throat was all but closed. 'Go!'

Miles heard me. He touched the legate's horse with the point of his sword, and the animal bolted.

There were shafts in the darkness, arrow shafts, shafts of firelight. It might have been distracting ...

Ned Cooper moved with me, loosing shaft after shaft. He grunted when he loosed.

Things hit me. A shaft, spent and pin-wheeling through the darkness, another stone off a sling I could hear spinning in the dark, a thrown spear. The last of the three was ill-thrown, and yet it slammed across my knees and wounded Cooper behind me. In daylight, spears aren't so dangerous. In the dark ...

Christ, I was scared. Fear is fatigue. Fatigue is fear. Thirst, hunger, bone-ache ...

There was nothing to fight.

But when Ned went down, I got an arm under his, and dragged him. The legate was past us, and I couldn't even see his horse. Gawain was across the avenue, head up.

A good warhorse is a gift from God. I had no other plan; I was the target for every archer in the ambush. I decided, as if from very far away, that if I could make it to Gawain, I'd ride away.

I made it halfway across the avenue and Gawain met me halfway, bless him. I didn't really think about the consequence – I got Ned up into the saddle.

He wasn't unconscious. He screamed as his right knee got knocked around, but the spear came free and fell to the road.

'Jesus *fucking* Christ the Saviour of *fucking* mankind,' he shouted into the night.

'Ride for it,' I said.

I slapped Gawain.

About then, I realised that I hadn't taken a blow or an arrow in what seemed like a long time. I had no idea why, but I had been in enough desperate fights to know that something had changed, and Ned and I were no longer the centre of the enemy's attention.

My visor was still up. I let go of Gawain's stirrup – I had had some notion of holding the stirrup and bouncing along like a man with ten-league boots, but I was too tired. And I had some notion of occupying the enemy while the legate escaped.

Unless, of course, he was dead, which was one awful explanation of why the enemy fire had shifted away from me.

But that made no sense, even to my fatigue-addled head. Men in a fight will go after one opponent until he's down and only then go for another. That's the law of the forest.

Kill the thing you can see.

What in the hell of Alexandria was going on?

The night was still a literal inferno. Fire and darkness ... smoke, that makes darkness even more deceptive. And can choke you. Only in full night can you stumble into smoke you never saw and cough your lungs out.

A man was coughing, just to my left.

I picked up the spear that had come out of Cooper's thigh. It was a surprisingly good spear – you know when you pick one up, line a sword. It was light and responsive in my hands, the haft slim and well balanced, the head light. I used it to feel my way. The cloud of smoke was drifting, I assume, because for me it was like a choking fog covering the moon. I could see a little at first, and then nothing.

I wanted cover. The smoke was killing me, but it *was* cover. I couldn't breathe, and my eyes were watering. My armour weighed like lead.

Yet, I was unwounded.

I moved one step at a time.

A man screamed – and his scream was answered by a feral chorus from behind me, too far away to be part of this small thread in the tapestry of violence.

I made it to the foot of one of the minarets. I knew the stonework in a glance, and there was a ruddy glow from inside that lit the smoke.

There was a man. He came at me, or merely crossed my path, and my spear went into his throat with the unerring accuracy born of practice.

I have no idea who he was, or whether he was part of the ambush. But he was armed and had mail on. I dropped him off my spear point.

Another step and the feeling in front of my face was replaced with a comparative cool. I essayed a breath, and then put my back to the low wall and heaved. I had inhaled too much smoke.

Another scream. And a shout. And coughing. All this so close that I whirled, head up, fatigue forgotten-

Three spear-lengths away, a man broke cover from a decorative shrub on the grounds of a tall facade to the west. He took two steps, grunted, and fell. In the smoke-shot dark, I had no idea why he fell, but he wore armour.

I alternated curses and prayers.

But the man who broke cover was not one of mine, and the mere fact of his being in cover said he was one of the ambushers. He thrashed to death like a crushed bug, his armour reflecting the inferno around him.

I ran towards him. Or rather, I stumbled. I tripped at least once, went down in an armoured sprawl, rose and plunged on, across another belt of smoke and heat. I couldn't see the ground, which was broken and full of stones. Someone's decorative border. I hurt my hands.

The man who had broken cover was a routier in a stained surcoat and looted harness, and he had a Mamluk arrow through his throat. His surcoat was blue and white.

I made it to the relative cover of the tall facade – marble in front and brick behind. By then, my head was running very fast. I had to hope it was one of John's arrows. If there were Mamluks loose in the city, the crusade was doomed and so were we. Although there was irony in that.

But odd as it sounds, the dead man with a Mamluk arrow told me what was going on. John and Maurice and George were behind the ambush, wreaking havoc. Otherwise, I'd have been dead in the road, and Gawain would have been filled full of arrows. If they had broken the eastern hinge of the ambush, then I was now moving with them, or behind them.

I offer you my thoughts, because fighting at night in a burning city carpeted in dead men is more difficult than it sounds.

I moved across the tall building's facade. It was not afire, nor was the next building to the west, which had rose bushes in a hedge around its entrance.

I guessed that the rose hedge was the basis of our ambushers' position.

And God performed a miracle for us. Fiore stumbled out of the darkness to my right. Never were the Order's surcoats more valuable.

'Close your visor,' he said. There's friendship for you.

'Hedge,' I said.

He nodded. I slammed my visor down, and we went at the hedge.

It may seem impossible to you that our adversaries didn't see us coming, but they did not. Nor do most men know that, in a full harness, a man is immune to thorns.

I knew, and so did Fiore.

We burst through the rose hedge like the vengeance of the angels. There were three or four of the Hungarian's men there, and the man himself. I had him immediately. He was in maille, with a black brigandine over it and I saw his face when he turned. I was just pulling my spear out of the crossbowman I'd encountered first.

I thought he'd run. Instead, he stepped back and drew.

To my right, Fiore was fighting three men, one of whom had on a great deal of armour. Another brigand slammed out of the dark and thrust at me with a spear. I slammed the spear clear of me and struck a clumsy blow, made worse by my butt-spike catching in the roses..

The Hungarian struck at me. His edge caught the rim of one of my gauntlets. His timing was perfect but his point control a little awry in the dark.

As a result, the spearman and I went close, and the Hungarian danced away.

In that beat of my heart, I knew he was a good swordsman, and that he was going to kill me. But I had my point under my other adversary's right arm. I released my top hand – my left – punched him in the head with my mailed fist, reached past his shoulder and caught the point of my spear as his head snapped back, which changed everything. I threw him. In fact, I ripped him off his feet and tossed him at the Hungarian. He went down hard and the Hungarian went down with him.

Fiore put his pommel into one man and pivoted on his hips, parrying his second opponent as if he'd practiced fighting three men all his life. Having made his cover, he brought his sword back up; not a very strong blow, but he made his second opponent stumble even while the first collapsed.

All that while I caught one breath.

I put a steel-footed kick into the downed spearmen and the Hungarian regained his feet while I pulled out my spear point in to finish my foe.

That's what you do when you are outnumbered. Make sure the men who are down stay down.

The Hungarian had a steel cap on over his maille hood and there was enough light, reflecting off smoke, making everything a ruddy haze except our blades that flickered like red-hot iron, that I could see his face clearly, his high cheekbones, his heavy, long moustaches, and his smile.

'Ah, Sir William,' he said.

He cut at me. He made three simple blows – mandritto, reverso, mandritto, just as Fiore drilled us, and I covered all three. I had my spear point low, the butt high in my right hand – one of Fiore's guards. In this guard, and with my good steel arms, I could ward myself all night, as long as I had the strength to keep the spear steady. With my advantage in distance, the Hungarian was limited to fast attacks and withdrawals.

I thrust low, at his hands.

He leaped back and I stumbled after him – armour is heavy, and I had forgotten the spearman on the ground.

The Hungarian thrust with one hand: I made my cover high and late, and his point slapped my visor.

Dead, except for my armour.

I cut; a simple, heavy fendente with the spearhead to buy time. He was faster than anyone I had ever faced – faster than Fiore, faster than Nerio. As fast as the Bohemian I had fought in Krakow.

But my simple fendente slammed into his outstretched sword even as he was withdrawing it, and knocked it well to the side. I passed forward, and so I was in a good low guard when he hurled his sword like a thunderbolt. Against an unarmoured man, in the darkness, it might have proved decisive, but I slapped it aside with my spear and cut at him.

I was standing at the top of a low wall, and he'd leapt to the bottom.

In the red darkness, I could see him crouch. I was wary; I saw the corpse and then the crossbow.

I ducked back. Behind me, Fiore was down to just two. I turned and stabbed one of Fiore's opponent's in the neck. My spear didn't penetrate his aventail, but I assume I broke his neck.

I turned back to the wall, but the Hungarian was gone.

Fiore and I were still panting like horses after a race when John the Turk rode up outside the rose garden and called out.

He had Ned Cooper and Gawain. He also had a dark bay – someone else's horse adrift in Hades.

We collected George and Maurice at the back of the tall building that was now shooting flames fifty feet into the air. They were stripping dead men of their purses like the professionals I'd taken them for and I was impressed that Maurice tossed a purse to John.

George nodded to me. 'Get the Hungarian?' he asked.

'No,' I admitted.

He laughed.

'And the legate?' I asked. All my best men except Nerio were there. And the legate was *not* there.

George just shrugged. But he handed me a gourd canteen, and I drank my fill. John the Turk gave me garlic sausage, good Italian sausage, and I sat there, surrounded by corpses and dying men, and ate sausage and drank water for as long as it takes a priest to say a quick Mass. Fiore joined me and we all ate and drank. The Hungarian could have killed the lot of us, but we were done in like knackered horses, and we had a little hole in the smoke in which to breathe.

But soon, too soon, I could feel the press of my fear for the legate.

We rode with the hot wind of the burning of Alexandria at our heels. We missed our way twice; once where the Avenue turned south and we should have taken a cross street. The second time, we missed the Great Mosque in the smoke.

But the city on fire reflected like dull bronze from the distant pillars of Pompey. We reached the wall in a huddle of hovels. We were nearly lost, desperate – and dawn was close. I was certain by then that Nerio and Miles and the legate were dead or taken.

Every decision I had made all evening came up like bad food.

George climbed the wall, cursed for a while, and climbed down. 'No idea,' he said. 'North, or south?'

I hate guessing. 'North,' I said. And probably something like, 'Is that north?'

In the dark and smoke, even with the pillars, everything seemed wrong. Perhaps it was just fatigue. But I was hearing voices – Emile, Father Pierre, my sister. And the endless sound of sighing, as if there was a choir in Hell.

Two miserable streets later, we crossed fresh corpses. We followed the trail of dead – there was a spearman, there and archer.

The Customs Gate rose out of the bloodshot murk. And in the relative safety of the tunnel was Nerio, his helmet off, and Miles, supporting the legate.

'Never do that to me again,' Nerio said. He threw his arms around me and tried to crush me – me, and Fiore too. 'Leave me to die and ride away. It would be kinder.' He spat, and handed me a canteen. I took a pull. It proved to be Malmsey, but it tasted like the nectar of the gods of Greece.

It also proved to be the last surprise of the night. By the time our exhausted column crossed the sand where the crusaders' ships were beached, the sky was grey and we could see men asleep on the sand.

We didn't stop. But neither did we gallop. We didn't have a horse capable of the effort among us.

The Order's admiral was awakened at once. I lay down in one of the Order's tents and slept for perhaps ten minutes. It wasn't much lighter when I was awakened and Fra Ferlino di Airasca ordered wine brought.

'We know very little here,' he said. 'And the legate took most of the Order away into the city.'

I outlined the facts as I knew them, so tired by then that I was sick to my stomach. But two slaves brought food, fruit, and bread and cheese, and I devoured it.

The admiral said nothing while I spoke, except to curse when I said that Fra Peter Mortimer had been wounded.

'How is the legate?' I asked.

Fra Ferlino shrugged. 'Well enough. Better when we can let him sleep. His eyes are better.' Knights of the Order have a great many healing skills – the Hospital is as much part of their trade as the sword – and they tended to speak in tropes. But I knew from Fra Peter that a man with a bad blow to the head shows it in his eyes.

He looked at me. 'Can the Cairo Gate hold? Where is the army?'

I shook my head. 'The army ...' I was tempted to blasphemy. 'The army is raping and looting the city. They man no towers, and they kill only—' I snarled.

Fra Ferlino cocked an eyebrow at me. 'You are a virgin of sieges? What did you expect? A parade?' He held out a hand. 'Yet we must hold those gates if we are to hold the city. And the army of Cairo?'

'We went out with the king last night,' I said. I stumbled in my speech – was it only last night?

'We hear the king is in the Tower of Pharos,' the Order's admiral said. 'But nothing more.'

'He needs to know that the Cairo Gate is held, and the main enemy army retreated,' I said.

'I'll see that he knows,' the admiral said.

And then they let me sleep.

*

That lasted three hours. Perhaps a little more.

I was *still* in my harness. I had no squire to get me out of it, and I was too tired to touch the laces and buckles. I think I tried – I have the vaguest impression of scrabbling at an arm harness just before collapse and I woke to a variety of aches and pains that I would associate with the results of a torturer's rack.

The man standing over me was the king. He looked as neat as a newly forged sword. His harness was clean and polished.

'I'm so sorry, Sir William,' he said. 'But the admiral tells me that the Cairo Gate is held, and the enemy army has slipped away. I need to know.'

Muzzily, I told my story again.

The admiral had a quick conference with the king and I caught enough words to know what they proposed. My heart sank: I've heard that phrase used a hundred times, but then I knew what it meant.

They needed me to lead a column of reinforcements back through the city.

The king embraced me. I almost laughed. *He* wasn't going.

When I got my harness cleaned up a little – the king's squire came and helped me, bless him – I drank some water and pissed it away, drank some more, and stumbled out into the sun, which hit me like the blows of a deadly opponent. Two serving brothers armed me, and the metal going back over my bones was like the bite of weapons. But when I reached the Order's parade – really, just a little area of gravel and old kelp in the centre of a three-sided wall of tents – there was Nerio, there was Fiore, and there was Miles.

I don't remember if I cried. But I do now. By our saviour, we were ...

We were. And Juan was dead.

'Let's get this done,' I said.

We rode into Alexandria, and nothing waited for us but the rotting horror of the spectacle. No dogs, no wolves, no brigands prowled, and no feral Alexandrines slaughtered. The streets were dead. And littered with meat that had been men. And women. And children.

When we reached the site of the ambush, Maurice gave me a sign, a wave, and he and George and John rode away without further explanation. I assumed that they were looking for signs of our attackers.

I was wrong.

I rode under the arches of the Cairo Gate with nothing endangered but our sense of man as a redeemable sinner. John and his companions came back an hour later, or so I hear, but I was, thank God, asleep.

I slept in one of the Cairo Gate towers. I slept yet again in my harness, and woke to an alarm that proved false. Then I slept again.

When I woke for the third or fourth time, it was to the terrible realization that I had not unsaddled Gawain, nor seen to him in any-way. Only that would have dragged me from some dead Mamluk's straw pallet – clean as a whistle, by the way.

Under my sabatons, my shoes were scorched and sticky with blood. My feet hurt – the arches ached. The armour was a worse enemy than the infidel. I felt I'd broken my hips while asleep.

Gawain was in the gatehouse stable, lying in clean straw, exhausted. He opened his eyes, snorted, and closed his eyes again, his derision for the whole of the human race clear to anyone who knows horses. Pressed against him was Fiore's charger, also curried and clean.

'Good knight, bad horseman!' John the Turk said. 'Jesus love animals. Knights not so much.'

I clasped his hand.

He nodded.

'Thanks, John.' I saw that he had Fra Peter's Mamluk horse groomed. The animal had a headstall and two reins through ring bolts.

'Stallion!' John said. 'Want.'

I'd have laughed, but all I wanted was sleep. John got my armour off me in the straw, and I collapsed by my horse as he told me that Fra Peter had been taken to the ships.

I slept again, guarded by a new Christian convert whose brethren were sitting across the river. Had John not been loyal to his word, I'd have been dead many times, that campaign.

But Tartars – Monghuls – do not lie.

Thanks be to God.

I awoke in the darkness. I could not move: it took an effort of will to make my eyes open, much less to move hands or feet. Straightening my spine was an incredible effort, as was extending my legs.

But, like climbing a mountain, every bit helped. I began to gain control of my limbs, and I rolled to my feet like a badly wounded man. I was not. To crown the miracle of the taking of Alexandria, my

fevered wound had closed and gone cold. I think – I like to think –
that when I lifted the legate, his flesh healed mine.

Say what you will, Chaucer.

It was almost fully dark outside when I was dressed and armed,
filthy, tired, and afire with the pains of two days of combat. John
armed me in silence and sent a boy for Fiore. I found Fra William de
Midleton in the yard.

'We are ordered to hold,' he said heavily.

The city was oddly silent. No cock crowed. No music, no muezzins.
Of course. And yet, the silence was terrible.

I think you need to know that despite the encounter in the smoke,
I didn't give a rat's arse for the Hungarian or d'Herblay in that hour.
Essentially, I forgot them. Holding the gate became our goal – there
was nothing else. You'll see.

I looked at the open gate. 'We should rebuild the gate. The ships
have carpenters—'

Fra William shook his head. 'There is a Moslem army just over the
bridge.'

'Not any more,' I said. 'My lord, did no one tell you?'

Fra William started. 'How do you know?'

I was too tired to argue. 'Fiore and I rode to find Fra Peter. Then we
went and looked at the bridge. The Saracens were fleeing.' I paused.
'That was – a day ago? Hasn't the bridge been burned?' I asked.

Fra William shook his head heavily. He was as exhausted as I. 'No,'
he said.

'Scouted?' I asked.

'No, Sir William!' he said. 'Nothing has been done. They say that the
king is surrounded by counsellors who say the city must be abandoned.'

I think I ignored him or didn't believe him. I knew, I, a young
knight, a Corporal, that by taking Alexandria we had cut the Sultan
off from all his trade, shattered his resources, and severed his main link
with Palestine and all his garrisons. Saint Louis had never struck such
a stroke. Indeed, since the taking of Jerusalem herself, no Crusade
had ever accomplished as much. With the fleet in the harbour and
possession of the walls, in effect, we had crippled Egypt. And when
the rest of Europe heard, when the Green Count came at our backs,
we would have the whole of Egypt, and the Holy Land as well. King
Peter's strategy was solid. We had *won*.

I was also wise enough to see that Fra William was more shattered than I. Even while I stood there in my harness, besmottered with blood and offal, I was growing stronger, as young men do. 'Let me see to it,' I said.

He spread his hands. 'Be my guest,' he said. 'I need to sleep.'

We had forty Hospitaller knights in various degrees of fitness at the gates, and another fifty sergeants and turcopoles. By the odd flow of the currents of war, we also had Lord Grey's retinue without the man himself; Miles Stapleton had taken command of them. That included Ned Cooper and his archers, who had ridden back with us.

'I ain't leaving you till I see my ducats,' Ned Cooper said. The wound in his thigh, so devastating in the heat of the fight, proved to have barely penetrated the skin to the muscle of his leg.

From Ned and John – and Maurice and George, now much less taciturn than they had been before – I learned more of the ambush in the dark. At the same time that John feathered one of the spies following us, Ewan had seen the rose hedge and made the correct assessment. He'd dismounted and put a heavy arrow into the hedge.

The night had exploded, but the Hungarian's hastily laid trap had failed to touch the legate, who'd ridden past without a scratch. Maurice and John had tried to counter the ambush from behind and everything had degenerated into a smoking tangle of chaos, in the best tradition of war and complex plans.

At any rate, in addition to my people – well, really the legate's and Lord Grey's, we had a dozen of the surviving Scots, including the Baron of Rosilyn, who outranked me, and we had most of Contarini's oarsmen, a disciplined body, under Carlo Zeno.

This was less a miracle than it seemed. In battle, men follow men they know. We all knew each other: the Scots followed the Hospitallers, and the oarsmen followed the English archers. But it gave us a good garrison, and when Fiore and I found Master Zeno, we quickly came to an agreement about employing his oarsmen to fortify the gate.

He made a wry Italian face. 'I wish I could send to the admiral,' he said. 'We have carpenters and tools. But that city ...'

'Hell come to earth,' I agreed.

Outside the walls of our gate castle, men continued to behave like animals. And, as I had seen in France, perhaps the worst of it was that local men joined the riot, killing their own, or the Jews – always the poor Jews – only to be massacred by our brigands and crusaders. Men set fire to their own houses. Men slaughtered their own families in despair.

And that was by day.

Night was worse.

Nonetheless, we worked by torchlight. Zeno was tireless, and if he was a mocking villain in the streets of Athens, he was a hero in the Stygian dark of Alexandria.

We made the courtyard behind the first gate a trap. We dug up the cobbles with pickaxes and trenched it, raised a rubble wall and put palm palisades atop it. We relit the fires, made food, and served it to our soldiers.

In the midst of all this, we were interrupted by a terrible dilemma. A Greek patriarch came to the gate and begged us to admit several hundred Greeks.

It was clear that the enemy was coming, and Fra William's sense – and he was a good soldier – was that the Mamluks and their infantry were coming across the river and striking against any Christian they could find. But we couldn't feed the Greeks. And the riot of the sack continued, so that we had the threat of Mamluks from the south and the threat of our own crusaders from the north.

Syr Giannis went to Fra William and knelt and begged him to save the Greeks. Fra William was standing on the walls, watching the city burn – and watching a small army of looters approaching.

But he was a Hospitaller. He opened a side gate, even while he sent a sortie – me, of course – to order the looters away.

I went out with a borrowed poleaxe in my fist, and walked along the so-called 'street of pepper' with Fiore and Miles and Nerio and Syr Giannis until we reached the main avenue, where the looters were coming.

They had a dead Moslem's head on a pole, and they were carrying a woman – or what was left of her. They were all drunk, and they looked like souls basking in the warmth of hellfire.

The five of us didn't even cover the street.

Fiore had his visor open. 'What do we intend to do with these dogs?' he asked.

They were slowing. Behind us, the Greeks were filing into the Cairo

Gate fortress, but they could only go single file. We had archers on the wall, and Fra William was preparing a sortie.

It was all too slow to save the Greeks. And the looters – the crusaders – were numerous and well armed.

The Count d'Herblay shouted my name.

'*Bon soir*, William the Cook!' He laughed. He had his armour on and his hose down by his ankles. He had a poleaxe in his armoured fists and fresh blood on the knuckles of his gauntlets. He didn't look like the angry, weak man of Genoa. The one who'd flinched from my beating.

In fact, he looked drunk, and insane.

I was in some way pleased. I admit this. It made what I intended easier.

I raised my axe. 'Halt,' I said. 'You may not come further, on pain of death.'

'Who the fuck pretends to give us orders?' asked a Gascon.

'I do, in the name of the Hospital. Go rape children somewhere else,' I said. In that moment, I hated almost all the men on earth.

They didn't like that.

No one does.

D'Herblay laughed, but it was hollow. His face was a terrible thing of rage and pain, fatigue and fear. He had lines that made him look like a damned soul, and his face was near black with smoke. He came forward without troubling with his visor or his hose. God only knows where his leg harness was.

Conversationally, he said, 'You know, Camus will kill me if I kill you. He wants you *so* badly.' D'Herblay laughed. His laugh was – terrible. Even – sad. 'But he's not here and I am. If you run away, we won't kill you.' He shrugged. 'Or we will.'

'Last chance, my lord,' I said. 'I'm tired of killing. Aren't you?'

He stopped, just out of range. Then he spat. 'You know,' he said, 'All my life, I have been afraid. All my life, I have wanted ...' He frowned. 'Do you know what I've found here? *Nothing* matters. It's all just shit. You ... my whore of a wife ... the king ... Camus ...' He croaked his laugh. 'Here, it just doesn't matter. I can be ... anything.'

I didn't think that I was talking to the Count d'Herblay. There was no vanity, none of the puffed up crap. No sarcasm. His voice was stark – and horrible.

'I don't even want to kill your damned legate any more,' he said. 'But it is all blood and smoke. Isn't it?'

He was shifting his weight.

I tried one more time. 'Disperse!' I shouted. Or perhaps I merely coughed it. 'Turn back, or be the enemies of God.'

'I *am* the fucking enemy of God,' D'Herblay said. 'So save your sanctimonious shit.'

One of his blue and white men at arms laughed at that – and then they all came forward at us.

There is an enormous difference between killing helpless townspeople and fighting a knight. I hope d'Herblay learned that when I broke both his hands with one blow. The steel of his hourglass gauntlets protected him from the edge, and he didn't lose the hands.

He just lost their use.

His spear clattered to the cobbles. He didn't growl – he screamed, and I put my axe head behind his heel and pulled, dropping him with a clatter.

I put the spike atop my weapon to his unvisored face. I stepped on his broken left hand. He screamed.

'I am not killing you,' I said. 'I do not want to kill another man. Not today. Go. All of you.'

Something in me was broken. Or had never been right. I *wanted* to kill him. In fact, I wanted to kill them all. I wanted to kill all the bad men, on and on.

But I had listened to enough of Father Pierre to begin to doubt if killing them was the way.

D'Herblay lay in the road and screamed. I ignored him. In Gascon French, I said, 'Are any of you knights? Are you not ashamed? Is this your war for the gentle Jesus? Is this all we are? Go hold a tower. Go and fight the enemy. The *armed* enemy. Or we are nothing but reivers and bandits?'

I suppose I thought that they would turn away, ashamed.

Instead, they simply attacked.

Fiore laughed. 'Well done,' he said, as his pole arm flicked out.

We were five against twenty, and from the moment the blue and white in front of me came forward, I remember little. But I remember passing my iron between a man's legs and lifting him, and his screams.

I remember slamming my poleaxe two-handed, a full blow like a man splitting wood, into another.

I confess I put another down after he had turned to run.

They still talk of that fight, in the Hospital. They could all see us from the walls of the gate castle.

Of course, they lie, and say that the five of us fought a hundred Mamluks. When in fact, we fought twenty men-at-arms who wore the same cross as we wore ourselves.

And then it was done. The survivors ran like rats, leaving their loot on the road.

And then – I'm not ashamed to say – John the Turk and Maurice and George shot them down. As they ran.

And I confess, too, that killing d'Herblay would have given me more pleasure than any of the poor devils of infidels I killed in Alexandria. But I did not.

I walked back to him, and someone had killed him. On the ground, his hands broken, as helpless as a babe.

And Nerio said, 'You are too good to be a mortal man, William Gold.' He raised an eyebrow. And flicked his sword at me like a salute.

The next morning, we fed the Greeks – and their Jewish and Moslem friends – what food we had. About an hour after sunrise, we were probed by Bedouins. They came in close but we were silent as the grave and we didn't allow them into the courtyard through the gate: Ewan and John and Ned Cooper saw them off, leaving a dozen corpses.

Then John followed Fra William and twenty turcopoles out the gate on his little Arab. They were gone an hour, and then John took the English archers and they were gone another hour.

The next troops to come at us were Sudanese. They were not well-disciplined, and I suspected they were being used to count our swords, so to speak. But they were fanatics, or possibly full to their eyeballs with opium. There were several hundred of them.

They died in front of the towers, and then they died in the gate tunnel, and then they died in our fortified trap in the courtyard, and they never stopped stabbing and chanting and screaming their name for God.

After their attack, we watched from the tower as three or four thousand soldiers, the Sultan's professionals, made camp on the other side of the suburbs.

I won't say we were smug. But we had a good garrison and a fine position. The courtyard trap was *better* than a gate, because we could sortie whenever we pleased and the Venetians and the English – and John – gave us a power of archery I've seldom had in a siege. We were going to run out of shafts in a few days, but we had the largest city in the world at our backs. I was no more worried than an exhausted soldier in a siege usually is and Fra William de Midleton was positively exuberant. He'd led the counter-attack on the Sudanese, axe in hand, and now seemed ... bigger.

That was evening of the third day.

By then, Fra William had organised watches. I no longer had a command – my group of volunteers was spread to the winds. We had casualties; Juan, of course, and others; and we were missing men. Volunteers of the Order were as likely to loot as others. And Nerio had taken men with him when he took Fra Peter back to the galleys. More had escorted the legate that hellish night.

Fiore and Nerio and I served with the Scottish knights. They were good men, and they followed Baron Rosilyn. He was no older than I, and very proud, but a fine fighter. I'd like to say we got along, but in fact, we never spoke beyond 'That wall', and 'Here they come'.

On the morning of the fourth day, Nerio took a patrol all the way to the ships, and returned in the evening with twenty Knights of the Order and all the rest of the available turcopoles and volunteers. They marched in just in time, for we had the first probing attack from Mamluks at dusk. We repulsed it easily.

Nerio had canteens of wine, and he shared them with us, so we were sitting on our haunches like beggars in armour, drinking Venetian wine from canteens. Nerio shook his head.

'Turenne, that man of steel, says this gate cannot be held. He is demanding that the city be abandoned.'

I shrugged, having heard the same. There were brigands and crusaders trying to join us by then. Fra William sent them to hold other gates. A few even did. We admitted none of them to our towers.

Nerio shook his head. 'No, I mean it. Most of the crusaders wish us to sail away. There was a rumour today that these gates had fallen.' He looked at me. 'The legate is in a bad way, my friend.'

I nodded.

Nerio frowned. 'Someone has told the king that you attacked d'Herblay and other crusaders – that you are a secret pagan, a traitor.'

Fiore grunted.

'I wish I had a better quality of foes,' I said. 'Camus and d'Herblay – ugh.'

Nerio's eyes slipped past Fiore. I was going to say more, but Fiore turned his head to look. It was a Greek girl, bringing water to the soldiers.

Nerio rose. 'Sabraham wants to speak to us. He said something to me,' he said, 'But I forget what it was.' He laughed, and went to chat to the Greek girl, apparently untouched by the horror around us.

The next day, the Mamluks prowled for a weaker gate.

The king came and told us that we were the pillars on which the crusade rested.

He had a complete collar of the Order of the Sword, and he put it on me. He waited with us for the daily visit by the Sultan's army, but it did not come, and eventually he rode away. He looked tired, and harried – we all did.

But de Mézzières had a conversation with Nerio and Fiore while I was invested with the order.

And when the king was gone, I put a hand on Nerio's shoulder. 'Brother,' I said, 'we need to bury Juan.'

Nerio shook his head. 'Not here,' he said. 'I have him on the galley. Wrapped in a shroud. He's not the only dead knight.'

I shook my head. 'He died in the Holy Land,' I said. 'Surely …'

Fiore looked down. 'We're leaving, Will,' he said.

Nerio wouldn't meet my eyes.

I sat. I don't think I decided to sit. My knees just gave.

Nerio finally looked at me. 'The king tried. The legate tried.' He shrugged. 'Listen, William, Admiral Contarini tried. He has been against this attack from the beginning, and he argued that now that we had raped the city and broken it for trade, the least we might do is hold it and march on Cairo.'

Zeno was drinking our wine – or, given that it was Venetian wine, possibly we were drinking his. 'Cairo?' he asked. 'Christ on a cross, this army!' He spat. 'Every fighting man in this army is right here,' he muttered.

411

Nerio made one of his Italian faces. 'We are leaving.' He put a hand on my shoulder. 'For you, I'm sorry.' He shrugged. 'For me ... I never want to see this place or these animals again.' He flicked his eyebrows up, and shrugged. 'Perhaps I am a banker at heart, but what have these infidels ever done to me? Nothing. But our crusaders?'

I was not the veteran captain then that I am today, but that city could have been held.

Instead, our crusaders made a real effort – not to fight, but to enrich themselves. You'd have thought, from the charnel house of death, that every living thing in the city was dead, but some people had been rescued – to be made slaves.

When we sailed away – with the loot of a rich city, ten *thousand* slaves, and two shiploads of Alexandrine Greeks who begged not to be left to the counter-sack of the Mamluks – when we left, the Egyptian Army had stopped attacking because they'd lost a thousand men for nothing.

We killed a great city.

Also – for nothing.

Two days later we landed in Cyprus. The 'crusaders' were eager to trans-ship their plunder and there were men sailing for Italy before Mass on Friday.

I have nothing more to say, except that those days, the voyage from Alexandria to Famagusta, and the days that followed, were perhaps the blackest of my life.

Nerio had saved his Greek girl. He was well enough. And he and Fiore tried to comfort me. And Miles, who was as disconsolate as I.

What do you make of the ruin of all your hopes?

What is knighthood, when crusade is but a word for rape?

We buried Juan in the cathedral of Famagusta. You can still see his arms there, in alabaster, painted. I have been to visit him a few times. Sometimes I sit on his tomb, and talk to him, though I realise this is foolish.

Sometimes I weep.

I certainly wept that day.

It was Nerio – Nerio, for whom religion was an inhibition on his carnal pleasures – who saved me. The four of us we standing over the tomb, no alabaster yet, and we went to the altar to pray.

And Nerio said, 'Let's go to Jerusalem anyway.'

The four of us rose, and swore – four swords on the tomb.

The crusade broke up with frightening rapidity. The English were gone in less than a week, and the French immediately began to spread a rumour that the English and the Hospital had deserted the walls first.

I got to listen to the process by which a military disaster that was a catastrophe of cowardice, indecision and greed was transformed into a Christian victory, a blow to the infidel. I got to hear black told as white, the admiral of the Hospital called a coward for attacking the Pharos Harbour, the Hospital accused of deserting the king on the beach.

There was worse to come. But luckily, in the atmosphere of recrimination, I took my leave of the king and de Mézzières in a rose garden. I didn't have to listen to the French, the Bretons, the Savoyards or the Gascons justify themselves.

King Peter looked drawn, his face pinched. Men said that he had come home to a cold bed and a distant welcome. Men said all sorts of terrible things. I saw the queen at a distance – but more on that later, if we sit together another night.

King Peter, true to his word, made me put my hands between his and accept a barony. Men told me it was a fine piece of land, would support ten knights and I swore to be his man and to serve him with three knights whenever he desired.

It did not lift the black fog entirely, but I had never held any land before. I was a lord.

By the grace of God.

The king gave me his leave to depart; not that, as a volunteer of the Order, I needed his leave. And he gave me his passport to Jerusalem.

He put a hand on my shoulder and sighed. 'Some of the English go to Jerusalem. My people say that the Sultan is so discomfited by the overthrow of his army at Alexandria that he has withdrawn his garrison.' His eyes met mine, and they were red. '*Where did we fail?*' he asked.

'The crusaders failed you, my lord,' I said. 'But for them, we should have won.'

He shrugged. His bitterness was immense. 'You will see the Countess,' he said.

My spine stiffened.

He looked at me. 'I am told,' he said, 'that her husband did not survive the sack.'

'I didn't kill him,' I said, probably too quickly.

He smiled grimly. 'As for that, Baron, I care nothing one way or another.'

I bowed, knee to the ground.

'Will you wed her, Lord Gold?' he asked. It was not the question, which was perfectly correct, but the manner of his asking – wry and discordant.

'I will, with God's help,' I said. Oddly, one of the answers we gave in Church.

He looked down, and shrugged. 'She is a wonder. When you see her,' he said, 'Tell her that she was correct in her surmise. Only that.' He shrugged. 'I never wanted to command the crusade.'

'No, your Grace,' I said. I accepted his kiss of peace, and I withdrew.

I will not say he was a broken man. I will only say that his light was dimmed. The fire that burned so hot in the lists at Krakow was almost gone. He knew – and I knew – that something was broken and would never, ever be restored.

The next day, we sailed for Rhodes, and the passage there was brutal, nine days of storm-tossed seas and fear. But by God's grace, on the tenth day we raised the twin harbours and the fortress, and we landed in the sunset.

There were a great many people on the beach. They began to cheer as we came ashore: the galleys turned and landed stern first, and the oarsmen marched off, followed by the deck crews, and then the volunteers and last the knights, and we paraded on the foreshore in the sand. And Raymond Bérenger, the Grand Master, walked along our ranks as the people cheered us.

Marc-Antonio was recovering – yet another miracle. He appeared beside me with our horses in his fists, and John with two more. John the Turk was grinning.

Nerio was grinning.

We were, after all, alive. When you are young, horror does not last, thank God and all the saints, otherwise we would all run mad.

Fiore hugged me, and Nerio shook his head. 'Turn around,' he said.

I did.

Emile was waiting, and without, I think, considering her action, she threw her arms around my neck. And her lips were on my lips and I suspect that this was not a common display in front of the knights.

'Will you come with me to Jerusalem?' I asked.

She laughed her good laugh. 'My love, we were always going to Jerusalem,' she said.

EPILOGUE

Chaucer was toying with his wine cup, and Froissart looked dismayed over his.

'But this is not what we hear of the great taking of Alexandria!' he protested. 'Percival de Coulanges is a great knight! And de Mézzières—'

'De Mézzières wants another crusade, led by the king of France, to avenge the last one, and to wipe away the stain it left on all of us,' Gold said. He sat back.

Chaucer smiled. 'You are quite the hidden man, William. I had no idea you held a barony on Cyprus.' He raised his cup to me. 'That was a fine tale. I think I even believe parts of it. Did you go to Jerusalem?'

Gold nodded. 'We did. But you know Sabraham, so you've heard all this before,' he said.

Chaucer laughed. 'I don't need your word on it to know that a crusade manned with the same mercenaries who burned France would come to a bad end,' he said. He set his wine cup down with a click. 'But you haven't made it to the Green Count's crusade or the Italian Wedding yet, much less to being the Captain of Venice.'

'By God's grace, Master Chaucer! Why not regale us with your own Spanish War? You spin words at least as well as Messire Froissart. And you were, I think, with the Prince in Spain?'

Chaucer nodded. 'Aye, William. We know all of each other's secrets.'

Sir William laughed. 'Not all, I think, Geoffrey.'

Froissart finished his wine. 'I would very much like to hear of the tournament at Prince Lionel's wedding – from a participant.'

Sir William nodded. 'The one held in the lists, or the one where we murdered each other behind the curtains?' he asked.

Froissart looked dismayed.

Chaucer guffawed. 'Now there's a tale!'

HISTORICAL NOTE

I am not a professional historian. Or rather – I am occasionally and in a very small way a professional historian, and writing these books about William Gold has made me want to write an academic book on the War of Chioggia (William Gold's greatest victory, I suspect.) But that aside, I'm a novelist first. While I care deeply for authenticity, I want to have a story that will move you. I try to make the experience real by practicing these things myself. I'm a reenactor and a collector, a patron of craftsmanship, and an amateur martial artist. I ride horses, I shoot bows, I cook at campfires, and I listen to music and read the languages and even fish with the period fishing tackle. But none of these makes for a story.

What does make for a story is my experience of humanity, and the people I see about me. I am not foolish enough to believe that the people of the fourteenth century were just like us; nor blind enough to think they were so very different, and that is merely one of the paradoxes that litter the work of the historical novelist.

It is essential to understand, when examining this world of stark contrasts and incredible passions, that people believed very strongly in ideas – like Islam, like Christianity, like chivalry. Piety – the devotional practice of Christianity – was such an essential part of life that even most 'atheists' practiced all the forms of Christianity. Yet there were many flavors of belief. Theology had just passed one of its most important milestones with the works of Thomas Aquinas, but Roman Christianity had so many varieties of practice that it would require the birth of Protestantism and then the Counter-Reformation to establish orthodoxy. I mention all this to say that to describe the fourteenth century without reference to religion would be – completely ahistorical. I make no judgement on their beliefs – I merely try to represent them accurately. I confess that I assume that any professional soldier – like Sabraham or Gold – must have developed some knowledge of and respect for their opponents. I see signs of this throughout the work of the Hospitallers – but that may be my modern multi-culturalism.

The same care should be paid to all judgments on the past, especially facile judgements about chivalry. It is easy for the modern amoralist to sneer – The Black Prince massacred innocents and burned towns, Henry V ordered prisoners butchered. The period is decorated with hundreds, if not thousands of moments where the chivalric warriors fell from grace and behaved like monsters. I loveth chivalry, warts and all, and it is my take – and, I think, a considered one – that in chivalry we find the birth of the modern codes of war and of military justice, and that to merely state piously that 'war is hell' and that 'sometimes good men do bad things' is crap. War needs rules. Brutality needs limits. These were not amateur enthusiasts, conscripts, or draftees. They were full time professionals who made for themselves a set of rules so that they could function – in and out of violence – as human beings. If the code of chivalry was abused – well, so are concepts like Liberty and Democracy abused. Cynicism is easy. Practice of the discipline of chivalry when your own life is in imminent threat is nothing less than heroic – it required then and still requires discipline and moral judgment, confidence in warrior skills and a strong desire to ameliorate the effects of war. I suspect that in addition to helping to control violence (and helping to promote it – a two-edged sword) the code and its reception in society did a great deal to soften the effects of PTSD. I think that the current scholarship believes that, on balance, the practice of chivalry may have done more to promote violence than to quell it – but I've always felt that this is a massively ill-considered point of view – as if to suggest that the practice of democracy has been bad for peace, based on the casualty rates of the twentieth century.

May I add – as a practitioner – that we as a society have chosen to ignore the reality of violence, and the hellish effect on soldiers and cops – and we have done so with such damning effectiveness that we have left them without any code beyond a clannish self-protection. Chivalry should not be a thing of the past. Chivalry is an ethic needed by every pilot, every drone controller, every beat cop and every SWAT team officer, every clandestine operator, every SpecOps professional. I often hear people say that such and such act of terror or crime justifies this or that atrocity. 'Time to take off the gloves.'

Crap. If you take off the gloves, *that's who you are.* Whether you do it with your rondel dagger or your LGB or your night stick. There need to be rules, and the men and women facing fire need to have some.

Rant off.

A word about the martial arts of the period. The world sees knights as illiterate thugs swinging heavy weapons and wearing hundreds of pounds of armour. In fact, the professionals wore armour that fitted like a tailored steel suit to the individual, and with weight evenly distributed over the body. We have several manuals of arms from this period, the most famous of which is by a character in this series – Fiore di Liberi, a northern Italian master who left us a magnificently illustrated step by step guide to the way to fight in and out of armour, unarmed, with a dagger, with a stick, with a sword, with a two-handed sword, with a spear, with a pole-ax, and mounted with a lance. The techniques are brutal, elegant and effective. They also pre-date any clear, unambiguous martial manual from the east, and are directly tied to combat, not remote reflections of it. I recommend their study, and the whole of Fiore's mss in the Getty collection is available to your inspection at http://wiktenauer.com/wiki/Fior_di_Battaglia_MS_Ludwig_XV_13. If you'd like to learn more, I recommend the works of Bob Charrette and Guy Windsor. Guy's School is at http://swordschool.com/ and Rob Charrette's superb examination of Fiore's techniques is available at http://www.freelanceacademypress.com/. Fiore Di Liberi was a real man, and his passion for his art shines through the pages of his book.

Sir William Gold, like Arimnestos, was a real person. He was a lieutenant of the White Company and often, but not always, followed Sir John Hawkwood. He had a fascinating career, and I suspect I'll render it more exciting yet – but the events described, whether Poitiers and the dismemberment of France in the middle of the century, the Italian wars, or the Alexandria Crusade – all of them are real events. Most of the characters are real people, and when I've created characters, I've used sources like Chaucer's remarkable 'Canterbury Tales' to make them live. Geoffrey Chaucer was a squire and a member of the Prince Lionel's household. He knew Scrope and Sabraham and in fact was at a chivalric trial where Scrope, Sabraham and Stapleton all discussed the Siege of Alexandria. Boccaccio and Petrarch and all the officers of the Hospitallers were real men. I have tried to be faithful to what is known of all their lives (Sabraham I have embroidered a bit …). I hope that I have been faithful to the period and to the lives of these great men and women (great and terrible – Hawkwood was no man's hero) and I do hope that my readers learn things. I think a good historical novel should teach, and I'm unabashed to say it.

But I remain a novelist first, and I hope that I have taken the bones of history and made a good story. Each of these books is about chivalry in some way – the laws of tournament and war, the rules of courtly love, and the ethics that ruled a world where violence was a commodity and money was of little importance except as a tool.

Finally, a word on this series. I would like to write three more – but that can only happen if you, my readers, support it. Please consider pushing it on your sword-swinging friends … I'd really like to tell the rest of this story!

ACKNOWLEDGEMENTS

My greatest thanks still have to go, first and foremost, to Richard Kaeuper of the University of Rochester. The finest professor I ever had – the most passionate, the most clear, the most brilliant – Dr. Kaeuper's works on chivalry and the role of violence in society makes him, I think, the preeminent medievalist working today, and I have been lucky to be able to get his opinions and the wealth of his knowledge on many subjects great and small. Where I have gone astray, the fault is all mine. This book I must add the works of Professor Steven Muhlberger on chivalry and the minutae of the joust and tournament, as well as the ethics of chivalry themselves. Several hours of conversations with Steve have not only been delightful but helped me with some of the themes of this book.

Not far behind these two, I need to thank Guy Windsor, who introduced me to the Armizare of Fiore di Liberi and profoundly informed my notions of what late-Medieval warfare was like among the skilled. Guy runs a school in Finland and I recommend his books and his research and offer my thanks. I'd also like to thank the other two masters with whom I've studied and trained this last year – Sean Hayes of the 'Northwest Fencing Academy' and Greg Mele of the 'Chicago Swordplay Guild'. To these three modern masters this book is dedicated. I'd also like to thank all the people with whom I train and spar – the *Compagnia* mentioned below. Reenacting the Middle Ages has many faces, and immersion in that world may not ever be a perfectly authentic experience – but inasmuch as I have gotten 'right' the clothes, the armour, the food or the weapons – it is due to all my reenacting friends, including Tasha Kelly (of Cote Simple, a superb web resource) Chris Verwijmeren, master archer, and Leo Todeschini and JT Palikko and Jiri Klipac and Peter Fuller, master craftsmen. I cannot imagine writing these books without all the help I have received on material culture, and I'm going to add more craftspeople

– all worth looking up – Francesca Baldassari and Davide Giuriussini of Italy, and Karl Robinson of England.

Throughout the writing of this series, I have used (and will continue to use), as my standard reference to names, dates, and events, the works of Jonathan Sumption, whose books are, I think, the best un-biased summation of the causes, events, and consequences of the war. I've never met him, but I'd like to offer him my thanks by suggesting that anyone who wants to follow the real events should buy Sumption's books!

In this volume, which leaves the 100 Years War for Italy and the Holy Land (is Egypt part of the Holy Land? Medieval men thought it was) I have turned, for Italy, to the works of William Caffero for inspiration, and I cannot recommend them too highly. And for the taking of Alexandria, I have used many sources. There is an 'almost' eyewitness account in Medieval French, by Guillaume Machaut, the first well-known musical genius of the Western world and really, one of the most interesting men of the era. I have used it, both as a source and as a source of understanding prejudice and the sheer alienness of the enterprise. But I also read translations of the Arab Egyptian accounts, and I made the best I could of the many and conflicting sources. Those who think of Alexandria solely as a terrible massacre should also temper that view with the knowledge that anti-clerical, anti-papal factions later used it as a vehicle to attack the idea of crusade. The Egyptians were not unarmed. There was a good deal of fighting. Beyond that, and the stupefying horror of the sack – there's not much hard fact. I did my best.

As Dick Kaueper once suggested in a seminar, there would have been no Middle Ages as we know them without two things – the horse and Christianity. I owe my horsemanship skills largely to two people – Ridgely and Georgine Davis of Pennsylvania, both of whom are endlessly patient with teaching and with horseflesh in getting me to understand even the basics of mounted combat. And for my understanding of the church, I'd like to first thank all the theologians I know – I'm virtually surrounded by people with degrees in theology – and second, the work of F. C. Copleston, whose work 'A History of Medieval Philosophy' was essential to my writing and understanding the period – as essential, in fact, as the writings of Chaucer and Boccaccio.

My sister-in-law, Nancy Watt, provided early comments, criticism, and copy-editing while I worked my way through the historical problems – and she worked her way through lung cancer. I value her commitment extremely. As this is her favorite of my series, I've done my best for her. I'm pleased to say that after two years, she is still alive and reading – and working.

And finally, I'd like to thank my friends who support my odd passions and my wife and child, who are tolerant, mocking, justly puzzled, delighted, and gracious by turns as I drag them from battlefield to castle and as we sew like fiends for a tournament in Italy.

This year, we formed the 'Compagnia della Rosa nel Sole' and we now have 70 members to recreate a Company like John Hawkwood's fighting in Italy in the late 14th century. Our company has given me (already) an immense amount of material and I thank every member.

William Gold is, I think, my favorite character. I hope you like him. He has a long way to go.

Christian Cameron
Toronto, 2014

The spectacular climactic novel
in the acclaimed Long War series.

Salamis is out now
in Hardback and eBook.